Celine's
Landing

ALSO BY STEVEN A SEGAL
Ida's Story

Celine's Landing

by
Steven A Segal

ISBN: 0615998771
ISBN 13: 9780615998770
Library of Congress Control Number: 2014906963
Steve Segal, Scottsdale, AZ

DEDICATION

Dedicated to the bravery and determination of the citizen Resistance fighters who gallantly gave so much in their struggle against tyranny following the surrender of France to Germany on June 22, 1940.

IN APPRECIATION

Of my wonderful wife, Lavonne, who attentively listens to evening readings of my prose additions of the day, encourages me with her praise and improves the story with her suggestions.

War is [simply] a continuation of politics by other means.

General Carl von Clausewitz, Prussian Army
Lived: July 1, 1780 – November 16, 1831

I hate war as only a soldier who has lived it can, only as one who has seen its brutality, its stupidity.

General Dwight D. Eisenhower, Supreme Allied Commander
A comment made January 10, 1946

War continues its damage far beyond its initial devastation; it robs the world of all the future contributions of those who perish in its wrath.

Steven A Segal, Author
Celine's Landing

CHAPTER 1

HMS *Triumph's* steersman was working hard to keep the huge carrier headed into stiff shifting winds in anticipation of the takeoff of the ship's small but powerful single-engine modified Lysander Mk II-SBS. The Lysander's pilot was good, damn good, and would need every ounce of his brash confidence this afternoon. The Triumph had steamed through the Straits of Gibraltar two days earlier on its way to support British General Bernard Montgomery's forces struggling in Tunisia. Monty's Eighth Army Tank Division was finally making strides against the Nazi's Panzer Corps under the direction of Erwin Rommel in North Africa, and the carrier group anchored at Tunisia would supply the air and artillery support that Montgomery had been screaming for. For the moment, though, to the disgust of the carrier group's Commodore, the mighty naval flotilla was treading water in stormy seas off the coast of southern France in an attempt to covertly deliver Celine Duval-Rousseau back into France.

Commodore Reuben Bentley, 45 year career naval officer, responsible for the carrier and its accompanying flotilla, had strenuously objected to the assignment's required deviation in route to Tunisia. The detour had pulled the fleet some 750 nautical miles northwest of that final destination in order to get within a reasonable proximity of the southern coast of France for Rousseau's flight home. Steaming into these northern Mediterranean waters substantially increased the risk to the carrier and its defensive cruisers and destroyers—not to mention the risk to the pilot who would be flying over Nazi-occupied France. The whole idea of jeopardizing so much to get one female Resistance fighter back into France had deeply irritated Bentley from the moment he'd been handed the assignment.

Bentley and his second-in-command stood on either side of the steersman, scanning the horizon through their binoculars in search of the two cruisers and three destroyers somewhere out there in the foggy rain and 12-foot seas. The fleet was on radio silence. Bentley wanted a visual on the escort ships—just his normal need to know where his boats were. *This bloody storm. Storm? Hell, gale.* He felt a bit of nervous relief as his sharp eyes caught sight of one of the cruisers bobbing up out of a trough 800 yards off the starboard. All five of his escort ships enjoyed the new high-powered sonar units from the Americans. Good stuff. Able to pick up subs a lot farther off than the old T3 units. *So far, no Nazi U-boats.* Bentley feared the German subs that prowled the Mediterranean. Not as many as a couple of years before, but it only took one. *All to get this little bitch back to her French sewing circle,* he grumbled to himself.

"I got the Panther in sight, Sir," Bentley's Captain broke the Commodore's sullen mood. "She's off the port bow about 600 yards."

Bentley grunted his acknowledgement, his thoughts still fuming at his untenable situation. He'd have to hold the fleet at this position for hours while the plane made its trip to the drop point high in the Alps, dumped off the woman and then returned. *Hell,* he mulled, *according to every damn report I've seen, we've got the Nazi bastards on the run. Bombed hell out of a couple of their war production plants up in the Ruhr Valley just last month. Can't understand taking this risk. Just can't understand it.*

"There's the destroyer Loyal—just off the aft port side," the Captain beamed, taking pride in spotting the escort ships before the old man found them.

Bentley looked over at the younger officer, "Okay, that's two to one. Chalk it up to youthful eyes. I'll get the last two afore ye."

The banter didn't relieve his irritation. *The damn war's turning against the krauts. Why in the name of Jesus do we think we have to train a bunch of girls to soften them up before we blow them the hell out of France? Absolute insanity.*

Women on ships-of-war. Bad luck. Don't think much of the French as fighters, anyway, much less spending 11 months and a ton of time and money trying to train one of their girls in guerrilla warfare tactics. If she's as gutless as the French men at Saint-Quentin during the last war, it's a bloody waste of pound sterling. French bastards ran off. Got my whole damn regiment shot up.

—⊸∞∞⊶—

Celine had pretty much kept to the cramped quarters assigned to her when they shipped out of HMNB Devonport, England. One of the carrier's ranking officers had voluntarily given up his stateroom to her for the trip. She only ventured out for meals—tried not to look uncomfortable with the stares and occasional hoots and whistles as she made her way down the narrow passageways to the officer's wardroom. Not pleasant being the only woman among the 1,879 men onboard. The officers were gentlemen, dignified, clearly working to make her feel comfortable. The pilots, a bit more rowdy than the staff officers, did their best to behave in her presence. Commodore Bentley was never present, his seat at the head of the table defiantly vacant.

The time onboard, sequestered in her small iron-walled room with its constant smell of machine oil, male sweat and the throbbing of the ship's engines had been a blessing of sorts. With no book to read, nothing to take her mind off of the reality she was going home to, she had time to reflect. Time to try and put the whole miserable war into perspective. Find some reason for it all—some hope. Some way to quell the anger seething inside her.

CHAPTER 2

Celine hadn't always been angry. Her youth was blissfully happy, spent in the magnificent Alpine wonderland surrounding her picturesque medieval village of Treaire. Her parents were soft, loving people. She adored her younger brother and her devoted friends—Remi Rousseau, Amaury Cheever, Alexis Beauvais, Felicien Naffis and Daniel Laurent. The thought of them brought a nostalgic smile.

Remi the consummate leader, the King Arthur of the group—her darling loving, magnificent Remi. She chuckled thinking of Felicien. Carefree Felicien, the flippant embracer of life. Amaury, sophisticated, educated, oblivious to his wealth, stalwartly dedicated to whatever he felt a just cause. Daniel the intelligent, the cynical, the perfectionist—Remi's reverent antagonist. And then, of course, Alexis. Big, sweet, adorable Alexis—so massively powerful, so innocent, so loveable. Her friends, her beloved friends who she would soon embrace. Who would once again surround her with the love and security they had provided for as long as she could remember.

The *friends*, as they came to refer to their unique tight-knit band, had all been born within 12 days of each other. The most births within a 12-day period in the known history of tiny Treaire.

The town's 1,400 inhabitants affectionately teased and talked about the rapid series of births for weeks after they took place, recalling that just nine months before, the *friends'* parents had all attended the gaily raucous 1918 Marquee de Cheever birthday celebration, held annually at Le Duc de Richelieu Bistro, located on the east edge of Treaire. The six couples, all lifelong residents of Treaire, had hung around together for years. They were all young, recently married, ecstatically in love. World War I had just ended. The future looked bright, the evening crystal clear, the music enchanting, the wine flowing freely. They laughed, danced, mingled with friends and neighbors, had a joyous time, and lingered into the wee hours of the morning. Nine months later, Treaire's only doctor spent the busiest two weeks in his 36 years of caring for the town's citizens.

Now, Celine thought wryly, *the Marquee's birthday celebration is no more*. Gone, like so many things she held in affectionate memories. After Amaury's grandfather died, the Cheever family dispensed with the annual September 5th event. It had been held at the family's Bistro for as long as anyone could remember. The street closed off. The town's band hired. Free wine and food for whoever showed up. The celebration commemorated the Marquee Douzième Chapiteau de Cheever, the family's 12th-century relative who spent the years between 1149 and 1185 working tirelessly at cheating local peasants out of their land—a life's dedication to fraud, which put the Cheevers solidly on the road to massive wealth.

The parents of the *friends* remained close through the years, resulting in the 12-day sextuples growing up together. The families frequently joined each other for outings and local events. The children played together as infants, totters and on into puberty, which fostered a growing feeling of unity and mutual affection as they matured. In school, the six interacted much as siblings do. There was something special about them—a symbiotic synergy, a unique understanding and appreciation of each other. Early on, the six started referring to themselves as the *friends*. Found comfort in its depiction of their camaraderie, enjoyment in its subtle exclusion of all others.

As the only girl in the group, Celine had a unique influence on the *friends*. Rambunctiously cute as a child, she was devilishly tomboy as an adolescent and strong, beautiful, and cheerfully optimistic in her teens. She brought something to the group that would not have existed without her. The boys adored her— were often challenged physically trying to keep up with her—and respected her. They quickly learned she resented being treated different from the rest, but despite her independence, they would come rushing to her aid like a troop of irate brothers whenever they felt Celine was under the slightest threat. She was protected. Special. Had something other girls her age didn't. And she secretly liked it.

To the boys, Celine was a binder of sorts. Filled in gaps that could have irreparably broadened with time. She never entered into the frequent arguments that erupted between Daniel and Remi, yet always had a reasonable compromise to satisfy them both. She provided the patient affection Alexis needed to accept and cope with his mental slowness. She took Felicien's teasing in stride, dealing back subtle barbs that often got the two of them laughing uncontrollably. She was not impressed with Amaury's immense wealth, making it okay for him and the others not to be either. She respected and admired Remi...had been secretly in love with him for as long as she could remember.

The *friends* spent as much time together as possible. Their childhood play often centered on acting out one of Remi's fantasies of the glories of French military history. He would lead them in make-believe battles in the defense of France, or if not in the defense of France, in the defense of a cause that he defined as being good for France. Whatever history story Remi was infatuated with at the moment, the *friends* would act out in the pristine countryside surrounding Treaire.

Remi was blind to the decades of pomposity, death and corruption permeating the disorderly political history of France. To him, the French way was the way God wanted the world to be. Daniel, also a student of history, tended to take a more critical view of France's past. Remi was the undisputed leader of the group, and Daniel's more cynical interpretation of the nation's history often resulted in conflicts between the two.

One glorious spring day the *friends* had gathered in the foothills of the Alps, ready to play act another battle of Remi's choosing. The hike to the playing field had been breathtaking—warm morning sun, sweet spring grass, meadows aglow in a burst of delicate wildflowers.

"I have been reading about the Battle of the Bastille, a glorious time in French history," Remi addressed the group, "a time of liberation. The advancement of freedom for all of France. Young idealist rebels, demanding their rights, rose up against King Louis XVI, threw off their shackles, and successfully stormed the Bastille..."

"That story is self-defeating," Daniel complained. "It's French against French, Remi. There's no glory in it. It's just us French beating the crap out of each other. The whole revolution was us fighting us." Daniel glumly continued, "Winning battles by beating your fellow countrymen to a bloody pulp is just not very uplifting. I want to play something where we beat hell out of somebody besides ourselves. Like one of Napoleon's victories where he beats the shit out of the Russians or the Italians or one of those other pitiful countries."

Even in their conflicts, Daniel held a deep respect for Remi's enthusiasm for great causes, his buoyant, uncompromising pride in France. Remi saw historical events on a broader plain than most youngsters. He saw the bigger picture. Taught the *friends* to think beyond themselves and see purpose beyond their self-centered individual worlds.

Daniel and Remi stepped a few feet from the group to argue out their disagreement. Felicien rolled over where he was lying in the soft spring grass next to Amaury, Alexis and Celine. Resting his head on his propped up arm, he rolled his eyes, "Well, here we go again. Might as well relax while King Remi and Lord Daniel work out the details. I never understand why Daniel and Remi have to be so particular about whether the battle we're going to play out has glory or not. Who cares? I just like stabbing pretend enemies, no matter who they are." He spit out the stalk of grass he had been chewing on, reached into his pocket and pulled out a pack of cigarettes.

"Are you still stealing those from Mr. Dumont's pharmacy?" Celine frowned.

"Yeah, he's so old he can hardly see or hear anymore," Felicien smiled, looking lovingly at the pack. "He's my best source now."

"Can I have one?" Alexis asked.

Just as Felicien held the pack out to Alexis, Remi and Daniel returned. "Put those damn cigarettes away, Felicien!" Remi snapped. "We're only eight years old. You shouldn't be smoking, and you sure shouldn't be teaching Alexis to smoke. Besides, we have agreement on the battle for the day."

Daniel proudly announced, "We agreed on the Battle of Amstetten."

"Never heard of it," Amaury lamented.

"What kind of battle was Amstetten?" Alexis asked. "I want to play a battle where we all charge across the Russian plains. Remember when we..."

"Okay, okay, just wait a minute and I'll explain," Remi interrupted. "We are mounted grenadiers and we race our mighty warhorses down the hill and attack the Russian Jägers and the Austrian cavalry holding the city of Amstetten hostage."

"I like when we pretend a mounted attack," Alexis grinned. "Running with swords drawn is neat."

Encouraged by Alexis' enthusiasm, Remi expounded, "I'll be General Nicolas Oudinot, and you all will be my mighty grenadiers. We'll charge down the hill on our sure-footed warhorses, specially bred steeds of fearless strength. Massive animals, which have tasted the sting of battle many times while carrying their grenadiers to countless victories."

Remi saw the growing enthusiasm on the faces of his team of grenadiers for the run down the hill. Pointing to a distant outcrop of rocks, he added, "We'll attack the cowardly Austrian cavalry and the Russian Jäger Corps there, hiding behind those rocks at the bottom of the hill. We are outnumbered ten-to-one. When we arrive at the rocks we will battle them face-to-face, hand-to-hand, our ferocity sending them running in retreat. Then, triumphant, we will ride majestically into the arms of the liberated citizens of Amstetten.

"Our charge must be chilling, ferocious and instantaneous, so mount up, my trusty grenadiers. Prepare for battle!"

Envisioning the glory, the excitement of battle, the adoration of the cheering citizens of Amstetten, they all jumped to their feet, mounted their imaginary stallions, raised their wooden swords and prepared for battle. Emotions surged. The muscled legs of their pretend warhorses restlessly pranced, eager for the order to charge. Celine had to pull on her nervous steed's fictional reins to control the powerful animal. Alexis made a snorting then a whinnying sound. Amaury's legs pranced, filling in for his fantasy stallion. Remi and Daniel mounted up. Remi looked down the line of his readied grenadiers, "Charrrrge!"

Illusory chunks of earth flew as steel-shod hoofs sprang into action, digging deep into the soil. The line leapt forward. No fear. No hesitation. There was a thunderous roar as the *friends* led hundreds of fictitious mounted troops to battle an evil enemy and free the enslaved men, women and children of Amstetten. All for the valor of war. The glory of France. A sense of victory electrified the air.

Half way down the hill, Felicien stumbled, falling full force against Celine, the two of them sprawling head over heels down the grassy embankment. They rolled helplessly entangled in each other. Felicien began forcing the roll increasing his laughter at what a farce they had made of the charge of General Oudinot's fearsome grenadiers. The more they tumbled, the more they giggled, finally stopping at the bottom of the hill in breathless fits of laughter.

Alexis and Amaury ran to join the fun, the charge of the fearless grenadiers forgotten as they headed in the direction of the howling fun of their comrades. Remi and Daniel stopped. Stood motionless. Disgusted. Then Daniel looked over at Remi and grinned, "Well, so much for laying siege to the cowardly Austrian cavalry and the Russian Jägers on our specially trained sure-footed steeds of fearless strength and dexterity."

Remi burst into laughter. The two raced down the hill, jumped on the pile and became part of the raucous joy. The *friends*. Laughing hysterically. Giggling in a heap. Immersed in each other's carefree euphoria on a spectacular spring day in the majesty of the warming French Alpine countryside.

With the fond memory comforting her for the moment, Celine didn't hear the throbbing of the ship's engines. Didn't smell the sweat and machine oil. She lay on the cot. The wondrous fun of her beloved *friends* soothing her mind. She smiled. It seemed only yesterday. So missed. A twinkling glow in time.

Remi was the most adventuresome of the *friends*. His parents, not demanding of his time, allowed him many days alone when the rest of the group was occupied with daily chores. Highly inquisitive, blessed with a vivid imagination, always needing to know what's just over the hill, around the next bend in the road, Remi enjoyed these alone times. Free to do whatever he wanted without having to bow to the demands of the others. He used every spare moment exploring everything he could climb, wade, swim, ski on or burrow into for miles around Treaire.

His heart thrilled to the majesty, the breathtaking splendor of God's world. He embraced its grandeur. Reveled in the cool Alpine air, filling his lungs with it. Standing alone, high above the lush valley nestling Treaire in its palm, he was enwrapped in a boundlessly glorious force, splendid beyond understanding. He felt it, spoke to it, found security in it. He immersed himself in this majesty as often as he could.

It was late in the afternoon the week following his ninth birthday that Remi made his most exciting discovery.

The several acres behind the 500-year-old Le Duc de Richelieu Bistro grew wild. It was unusually overgrown for a Cheever-owned property, but understandable since the area abutted the east edge of town with nothing but forest beyond. The area that stirred Remi's curiosity lay behind the Bistro's ancient stables and outbuildings. Totally unkempt, it thickened from tall grass into brush and thicket, eventually giving way to a forest of ageless mammoth pines.

He had experienced a magnificent day in the woods. Sat for over an hour watching three beavers gnaw down a good sized aspen. Practiced hitting puff-ball mushrooms with his homemade bow and arrows, taking pride in his improving accuracy. Altogether, a splendid day. Happy and fulfilled as he bounded down the dirt road leading into Treaire, he glanced over at the overgrown acre-age. *Wonder what's back there. Why haven't I had a look before now?*

Bow strapped across his chest and arrows tucked in their crudely stitched quiver, he cut into the thicket making his way along a dry creek bed. An outcrop-ping of smooth, weathered rock rose on his left, gaining in height as he moved along until it became a sheer cliff some 20 feet high. Massive vines encrusted its top, spilling their leafy plumage to the creek bed below. The opposite side of the creek bed was thick with elephant-sized bushes, which completely concealed the back of the Bistro from view. *Wow, what a great place. Can't believe I've passed this up for so long. What a neat place for us to build a secret fort.*

Remi surveyed the vines dangling from the cliff. *Perfect for swinging.* He pulled hard on several of the smaller ones, dislodging them from their tenuous hold high above and showering him in a rain of dirt as they plummeted down, snak-ing in piles of leafy green at his feet. He moved toward a group of larger vines. Testing one, he felt a rush of cool air on his face. Parting the vegetation, he gasped in frightened excitement. A cave.

He stood motionless as the yawning blackness hypnotized his anxious at-tention. The entrance arched some 10 feet above the ground pushing a musky breath on the cool draft exiting the darkness. A tingling foreboding washed over Remi as he parted the heavy vines and cautiously moved forward.

Taking several steps into the opening, the eerie blackness closed in. *Wait for your eyes to adjust.* Held his breath. Listened intently. Nothing. Several more steps. The gloom deepened. He held out his hand, barely able to see its outline. Paused again, listening. The silence had intensified. Musty, like the air he smelled once when he had peered through a slot in the side of one of the crypts in the cemetery. The same chill shivered through his body as on that day. That day he ran in terror. Two years ago. He was older now. Braver.

He stepped forward several steps. *Easy. Careful. Don't fall in a hole.* The heels of his shoes echoed as they met the stone floor. *Damn, too much noise. Don't wake anything. Slow down, be quiet.* He stretched out his hand, fully extending his arm, and could barely make out his fingers. Natural sounds from the outside world had now completely faded. A stuffy silence intensified the blackness.

All at once, a rushing crash split the air. Remi stumbled back in terror. *It's going to grab me!* Tripping, he fell hard on the stone floor. *I've got to get out!* Scooting fast on his butt. The jagged floor grabbed at his pants pockets, holding him, slowing his escape from the terror of blackness swooping to engulf him. *God help me... got to get the hell out!* He pushed hard tearing his pockets lose. *Oh, God, get me out of here. Where the hell is the opening?* Struggling to his feet, he leapt for the opening. Crashing through the vines, he tripped, staggered, and fell heavily on the round stones lining the creek bed. Daylight. Safety.

His heart pounded as he lay there. Another cluster of the vines he had pushed aside readjusted themselves back to their natural position overhanging the cave opening. Made the same noise. Remi smiled, *You chicken shit.* Laughed. *Come on, Remi. You're nine now. Grow up. Get some balls.* In spite of his self-coaching, he decided that further exploration would definitely be better pursued in the company of the others. He smiled at the dark opening, "I'll return. The *friends* and I will find out what you're all about."

Two days later, Remi brought the group to the road side where he had first begun following the creek bed. He led them through the thicket, out of sight of the road, and gathered them around, "I am about to show you the greatest discovery ever made. You must all swear a blood oath that what I am about to reveal you will never tell anyone. Not your parents, not your brothers or sisters—no one, ever."

They were all used to Remi's flair for the dramatic, but had never before seen quite this level of seriousness.

"What if we don't swear?" Alexis provoked.

"Then we stop here and I take the secret to my grave."

Alexis, still in search of clarification, persisted, "What if I swear and maybe Amaury and Celine swear, but Daniel and Felicien don't?"

"Oh, for the love of God, Alexis, I'm going to swear," grumped Daniel.

Remi grew even more serious, bending into the circle and speaking almost in a whisper, "Everyone swears—and not only swears but swears a blood oath, or we don't go a step farther."

"Come on Remi, cut the dramatics and get on with it," Daniel pleaded. "Hang up all the Shakespearian melodrama and show us this so-called Greatest Discovery of All Time."

"No... a blood oath or nothing. I brought a needle and we will all prick our thumbs then mingle our blood and swear an oath of secrecy."

"I'll do it." Celine grabbed the needle and pricked her thumb.

"Okay, me too," Alexis followed.

They tightened the circle, rubbed the spots of blood on each other's thumbs. Remi said, "Repeat after me, 'I, Remi Rousseau, swear...'"

Remi halted, speaking pointedly to Alexis, "Alexis, when I say I, Remi Rousseau, you say your own name, not mine."

"But you said to repeat what you said."

"Yes, I know, but blood oaths are always done like this or they don't count. Okay, once again, I, Remi Rousseau.... swear on the sanctity of life... I will never reveal what I am about to see... will never disclose its location... and will hold this knowledge forever until my death."

Remi once again looked them all in the eyes, then boasted, "Don't be afraid when we get there. I've done some preliminary exploration. It's safe."

Daniel rolled his eyes, "This better be good."

It was better than good. They stood mesmerized as Remi parted the vines, exposing the gaping opening. He paused for a moment, letting the full effect of what they were staring at soak in.

"I hid some torches here that I made from sticks and oil-soaked rags," Remi said as he reached behind a bush and handed each a torch.

"You were pretty sure we were all going to go along with the swearing and bloodletting," Daniel laughed as Remi lit his torch.

"Sure. We're the *friends*. There was never a doubt in my mind."

With Remi leading, they crept in.

Amaury, his eyes wide, gasped. "I can't believe this is on one of our family properties and I've never heard of it. I don't think my folks know it's here. Look how it's carved out in a perfect arch. I think this is man-made."

Twelve yards in, the tunnel turned abruptly to the right. At this point, its floor, walls, and arched ceiling became tiled with square stones packed so tightly together the thin blade of a knife could not be wedged between them. Twelve more yards and the tunnel took a 90-degree turn to the left, revealing the most astounding surprise of all: a large room.

They entered in wonderment. The room was 14 feet wide and 18 feet long with its arched ceiling soaring to 15 feet at its apex. Four huge wine casks rested on rough-hewn timbers on each side and rusty iron torch holders were bolted to the walls between them.

"Look," Celine pointed, "there's a door at the far end."

Moving through the door, they entered a second room of similar size. In its center stood a massive ancient wooden table with eight heavy chairs pulled up to its ends and sides. Iron torch holders lined the walls, and centered in the middle of the left wall, another arched doorway led off into blackness.

"My God, we've found a castle," Felicien whispered in amazement. "I can store every pack of cigarettes in town in here."

"Not a castle," corrected Daniel, "but certainly the neatest hideaway in all of France. I've got to hand it to you, Remi. This is fantastic. Almost worthy of all the crap you put us through, even though I still think the bloodletting was a bit much."

"Let's see where that door leads," Celine urged.

"Not today," said Remi. "The torches are beginning to run low and I don't want us getting halfway through wherever that goes and find ourselves in the dark." He started counting the iron torch holders on the walls. "Okay, there are 12 torch holders in this room and eight in the other. I'll make better torches over the next few days and well come back next Saturday and light the place up. We'll search that corridor then.

"Remember, not a word, not a hint, not a whisper to anyone—ever. This is ours, only for the *friends*. No parents, no one can ever know.

"Amaury," Remi turned. "Can you find out if any of your family members know about this without revealing what you're talking about?"

"I think so. The folks usually down several bottles of wine with dinner and often don't remember much in the morning. Grandfather is so forgetful I could ask him outright about the ancient wine cellar on the Bistro property and he wouldn't remember talking about it before he finished his answer," he laughed.

The following Saturday, the six eager explorers slipped Remi's torches into the wall holders and brought the rooms to light. The rooms were remarkably clean, except for an abundance of cobwebs clinging to the ceilings. While Celine and the others dusted and swept, Remi and Amaury ventured into the unexplored tunnel. It proceeded in a straight line for several hundred feet, took a bend to the left, then another turn to the right, ending at a point where several stone steps rose to a sealed doorway. They eased up the stairs. The doorway was tightly blocked with heavy wood planks. They pushed on the planks. No movement. Then Amaury whispered, "Wait! Listen!"

They stood silently, straining their ears to hear the murmur of voices on the other side of the planks.

"Remi," Amaury whispered, wide eyed, "that's coming from the Bistro. Listen."

They placed their ears against the planks. The voices remained undecipherable but there was the unmistakable clattering sounds of a busy restaurant kitchen.

"My God, this door leads either into the kitchen or into the hall adjoining it," Amaury said. "It must have provided the Bistro access to the wine cellar years ago."

Remi looked terribly disappointed, whispering, "Then surely your folks, or at least your Grandfather, know about all of this."

"No. I questioned them several times. I'm convinced no one has any idea. A long-dead relative won the Bistro from its owner in a card game over 200 years ago. Before it was a Bistro, it was an inn, and before that, a monastery. Remi, the buildings that make up the Bistro and the stable behind it are over 500 years old. I'm convinced this access to the cellars has been sealed for hundreds of years— maybe even sealed by the monks before it became an inn. We're safe, Remi. I'm positive."

The rest of the summer was devoted to dressing out the cellars. Celine made four brightly colored banners with a coat-of-arms insignia and the Latin words 'Fratres In Aeternum' (Friends Forever) circled above a roaring felt lion and the inscription 'Qui In Aeternum' (Forever One) circling below a multi-patterned shield. Remi and Felicien perfected the wall torches, extending their life and reducing the smoke they produced. Felicien and Alexis found that two of the casks still held wine. Although a tad on the sour side, when cut with a bit of sugar water, and strengthened with strong resolve they found it drinkable. Daniel spent hours in Treaire's tiny town library researching the history of the Bistro, but found no mention of the wine cellar.

On the afternoon of September 21, 1927, with torches illuminating the room, Remi stood at the head of the table under the largest of Celine's gaily colored coat-of-arms banners. He raised his cup and the others followed in unison.

"Fratres In Aeternum, Qui In Aeternum," he loudly proclaimed. "I, Remi Rousseau, do hereby declare and create the Order of the French Knights of Treaire, a band of friends dedicated to the support and defense of each other and their fellow countrymen in good times and lean, dedicated to the preservation of France and committed to the honor and liberty of its citizens. Vive la France!"

"Vive la France," the *friends* sang out in united response.

Celine couldn't take her eyes off Remi during those wonderful childhood years. She loved his look of bravado, his confident determination, his endless curiosity. In their games of pretend, she and the others were there for the fun. For Remi, it was different. She could see it in his eyes. To him, the games were real. He was there, charging across the wind-swept plains of a battlefield, leading not just a few ragtag children, but an army of thousands. In his beautifully creative mine he was a knight in the Order of the French Knights of Treaire. He lived it. Lost himself in the fantasy. Felt the majesty of the cause, heard the call to arms—the call to right the world's wrongs. His world fascinated her.

She was too young then to understand the feelings he stirred within her. An excitement that was wonderful and painful all at the same time. Her feelings intensified as they matured.

Then one afternoon, in their 16th year, walking home from school, in the warm air immersed in the yellow-orange glow of early fall, at the iron gate in front of her house—he kissed her.

Shocked and delighted, she gasped, "Why did you do that?"

"Because I have wanted to for a long time," he smiled.

"You have... For how long?"

"For a couple of years, I think. I don't remember the first time I thought about it. Probably at least a couple of years."

Bursting with joy, wanting desperately not to spoil the moment, she looked into his eyes. "Why did you wait?"

"I was afraid you wouldn't like it. Afraid you'd be unhappy if I treated you any different from the boys. That it would change everything somehow. Maybe change it so you wouldn't respect me as much anymore." He dropped his eyes, nervous that those very results might be unfolding.

"Oh, Remi, no. I have always been pleased that you respect me just like the others, but I loved the kiss. You always make me feel so special."

He smiled, a feeling of relief sweeping over him. His smile grew into a delightful boyish grin, "Okay, then... good. See you tomorrow." And with that, he turned and jogged down the street.

Celine watched him disappear around the corner. *He loves me,* she smiled, a little unsure of how to accept that realization. *Will he treat me differently when the friends are together? I hope not. I desperately hope not.*

The tight unity of the *friends* remained as the six matured. Felicien's marriage at the age of 18 seemed to change little in his relationship with the group. His divorce seven months later also did not seem to have significant effect on his position among the six, nor did his second marriage at the age of 19 and a half. After all, that was just Felicien. Spontaneous, carefree Felicien. His new wife joined the *friends* in their get-togethers as did his ex-wife, with whom he and his new wife remained close friends. While often included socially with the *friends* they were never taken to the cave.

As the years passed, Remi and Celine blended into a beautifully unique singleness of mind and purpose. They openly celebrated each other to everyone. An invisible force developed between them that they found supportive, strengthening. They felt somewhat diminished when apart. Something went missing. They were each a little more vulnerable.

Among the *friends* their unity brought strength and reason. The magnet that kept all of the pieces together.

In April of 1940, they married. The bond was acknowledged for all the world to see. Celine and Remi—united forever.

Threatening clouds were rising on the horizon that April in 1940. Germany's powerful military had conquered Czechoslovakia, and both the Nazis and the Russians invaded Poland, meeting in the middle and splitting up the country between them. The Nazis signed the Pact-of-Steel treaty with Italy's fascist dictator Benito Mussolini. Canada declared war on Germany. The Soviets attacked Finland, and there was talk that Germany was incubating further aggressive ambitions of flexing its powerful military muscles. Nothing felt safe, nothing secure.

A month before their wedding, Remi had commented to Celine that perhaps they should wait. "Just a while," he said, "just until we see how things are going to play out." She had been crushed by his comment, tried to look positive and supportive, but had failed miserably. He saw the devastation in her eyes, immediately took her hand, "Oh, Celine, that was foolish of me. If we keep waiting until things play out we will be old and tired. We'll go ahead. Just like we've been planning." His fears lingered but she was right. To postpone their lives, the joyous excitement of their love because of circumstances far beyond their control would solve nothing.

Celine too was concerned about the terrible events unfolding in Europe. Uncertainty was the only constant of the day. Everyone hung on the hope that the British efforts to negotiate with Hitler, talk him out of his seething desire to take ever more land from his neighboring countries, would be successful. Spirits soared when Britain's Neville Chamberlain returned from meetings in Berlin, making statements that he was encouraged with the peace negotiations taking place between him and the Führer. But the wishful longings were for naught. On May 10, 1940, just six weeks after Celine and Remi married, Germany invaded France. Three weeks later, the Germans bombed Paris and on June 14th Hitler accepted Philippe Pétain's surrender of the nation.

So much had happened since that terrible day. Events Celine would never have believed possible came crashing down upon her with incomprehensible speed—events that filled each day with anxiety, snuffed out the carefree romance of her new marriage and bent the fabric of daily life into a disorienting tangle of fear and uncertainty. Nothing was the same after the Germans took control of France.

She thought back to how terrified she had been when the Nazi invasion brought France to its knees. Germany's soldiers had poured into the country and now were ubiquitously injecting their reign of terror into every crevasse of life. They tromped through France with brutal disregard. The slightest resistance was met with atrocious force. In several towns where city authorities argued with demands of German officers, they were dragged into the streets and shot, their bodies left for the town's folk to dispose of.

The Nazis expressed no remorse for the damage they inflicted, imposing their agenda of cruelty without hesitation. Their objective was to bring the citizenry to heel, and whatever tactics were necessary to achieve that end were implemented instantly and with total detachment. To the Nazis, everyone else was inferior, unworthy of their consideration. French citizens were things to be used and discarded. The Germans took what they wanted, returning only grief, despair and agony in the settling dust from the tramping of their jackboots.

These terrible events had created the anger that now raged within Celine—an anger that disgusted yet permeated her like a cancer. Hitler's Nazis had stolen her youth, her optimism, destroyed her every fantasy. Her dreams had been put on hold, and now, after so many years, had begun to fade, taking with them her innocence and any hope of getting it all back It left her feeling vacant, abused, and unlovable, a vision of herself she had never thought possible.

The tragedy of it all welled up in her heart. The unceasing clamor from the ship's engines pounded in her ears as the odors of sweat and machine oil filled her every breath. She rested her head in her hands and quietly wept.

CHAPTER 3

In the first few months following the surrender of France, the Germans focused their attention on consolidating their power in Paris and northern France. German military presence in the south was sparse—virtually nonexistent in and around Treaire. Life continued much the same as it had before the occupation. If not for the rationing of various food stuffs in the markets and the news articles reporting tensions in Paris and cities to the north, it was almost as if the Germans had never entered the country.

Deeply in love and protective of their new marriage, Celine and Remi worked hard to shut out the politics of the nation's capitulation to the Nazis. They both wanted to be left alone, free to bask in the tenderness of their love, the beauty of their joy. They fought against any distractions, savoring every moment of being husband and wife, turning their apartment into their sanctuary from the world, reveling in the thrill of each other. They were successful at first, able to put the war on hold for the first few months. There were days, sometimes even a week or more, when there was no mention of the Nazis, the deteriorating economic conditions in France or Germany's continued military expansions now embroiling all of Europe and spilling into Russia. That all changed in late September.

Rumors were growing that the Germans were about to establish a major military base in southern France, specifically involving the area around Treaire. Such rumors had existed ever since France surrendered back in June, but as of late they had become more persistent. Tradesmen who had recently traveled through Chambéry, a medium-sized city 20 miles north of Treaire, reported a noticeable increase in German troops and equipment there. Then, on September 25, 1940, Lieutenant-General Franz Fettler rolled into Chambéry with 300 troops.

The Chambéry evening newspaper's lead story left nothing to question. The Nazis were taking over the vast Chambéry railroad switchyards and adjacent supply buildings. They would be doubling the size of the existing supply depot and would use the railhead as a staging point for funneling troops and equipment to their forces in Italy. Chambéry would be established as the Headquarters of the Deutsch Heer's Quartiermeister Einheit in Südfrankreich (German Army Quartermaster Unit in Southern France).

Apparently, the mayor of Chambéry, known for being fearlessly outspoken, confronted General Fettler, expressing his objections to having the troops stationed in his city. He wanted to discuss the matter with Paris German command, demanding the troops be housed outside Chambéry city limits until the matter could be resolved.

On September 30th, the Gestapo unit accompanying General Fettler's troops rousted Chambéry's mayor, members of the city council and a handful of hapless city clerical workers out on to the street and shot them. They performed the heinous act in broad daylight in the city's plaza filled with horrified onlookers. The Gestapo officer in command walked up to the mayor, whispered something in his ear, stepped back and shot him in the head. He then stepped to the side and ordered his men to open fire. Eleven people were shot down that day. There had been no warning, never an explanation, no newspaper coverage, not a word. Just the bodies left dead and dying in the city plaza as the firing squad marched away.

Celine's younger brother, Phillip, a minor clerk in Chambéry's utility offices, died in that murderous display of Nazi power. Her mother never recovered from the shock, taking her agony to her grave within months of the vicious travesty.

Treaire had been spared such a calamity, but tentacles of the murderous Chambéry incident quickly slithered the 20 miles that separated the towns, ensnarling Treaire's citizens in its grip of fear.

Within a month of establishing the German supply depot at Chambéry the Nazis sent an 80-man garrison into the tiny village of Falauge, just two miles east of Treaire. Falauge also had a rail switchyard, albeit much smaller than the one at Chambéry. But Falauge was immediately adjacent to the Saint Laurnee Gorge and its strategic rail trestle and tunnel—the key link to transporting enormous shipments of supplies and equipment into Italy.

The highway heading south out of Falauge into Italy was incapable of han-dling the massive convoys of equipment and supplies needed by the German battle groups stationed on the Italian Front. Just to the south of Falauge, the deep Saint Laurnee Gorge cut east and west, creating a natural barrier to ground traffic. The Romans had cut a roadway into the mountainside adjacent to the gorge almost 2,000 years before, when they expanded their empire north into France. The ancient road was still passable, but it narrowed in spots to one lane, and its bridges were much too weak to support heavy German tanks and artil-lery pieces.

In 1878, the French government, desiring to increase trade between France and Italy, started construction on a railroad line to circumvent the old Roman highway between the two countries. Two miles south of Falauge, they built a trestle over the 1,500-foot-deep gorge, and where the tracks met the vertical rock face on the opposite side of the gorge, they blasted out a mile-long tunnel through solid granite. When the rail line was completed in 1899, it was hailed as a great engineering accomplishment. The combination tunnel and trestle became known as the Saint Laurnee Passage, a point of critical military value to anyone needing to ship equipment and troops south into Italy or north from Italy into France.

As the first inhabited location after crossing the Saint Laurnee Passage, the town of Falauge provided a natural location for the establishment of a rail yard where cars could be switched or parked prior to their movement through the Passage. The rail yard had expanded steadily over the years, employing the ma-jority of Falauge citizens and quite a few men from Treaire.

Not trusting Frenchmen to load their military equipment on to flat cars for the rail trip into Italy, the Germans fired the French rail yard workers, replacing them with their 80-man garrison. Equipment convoys would motor to Falauge from various locations in northern France, including the huge Chambéry supply depot, then were loaded on to rail cars for shipment into Turin, Italy. Members of the Falauge garrison also manned anti-aircraft guns at several strategic points in the surrounding mountains to protect the Saint Laurnee Passage from any at-tempt by Allied war planes to destroy the vital transportation link.

In reality, the Allies had no intention of destroying the Passage. They were convinced that sooner or later they would push the Germans out of Italy, and when that day came, they wanted the Passage in tact to ship their own supplies and troops north.

The establishment of a German garrison just two miles from Treaire resulted in German troops and officers constantly in and around Treaire, bringing perpetual tension to every moment of daily life.

CHAPTER 4

It was Remi's obsessive loyalty to France, his love of the culture, his devotion to French liberty that had always attracted Celine. From her earliest remembrances of him he exuded a passionate love of country. This fervency for France, his commitment to values beyond himself, and his willingness to fight for his beliefs was about to draw them intensely into conflict with their German conquerors. Because of the times, Remi's passion would bring them face to face with the enemy and set them on a course of no return. At the same time, it would deepen their unity and bind them to the *friends* more passionately than ever before.

Immediately following France's surrender, Premier Philippe Pétain, with the permission of the Nazis, set up a new French government in Vichy, France. While the Vichy government claimed sovereignty, it was nothing more than a puppet of Germany. Pétain collaborated with the Germans, believing Hitler would successfully conquer all of Europe and hoping the Führer would then look favorably on France as he ruled to the conquered nations.

Under the direction of the Gestapo, Pétain turned the defeated French army into a national police force, the Milice française (French Militia), and set them to work carrying out the Nazis' underground war against French Jews and any non-Jewish French citizens causing problems for their German conquerors. Despite their protests, the majority of honorable men who had served in the French army prior to surrender were required to serve out their conscriptions in the Nazi controlled Milice. The moral men left the Milice units as quickly as their conscriptions ran out leaving behind the thugs and bullies who relished the power their Milice uniforms gave them over fellow citizens. In time the Milice française became an army of sadists even more brutal and assaultive than the Germans.

They were feared and despised by the majority of French citizens, considered traitors and persecutors of the nation's brave Resistance fighters and killers of innocent Jews.

With the establishment of large German military units in both Chambéry and Falauge, the Nazi presence in the area increased dramatically. Soldiers and officers of the Third Reich became common on the streets and a Milice enforcement unit was established in Treaire.

Celine and Remi continued their resolve to isolate themselves from the tensions. Being confronted and intimidated daily by Nazi soldiers and local Milice members placed ever increasing strained on that resolve, particularly on Remi. He seethed at the indignity of having to show his papers whenever one of the Milice regulars demanded he do so. Most of the local Milice members were the same bullies who had been problems when the *friends* were growing up... the same characters who got attention by beating up weaker kids, starting malicious rumors and blaming their faults on everyone but themselves.

Remi's resolve collapsed the night five Milice thugs surrounded him on his way home, heckling his unwillingness to join their police unit and roughing him up a bit—just for the fun of it. As he walked through the front door of their home, Celine knew immediately something was very wrong. He went directly into the bedroom to change. No smile, no warm greeting, no hug.

She slowly pushed the door open, "What's wrong, Remi?"

"Nothing," he snapped, immediately regretful for the tenseness in his voice. "I'm sorry, Cel. Just a bad day at work," he lied, keeping his back to her as he stripped off his shirt.

She hesitated for a moment, then silently left the room closing the door behind her. Moments later, Remi came into the kitchen.

"Cel, I can't go on pretending I don't care about the Nazis and the bastard Milice pushing everyone around like animals. I am so bottled up trying to act as if it doesn't matter. It's killing me." He stood shirtless, leaning against the doorway, looking at her with angry yet pleading eyes. "I can't stand it anymore. I've got to fight. I've got to stand up to these bastards. They're sucking the life out of our people and worse, they're starting to suck the life out of me. I've got to resist, to fight back—destroy them if possible or they will destroy us."

Celine wiped her hands on her apron, came to him, put her arms around his waist and laid her head against his chest. She felt his arms encircle her, squeeze her. He softly kissed the top of her head.

"I'm sorry," he whispered. "All I want is for you and me to be together, left alone to live our lives."

"I know," she whispered, "it's what I want, too." As she faced the reality of how innocently hopeless that dream was, a tear filled her eye. "Remi, I love you with all of my heart and soul. Marrying you was a dream come true, something I have longed for so many years." She looked into his eyes, which had also welled up. He bent his head and softly kissed her.

"You are my soul mate, Cel, my magnificent forever girl." He held her silently for a moment, then took in a long acquiescent breath. "I'll try to settle down. I am sure if I just..."

She interrupted, softly placing her fingers on his lips. "No," she whispered, "you are right to be angry. You are right to be passionate about what is happening. I wish it were not happening *now*, but there is nothing we can do to change that. We cannot pretend it is not affecting us—wishing it would just disappear.

"I know you, Remi. I know how deeply you feel about France, about our people. I know how violated you feel."

He told her of his encounter with the Milice. They both knew two of the Milice regulars who had been involved. Two of the same punks they avoided when they were growing up. Celine saw the deep anger boiling in Remi as he related the incident. "It's only going to get worse as time goes on, Cel. Eventually, they'll goad me or someone else into fighting back, then they'll cart us off to prison or one of the bastard Nazi concentration camps. They roughed up Felicien day before yesterday. I'm damn surprised he didn't haul off and deck one of them. Thank God, he didn't."

"It's time to fight, Remi. There's no avoiding what is happening. It's time for you to fight and I will fight alongside you. *We* will fight, you and I."

Her tone was strong. He felt her commitment. This was not a moment in time meant to temporarily appease him. She had come to the same conclusion—they could no longer act as if their world had not changed. It had, and she was ready to unite with him in dealing with it. Whatever it took.

He slowly rocked side to side, holding her in his arms, resting his lips softly on her head. "God, my dear God, what a beautiful woman you have given me," he whispered. He repeated his love prayer silently over and over in his head as they stood there in each other's arms.

Yes, she decided, she would fight alongside Remi. She would follow him into the face of death if need be. That night bound their marriage together on a whole new level of commitment. For the first time in months they were excited about the future—a future *they* would design and control. A future they would share in a common cause. Yet, a future where rapidly unfolding events would determine their destiny, lead them down tenuous passageways and unchartered backstreets of terrifying consequences.

❦

For the next 14 months, Celine and Remi were cohorts in arms. They created the Tristan Freedom Fighters and enlisted the *friends.* Once again, Celine, Remi, Amaury, Alexis, Daniel and Felicien became inseparable, re-igniting the deep bonds of their lifelong alliances. Amaury, Alexis, Felicien and Daniel were the body of the Tristan; Celine and Remi were its brain, its heart and soul.

The unity between them since birth had evolved, creating a group so mentally synchronized they interacted almost on a supernatural level. They understood each other's moods, played off each other's strengths and balanced each other's weaknesses. A harmonized unit, all six instinctively assisted each other in both simple and complex situations. It often took little more than a glance, a gesture, an expression between them to provide sufficient communication to elicit a desired response.

When this unique interactive relationship came together as a Resistance cell against the Nazi occupiers, the results were dramatic and devastating. The Tristan Freedom Fighters were destined to become one of the most sought after rebel bands in all of occupied Europe.

CHAPTER 5

During their first year the Tristan cell was invincible. Every action went flawlessly. Celine, Remi, Felicien, Amaury, Daniel and Alexis operated in perfect synergy. The ease with which they carried out their destructive attacks against the Nazi occupiers seemed as if their childhood games of fighting imaginary battles in defense of France had magically morphed into the realism of adult warfare.

Their stealth was impenetrable. Even the name 'Tristan' was known only to the six. Citizens for miles around proudly whispered of the mysterious Resistance group that had sprung to life, but no one knew who was behind it. It was as if a ghostly residue of the Three Musketeers had seeped from their mythical graves, spreading its phantom mist in the defense of France while leaving no trace of its origin. Speculation ran rampant; the joyous excitement of the local citizens grew with every successful Tristan raid. Their mystique added to the romance of it all, kindling a flame of exhilaration among the people. More than just disrupting Nazi activities, the Tristan was reawakening the spirit of the people. The 'Friends of France', as they came to be reverently referred to, were on the lips of everyone.

Remi delighted in their furtive hero status, eavesdropping intently on citizens' excited exchanges of praise for whoever was causing the Nazis such grief. The Tristan's seeming invincibility lent an atmosphere of superhuman invulnerability to their baleful activities. It was almost as if the 'god' that Remi felt approved of everything French, had somehow created an impenetrable dome of protection around them.

With each successful raid, the 'Friends of France' status grew, as did Remi's confidence. The Tristan destroyed bridges, blew up storage facilities, devastated food supplies, confused troop movements, disrupted power at military facilities and stole German arms and ammunition—all without so much as a scratch to any of them or a trace of evidence left behind.

The Germans were furious and perplexed. The skill and deftness with which the raids were implemented indicated detailed planning and insightful knowledge of German activities in the area. The attacks came with total surprise, were enacted at both vulnerable and heavily guarded locations, and were carried out with professional speed and efficiency.

There was even speculation among some high-ranking Nazi officers at both Falauge and Chambéry that a British or American commando team had somehow infiltrated the area. Gestapo Intelligence discounted that theory, maintaining that it had to be Frenchmen. They argued that, regardless of the level of fluency in French, Englishmen and Americans could not vanish into the local population with such undetectable amalgamation. German frustration with the situation was quickly reaching a boiling point.

While the *friends* basked in the rising glory of their reputation among the local citizenry, they remained naïvely innocent of their escalating infamy within the German high command. Their notoriety had even reached the Nazi General Staff's attention in Berlin. The Tristan, along with one other Resistance group operating out of Versailles, had risen to the status of the most wanted criminals in all of France.

CHAPTER 6

Reichsmarschall Hermann Göring, second in command to the Führer himself, called for a personal briefing on the 'French Problem', as it had become known within the Nazi hierarchy. By the conclusion of the briefing, Göring was emphatic that the rebels operating in the south of France were of the highest priority.

"Screw the Versailles bunch. They are nothing but a bunch of aging whores compared to the sons of bitches in the south," he growled at his aide-de-camp. "It is the bastard rebels in the south we must crush," he screamed, slamming his meaty fist down on the gleaming conference table. "They are the problem and they are operating in the area of the Saint Laurnee Passage."

The report had thoroughly described the horrendous damage the Tristan was inflicting on German military installations in and around the Chambéry supply depot, Grenoble, Lyon, and the critically strategic Falauge railhead. Most terrifying to Göring was the potential for destruction of the trestle crossing the Saint Laurnee Gorge, a blow that would be devastating to Germany's ability to supply its forces in Italy.

Placing his knuckles on the table, Göring pushed his weighty bulk to a standing position. He stood hunched forward, glaring at his officers allowing his anger to rise toward its legendary boiling point. Slowly, he turned and paced the length of the conference table, his boots generating a menacing echo in the massive room.

The seven officers sitting around the table dared not look at him. From previous experience with Göring's tirades, they knew his face was red with rage and any eye contact could direct his fury at the observer. He halted behind Franz

Fettler, leaned his belly against the back of Fettler's chair, and glowered down at the balding 58-year-old General. Fettler felt Göring's eyes penetrating his being. He sat, hardly breathing. Göring let a full minute pass as he stood behind Fettler, the silence broken only by the ticking of a massive grandfather clock sitting in the corner. Keeping their heads bent low, several fellow officers inquisitively stole glances in Fettler's direction. He continued to sit motionless, staring down at the report in front of him. Göring leaned into the back of Fettler's chair, causing it to slide uncomfortably toward the table as he broke his silence.

"Do you consider yourself an accomplished officer, General Fettler?"

"Jawohl, mein Herr."

"How long have you been Commandant of the French Southern District?"

"One and a half years, Sir," Fettler spat back his clipped answer, attempting to mask his rising anxiety.

"And inform us, Herr Fettler, when was the first raid perpetrated on the Chambéry yard—the supply yard directly across the street from your lavish office, the yard that your southern windows face, allowing you to survey the entire 50-acre site—the raid in which five troop trucks and two Tiger I assault tanks were destroyed at approximately 2:37 on a sunny spring afternoon?"

"It was a 10 months ago, mein Herr." Fettler shifted awkwardly in his seat, pulling a handkerchief from his pocket and dabbing sweat beads from his upper lip.

"And, Fettler, did you witness the trucks and the tanks burning in the depot yard as a result of that raid?"

"No, mein Herr, I was on leave... here in Berlin, visiting my wife and sons."

Göring leaned a bit harder, squeezing Fettler's chair still tighter to the table. "Ahh, you were here in Berlin, having a little family get together. Do you often leave your post at Chambéry to return to Berlin for warm and loving family visits?"

"No, Sir. Just that once... only that once since I have been assigned to Chambéry."

"Hmm. Interesting that you were in Berlin on the exact day of the raid on Chambéry depot," Göring's voice began taking on an almost playful tone. "Almost as if the perpetrators knew you'd be absent."

Göring paused, allowing the ticking of the grandfather clock to once again take control of the room. He bent his head back, staring at the ceiling, then looked back down and pushed hard on Fettler's chair, pinning the General tight against the table.

"And, Herr Fettler, how many raids have taken place since that initial disaster?"

"Reichsmarschall Göring, I beg of you... please, Sir, let me explain what we have been doing. The progress we have made in tracking these..."

Göring slammed hard against Fettler's chair, jamming the General painfully against the table's edge. "Answer the question, Fettler," he screamed, jolting everyone in the room to terrified attention.

"Thre... three, three more since the first," Fettler coughed.

"And, General Fettler, tell us when the most recent raid took place." Göring's voice now dramatically increasing in pace and anger as he continued, "The one in which four German soldiers were killed in the supply building that was blown up in Grenoble... the raid in which 700 assorted rifles, machine guns, mortars, hand grenades and thousands of rounds of ammunition were destroyed."

Franz Fettler was descending into stark terror. His hands palsied as he brought the handkerchief to his mouth. His voice cracked, "It... it was last... last month, Reichsmarschall Göring. But please, Sir, I beg you... please, allow me to explain." Fettler tried to twist in his chair, in a futile effort to look Göring in the eye. "We are... *(cough)*... closing in on the... *(cough)*... responsible group. We now know... they operate out of the small village of Allevard and we are prepared to..."

Göring smiled down at the stricken officer and in a soft, almost sympathetic voice interrupted his pleading, "What a shabby end to a family history of distinguished military service to the Fatherland, Mister Fettler."

Göring leaned against the back of the chair with such force Fettler had difficulty breathing. He withdrew a small-caliber revolver, pointed it straight down on the top of Fettler's head and pulled the trigger. Fettler's eyes shot wide in shock. His mouth sprang open as if to cry out, but no sound emerged. He continued sitting erect, wedged in place, as blood trickled down his forehead and he stared across the table through dead eyes.

Göring replaced the pistol in its shoulder holster, walked to the head of the table and settled back into his seat, facing his shocked officers. "Now, gentlemen," he smiled as he surveyed his near panicked audience, "which of you is to take Fettler's place as Commandant of the French Southern District?"

The six remaining officers sat rigidly, staring in horror at their dead fellow officer.

"Please, gentlemen, give me your undivided attention. Though fascinating, I think you'll find Fettler quite unappreciative of your notice of him." The officers turned to look at Göring, the man who held their fate in his hands.

"I am pleased to announce Generalleutnant Horst Hofstetter will replace Fettler as Commandant of the French Southern District." Göring smiled, almost as if expecting jubilant applause.

Hofstetter mentally shuttered as he contemplated being thrust into the high-profile situation his friend Fettler had just died for, yet he did not let his military façade reveal his loathing of Göring and his terror of the assignment. Hearing Göring name him, he bolted to attention, gave the Reichsmarschall a crisp Heil Hitler and said, "You may rest assured, Herr Reichsmarschall Göring, the criminals who are disrupting German operations in the south of France will be tracked down and annihilated within two months of taking my post at Chambéry."

Göring broadened his grin, eyeing all of the men. "Now, then, that wasn't so difficult, was it, gentlemen?" He rose, turned his back on his men, and left the room.

CHAPTER 7

9:55 pm, 19 April, 1942
35 Rue Beudant
Treaire, France

Seven hundred miles to the south, buoyed by the Tristan's string of unhampered successes and invigorated by all the comments of reverent awe from fellow citizens, Remi was convinced the Tristan should increase their activities. His love of adventure sparkled in his eyes as he described his vision to Celine.

"Cel, it's time we expand. We are doing so much more than causing the Nazis problems. We're changing the attitudes of the people. We hear it everywhere. The conversation we overheard today at the grocery…remember? The two old men laughing at the bumbling Nazis and wondering when the next 'Friends of France' raid would take place? The spirit of the people is growing positive once again." It was typical Remi. Seeing the romance and excitement of a much larger picture. Perhaps even fanaticizing an image of the people rising up in rebellion and overthrowing their German oppressors.

Celine caught the exhilaration in his tone, delighted in the eagerness sparkling in his eyes. She longed to follow blindly along, but this was not simply an extension of their fanciful childhood games. Recently there had been a sense of foreboding growing within her. She was thankful the Tristan's ventures had all gone flawlessly, but not convinced that trend would continue.

"I'm not so confident, Remi. The Germans are committed and cunning. They are not bumbling idiots, regardless of what people think. We've seen an increase in Nazi Commissioners and Gestapo agents in Treaire lately. People are being stopped and interrogated every day. You've heard the reports from Grenoble, Lyon and Falauge. They're all experiencing increased Gestapo pressure. I just heard the Nazis are probing around Allevard and Albertville. They're angry, Remi, and they are determined to find us."

"Of course they're angry…more like *terrified*," he added, smiling at his far-fetched vision of scaring the entire German army out of France.

Celine remained pensive, "Call it whatever you want. You know what they are capable of. Next they'll be dragging innocent people out into the streets and shooting them until someone comes forward and identifies us…or worse, confesses to the attacks in order to save their family.

"We're all alone out here, Remi. Sooner or later, we'll make a mistake and someone will find out who we are. If you want to expand, perhaps we should affiliate with the de Gaulle National Resistance organization. What about contacting Jean Moulin? He's working with de Gaulle to unite all of the various Resistance groups into an integrated force. That would give us some outside support."

Celine's hesitation slightly dampened Remi's enthusiasm, "The problem with all of those groups—the Moulin effort, is they have no unified sense of purpose. They spend hours sitting around arguing their conflicting ideologies, accomplishing nothing. We're doing real damage to the Nazis—damage that stings, makes those Hun bastards think twice about being here. I don't want to play at being a freedom fighter, I want to inflict real pain…kick 'em in the ass, bloody the sons of bitches." He paused, looked over at her and smiled, "We're so damn good at it, Cel."

She sipped her wine, considering his comments. His expression shouted the dedication and enthusiasm she so admired. *Is he right? Are we unique? Somehow divinely destined to play a major part in defeating Germany's desire to subjugate the world?* She wanted to believe, to follow along unquestioningly. *No…sooner or later they will find us. They will kill us. Torture our families. They are determined to crush us. They're getting closer every day. I can feel it.*

"Remi, the Nazis have conquered all of Europe. My God, half the French government is sympathetic to their cause. They are not going to be routed by us, no matter how much damage we do to them, and they are not going to sit by idly allowing us to kill their soldiers and destroy their equipment.

"They're snooping around, questioning more people and…"

"And getting nowhere," Remi injected, "because no one knows who we are. Hell, the krauts don't even know we operate out of Treaire. The last I heard, they think we're a cell operating out of Allevard."

"That's exactly my point, Remi. They don't know who we are. Anyone we bring into the Tristan increases our exposure. There is no one we can trust like Amaury, Alexis, Felicien and Daniel."

"There are others we know almost as well, Celine. Besides, we've got the Germans on the run…"

"You can't believe that," her interruption disclosed more irritation in her voice than she had intended.

"Can't believe what?"

"You cannot sit there and tell me you believe we have the mightiest military force in all of Europe on the run."

"I didn't mean on the run," he apologized. "But we've got them concerned. They think Frenchmen are a bunch of cowards because Pétain folded to them without so much as a good fight." Anger flashed in his eyes. "Their officers laugh about what a bunch of cowards we Frenchmen are. We're changing that misconception.

"Cel, we've made them see they are not going to get a free ride in France… that we are not going to simply step aside and let them tramp us into dust."

"That is just the point, Remi. They've got to be mad as hell. The minute there is the slightest suspicion of who we are, they'll bring the wrath of hell down on us. The fact that they don't know, and that we can trust our *friends* that they will never know, is our only safety. Recruiting outsiders will bring us down, Remi, I'm convinced of it."

Remi had to admit he, too, was seeing signs of increased Nazi agents probing around Treaire. He had heard reports of similar activity in the other towns Celine had mentioned.

No doubt, the Tristan was probably high on the list of Nazi irritations in southern France, maybe even center stage; but that was exactly why he felt they should make a major push now— before the Germans started terrorizing every town for miles around.

He lit a cigarette, refilled their wine glasses and rested his head on the back of the sofa. They both sat in silence, staring at the flames dancing in the fireplace.

"What about Max Dulac and Damian Descoteaux…or how about Camille Laurel?" Remi almost whispered. "We've known them all of our lives. They're our age, loyal to France and all have families that have lived in Treaire for generations. It is only a few, Cel, just a few that we would consider—people we know well."

"Why them?"

He looked over at her. The milder tone of her question offered hope she was at least open to consider the trio.

"Because Camille, being a waitress at the Bistro, and German officers frequent the place—she hears everything. Damian, managing the telegraph at the post office, is privy to every bit of news coming in and going out of Treaire, and Max's position at the apothecary gives him access to drugs and chemicals we can use," he paused and couldn't help but chuckle. "You know, he could steal cigarettes for Felicien and drugs we can use to poison the Hun bastards."

She had to admit they were all bright, dedicated, and committed to France and Treaire, and had been close friends since childhood. Still she couldn't overcome her gnawing uneasiness.

She looked over at Remi, yearned to support him. *Perhaps*, she thought, *I am too cautious. Had it not been for Remi I would never have started down this path in the first place.* Her thoughts pacified her, but did not ease her deepest concerns.

She sighed, reached over and laid her hand on his, "Those are good people, Remi. I have to admit. They are people I feel we could trust. But I can't shake the feeling the Germans are livid about what we're doing. It's almost as if I can feel their eyes on me all the time. We raise our risk by going outside of the *friends,* and I question whether it is wise for us to increase our activities right now. If anything, it might be a time for us to back off for a while—give the Germans a reason to lower their interest in us."

She made her point. At the same time, he was inwardly encouraged by her agreement that Max, Damian and Camille might be good choices, and were people she considered trustworthy. He breathed deeply, took a last drag on his cigarette and downed his remaining cabernet.

"Perhaps you are right," he stretched. "It is time for bed. Let's think about it and discuss it more tomorrow."

Celine felt she had raised his caution but had not convinced him not to proceed.

Camille Saurel left the Bistro, locking its ancient door for the night. It was 2:30 am, the night air chilly as she hurried through the dark streets. Regardless of having made this trek countless times, she was never able to throw off the apprehension the blackness of night brought on. She wrapped her hand around the switchblade stiletto in her pocket, determined she would not be taken down again.

She pulled the knife quickly from her pocket pleased it emerged open, its blade locked in position and ready to strike. She had practiced often since the incident and could now draw and flash it open instantly. She closed the blade. Pushed the weapon back into her pocked and quickened her pace.

About to practice once again, her heart leapt as a black sack was thrust over her head from behind and yanked down to her waist. Strong arms wrapped around her, pinning her arms to her sides. She stumbled forward in panic and the arms held her from falling to the street. A deep voice whispered, "Do not be afraid. I will not hurt you. I am a member of the group you know as the 'Friends of France'. We want to talk with you."

Her terror eased slightly. The massive arms holding her, while powerful, were not assaultive. The speaker, although attempting to disguise his natural pitch, was calm and reassuring. Still, her voice trembled in its reply, "When? When do you want to talk with me?"

"Now. If you are agreeable to meet with us, I will wave for a car to pull up. We will take you to a secret place where we will explain what we want. You will not be harmed. We would like you to work with us. Once you have heard our proposal, you can decide what you want to do."

The thought of joining the 'Friends of France' excited her. She had fantasized about the honor she would feel being one of them. Still, she hesitated, victimized by the debilitating terror of what might happen if she refused.

The man waited patiently, still holding her supportively in his arms, "Your answer, Camille," he whispered.

"Yes…okay, I will talk."

"When I ease my arms from around you, do not turn around. Keep your back to me and do not try to remove the sack."

A car approached. She was assisted into the back seat between her assailant and another man. They drove in silence for 20 minutes, making multiple turns before finally coming to a halt.

The same voice said, "I will place my arm around your shoulders as we walk. Relax. Let me guide you. We will be walking on a path, so I will be guiding you left and right as the path meanders. Do you understand?"

"Yes, okay."

Dried leaves rustled at her feet as they made their way along the path. Someone was in front of them and another was keeping pace directly behind. Her footsteps then seemed to be on pavement of some sort and the sounds of their movement echoed as if they were walking down a twisting hallway.

"We are going to stop now," the voice instructed. "I will slide a chair up behind you." The rim of a chair touched the backs of her legs.

"You may sit down now. Stare straight ahead. As you sit, I will remove the sack. Do not turn and try to look at me."

The sack was lifted causing her to blink painfully. Intense white light shone directly into her eyes.

She was sitting in the center of a six by six-foot square defined by black cloth panels on all four sides. Bright lights shone down from above at the corners of the drapery. She could feel the heat they generated. The floor was roughhewn stone...a tile of some sort. A humid dampness filled the air. Musty. The room was eerie in its silence, yet she sensed there were people behind the cloth panels, viewing her through the material. From her side, she saw nothing but the occasional rustle of the black drapes.

A different voice spoke. Calm. Strong and reassuring. "Please sit quietly and do not interrupt. You are in the presence of the group you know as the 'Friends of France'. We have observed you and believe you are trustworthy. A dedicated patriot of France. We believe you could be of assistance to us, should you be willing to join with our organization.

"You work at the Bistro in Treaire. You hear many things there. When you hear comments you feel we should know about concerning the Germans, the Milice, or anything you feel would be important in our battle against the Nazis, you will call for a meeting by wearing a red, yellow or green ribbon in your hair at the Bistro. You will be observed daily.

"When we see the red, yellow or green ribbon, you will be contacted by one of us as you proceed home at night. We will intercept you at varying locations along your night route. Our contact will approach you from the rear as you make your way through the streets. Even though our contact will be dressed in black and wearing a black ski mask, you will keep walking, facing straight ahead, and upon instruction will whisper your information as you proceed on your way. If we do not make contact on the day you wear one of the ribbons, do not be concerned. Contact will be made at a time we deem safe for you and for us."

She sat quietly. There was a long pause, then the voice continued.

"You will never be allowed to see any of us. What we are asking you to do is dangerous. Should the Nazis or the Milice become suspicious, they will interrogate you, perhaps even torture you. Most likely, we will be unable to come to your aid should that happen. Also, you must understand that if we ever gain proof that you are working against us, we will not hesitate to kill you."

Another pause.

"We want to know if you are agreeable to these rules. If you are not, we will return you to Treaire, where you can proceed home and you will never hear from us again."

Whatever romantic ideas Camille may have fantasized about being a member of the 'Friends of France' vanished in the cold verbalization of the instructions.

She took in a long breath trying to calm her thoughts as she sat staring at the black curtain. "Can I think about this and give you…"

"No. You must decide now."

"What about my parents, my brother and sister? Will they be in danger if I do this?"

"If you are exposed, everyone you know will be in grave danger—interrogated, most likely tortured, and perhaps killed. We are considered terrorists by the Nazis. They are unwavering in their determination to find and eliminate us. We will do everything in our power to protect you from suspicion, but you must understand that you will become an extension of us through your cooperation. What is your decision?"

She sat silently. The proposition was so one-sided, so fraught with danger, yet she had come to passionately hate the Germans. The flashback of being grabbed, dragged into the woods behind her home and assaulted by the two German soldiers screamed through her mind. In the months since that horror she had struggled to bury the humiliation as deeply as possible. No one knew. Not her mother, not even her sister in whom she confided everything. She had not seen the two soldiers since.

The flashback inflamed the anger she had fought so hard to overcome. Brought back every moment of the rape. But this time, there were no tears, no self-pity—just seething rage screaming to lash out, to get even.

"Yes. Okay. I will do this," her voice was powerful, her anger unmistakable. "But I have one condition."

"State it."

She breathed deeply, "When I prove my worth, my reliability. . .when you feel you can trust me, I want in. I want to be more than just an information gatherer. I want to participate in the destruction of these Nazi pigs."

No one saw the smile behind Remi's mask, but Celine knew it was there. "Fair enough," he said.

The same interrogation procedure was used to interview Maximilian Dulac and Damian Descoteaux. They, too, committed.

CHAPTER 8

1:33 pm, 23 April, 1942
Chambéry air strip
Chambéry, France

General Horst Hofstetter landed at Chambéry in a dismal mood.
Göring's sickening and cravenly murder of Franz Fettler exemplified everything Hofstetter had come to despise about the lunatic group presently in control of Germany's government. Nazi terror squads gave the German populace little choice but to keep quiet and hope for the best as the country pursued its dictator's perverted plans for the world.

Hofstetter's following his family's long military history of serving the Fatherland found him caught up in a war he did not feel Germany could win, fighting for a cause he did not support, under the command of leaders he did not respect. Now he was facing an assignment he was not convinced he could successfully accomplish.

He disembarked the transport plane alone. No aide at his side, no fanfare. He wasn't even sure the Chambéry staff was aware Fettler had been replaced, much less knew their General had been murdered. The surprised look on the face of the driver at the airport confirmed his suspicions.

"I am General Hofstetter, young man. Take me immediately to Chambéry headquarters."

"Jawohl, Herr General," the driver snapped, burying his confusion at not seeing General Fettler.

Hofstetter walked briskly into the Chambéry headquarters building and up to the information desk, "Direct me to General Fettler's office."

Fettler's aide sat at a reception desk immediately outside the General's office and sprang to his feet when Hofstetter pushed through the door.

Not slowing his pace, Hofstetter said, "I'm your new Commandant, Major. What is your name?"

"Beinholt, mein Herr," came the crisp reply.

Hofstetter threw open the door to Fettler's office. Over his shoulder, he instructed, "Bring me every bit of information that exists on the terrorist raids that have taken place against our forces within a 100-kilometer radius of Chambéry over the past 18 months. Then, prepare to spend a long night going over them with me."

At 1:45 am, Hofstetter crushed out the foul-tasting cigarette he had unconsciously just lit. "There is nothing here, Beinholt. Not one hint of who these people are. Not the slightest indication of where they operate from—nothing! How in hell can a group do so much damage without leaving a trace of evidence?"

Beinholt hesitated. It was in his best interest to remain as distant from this quest as possible, but in the few hours he had spent with his new boss, he liked Hofstetter. He saw passion in the man, willingness to apply himself to a task he dreaded simply because it was an order. Beinholt deeply respected such military bearing.

"I believe they operate either out of Grenoble or Treaire, Sir."

Hofstetter shot the Major a questioning look. "Why in hell did you wait until now to bring this up?"

"It is only a theory, Sir. Based on my observations of where the attacks have taken place and the most logical escape routes the saboteurs would have to take in order to vanish so quickly and completely each time. I brought this up to General Fettler and the Gestapo."

"When?"

"About eight months ago, during a briefing of Hauptsturmführer Barbie in Lyon. Captain Barbie and his aide dismissed my idea with such distain we dropped it immediately. General Fettler never brought it up again, so I just let it go. Hence my reluctance to repeat it now."

Hofstetter leaned forward, pushing aside the array of files in front of him, "Show me."

He sat patiently for the next 20 minutes as Beinholt presented several maps on which he had drawn circles around trails and back roads leading away from attack sites. On each map he had highlighted routes of possible escape. In every case, only Grenoble or the area surrounding Treaire offered plausible opportunity for rapid and undetectable escape.

Hofstetter pinched the bridge of his nose in an effort to subdue his exhaustion. "Tomorrow, Beinholt, you and I will pay a visit to the Milice units in Grenoble and Treaire."

<hr/>

The French Milice units were often considered more dangerous to French Resistance fighters than the Gestapo. Made up of Frenchmen, the organization's members had intimate knowledge of their community areas, understood the subtleties of the culture and, with their members being citizens living within the local environment, little escaped their notice. They were often the first to recognize if anything were out of order.

Jacques Madure, the ne'er-do-well ranking officer of the Treaire Milice unit, was startled when his aide announced General Hofstetter, the new Commandant of the French Southern District, and his aide-de-camp were waiting in the lobby. Madure's initial concerns were about to intensify.

General Hofstetter immediately cut to the point, "I am here, Colonel Madure, to find the source of, and put a permanent halt to the sabotage activities taking place in this area. I do not have to detail the devastating attacks that have taken place on German installations in the area over the past 18 months. I will further point out that I am disappointed in you and the performance of your unit in not having turned up a single clue as to who the perpetrators are, how they operate or where it is that they crawl back into hiding."

Madure sat nervously intent on the threatening tone in Hofstetter's voice.

"I have reason to believe these terrorists are operating out of Treaire or Grenoble. My orders to you are simple. Find them, infiltrate their organization and expose them to me. I expect this to be accomplished within the next eight weeks. Should you fail to meet this timetable, I will have you sent to a concentration camp, replace you with another of your countrymen, and begin the process over once again.

"Any questions?"

CHAPTER 9

Max Dulac was excited about having been recruited into the 'Friends of France'. Despite the fact that he still did not know who any of them were, he was honored this heroic group had sought him out. Definitely a compliment to his patriotism and their trust in him. Max was several years younger than the *friends,* but they had all known him and his family for years. He was bright, hard-working, still living at home, and extremely protective of his adolescent sister and brother. She was a delightful girl of renowned beauty and his little brother revered Max, constantly working to earn his big brother's respect.

Max, himself, was fiercely loyal to France, almost as vehement in his loyalty to the country as Remi. He hated the Germans. Hated the Milice even more. To Max, the Milice were gutless Frenchmen—despicable traitors. Of their three new recruits, the *friends* were most pleased with Max. It was only through his growing respect for Max and Max's constant badgering to become more in-volved that Remi allowed him to accompany the group on several minor raids. Even then, with the members all shrouded behind ski masks, Max was kept in the dark as to their identities.

While the *friends* welcomed their new recruits, they shared little information with them. None of the new members knew the identity of the *friends,* nor did they know of each other's involvement. Camille and Damian were strictly used as informants, never brought together with the group.

Shortly after Max joined the Tristan, one of the Milice regulars got wind that Max might be participating in some Resistance activities. It was just a hunch—nothing substantial—but Colonel Madure was in no position to be picky about substantial proof. Any hunch satisfied his panic to get some information he could hand back to General Hofstetter. He jumped at the chance to interrogate Max Dulac.

Returning home from work one evening, six Milice regulars grabbed Max and dragged him to Milice headquarters. He was tied to a chair and roughed up—nothing serious enough to leave tell-tale bruising, but inflicting sufficient pain to get his attention.

"We know you're a member of the 'Friends of France', you little bastard," lied Madure. Although a bluff, the statement was delivered with sufficient conviction to give Max concern that somehow his cover had been compromised.

"You're going to start cooperating with us, Maximilien Dulac, because if you do not, that cute little sister of yours is going to be hauled into the woods one of these days to romantically entertain a group of our members, after which we'll see that her lovely face gets rearranged."

Madure was smiling as he delivered the message. No idleness in the threat. Because of their close association with the Germans the Milice could carry out such atrocities with total immunity. They left Max alongside the Chambéry-Treaire highway, painfully doubled over from the final stomach punch delivered when they ejected him from the car.

———— ✦ ————

At first, Max leaked as little information as possible—just enough to keep his sister safe from the threat. But Jacques Madure was on a tight timetable and quickly grew impatient with Max's reluctance to pass on anything meaningful. He broadened the threat to include Max's entire family and demonstrated his commitment by having Max's grade school-age brother beat up by Milice regulars as he returned home from school one afternoon. It wasn't a severe beating. Just enough to terrify the little boy and leave a scar just above his right eyebrow.

Max began to divulge the information Jacques Madure needed, and things immediately deteriorated for the Tristan.

The first Tristan tragedy was Daniel, Handsome, courageous Daniel—the *friend* who gave prudent advice to Remi, was always a gentlemen to Celine, kidded Alexis, poked fun at Amaury's vast wealth and had perfected the art of cigarette smoking with the diligent help of Felicien. He fell, critically wounded, in the doorway of the Milice armory the instant he entered.

Being forewarned of a Tristan raid, the Milice met the *friends* with a barrage of gunfire as they broke into the building. The Tristan had stolen from the armory before. It was always carelessly unlocked and unguarded— an easy target. The raid was to be a quick in-and-out operation…steal a few weapons and ammunition then quickly vanish into the night. Daniel was first through the door, catching two bullets in the chest. They managed to get him back to the cave, where he looked into Remi's eyes with brotherly love and died.

For the first time since they had started their self-proclaimed war against the Nazi occupiers, the Tristan tasted the acid sting of personal tragedy. Daniel's mournful death marked the beginning of a series of devastating setbacks. Over the next six weeks, nothing went right. Assaults on German installations were thwarted when both German and Milice troops would show up expectantly. Amaury incurred a flesh wound as the group ran from an interrupted raid attempting to blow up a section of railroad track. Celine was separated from the group in a mad dash for safety in a power line-cutting operation. She didn't show up for a day and a half, forced to implement a series of complex maneuvers through the back country to elude her pursuers. A week later, Damian Descoteaux was murdered. His bloody body found slumped over his telegraph machine by fellow postal workers as they arrived at work one morning.

The day following Damian's death, Max Dulac put a gun to his head, ending his torment and the Milice's source of information.

All of a sudden, the Tristan's activities were no longer a game. The excitement of the untouchable Tristan Freedom Fighters vanished, the romance of the 'Friends of France' drained away in the blood of reality, and their world changed forever.

CHAPTER 10

Remi took the blame upon himself for the series of tragedies, as he always did when people he loved and respected came to harm. Three days after Max's suicide, he and Celine asked the *friends* join them at one of their favorite childhood haunts deep in the woods. The sitting stones they had gathered in a tight circle as children were just as they had left them so many years before. The serenity of the woods surrounding their circle was calming in its natural beauty.

Remi was repentant and serious. "I will never fully recover from the pain of the recent past. My heart has never before felt broken. I am racked with remorse and I apologize to each of you for talking you into all of this."

He paused, regaining his composure, "My love for each of you is deep and constant. You have been the anchors in my life. You have returned my love, yet I have placed all of you in peril. I now realize the seriousness of the risk I have exposed you to. It is a risk I resisted allowing myself to fully comprehend. It exposes not only you, but everyone you love to the wrath of an enemy of power and relentlessness far beyond our means to control.

"They are without pity or guilt, and will stop at nothing to destroy us. I am convinced they still do not know who we are or how many of us make up the Tristan. We were successful in passing off Daniel's death as a work-related accident. The citizens of Treaire accepted that story, and there is no reason to believe the Nazis or the Milice believe any differently. But they now know we operate from out of Treaire. If we continue, they will begin indiscriminately torturing and killing our friends and neighbors.

"We are small. We will never defeat them. All we can hope to do is further irritate and enrage them. They do not fear us. They have taught me that *I* must learn to fear *them*. Our continued efforts are not worth the price they will exact."

All eyes were cast toward the ground as Remi spoke. He paused. Breathed deeply. Sat in sadness with Celine and the men he considered brothers. He looked up at them with a pained heart, "It is time for us to go our separate ways. Go home to your families. Forget you were ever a member of the Tristan. Forget your hate for the Germans. Bury it. Forget your passions for France. Rely on God. He will eventually deliver us from this evil."

His words fell heavily. They sang of defeat, a song none was prepared to hear. They burdened the forest with their weight crushing down on the listeners. Tears welled in Alexis' eyes as he continued staring down at the soft grass. Remi slowly bent his head into his hands and wept. Tears dampened every face—shed not only for their fallen comrades but also in painful defeat of their love of France...the France they had so joyously banded together to protect and liberate. Now it was over.

They remained huddled there, surrounded by the soft peacefulness of the scent of the pines and the distant call of ravens watching the gathering and wondering at its meaning. After many hugs and soft words between them, they went their separate ways, their minds numbed by the crushing realities of war.

There was no contact among them for three weeks, the longest period of time the *friends* had remained apart since birth. They carried on their separate lives in mourning, the burdens of the world weighing heavily on each.

Celine, making her way home one afternoon, was approached by Felicien, "We want to meet with you and Remi. Amaury and I have been talking and we want everyone to meet. At the cave tomorrow evening at eight. I will contact Alexis."

The following night they gathered around their ancient oak table, sequestered in their private catacomb. Felicien set glistening, long-stemmed glasses before them, each twinkling the reflections of yellows and golds of the dancing flames from the wall torches. He carefully filled each glass with a magnificent Cabernet that Amaury had selected from the Bistro. Amaury stood behind his chair and raised his glass. All rose in unison.

"We raise our glasses in respectful memory of comrades lost in battle. Many years ago, Remi taught us to look beyond ourselves, to see purpose, dignity and honor in the morality of the greater cause. Those of us who have died—Damian, Max and Daniel—gave their lives for freedom. For the freedom and liberty of our oppressed people. Felicien and I have assembled you here tonight that their families not mourn their loss in vain. That their lives not be forgotten. May their souls look down on us with pride.

"To our fallen companions."

"To our fallen companions," echoed the assembled.

Felicien remained standing, turning to Remi and Celine, "Amaury and I have been discussing things. We have also talked with Alexis, who is in agreement with us.

"We understand the burden you have chosen to carry, Remi, but we, and those we have just praised, were not led into this fight as naïve school children. We are at war with a mighty enemy, a brutal enemy that does not care if we survive. They do not care if France survives, and we are convinced that if they prevail, they will destroy not only France but all of Europe.

"Alexis, Amaury and I want to carry on…to fight them whenever and however we can. The Nazis are taking thousands of Jews from Paris and exporting them to work camps in Germany. It is only a matter of time before they do so here, in Treaire.

"The English and the Americans are beginning to make gains in Africa against Rommel's forces. The Russians are pushing the Nazis back from Stalingrad, and the German offensive at Kursk has failed. These bastards are not invincible. They can be beaten and we want to participate in their demise."

Amaury looked at Celine and Remi, "We are willing to fight, but we need the two of you to lead. Your planning kept us out of trouble for over a year after we started up. Felicien, Alexis and I do not have your skills. We cannot continue on if you do not come with us. We understand your remorse but, Remi, your guilt has no place here. Your guilt is arrogant and disrespectful of us. We are not children. We knew the danger. So did Daniel, Damian and Max. If we quit now, those men will have died for no good reason. Damian's wife and child will have given him for nothing."

Alexis chimed in, "Yeah, me, too. I think we should keep doing this, too."

Remi smiled at Alexis' addition to the eloquence. He looked at Celine. She nodded, giving him an encouraging smile.

"Okay," he sighed. "I will stop being so depressed. You are all brave and I respect your wishes, but we must not move on immediately. I made a mistake in trying to move too fast. We must let things cool off...make the Germans think they have crushed us. I have not been totally idle. I went to Lyon and met with Jean Moulin, who is coordinating things for General de Gaul. He told me last year the Americans and the British established a special training camp somewhere in England. They are training members of various Resistance cells from each of the occupied countries. Their first trainees will graduate soon and they are filling slots for the next training session now. Moulin said they will take one of us if we are interested.

"Trainees are smuggled out of their respective countries, brought to the training camp and schooled in every aspect of Resistance warfare. The training takes the better part of a year. Each trainee will be expected to return to their Resistance cell and pass the training on to their comrades. They will be supplied with weapons and ammunition by the Brits and Americans upon their return.

"If we're going to continue on with our battle, I want us to send someone to this training. We will choose who will go and the rest of us will suspend all activity until our chosen one returns. Dropping out of sight for an extended period will take the heat off, get the Germans to lower their guard and set the stage for when we start up again."

Excitement burst forth, filling the room with toasts, backslapping and several conversations going at once. Alexis interrupted loudly, "Who's going?"

They all turned as he added, "We have to choose who's going to go to the training."

The next hour was filled with argument as to who would be the best candidate. It was Celine who finally suggested they draw straws, and it was she who drew the short straw.

"Wait," Alexis said, looking fearful, crushed, "This is not fair. She is too little and will get hurt."

Remi turned toward his big friend, "We have never made exceptions for Celine, Alexis. She is as capable as any of us. God knows I will miss her more than anyone, but it would not be fair, either to Celine or the rest of us, if we made her an exception now. She won't get hurt, Alexis. She's strong in so many ways. She is one of the *friends*, an equal. She'll do fine." Remi's words masked the ache in his heart, his own worry for her safety and the dread of loneliness he knew he would face.

Two weeks later, on an isolated patch of road high in the Alps, a British Lysander Mk III touched down and remained stationary on the road on the road for under 30 seconds. Celine dashed to the plane jumped into the single passenger seat and the plane roared up into the night carrying her off to an unknown destination to learn the skills of war.

Two days after Celine's departure, Remi, Felicien and Amaury carried out one more operation. They kidnapped Jacques Madure and his top two Lieutenants, drove them to the edge of the Saint Laurnee Gorge and shot them. Their bodies were never found.

General Hofstetter shut down the Treaire Milice branch upon learning of the disappearance of Madure and his henchmen. Hofstetter was personally glad to be rid of the incompetent Treaire Milice.

The Tristan went dormant.

The *friends'* lack of activity over so many months brought renewed confidence to the Germans. They mistakenly believed they had intimidated the Tristan into extinction. All of that was about to change.

CHAPTER 11

4 June, 1943
Mediterranean Sea
50 miles south of Montpellier, France

There was a tap on Celine's steel stateroom hatch, "Time for your flight, miss," the Petty Officer called over the pulsing hum of the ship. "Just head up to the ready room. I'll bring your duffel," he smiled as she pulled open the hatch.

She knew the way. Down the narrow passageway, third hatch on the right up the ladder, two hard rights up another ladder and into the ready room. As Celine emerged through the hatch, the Captain smiled and came over to her. "Not a very good evening for a flight, Mrs. Rousseau, but under the circumstances, it's the best we can do. On a bit of a tight schedule. Trying to make it down to Tunisia, you know."

The young pilot who would be flying Celine stood at the other end of the room. The Commodore was lecturing him and the pilot was repeating, "Yes, Sir," at appropriate spots in the one-sided conversation. Celine smiled at the Captain, "The Commodore doesn't think much of me, does he?"

"Oh, don't let that worry you, ma'am. Commodore Bentley is of the old school. Bad omen, women on ships of war, and all that. Nothing personal, I assure you."

The conversation between the Commodore and the pilot ended and the Commodore turned his back to leave the room. Celine called out, "Commodore, excuse me. May I have a word with you?" The old man froze, then slowly turned as Celine moved toward him. His face reflected his discomfort combined with irritation.

"I want to express my gratitude to you, sir. I respect your military bearing, the discipline that allows you to carry out an order you find distasteful, yet carry it out with the same dedication to its success as one that would bring you great joy. I, and the people I will be working with, will fight and, if necessary, die to assist you and the Allied forces defeat Germany. The training I have received from your countrymen and the Americans has been invaluable. It will help us avoid losing more of our Resistance fighters than the three we have already lost. Thank you, sir. For all you have done to get me back into the fight."

The discomfort still predominated Bentley's expression. The irritation was gone. "You're welcome, young lady," he reached out and shook her hand. "God be with you."

⸺⚬⚬⚬⸺

From the pitching of the ship Celine experienced below decks, she figured the weather was bad. She had not been prepared for quite how bad as she stepped out onto the carrier's wet flight deck. The early summer storm was approaching Force 8 wind gusts, and seas were measuring 14 to 16 feet. Heavy rain was blowing horizontal at times.

The powerful little single-engine Lysander Mk SBS, a modified side-by-side two-seater airplane, strained on its tie-down lines in the shifting winds. The June wind was cold, filled with the taste of sea salt and pelting rain. A sailor came around the far side of the plane, slip-sliding toward Celine and shouting over the howling gale, "Duck back into the passageway, missy. The pilot's just now coming to the flight deck. Let him get to the plane, then we'll get you on board."

She watched her pilot bracing against the wind, trying to keep his footing as he made his way to the plane. He struggled with the door against the wind. He was in. Two sailors came across the deck toward Celine, "I'm okay," she shouted, "don't need assistance." The men grabbed her under each arm and literally carried her to the plane. *Oh, what the hell. Why fight it?* she mused to herself. A following deckhand stuffed her duffel into the plane behind her as the two lifted her into her seat. They slammed her door just as the pilot hit the starter. The Lysander's nine-cylinder, 636-horsepower radial engine exploded to life violently, shaking the airframe. It's three-blade aluminum propeller instantly jumped from dead stop to 2000 rpms. Celine looked out of her side window.

Four sailors were holding fast to the plane's tie-down lines. The pilot stood on the brakes, revved the engine up to 2800 rpm, waved the sailors off, pushed the throttle past 3400 rpms, and released the brakes. The plane shot forward, a strong up draft caught the wings and the plane leaped into the air. A down draft followed bouncing the Lysander's rugged landing gear down hard on the deck. The pilot shoved the throttle past it's red line, pulled back hard on the stick, and the plane rose in the turbulent winds and slowly began to climb as it left the end of the carrier's deck.

The pilot looked over at Celine, his boyish face breaking into a broad grin, "Not too bad, considering the conditions." Celine's ashen expression remained frozen. She clutched the safety bar on the dash in front of her with her left hand and held the structural steel bar beneath her seat so hard with her right that pains began shooting through her arms. The Mediterranean disappeared instantly in the shroud of thick white haze as the little plane bounced ever higher toward its 7,000-foot planned altitude. Lightning flashed with an ear-splitting crack, lighting up the angry clouds that Celine was sure were about to swallow them. Another flash. Louder. The plane jerked up on a strong updraft, hit its peak and dropped sharply before bottoming out with a hard jolt as it hit the next updraft.

"Windy little bugger, this cloud," the pilot's voice chimed through Celine's headset. "Nothing to worry about, miss. We're climbing through 3,500 feet. Running through some of this cloud's up and downdrafts. This is a rugged little plane. Takes a lot more than a stiff wind to take her apart."

His matter-of-fact tone coming through her headphones was calming. She cautiously eased her hand from the safety bar and released her grip on the seat, thinking, *Why in the hell am I holding on to the seat? If the damn plane goes down, this seat is going with it.*

His voice cracked through again, "Just passed 4,300 feet, miss. Might be a bit smoother once we get up around 7,000. You doing all right?"

"Yes, I'm fine," she lied, fighting hard to quell the bit of nausea she was feeling.

<hr />

Two hundred and thirty eight miles to the north, Remi, Amaury, Alexis and Felicien were already at the drop site. Remi had selected the coordinates 45° 15' 0.9318" x 6° 40' 46.9128", an isolated 2,000-foot stretch of straight gravel road high in the Alps, for the Lysander to land and return Celine to French soil. The British had received the radio message sent by Remi and Felicien a week ago specifying the latitude and longitude coordinates of the landing site. Within five minutes they had received the British acknowledgment specifying a date and time of Celine's landing. In that transmission the radio communication had worked perfectly. But that was not always the case.

Their dilapidated little radio transmitter often was not reliable. Sometimes it got messages through to the British, sometimes not. Even when messages did get through, their receiver did not always pick up the British acknowledgement. Remi and Felicien had come to realize that not receiving an acknowledgment did not necessarily mean the British had not received their message. It just might be that their receiver didn't pick up the acknowledgement signal. It was a frustrating situation that always left them in the dark as to whether or not their message got through.

This day had been one where they sent a message and did not receive a return acknowledgement. Early in the afternoon they had radioed the British that a severe storm had moved into the Alps, the same storm Celine and her pilot were fighting as their Lysander struggled toward the French coast. The message had suggested postponing the landing attempt. Remi knew that even in good weather, the landing site would be tricky. He chose it because its isolated location was safe from enemy eyes. But the narrow gravel road was located in the middle of a half-mile-wide valley sandwiched between mountain peaks rising over 2,500 feet on either side.

Finding the road would be like finding a needle in a haystack and landing at night in this storm like trying to thread it blind. It would take one hell of a pilot to pull that off without splattering himself and Celine all over a mountainside.

Because they hadn't received an acknowledgement to their first message, Remi and Felicien sent a second. They waited another hour, listening to scratchy static. No acknowledgement. They had no choice but to drive to the designated landing site and wait. Remi prayed that the message had been received. The plane would not show up. Try another time, wait for safer conditions.

As the men made their way toward the landing site, the weather continued to deteriorate. Climbing higher into the mountains, the rain turned to sleet, to snow, and back to rain again. Now, standing in the middle of that gravel road in the quickly fading late-afternoon light, Remi took hope in the fact the rain had stopped. He looked up at the black clouds racing overhead and pulled his jacket up around his neck in defiance of the cold wind. *Those clouds can't be at any more than 700 feet.* The thought sent a chill deeper than any the wind could manifest. *What a hell of a night. They'll never pull it off,* he thought. *God, dear God, be with her.* An unshakable foreboding churned inside him. *This isn't going to work, no way, not tonight, not under these conditions. The cloud ceiling is insufficient. God, please let our message have gotten through. Please don't let that plane show up.*

To give the pilot a visual on the landing strip they set pots filled with gasoline on each side of the roadway. As soon as they heard the plane's engine they would light the pots outlining the makeshift runway. But under these conditions, the plane would have to be at less than 700 feet above the valley floor before the pilot could see the burning pots. He'd be thousands of feet below the peaks on either side before he broke out of the clouds. Remi kept silently begging God not to let that plane show up tonight.

He gave the clouds another troubled glance as they darkened in the fading twilight and decided to through in a cover-prayer just in case they did show up—*God, if they do show up, please make that son-of-a-bitch at the controls the best you've got.* He shuddered, pushing his hands deep into his heavy jacket pockets. They had no option but to wait, pray, and listen— straining eyes in futile attempt to see through the black haze and straining ears for the drone of an airplane Remi desperately hoped was not on its way.

He moved on down the road toward Felicien. No reason to check on Felicien. He always came through perfectly. Just something to do to pass the time. Besides, it was virtually impossible to talk with Felicien and not have him cheer you up.

In spite of the fact that Celine might be coming home after almost a year's absence, his worry for her safe landing combined with the miserable conditions the Nazis were inflicting on life in Treaire had him in a rotten mood. The Germans had rationed everything—food, petrol, fertilizer and even the city's water supply.

Remi was employed by Maurice Pippen, who owned the private water pumping utility that supplied Treaire. The plan was for Remi to work toward purchasing the utility from Pippen over the next 12 years. A good plan for both of them. It gave Monsieur Pippen a way to comfortably retire and allowed Remi to one day own his own business. Two months ago, the Nazis came to the water utility and placed restrictions on water delivery to two hours between 6 am and 8 am and three hours between 4 pm and 7 pm. With those restrictions, it was impossible to generate sufficient income to cover expenses. Remi was now working for half pay and had to take a job with Amaury, driving one of his trucks supplying the Bistro. He knew Amaury didn't need the help, and just employed him so Remi could make ends meet. He needed the income, but Amaury's well-intended kindness made him feel like a leach. Without the income, however, he wouldn't be able to support Celine the way he had before she left. They might have to give up their little house. Move back into a cramped apartment. His whole plan of someday owning the water utility was now at risk. Every time he thought about it he fumed with anger.

"You Nazi bastards come and take everything," he bitched to the wind. But that was life. They took everything in France these days. All Remi could hope was that this night didn't wind up killing the only woman he had ever loved.

CHAPTER 12

Somewhere over southern France
searching for coordinates
45° 15' 0.9318"latitude
6° 40' 46.9128"longitude

Celine was proud of herself. She was still grabbing for hand holds as the plane bounced from cloud to cloud, but she hadn't thrown up. She complimented herself on that victory. She looked over at the pilot, his face dimly reflected in the glowing lights of the instrument panel. His attention was keenly focused on those instruments. *Must be getting near the drop point,* she thought.

Wham! The plane hit a jarring updraft. In spite of her best efforts to remain calm, her heart was pounding. Her stomach lurched as the craft shuttered and then dropped sickeningly in the ensuing downdraft. A blue-white flash lit the cloud's inner churnings and a deafening crash of thunder sounded as if it had erupted just behind her seat.

"Thought we might run out of this tough weather," the pilot said. "Is it always so pleasant around here this time of year?" She didn't answer his flippant comment.

Outside, boiling clouds encased the tiny plane—another blinding flash! She spoke into her headset, her voice sounding feeble, "What is your estimated distance to the drop point?"

"My best guess, about 10 miles, miss. Just a few more boring minutes." He was working hard to keep things on a positive tone.

Celine knew the topography of the drop site. Part of her training had included basic flight instruction…just enough so she was familiar with the Lysander's instruments. As they forged on, groping their way through the shearing winds, she almost wished she didn't understand the instruments. They were in the western Alps, picking their way through narrow valleys. Rugged mountain peaks shot to 9,000-foot heights everywhere. The Lysander's altimeter was holding steady at an altitude of 3,000 feet.

The pilot rapidly glanced from compass to air speed to the map strapped to his leg. The red penciled line on the map flew them directly up the valley toward the drop point...not difficult in reasonable weather. Tonight, a major challenge. He was flying by dead reckoning, she was convinced of it. *Please, dear God, keep this little plane on that red line and the mountains safely on each side,* she prayed as she braced against another wind shear jolt.

Catching her intent focus on his map, the pilot attempted to reassure her, "It's okay, ma'am. We're in the Tarentaise Valley. I know right..." He paused during another breath-sucking jolt. The plane pitched violently as he fought to control it through the counter-shearing winds.

Then, a momentary calm..."As I was saying, miss, I know right where we are. No need to fret. Have you down in a jiffy."

"You going to climb soon?" she questioned, her voice a bit more shrill than intended.

"No, ma'am, I know this map by heart. The town of Modane is off to our right about five miles and Frene hamlet is directly ahead. We've got to stay low in this weather. We're in the valley. We're okay. The wind up above is really fierce. Trust me, we're doing fine. A bit bumpy, but we're right where we are supposed to be. I'll have you down safe on terra firma La France in about 10 minutes." She took heart from his youthful confidence, in spite of the glistening sweat beads covering his brow. For some reason, she did trust him, although she determined purposely not to dwell on what appeared to be his shoot-from-the-hip navigation.

He couldn't have been a day past 20. *So young,* she thought. *I wonder if he'll survive the war.* She shook her head with a resigned frown in silent defiance of the chaotic world that engulfed her—engulfed everyone she knew. Nothing was certain. Nothing could be relied on. *Hell, I wonder if any of us will survive the war.*

She pushed her thoughts away from the immediate terrifying situation, recalling her months in England.

The training had been tough. Brutal, really...unlike anything she had ever been through. From the instant she entered the camp, the threatening mindset of the instructors—their alpha-male hardness and the swim-or-drown-we-don't-give-a-damn-which attitude—had pervaded every moment of her life.

A large sign over the entrance to the camp canteen read: 'Toughen Up or Get the Hell Out – No Compromise'. At dinner the first evening, the commander, a ruggedly handsome Brit, defined the message.

"The sign over the canteen door says Toughen Up or Get the Hell Out – No Compromise. We'd rather you get the hell out. We're going to do everything in our power to train you how to fight and survive. We're going to teach you how to kill your enemies and keep them from killing you, your companions and your families. We will work you day and night, and for those of you who have the tenacity to stick it out, we will push your odds of survival up to around 50% once we dump you back onto your home soil. For any of you who have the slightest trepidations about this program, get the hell out now."

Some had wimped out. To Celine's disappointment, a Frenchman left the program after just four days, lending fodder to the sneering British attitude that all Frenchmen were chicken-hearted. She felt somewhat vindicated for French trainees when one of the trainees from Poland quit two days later. Their leaving was almost understandable. She had suffered many nights of muffled tears, when the exhaustion and feelings of humiliation from the continuous criticism of the yelling trainers was so severe she yearned for the peace of death. The instructors were relentless, constantly shouting demands and short tempered with the slightest lack of perfection in every activity. She took pride in having made it through, but the training had changed her.

Her innocence was gone, lost in her determination to live up to the canteen sign's demand to 'Toughen Up'. They taught her to hold emotions in virtual abeyance, desensitized her hesitation to taking another's life, and reprogrammed her to inflict bone-breaking martial arts with cold detachment. She was not the same woman who had left France just 11 months before. Remi would notice immediately. She was convinced of it. She worried about that.

"You might start looking for the fuel pots, miss. We should be smack over the drop coordinates," the pilot's voice barked through the headset. "I'm dropping down a bit now to see if we can get below these bloody clouds."

She looked over at the altimeter. They were dangerously low—800 feet. He flipped on the landing lights for a split second. The lights reflected back in a blinding gray-white glare—cloud cover, thick cloud cover, above and below. They began circling, descending to 500 feet, hoping to break out of the clouds. It was impossible to land without visually spotting the burning pots. Again, a quick on and off of the landing lights. Again, blinding flash back. The turbulence had substantially subsided. The pilot eased back on the throttle, slowing the engine to almost a wind milling of the prop.

Celine glanced at him, "You still sure about where those mountains are?"

"Not totally, now, miss," he responded. "I'm dropping down a bit more. See if we break out of these damn clouds." He flipped on a wing light...white flash back. The altimeter hovered at 250 feet. Celine desperately fought to find some of that cold detachment she had supposedly been trained in. She knew the valley would be clear of trees, but the pines on either side soared to over 80 feet and as the plane circled back and forth across the valley, they would surely be gliding over those magnificent products of Mother Nature.

Looking down, straining to find the dim burning runway pots, Celine forced herself to breathe deep in an attempt to calm her pounding heart. Nothing but pitch blackness below. The pilot pushed the throttle in, giving the engine some increased power as he banked hard to the left, positioning the plane for another pass over what he was sure was the valley of the drop point coordinates. The altimeter registered 175 feet.

"I estimate the trees surrounding this valley at about 80 feet," Celine spoke into her headset, unable to keep her frayed nerves out of the comment.

"Thanks for the input, ma'am. Believe me, I'm just as interested in getting through this as you. I think the valley is about half a mile wide. We're presently doing about 80 miles per hour, so we'll cross it every 20 seconds. I'll try to drop down below the clouds as we cross, so search for the fire pots."

———— ✦ ————

Remi dashed to light one of the pots as the Lysander roared overhead. Celine and her pilot had been crisscrossing the valley to the north of Remi's position and for some inexplicable reason, he had not previously heard the engine. Even now, he didn't see the plane, but the howl of its engine convinced him it was just several hundred feet overhead. He shouted, *"Amaury, get the pots lit! They're here."*

Amaury lit the first pot and ran full out toward the second, also hearing the sound of the plane's engine fade as it moved away, in search of the glowing pots. Off in the distance the engine growled to life as the pilot once again opened the throttle, banking hard for another pass across the valley. Amaury got to the second pot and ignited its volatile fuel into flame. He looked up, feeling as if he could almost touch the clouds now lit by the pot's flames. Alexis turned on the headlights of the Citroën, shining them down the road and hoping to provide some light for the pilot's searching eyes. Amaury reached the third pot and it exploded to life, then he raced on toward the fourth. Up the road, Remi and Felicien had their pots ablaze. The reflection off the clouds cast the valley in an eerie yellow-orange glow. The Lysander banked, its engine increasing in sound as it once again turned toward the road now lit for the drop.

"There," yelled Celine. *"There! Off to the right. I see them!"*

"Okay, miss, okay. No need to shout. We've got on headphones, you know." The pilot leaned the plane steeply into a turn, then abruptly leveled out in the direction Celine had indicated. He saw the pots as the plane shot across the road just two hundred feet over the Citroën. Alexis jumped into the roadside ditch in anticipation of an explosive crash, sure the plane was going down just ahead of car.

"I've got the road spotted," the pilot shouted louder than he had scolded Celine for. "I see the bloody pots. Okay, I've got our bearings.

"Hang on, miss. We're going to do a tight 180." The engine roared as he gave it full throttle in a climbing turn. Celine felt herself pushed down hard into the seat. The climb put them back up into the heavy clouds. With both the wing and nose landing lights blazing, everything once again went into a gray/white blur and Celine once again found herself holding on to her seat for dear life.

"Don't fret," his voice cracked through her headset. "I know you can't see the pots from here, but I know right where they are. I'll set us down within a foot of the first one."

"I won't hold you to that claim. Any successful landing point will be fine," she managed.

The plane shuddered as it reached the top of its tight-climbing turn. The engine screamed as the port wing dipped perpendicular to the ground. The pilot was pushing the Lysander to its maximum. Rattling vibrations shook everything as the little plane gave its all, straining to comply with the pilot's demands. All at once, they dropped in a nauseating fall. Celine shut her eyes hard in anticipation of the inevitable sickening crash.

The pilot jerked to horizontal position, slamming Celine against the passenger window, cutting the engine instantly from full throttle to just above idle. The plane slowed so fast it actually felt as if he had pressed down hard on the brakes. Celine was thrown forward. Her stomach reeled and she fought to keep it from ejecting its contents. The altimeter read 160 feet and was spinning toward its 140 mark. Still, the whitewash of fog was all that could be seen through the windshield.

"Now look directly ahead, miss," the pilot smiled confidently. "In about two seconds you are going to see those beautiful pots all lit up. Your little birthday cake set up to welcome you back home."

The clouds broke. Celine gasped as the black image of a treetop shot past just a few feet below her window. The pilot corrected, ruddering the plane to the right. Then, just as he had said, there immediately in front of them, with the plane's nose squarely centered between, were flaming pots lining both sides of the road.

He further cut power and steepened the dive toward the road. The plane plummeted down at such a sever angle Remi gasped sure of the ensuing impact.

The pilot pulled up hard and within three feet of passing the first of the fuel pots, the Lysander's soft rubber tires bounced violently on the gravel. He pumped the brakes hard, grinding almost to a stop just 25 feet beyond the first bounce.

With the Lysander still slowly rolling, the pilot reached across Celine's lap, unlatched the door and yelled, *"Now! Go now…out, out!"*

Celine rolled out of the open door, pulling the huge duffel bag with her. She hit the gravel with a thud. The Lysander's engine roared to life, sending chunks of wet gravel churned up by the prop wash peppering Celine's face. She ducked behind the duffel, shielding herself as best she could. The plane leapt forward, picking up speed as it closed in on the Citroën that sat in the road directly ahead of it. Alexis jumped into the car as the plane screamed toward him. Throwing it into reverse, stomped on the accelerator, hoping to keep the car on the invisible road behind him. Both Remi and Felicien hit the ditch as the plane roared past them. Its wheels reluctantly gave up their earthbound grip, lifting just several feet over the Citroën. The Lysander and its young pilot disappeared into the blackness of the night sky in search of their ship that waited in the stormy Mediterranean.

Remi ran to Celine, lifted her off her feet and squeezed her tight, "Thank God, you're all right. Thank God you are back." She clung to him, the tension draining from her body. Amaury and Felicien arrived in a run, throwing their arms around them both and Alexis massively bear-hugged the whole group as he yelled, "Vive la France. Vive la Celine! Vive la Resistance!

Celine had landed.

PART II

CHAPTER 13

Le Duc de Richelieu Bistro had been feeding hungry customers since 1650 and still served as the gastronomic social center of Treaire. The magnificent food prepared in its kitchen, the wide array of quality wines filling its cellars and its staff of friendly, efficient servers attracted a constant stream of patrons. In defiance of the strict food rationing imposed by the Nazis, Amaury's boundless personal wealth allowed him to pay the exorbitant bribes demanded by Vichy French government officials for fresh meats, vegetables and beverages sold only on the black market.

Bistro trucks headed out each morning before the sun peeked over the horizon, making their way to the surrounding cities of Chambéry, Lyon, Grenoble, and Saint-Étienne. Once at their destinations, they would ramble down back allies and pull into darkened warehouses where the drivers would meet the shady characters of the corrupt Vichy government, renegade Nazi officers and mafia figures of the wartime underworld. Huge sums of cash would change hands, after which the trucks would be filled with choice meats, fresh vegetables, fine breads and quality wines, whiskies and beer, thus assuring that the Duc de Richelieu's tables continued offering the finest in French dining. Dedicated patrons from Treaire and Falauge frequented the Bistro for their evening meals and filled its quaint bar with their jovial laughter and card playing long into the evenings as they sought to bring a bit of pleasure into their lives and forget the painful grip of the war. The Bistro was Amaury's hobby, its lack of profitability due to the outrageous wartime bribery expenses just accepted as a cost of temporarily bad times.

The building housing the Bistro had been erected in 1340, the date chiseled in its cornerstone. Over the next several hundred years a livery stable, maintenance shop and equipment hut were added in back. All of the ancient buildings were well maintained and made up of multiple nooks and crannies, narrow hallways and secret passages offering unique stealthy benefits to the cloaked activities of the Tristan. Being the only source of good food and drink for miles around, German officers frequented the establishment and after the wine and beer loosened their tongues, they proved a continuous source of reliable information concerning Nazi activities in the area. Locals contributed additional valuable information concerning Nazi and Milice for miles around Treaire. These unique qualities, combined with the Bistro's public transparency, made it the perfect hangout for Remi and Celine, who picked up invaluable information for planning their clandestine raids against their German oppressors.

⸗⸗⸗

The Bistro property had been in Amaury's family for 380 years, give or take a decade or so. Amaury's full name was Amaury de la Cheever le Douzième Chapiteau de Cheever, the "la Douzième Chapiteau de Cheever" part denoting the family's direct lineage to nobility dating back to King Henry IV—some 19 generations. Being an only child, Amaury had inherited everything on his 20th birthday. The inheritance was not related to his coming of age but rather to the fact that was the night his parents were both killed in an automobile accident. No one was really to blame since Amaury's parents and the driver of the car they crashed into were so equally drunk none of them knew what hit them.

Amaury, who respectfully feigned mourning, was inwardly relieved to be free of his meddling, alcoholic parents. The family estate left him a vast fortune in cash, precious metals, artwork, jewelry, an internationally respected winery, multiple operating farms and numerous commercial buildings in Marseille, Lyon and Grenoble. At the estate meeting with the family lawyer he was pleasantly surprised to learn he was the majority owner in one of the larger gold mines in Africa—a tidbit of knowledge no one in the family had ever mentioned.

Left alone to fend for himself, Amaury now rambled around in the 47-room Cheever château two miles south of Treaire. The 70 staff members who kept up the estate and tended the farms and winery had been employed by the family for decades, some were second generation Cheever estate employees and they all were as trusted and as well treated as if they were blood relatives. They lived with their families on the estate, rarely going to town. The estate was virtually independent of the world. Its farms produced livestock, milk, eggs, vegetables and fruits. There were several freshwater streams and numerous springs and fishing ponds. In reality, Amaury could have supplied the Bistro with its provisions from the estate, but felt it would be safer to project a less self-sufficient image and pay the Vichy and corrupt German officers their bribes for the restaurant's supplies.

Although Amaury despised the life-sized portraits of his long-dead scowling relatives dressed in their armor and absurd gowns hanging from numerous walls within the château, he was proud of himself for not taking them down immediately following the death of his parents. Painted by famous artists of the time, several of the portraits were of significant value. A few of lesser worth were in bad shape since Amaury often broke the monotony of lonely evenings by lobbing darts at them—an unmentioned annoyance to the staff who would have to climb a stepladder to remove the projectiles the next day.

Amaury had avoided developing the self-appreciating snobbery of his parents by embracing everything they felt was low class. His parents enjoyed the revenue brought in by the Bistro but felt frequenting such an establishment was below their social rank. They employed a professional manager for years. When the manager retired, Amaury insisted on becoming the new manager; to the great ire of his parents. He immediately moved out of the château, fixing out a room for himself above the Bistro and immersed himself in every detail of running the tavern. Of all his possessions, the Duc de Richelieu Bistro was Amaury's favorite.

He loved the jovial atmosphere of Treaire's citizens, who showed up faithfully to drink the wine enjoy the camaraderie, and rid themselves of the pressures of the day. He drank with the drinkers and ate with the eaters. He gossiped, was an intent listener and served as a compassionate supporter of those in inebriated need of moral support. Amaury was considered the personal friend of every customer who ventured into the Bistro, and he loved every minute of it.

He was particularly proud of the fact that the Duc de Richelieu had a reputation for outstanding food and magnificent wine for miles around. The *friends* and several local families Amaury knew were extremely hard pressed by the economic tribulations of the war ate and drank on credit—bills which he com-passionately discarded monthly.

———⊶⊷———

Once Amaury took over management of the Bistro, he searched for where the *friends'* secret cave tunnel adjoined the structure. He eventually found it behind a massive built-in cabinet in the hallway leading back to the kitchen. Working with Felicien and Alexis, they enlarged the cabinet into a walk-in pan-try and installed a false back panel that could be slid to the side to provide quick access to the tunnel. All of the work was done in the wee hours of the night. The access to the tunnel remained a secret known only to the *friends.* When Remi and Celine formed the Tristan, the group ran electricity from the Bistro into the cave, bringing electricity to the catacombs for the first time in their 400-plus-year existence.

CHAPTER 14

Celine hurried up the street. Tonight she would go over the contents of the duffel bag she brought back from the training camp, and she was running late. She worked at the bakery and hadn't been able to get away until 8:20—time enough to get to the cave for the meeting, but no preparation time.

She walked quickly down the main street toward the Bistro and turned left on Rue Vignemale in the direction of the path through the woods that led toward the cave. The cobblestone street was dark, just long enough to serve its five houses before becoming a dirt road leading up to several of the dairymen's summer grazing pastures.

She tensed. A Kübelwagen patrol car turned onto the street, its headlights elongating her shadow eerily in front of her. Her stomach knotted. It was after curfew. The only cars out would be German patrol vehicles. She slowed her pace. *Maybe they'll pass by, make a U-turn and head back into town. Please, God, let them do that.* The vehicle slowed behind her. She slowed further, trying to make it appear the street's hill was causing her exhaustion. The vehicle paced her. She was within 200 feet of the last house. *I'll have to go into the last house, make it look like I live there,* she thought. She knew the man who lived there, but he was very old, probably in bed—most likely wouldn't hear her if she knocked. *Good,* she thought, *I'll just go on in as if I live there. Dear God, please let the door be unlocked.*

The ugly Kübelwagen pulled several feet ahead of her. A Sergeant stepped out, blocking her path. *At the very least, they're going to want to know which of these houses I live in,* she thought. *Why I'm out past curfew. They'll want my papers. Damn, do I have my papers? Stay calm. Breathe deep, be humble.*

The Sergeant had a heavy German accent further complicated by his inebriated slurred words, "Sho, my little schatzi, vhat is such a pretty thing doing all by herself out valking this evening?"

The bastard's drunk. Not good. Not good at all. Celine primed herself. She said nothing, halting in front of the man. His breath was sour of rank alcohol as he stood grinning, weaving a bit and leering at her.

"You are prettier from the front, my little French Schöne," he mumbled. Three other soldiers exited the vehicle and closed in to her sides and rear.

The Sergeant continued grinning at her, inspecting her. "I think ve vill start the evening by seeing your papers, hübsches Mädchen. Then, ve shall decide how to proceed. You are out after curfew. Not good. You can go to jail for this. But maybe ve can vork something out so that does not happen to you," he licked his lips and smirked.

He moved closer, much closer. Swaying in his inebriation, his nose almost touching her, fouling the air with his breath. She pushed him back. The hand of the soldier behind her slid between her legs. She whirled, slapping him hard.

"Ah ha! Ve have a feisty one here," laughed the Sergeant, placing his hand on her breast.

Celine had the martial arts skills to take down all four men so quickly they would not have had time to react. She could have dropped them where they stood—fractured bones, ruptured joints—she could have killed them, all of them. A different aspect of the training kept her calm, thinking logically, tactically. Killing four German patrol guards would bring the entire Falauge garrison down on Treaire.

She spun back, knocking the Sergeant's hand away, "Get your filthy hands off of me, you pig. You are out of order, Sergeant! I am close to Colonel Andreas Nussbaum—*very* close. If you do not immediately return my papers and get your drunken self and these repulsive dogs back in that car, this incident will be reported to Andreas."

She prayed that Andreas Nussbaum had not been transferred during her long absence and was still the commander in charge of the garrison at Falauge. She knew of him only because the Tristan made it their business to know the names and ranks of all German officers in the area.

At her reference to Colonel Nussbaum as Andreas, the Sergeant went pale. *My God,* he thought, *we are messing with the Colonel's mistress.*

His face went blank with fear. He stiffened, stumbled back a step, stiffly thrusting out his hand returning Celine's papers. He stuttered, "Ah, my apologies, miss. All vas meant in jest…just a bit of fun. Ve simply vanted to assure that you vere safe valking in the dark. Ve vould be most villing to take you to your house if you vould like."

The ruse had worked.

Celine glared into the Sergeant's panicked eyes. His men were already scurrying toward the patrol car. "I see from your nametag your name is Steinholt. The next time I am with Andreas, you had better pray I do not mention this incident, Sergeant Steinholt. I know the rules of conduct Andreas expects of his troops. You and your men are totally out of order—totally revolting and assaultive. There is no question Andreas will have you skinned alive before having you and these other pigs shot if I mention this incident."

"Jawohl, miss. Please, I beg you…please, if you can forgive my bad behavior, I ask that you do not mention this to the Colonel. I have had too much to drink tonight, please."

"Get your pathetic ass back in that car and go, Sergeant Steinholt," Celine snarled. "If I see you or any of these men harassing anyone—women or men—I assure you, Andreas will get a detailed description of everything that happened here."

"Jawohl, miss. I am sorry. Please forgive," he repeated over his shoulder as he jumped in the car and motioned for the driver to quickly move on.

As the car quickly pulled away, the Sergeant leaned over its side and vomited. *Be sick, you stinking pig,* thought Celine, *be sick with fear and know we are coming for you soon.* She stood, watching the Kübelwagen do a screeching U-turn.

How many other women have been abused by this repulsive bunch? she wondered. Witnesses peering from their darkened windows had seen women raped by the patrols. They spoke of such incidences only in whispers among trusted friends. One young girl went missing several months ago and was still not accounted for. For the citizens of Treaire, there was no retribution for such offenses. No way to avenge the wrongs.

You will pay, Celine vowed, watching the vehicle carry away its load of thugs. *You will pay dearly, you miserable, arrogant bastards.*

Remi did a double take as Celine entered.

"Celine, are you all right?"

"Yes, no problem, Remi." She didn't want to go into the incident—not in front of the others. Didn't want this important evening to start out like this.

Remi came to her, gently turned her toward him, "Something is wrong, Cel. I can tell. What happened?"

She gave a resigned sigh; it wasn't fair not to address his concern. She spoke in a tone so all could hear, "I was stopped and sexually threatened by some drunken Germans on patrol, but everything is fine. I sent them away with the impression I am Colonel Nussbaum's concubine. They'll spend the next several weeks in tormented hell, wondering if their world is about to fall in on their pathetic heads."

Felicien burst into laughter, "Oh, lord, I wish I'd been there…a tiny gnat, sitting on your delicate little shoulder when you came up with that line. They must have gone white with terror."

Celine had to smile. Felicien always found the humor in everything, "You'll be happy to know, Felicien, the Sergeant threw up as they sped away."

Felicien doubled over, holding his stomach in laughter, "Oh, God, Celine—I can't believe it. You made the guy puke," he howled. "Why do I always miss all the fun in this war?" His laughter had them all smiling. All except Alexis. To Alexis, any affront to Celine was personal, painful. His love for her, his deep emotional caring allowed him no leeway to find humor in anything that caused her discomfort.

He frowned at Felicien, "It's not funny, Felicien. They were bad to Celine. If I had been there, I would have beaten the crap out of them. What they did to Celine is not funny."

Felicien slapped his big friend on the shoulder, still chuckling, "I'm not laughing at what *they* did to *her*, Alexis. I'm laughing at what *she* did to *them*."

"I still think they need a good beating," Alexis sulked. "I'd have given them a good beating."

"I'm sure you would have, Alexis, but they soon would have healed from a beating. This way, the bastards will spend the next six months in terror that at any moment they're going to be shipped off to the Russian Front. That was brilliant, Celine, totally brilliant," Felicien complimented.

Alexis didn't get the joke. To him, Celine had been assaulted. He felt her humiliation.

Remi had arranged the contents of Celine's duffel bag neatly on the table. There were six MP-40 machine pistols, two MG-42 machine guns, eight Lugers, two disassembled sniper rifles, sniper scopes, hand grenades, gas masks, knives, plastic explosives, detonators, flares, and an assortment of syringes and vials of liquids all marked with numbers and red skull and crossbones icons.

"My God! No wonder that duffel weighed so much," Felicien commented as he lovingly inspected one of the big MG-42 machine guns.

"Interesting that all of these weapons are German," Amaury observed.

"Yes," Celine said, "that way, if a weapon is left behind or lost, it will not raise suspicions that we are being supplied from the outside.

"More equipment is coming, too," Celine added. "Heavy weapons, explosives and a lot of ammunition. They were too heavy for the Lysander. They will be dropped by a light bomber. It may be a while before they can make that drop but I still want to send the Brits the coordinates for the drop point as soon as possible. This shipment will weigh over 900 pounds, so we are going to need a truck to transport it."

Amaury expressed concern, "Radioing the Brits may just have become pretty risky. The electrician, Jean-Claude Badue, was talking with me at the bar last night. The Nazis employed him when they installed a new radio receiver at Voiron. They've also installed updated receivers at Chambéry and Falauge. They didn't know Badue speaks German. He overheard some officers saying that when the new receivers are up and running they'll be able to pinpoint any outgoing radio message within a 40-mile radius and accurately identify its location within three minutes."

"We're safe," Felicien mused. "On that piece of junk we call a radio; *God* can't even pick up our messages."

"Still, I am telling you, we must be careful. Much more so than in the past. With that equipment, they will be able to find us when we broadcast."

"I wonder why they've focused the equipment on just a 40-mile radius right here," Remi puzzled.

"I'm sure it's because of the Saint Laurnee rail trestle and tunnel," Celine said. "One of the logistics experts at the camp spent time going over maps with me. The Saint Laurnee Passage is the most critical rail link between southern France and Italy. It's the only reasonable way for the Germans to keep their Italian troops supplied. They'll do whatever it takes to protect it… which means they want to be sure there are no active Resistance cells in this area."

Alexis smiled, "Then let's take a bunch of these explosives and blow up the trestle."

"That's exactly what I told the logistics guy at the camp," Celine responded. "The problem is the British and Americans are just as keen on keeping the Passage intact as the Germans. They are convinced it's just a matter of time before they push the Nazis out of Italy. When that happens, they want the Passage intact to move their supplies into France."

"It's okay, we can deal with this," Remi said. "We'll just drive out of the 40-mile triangulation coverage area when we want to send messages. What's important is that we do not alert the Nazis to the fact that we've become active again. We've been quiet so long they are convinced they've done away with us. We've got to keep it that way as long as possible."

"Training begins first thing tomorrow," Celine said, playfully slapping away Alexis' hand as he reached for one of the poison vials. "Be careful touching the liquid stuff. One drop of some of that in a cut or sore and you'll not only miss the rest of this evening but the rest of the war."

She moved to the table, picking up one of the vials. "This one's interesting. It contains a concentrated form of several snake venoms. They claim it will shut down a 200-pound man's breathing apparatus within seconds of injection. Oh, here's a nice one," she picked up another of the tiny bottles. "This one causes a stroke in its victim. Really remarkable stuff," she held up the vile to the light. "It is totally undetectable in an autopsy."

Pointing to the other side of the table, she continued, "Those over there, the ones with the blue caps, cause excruciating pain throughout the body but won't kill the victim. The pains can be stopped by injecting the yellow-capped liquid. They told me just the promise of being able to stop the pain is enough to get a person to tell you anything you want to know."

They continued through the duffel contents for another hour when Felicien stretched noisily. "My dear friends, all this talk of fun and creative methods of killing people has gotten me in a gaily festive mood. I have some great cigars and if Amaury can come up with a reasonably acceptable bottle of wine, I say we put away the toys for tonight and relax a bit."

"I've got the wine," Amaury said, moving toward the wine cabinet, "but I'm not sure your cigars will measure up. Are you still stealing them from Dumont's pharmacy?"

"Amaury, how disrespectful," Felicien chided. "You know old man Dumont passed many years ago."

"Yes, and from what I heard, he died worrying how he was going to afford to keep the pharmacy open, seeing how you were stealing his cigarettes faster than he could restock."

"Actually, supporting my tobacco habit was not what did him in. It was when I started stealing those little quarter-bottles of wine he sold at the counter. It was a real shame, too. Ever since he showed up at heaven's gate, you just can't find good quarter-bottles of wine around here. Too bad you are not able to procure the quality wine Dumont's pharmacy once offered, Amaury. But that is life. All good things eventually come to an end."

"The only thing I could come up with is a magnum of 72-year-old Bordeaux from Château Haut-Brion. Sorry, Felicien, it won't have the nice vinegar bouquet Dumont's quarter-bottles offered so you can opt out if you like.

"No matter how many times I do this," Amaury lamented as he pulled the cork, "I always feel some guilt opening a three-generation-old bottle."

"My exact feelings every time I opened one of Dumont's quarter-bottle delicacies," Felicien lamented.

The *friends* relaxed together for the first time since Celine's return. They smoked Felicien's cigars, drank Amaury's wine, laughed at each other's jokes, and sadly mourned their fallen comrades. The room filled with the delectable smoke of Felicien's fine cigars and the mood lightened with Amaury's excellent wine. Warmth and companionship emanated from the years of love and respect that had grown between them, bringing a momentary security—much like the comfort of pulling a soft, warm comforter around one's self by the fire on a cold winter's night.

Celine was home. She immersed herself in the love and security that flowed so easily among the *friends*. She had deeply missed this magnificent interaction, silently thanking God several times during the evening for the *friends* and her safe return to them.

In bed that evening, in the dark of the night, a counter feeling pervaded her thoughts. She once again felt rage for Sergeant Steinholt and his men. She was convinced she was not the only woman they had accosted, perhaps there were many, perhaps friends and acquaintances, perhaps they were behind the missing teenage girl. She determined she would be their demise.

She didn't realize she would get her chance much sooner than she anticipated.

The pressing need to contact the British with coordinates for the subsequent heavy drop delayed the start of Celine's martial arts training. Remi and Felicien left the village the next morning before dawn.

They drove to Oles Baraque, a tiny mountain village of not more than seven houses situated among massive pines that long ago had fed it's now decaying sawmill. Remi hoped the distance combined with the mountain peaks between their location and Treaire would be sufficient to prevent the Germans from picking up their radio signal. As an added precaution, they would send messages in short bursts of no more than several seconds of transmission. Once again, Felicien's extensive technical skills were tested seeing if he could get the beat-up radio to do its job.

The first of the message was instructional:

FROM: TCP-3.965
TO: HMN-O-37
15 June, 1943
Note – Germans have receivers in Chambéry, Falauge and Voiron.
Triangulation capability in effect. Respond only in short bursts 15 to 20
seconds
(>) more to follow

five minutes later -

Heavy package drop coordinates – 42.3600N, 5.3700E – Acknowledge
time/date
(...) end

They were in luck. Seven minutes later, the little radio barked to life:

FROM: HMN-O-37
TO: TCP-3.965
15 June, 1943
Heavy package drop acknowledged – 42.36N, 5.37E – 22to23hr
– 9/9/43date

CHAPTER 15

Celine was nervous. Tonight she would begin martial arts instruction. She had mastered the training—actually, more than mastered it. Excelled in it—received top honors in her class. But the responsibility of now having to teach those skills to men who might have to depend on them as a matter of life and death was very concerning. She had spent a sleepless night, first trying to mentally review the sequential steps the instructors had used in her training, then tossing and turning in frustration that her lack of sleep would cause her to be forgetful and exhausted for the training session. Her heart was pounding as she and Remi pulled up to Amaury's enormous château.

They met in the gymnasium. Amaury's father had converted what was once the great meeting hall, where his ancient ancestors threw dinner parties for hundreds of guests, into a gym. Amaury could never figure out why. Neither of his parents ever raised a sweat doing anything, except perhaps when fretting over which wine would go best with the meal they were being served.

Regardless of his father's reasons, the gym was superb. A huge high-ceiling room filled with an array of weights, exercise machines and various tumbling mats. Twelve life-sized portraits of Amaury's scowling relatives attired in their satins and ruffles hung some 15 feet from the floor, casting their disapproving looks at everything that took place.

Celine moved to the center of the floor where Amaury and the others had placed several of the tumbling mats. There they stood all outfitted in their tank tops and tight shorts—all except Felicien.

"Where are your workout clothes, Felicien?"

"Sorry, coquette. Just didn't have time to change from work. Might as well learn in these. After all, we're not going to be all decked out in gym clothes when we're kicking the crap out of krautheads," he laughed, jokingly poking Alexis in the ribs. Celine was annoyed.

She told them to line up at the edge of the mats, took her position facing them in the center and said, "Rush at me, Alexis. Try to knock me down."

He stood there, confused, staring at her. He was two and a half times her weight and towered over her by 16 inches. He loved Celine and had always felt an obligation to protect her and treat her with gentle respect.

"I don't want to, Celine, I could hurt you," he said, looking shyly down at the mat.

"Look at me, Alexis. This is a demonstration. You won't hurt me. I am choosing you because you are the biggest and the strongest of the men. You could easily take any one of them in a fight. Don't be concerned about me. You're going to be amazed at what they taught me at the camp. No matter what you do or how fast you come at me, you won't be able to hurt me—and I warn you, I will lay you out flat before you know what hit you. It is you who will not get hurt," she smiled, "because I will be careful with you."

Alexis beamed when Celine acknowledged him as the strongest of the *friends*. He loved being revered in her eyes, and her complimentary comments always brought confidence to his constant self-doubting.

He looked up at her and a shy smile emerged. "Okay. If you really want me to, I will." She nodded her approval. Alexis charged. Instantly, he found himself face down on the mat, his arm twisted up over his back in what could have been an excruciatingly painful hold had Celine applied pressure. She hadn't hurt him, but had dropped him with such speed that he and the others were shocked and clueless as to what happened.

He started laughing. "I feel glad you didn't hurt those German soldiers the other night when they were bad to you." Alexis seldom met his physical match and he found it hilarious to have just been floored by Celine.

Remi was next and had the advantage of knowing what to expect. Still, he was instantly thrown on his back. Felicien looked over at Amaury, gave him a smile, and they both charged immediately, finding themselves on the floor with Remi.

She repositioned the men at the edge of the mats and faced Felicien.

"Shake my hand."

He laughingly took a clowning step behind Alexis, "Save me, big brother, there's a mad woman loose here."

She turned to Amaury and commanded, "Shake my hand." Instantly, he was on his back, his hand now gripped by hers and twisted painfully at the wrist.

"I can now break his wrist with the slightest amount of pressure here, then immediately break his elbow by bending his arm over my knee." She applied minor pressure.

"Aaaah, okay, okay, I get the point," he grimaced.

She had Remi attack her from the back, threw him to the floor, grabbed his leg and held him in position, then looked up at the others. "With just slightly more pressure, his knee joint will snap. This all seems cruel and grotesque. We are offended by it because it goes against everything we are taught about being accommodating to people, but you cannot hesitate, you cannot shy from breaking bones. If you hesitate or become squeamish about snapping your opponent's joints, he will kill you."

Still holding Remi in the same compromising position, she continued, "When you get your enemy in this position, you must be willing to proceed. Break the knee, then, while he withers in pain, kill him. Shoot him. Knife him. Strangle him. Kill him however you can."

Her tone was chilling, matter-of-fact. No wavering, no compassion. She left no doubt she meant what she said and would not hesitate to proceed against an enemy combatant.

Over the next hour she meticulously demonstrated how to break legs and arms, incapacitate a combatant with a palm thrust to the base of the nose, how to dodge fists, and elude multiple attackers. The men were breathing hard, sweating profusely as Celine called one after another to attack.

"Hold this pistol on me, Alexis," she commanded. He did so.

"Grip it as if you are afraid I'm going to take it away from you."

He tightened his grip, determined to maintain his hold. In an instant, Celine was behind him, holding the pistol pointed directly at his head.

Again, he had to laugh. "It happened so fast, I didn't feel it. She is really good. You are really, really good, Celine. Can you teach me?"

"Yes, Alexis. I will teach all of you. "The techniques are simple once you understand them, but they take dedicated practice to perfect. You must learn to perform them flawlessly. You have to get so good at them they happen automatically, so skilled they happen as instinctive response to your attacker. That will only happen by practicing every single day. We are going to work here in the gym for three hours every evening and beyond that, I expect you to practice individually. Practice your moves in front of a mirror until you feel they are perfect. When you are not physically practicing, you have to be mentally envisioning these moves until you do them in your dreams."

Confidence radiated from her. She was totally in charge. Her command of the environment was forceful, the level of her seriousness new and different.

"We'll go for another hour."

"Another hour? Are you kidding, sweet coquettete?" Felicien complained. "My God, woman, I'm dying."

Celine jumped inches from his face, yelling, "You are *not* dying! That's just the damn point. If you don't get serious about this…if you sluff off, Felicien, if you take your normal flip attitude, you will die. This is not a joke, damn you. Get serious or get the hell out."

Turning toward the others, her anger continued to spew forth, "I am not here to make you feel good, boys. I am here to train you how to stay alive. I need you to get serious, get committed and stay that way." She threw down her towel in exasperation, turned and left the room.

"Good God, what's gotten into her?" Felicien scowled, "She doesn't have to skin me alive."

"Maybe she does, Felicien," Amaury corrected. "Yes, maybe she does."

—⁂—

The next month they carried on in uncompromising seriousness. Celine was cordial but unforgiving in her demands. Most of the time, she paired Amaury and Remi. She relentlessly worked Felicien and Alexis one on one. Amaury, Remi and Felicien began to catch on, their more agile physiques responding to Celine's demanding methodology. Alexis struggled with both the mental and physical demands of the lessons.

Mixed in with the unrelenting Aikido practice, the men were shown where to place the blade of a knife, a pencil, a pen, any pointed object at hand in the spine, the side, the abdomen, behind the ear, in the temple or the throat for a kill. She calmly demonstrated how to kill a person quickly and quietly when the only available weapon was your bare hands.

This was a not the same innocent girl they had known for so many years. She was critically demanding that every detail of the training be carried out precisely and methodically. She drove them to the point of exhaustion and demanded more. But more concerning than her uncompromising attitude was her emotional detachment in describing killing techniques. There was no hesitation, no compassion. She displayed a cold indifference—a mindset similar to the passive aloofness she so despised in the Nazis. Her mercilessness came through with disturbing consistency. Celine was not only more capable of defending herself than any of them, she had become a dispassionate lethal weapon.

Her mood was sullen, almost angry. She put them through their routines with rote determination. The normal amusing banter, so much a part of the *friends'* interaction, was not tolerated. The men looked at her in glum bewilderment. *Who is this person?* Her trainers had warned her this moment would come. It was time to address some very serious issues.

⤬

On the 33rd night of training, Celine entered the gym purposely late. The men were hard at work. No greetings, no pause in their activities— just another night in hell and Satan had just arrived. She watched for a few minutes. Remi and Felicien had come a long way, their moves fluid and swift. Amaury was right behind them, but Alexis still relied on pure brawn. *Perhaps that's okay,* she thought, *he has done pretty well so far in life. I'll just pray muscle will bring him through.*

She blew the whistle that now hung around her neck during the practice sessions. The men jolted upright, in acquired annoyance of the piercing sound. "What now?" Felicien murmured under his breath, wiping the sweat from his brow.

"It is time for us to have a chat…a chat about me and the irritation and confusion you are all feeling. Grab a towel, get some water and gather around the table where I can look into your eyes as I explain some things to you."

Still panting, the men pulled up chairs and sat in sullen silence, as they always now did in her presence.

She sat at the head of the table, watching them gather. They were her dear men, the men she loved. Men it terrified her to think may not survive the coming battles. She fought to calm herself. *Do not get emotional. Get your message across and don't let the love you're feeling right now cause you to break down.*

She took in a deep breath. "The training in England changed me. You see it and I know, my darling Remi, you feel it. That change did not come about accidently. It was planned. Designed into the training process. I cannot judge whether the change is good or not. Only time and the end of this hideous war will determine that. But it is important we discuss this change so you will understand who I have become," she paused. Their eyes fixed upon her.

"Much of the training focused on physical combat, martial arts, weapons, explosives, strategy. But it dealt with something else, too—something invisible. It dealt with attitude. Looking back on it, I can see this aspect of the training started the moment I arrived at the camp. It was subtle at first. But as time went on, it grew more intense. In the last few months, they worked with each of us in individual counseling sessions.

"These sessions focused on two things. The seriousness of what we were being taught and desensitizing our attitude about killing another human being. The mental training was every bit as intense as the physical, perhaps even more.

"The seriousness I have brought to these martial arts instructions has taken a toll on the fun-loving atmosphere that has always been such an integral part of us. I fear it may be lost forever." The thought of destroying that carefree interaction sent a pang of sadness through her.

She calmed herself and continued. "I am sorry for that. It is painful to me. I feel I am destroying something that has always come so naturally, the very spirit that has been an integral part of binding us so closely for so many years..." she faltered, her eyes filled with tears and she fought for control. The men saw emotions in Celine they had not seen since before she left for training.

They felt her deep passion—her concern, her love and fears for them. They began to understand the severity of the struggle she now faced in feeling their safety was solely in her hands.

They sat quietly, sadly realizing the demands of war was changing all of them.

She reached over and placed her hand on Felicien's and looked into his eyes, "My seriousness comes from knowing that if I do not teach you, all of you, well enough, my failure will get you killed," she pulled back, looking at all of them. "I lay awake at night praying I am doing an adequate job, praying that through my seriousness, you will realize this is not a game—this cannot be taken lightly. I pray that you will believe that if you do not take what I am teaching you seriously, you will die."

She paused again, bracing herself for what she now must get them to accept. She forced the loving passion of the past moment into the background.

"In the second part of my training, I am trying to desensitize you. To beat out of you any hesitation you might have to break your opponent's wrist, snap his leg and kill him with whatever means you have available. If I fail at this, I fail myself, and worse, I fail you. I cannot teach this detachment to killing in an atmosphere of playful joviality. We have killed German soldiers before, but there is a difference in shooting a man 30 yards away and looking into his dying eyes in hand-to-hand combat.

"They told us that human beings have a natural tendency to shy away from killing another person. That tendency causes a normal hesitation when we are confronted with killing a person, and even a moment's hesitation in a face-to-face combat environment most likely will get us killed. Hesitation in any combat situation is dangerous, but to hesitate in hand-to-hand combat is almost always fatal.

"I hope we are never confronted with hand-to-hand battle, but that is probably wishful thinking. If you are in a face-to-face fight, and I am with you, you must overcome any concern you may have that because I am a woman, physically smaller, you have to defend me. You have seen my capabilities. You know I can defend myself, so put any illusions of chauvinistic valor out of your heads.

"In hand-to-hand combat we always come to each other's aid, but only after we have eliminated our individual adversary. Never turn your attention from your adversary before you have them down and eliminated and when I say eliminated, I mean *dead*. Do not hesitate. Do not make the mistake of thinking a severely wounded adversary is eliminated. Do not assume an adversary who is unconscious is not a danger. Never leave an injured adversary. Never leave an unconscious adversary. Kill them! If you cannot accept this rule, I do not want to fight alongside of you because you will get yourself, and perhaps every one of us, killed.

"We have already killed German soldiers. You killed the Milice Colonel and his men after I left, so perhaps what I am telling you…what I am so concerned about…is a moot point. But the German soldiers killed in our early raids were killed at a distance and you killed the Milice out of deep revenge for the deaths of Daniel, Damian and Max. The distance, the premeditated revenge will not be present in hand-to-hand combat. Hand-to-hand combat comes on without warning, instantaneously. It is often a surprise, confusing, personal. You must assume your combatant intends to kill you so your only objective is to kill him first.

"Our goal as the Tristan, as Resistance fighters, is not to kill the enemy. We cannot kill enough of them to make a difference and we should avoid killing them if at all possible. We should avoid killing them because it heightens their resolve to track us down, and worse, killing as many Germans as we can holds the possibility of turning our own citizens against us.

"People understand killing in self-defense or killing a German soldier to protect them and other defenseless citizens, but indiscriminant killing will appall them. If we kill indiscriminately, the people will become fearful of us. We become savage brutes in their eyes. We will need their help at some time in the future—rest assured of that. But if we are looked upon as blood-thirsty bullies, they will not be compassionate to us. As Resistance fighters we must focus on disrupting and disabling the enemy's ability to fight. It is the responsibility of the Allied armies to kill them. Our job is to make it easier for them to do so."

Alexis raised his hand, "I thought you just said we should kill the Germans without hesitation. Now you are telling us we should not kill them."

"No, Alexis. That is not what I am telling you! In combat where an enemy can kill one of us, we must kill him first—without hesitation. You must not hesitate or think you can wound the enemy and get away. Most likely, if you do not kill your adversary, he will wind up killing you or one of us. But we should never set out on a mission strictly for the purpose of seeing how many Germans we can kill. That is not our objective.

"Our challenge is to operate with such stealth and in such a manner that our activities are highly disruptive and untraceable to us. If some Germans get killed in the process, they are simply victims of war and so be it."

Again, Alexis spoke, "So, then, why do we need to be trained not to hesitate to kill?"

"Because there will be times when killing will be necessary and some of those times we will probably be in very close contact—maybe looking the enemy right in the eyes." That image deepened the seriousness in the room as Celine continued, "We must not hesitate to kill in a situation where a combatant can kill us. I did not say we must not hesitate if the enemy *will* kill us; I said we must not hesitate if they *can* kill us."

They looked at her both in admiration and a growing understanding. Yes, Celine was different and now they understood how.

Remi had been staring at her. Ever since her return she had been different. It was subtle. There had been tension between them—at least, *he* felt the tension. She seemed remote to it, which amazed and confused him. She often seemed agitated, preoccupied, annoyed. Several times he had asked her if everything was all right between them and she had always responded with a somewhat surprised confirmation that it was. Still, he felt it. The last time he asked, she said, "Yes. Why do you keep asking me? Everything's fine." Her tone was petulant. Her answer turned him from concern to irritation. He simply turned away in frustration.

It was clarifying and disturbing to hear her explanation. *Could this be what's going on?* he wondered. *Could the training be the source of her tension?*

He gazed at her. Sitting across the table from him was his cherished Celine—so beautiful, so innocent in appearance, yet so transformed. He cursed himself for ever letting her go to England. They had changed her, brought a sharpness to her, stripped away her innocence…the soft innocence that so delighted him. *So, this is my new Celine. My God, what a price she and I have paid.*

He sighed in resignation, "Teach us, then. And to the best of our ability, we must try to avoid those close encounter killing situations you are describing. But if we do get ourselves into one, teach us how to respond."

Remi turned to the others, "Do we all understand what Celine is telling us?" They all nodded.

"Alexis, look at me," he demanded. "Do you understand what Celine is telling us? Do you understand she is trying to keep us alive? That she is fully capable of protecting herself and that if you and she are ever in a hand-to-hand fight with individual adversaries, you have to take your man totally out of the picture before you go to help her?"

Keeping his eyes cast toward the table, Alexis shook his head yes.

"Alexis, look at me and answer me," Remi demanded with more irritation in his voice than he intended.

"Yes, yes! Damn it, Remi, I understand. I will do as Celine says," Alexis shot back, still not looking up. "Now I would like to leave for a while."

Remi doubted Alexis really would follow Celine's instructions, but at the moment, he was just too tired to give a damn. "Okay," he said, pushing his chair back and rising, "perhaps we should all take a break."

—∞∞—

They regrouped at a table in the Bistro among the late-supper customers, all except for Alexis. They knew he would have to be off by himself for a while to process everything he had heard.

Alexis had driven back to town by himself, parked his car at his house then began walking the streets, trying to wrap his mind around Celine's message. He was angry with Remi for sending Celine to England. He could not understand why Remi had let her go, even after she had drawn the short straw. *Remi should have only let the men draw straws,* he mentally grumbled.

Deep inside, he realized even that would not have worked. Had he drawn the short straw, he would not have been capable of understanding the training. After all these years, it was still so difficult for him to accept the limitations his slow mind placed upon him.

He had been in love with Celine ever since he could remember, and he resented how the training had changed her—what Remi had allowed to happen to her. He was angry with Remi, but at the same time, he loved him, too. He knew that Remi would not carelessly put Celine in harm's way.

I don't understand how I can be mad at Remi and love him, he thought. *Sometimes, I am so stupid.* He pushed his hands farther down into his jacket pockets and trudged on down the dark street.

His thoughts turned to Celine. She was so beautiful, so kind and considerate of him. When they were children and other kids teased him, she was always there for him. She would defend him, telling the teasers Alexis was stronger than they, bragging that he was able to perform acts of strength they would never be able to do. Over the years, he came to understand he would not win her heart. He had come to accept that, but still he loved her so very much…his surrogate girlfriend, his pretend wife. He loved Remi and the others, too, and of the others, he loved Remi the most. Remi was his hero, his confidant, his make-believe brother. But his love for Celine was different. He didn't understand exactly what the difference was, just that his love for her was somehow more.

Right now, he wanted to sock Remi for sending Celine to the training rather than going himself or sending either Amaury or Felicien. He had told Remi at the time that it was he who should go because he was the leader and it was the leader's responsibility to get the training, then come back and prepare his team for battle. But the decision had been made, so it was Celine who went, and now look what they had done to her.

He stopped in the middle of the block, standing in the drizzling night rain. His hair was soaked. Droplets gathered and ran down his face, mixing with the tears filling his eyes. He cried because he didn't understand things like the rest of the *friends* did. He cried because he loved Celine, and because he simply felt so sad inside and, as always, didn't fully understand why.

CHAPTER 16

Celine's explanation did much to clear the air. The men worked even harder and she lightened up. Some of the fun returned. While Felicien once again began to show some of his natural lightheartedness, he remained serious about perfecting the skills Celine so clearly explained may keep them alive. He even spent time with Alexis, carefully explaining the subtleties of some of the more complicated movements. Felicien's ability to laugh at himself and make a joke out of his own ineptness soothed Alexis' feelings of inadequacy and he, too, began to catch on.

Then one night during practice, Felicien threw Celine to the mat. He sprang to his feet in shocked glee, "Yes, yes, now I see. Now I see how you do it!" Celine lay there on her back, gasping as she waited for her breath to return. Her pained face could not hide her smile. *They are starting to get it. Damn, that hurt.*

From that night on, Felicien began advancing quickly. He had always been athletic, consistently beating all the *friends* to the top of the hills and mountainsides they climbed as children. He immersed himself in practice, becoming so exacting in his moves that Celine was able to use him as an assistant, speeding up the teaching process. Both Remi and Amaury also began to excel, with Celine and Felicien coaching slight corrections as they perfected the various Aikido techniques.

Celine set up special sessions when she and Alexis would practice alone. He enjoyed the time they worked together. It was special for him and he did not feel so self-conscious about constantly having to compare his performance against the others.

In time, he began to repeat the more basic techniques with a reasonable degree of skill. What Alexis lacked in finesse, he made up for in strength. Celine was convinced Alexis had the strength to break a man's neck through sheer force. She had no doubt he *could* kill a combatant. The question was, *would* he?

Though Alexis' strength would save him in any combatant situation, his naïve and trusting disposition was of concern. To Alexis, people were good…all people. His approach toward others was compassionate, not combative. Celine seriously wondered if Alexis could bring himself to take out his opponent—even in a violent fight.

She talked endlessly to him about how important it was in hand-to-hand combat that he kill his foe as quickly as possible. She struggled to point out that anything less could get him and the rest of the *friends* killed. He would listen intently and nod his understanding while retaining the same sweet, agreeable smile he used with everyone about everything.

Each time they talked, Celine would pause, her heart melting as she stared into his soft brown eyes. They exuded such deep caring for her—for all of life. Alexis' heart shined through those eyes every day, gently affecting so many people in so many ways. There were very few people around Treaire who had not been helped over the years by Alexis, touched by his kindness in one way or another. He was adored—known for miles around as Treaire's helpful big bear.

❦

It was the seventh week of training. Celine and Alexis had been working alone at the château until late in the evening. He drove her back to Treaire in his oil-guzzling Citroën and dropped her at the bakery so she could finalize preparations for the early morning breakfast rolls before retiring for the night.

She left the shop about 12:45 am—long after curfew. She would stick to the shadows, be alert for patrols. As she climbed the hill on the dark and narrow Rue Bernoulli, two blocks from home, Sergeant Steinholt stepped from a doorway just a foot in front of her. She jolted back in shock.

"Out again after curfew—tisk, tisk, tisk. I am not drunk tonight, little girl. Ve have been thinking about you, pretty one, haven't ve, men?"

There were sounds of movement as three dark figures moved from the shadows and moved in behind her.

"Ve have been thinking vhat to do," the Sergeant smirked, "und have decided it is not vise for us to risk that you might tell Colonel Nussbaum about our little meeting a vhile back." His hand shot forward, grabbing Celine's arm hard and yanking her to him. His men pressed in tight behind her.

A calm fury built within her. Her eyes narrowed. Pulse quickened. Adrenaline surged through every muscle. The hair on her neck bristled. With her free hand, she pulled a pencil from her coat pocket, jammed its point into the opening of the Sergeant's left ear, and pushed in and up hard. His eyes burst open as if they would fall from their sockets. He gasped, released his hold on her arm, as his legs buckled.

The three Privates staggered back, watching their infallible Sergeant's knees hit the pavement with a crack as he exhaled his last dying breath.

Celine whirled, foot raised, her speed building tremendous force before connecting with the side of the first man's leg at the knee. It cracked loudly in the still night air. At virtually the same instant the heel of her hand impacted the base of the second man's nose, lifting him from his feet, shattering cartilage and sending shrapnel of thin bone fragments into his head behind his eyes. Blood shot from his broken face. He fell back, his head meeting the cobblestone street with a sickening thud.

She leapt clear, turning her focus to the third man, who stood dumbstruck. As she started toward him, two huge arms wrapped around his chest from behind, lifted him several feet in the air, turned him sideways and smashed him to the street.

"Alexis," she gasped.

He smiled, "I always watch to see you get home safe, Celine. Pretty good I did tonight, huh?"

She moved quickly around him, grabbed the head of the man with the broken leg and dropped the weight of her body full force down on his bent spine. His chest collapsed with a sickening sound. She immediately moved on to the man with the shattered face, whispering to Alexis as she moved, "Kill the man. Alexis, kill the man you threw on the ground."

He looked down at the man. The force of the impact had broken several bones. The soldier groaned in pain.

Celine put the man with the shattered face in a choke hold and applied all the pressure she could muster.

"Kill him, Alexis," she repeated in a whisper louder than the last. "Kill him now!"

Alexis glanced over at Celine, still holding tight to the throat of the faceless man. A sad fear developed in his eyes. As he glanced back toward his victim, he stared into the muzzle of a Lugar as it discharged its bullet into the side of his neck.

He fell back. A searing flash of pain shot up into his jaw. Blood gushed from the huge tear in his carotid artery. Celine released her grip on the now dead soldier's neck, sprang to her feet, grabbed the hand of the shooter, and stripped away the pistol. She smashed the gun down solidly on the man's throat, crushing his larynx—his suffocation complete in seconds. She rushed to where Alexis had collapsed, lifting his head on to her lap and jammed her hand down hard on the gushing artery. Already, he was growing weak. "What in hell are you doing here?" she moaned.

He looked up at her through glassy eyes, "I always watch to see that you are all right when you walk home at night from the bakery," he smiled. "Tonight, it was good...(cough)...tonight, it was good that I watcchhh..." A warm exhaustion eased over his body as if his angel had pulled up a soft blanket. His eyes slowly closed and he felt his body rising.

He opened his heavy eyes again, smiled his sweet Alexis smile, and whispered, "I love you, Celine." She bent and kissed his forehead, "I love you, too, Alexis...I love you, too."

She felt him relax and she sobbed quietly there in the dark street.

She remained with Alexis long after he passed—her tears falling, her heart broken. She had her answer. Alexis would hesitate; he would not kill his opponent. He would die because of his kindness and because of his love for his fellow human being.

A Kübelwagen's lights rambled slowly past the intersection at the end of the street, bringing her out of her mourning despondency. She was sure the patrols wouldn't come up Rue Bernoulli. It was a narrow street buttressed on both sides by workshops—no people to watch or harass. Not of interest to the night patrols.

She gently eased Alexis' head from her lap, then hurried home to Remi. They contacted Amaury and Felicien and rushed back to the tragic scene to remove the bodies. They buried the Germans deep in the woods on the Cheever estate, concealing the multi-body grave by covering the fresh earth with a thick ground cover of brush and dead leaves.

Alexis had no living family. After his parents died, he continued to live alone in the family home. No relatives ever visited, and he never spoke of extended family. To him, the *friends* had been his family. He had loved them, sometimes secretly watching over their safety at night, as Celine had learned he often did for her.

When she told the *friends* about his coming to her rescue, Felicien said, "Oh, didn't you know about that? Alexis often watched over all of us. If he knew one of us was out alone at night, he'd watch from a distance. I found out one evening when he brought our kids home from a function they had attended. On the way home, some older kids started badgering them and Alexis came out of nowhere to protect our little ones. I told him he didn't have to do that. He just smiled at me...you know how he does. I knew he was not about to give up the practice."

They buried Alexis the next day—not in the cemetery where his folks were buried. He was always frightened of Treaire's cemetery. They took him to a high-country meadow in the mountains. The little meadow came alive with dozens of varieties of wildflowers each spring. The mountain flowers continued their brilliant décor in the cool, green valley throughout the summer. It was a place Alexis loved. He had shown the meadow to the *friends*, telling them how he would sometimes drive there, lie down next to the stream and feel at peace. He said it was his place next to God.

They buried him near the stream. They placed no marker. The meadow itself would serve to identify his last spot on earth.

Remi stood, looking down at the fresh grave. Tears formed in his eyes, "We will miss you, brother. You were our heart, our kind heart—the one who brought compassion to us. You were always there, always faithful, always vigilant. What God denied you in thought, He returned multifold in demonstrating His love for all of us through you. You are irreplaceable. You will be missed every second of every day, by all of us.

"Rest now, our big brother. Take your smile, your love and your kindness into heaven and embrace the angles."

They lingered there in the early afternoon sunshine. They spread a blanket on the ground, ate cheese and fruits and drank a bottle of Amaury's best wine in honor of the Tristan's fallen gentle giant. Alexis would have enjoyed the picnic.

———❦———

Celine excused herself from the training the week following Alexis' death. She encouraged the others to continue, but said she needed time away from the war to settle her grief. They all shut down for a while. The pain of losing Alexis weighed enormously. A week later, Remi called them together.

"We cannot lose ourselves in grief and give up. Alexis and Daniel have given their lives. They died because of this war, because of the Nazis. It is not fitting for us to show weakness in response to their strength. I am calling us back to finish the fight we have begun." The mood remained solemn. He had not expected anything different. His heart, too, yearned to simply escape from what had become such a heartbreaking commitment.

He sighed deeply. With forced resolve in his tone, he continued, "The shipment of heavy weapons is scheduled to be dropped in two days. We have until then to lick our wounds, but then we must once again rise to our task of ridding France of her conquerors. I have confirmed the drop coordinates with the British. Everything is set for Thursday night. Be ready."

CHAPTER 17

Heavy equipment drop site
Alpine valley near Les Manuires
45° 19' 4.62"latitude
6° 31' 54.1272"longitude

Amaury drove one of the large box trucks used by his grounds maintenance people and met the rest of the *friends* on an isolated country road several miles outside of Treaire that Thursday. The heavily rutted farm roads up through the mountain passes made for slow going. It took well into the evening to drive to the drop site. The drop coordinates targeted a high valley surrounded by jagged snowcapped mountain peaks some 70 miles from Treaire.

Like Celine's landing site this one, too, would be tricky, as were all such acts of cooperation between Resistance groups and the Allied forces supplying them. It would once again demand a crack pilot to bring his lumbering bomber in over mountain peaks then quickly drop down toward the valley floor for a skilled bombardier to drop the cargo on target.

The *friends* rambled into the valley just before 8:00 pm. The air was cold and the sky clear. The pines glistened with feathery crystals of frost, causing them to gleam as they waved slightly in a light breeze, singing their eerie night melodies.

Now, the question was when—and even *if*—the drop would be made. The last message Remi had received indicated the drop was scheduled for between 10:00 pm and 1:30 am Greenwich Mean Time (gmt). Experience had taught him that could mean anything from an hour early to several hours late…and perhaps not at all. If anything went wrong on the British end, the plane simply would not show.

They set ten fuel pots in a circle roughly 100 feet in diameter in the middle of the grassy field and placed two more directly in the center. The vehicles were backed into the woods out of sight. Amaury grumbled that all of this camouflage was not necessary, but Remi insisted the vehicles be hidden. He had heard of attempted drops to various Resistance groups that had gone wrong—drops that had been detected by the Germans. They would send in Messerschmitt fighters and spray the area with 50-caliber cannon fire, destroying the vehicles, killing those in the crossfire and stranding any survivors miles from safety. He was not about to take that chance...not on a night when the temperatures were already below freezing and falling fast.

It was a cold and boring wait. The *friends* were positioned too far apart to talk among themselves, Each sat out in the open field beside their assigned fuel pots, ready to ignite then on Remi's command. Felicien cursed himself for not bringing another pack of cigarettes. Cigarettes were not all that easy to get since the occupation, but he always had a good supply, often taking them in payment for the handyman work he did for people in and around Treaire. Tonight, he was down to his last four. Not many to keep him company as he whiled away the hours.

He lay there, warm in his layers of winter clothing—enjoying the peaceful moment. *I really love smoking,* he thought. *I'm so happy it was invented. If I recall my schooling, I think I have the American Indians to thank for tobacco. Thank you, American Indians,* he smiled, lighting up one of the joys of his life.

Felicien took a long satisfying drag as he looked up at the moonless, star-studded Milky Way millions of miles above his head. His mind drifted back to when they were children. It was he who always stole cigarettes from the local stores for the *friends* to smoke in the cave as they drank their sour wine. *They were so lucky to have me. How mundane it all would have been without my stolen cigarettes and wine. Thank you, Mr. Dumont, wherever you are.*

He smiled again, enjoying the memory of how good he was at shoplifting. He got so good at it; he would test his skills just to see if store owners could catch him. He had stolen so many packs of cigarettes that the smarter shopkeepers began securing them behind the checkout counter. But he was even able to snatch a pack from those sheltered locations from time to time. He would wait until a customer asked for help. When the store owner went to the customer, he could be behind the counter, grab his prize, and be out again before the man even got halfway to the shopper. He pridefully recalled how stealthy his moves were—fast and silent. Monsieur Dumont was never as much fun because he never caught on. *Probably age,* Felicien thought. *I wonder if everyone becomes so stupid as they age? Nope, Dumont had a lock on stupidity—had successfully honed it to perfection,* he chuckled.

But all good things come to an end. Eventually, Felicien was caught and, sadly, his father let the local gendarme throw the book at him. From his first tottering footsteps, Felicien had been an adventuresome child. It wasn't that he was cruel or destructive, just inquisitive and always willing to see how far he could push the envelope. If trouble could be found, he was the first in and last out. If no trouble was in sight, he'd quickly become bored and create some.

At the time of his failed heist he was 11. By then, he had been sent home from school more times than his parents could count, and had been brought home by Pierre Bonney, Treaire's single police officer, so often that Pierre and Felicien's father, Charles, had actually became close friends. Felicien's mischief had his parents at their rope's end. His father was convinced the boy was destined to become a professional thief, doomed to spend his adult life behind bars.

Felicien's individual infractions were all relatively inconsequential, but they were also so numerous that scarcely a week passed without him being in some sort of trouble. When Pierre showed up at Charles' front door holding Felicien by his coat collar in one hand and a pack of contraband cigarettes and a stolen bottle of inexpensive wine in the other, Charles' patience was at an end. He told Pierre to take the boy to jail and slammed the door.

This was quite an inconvenience for Pierre since Treaire had no jail, but sympathizing with Charles' frustration, Pierre took Felicien home and locked him in his basement fruit cellar for the night. The next day, Pierre and Charles met at the Bistro and over several glasses of wine decided that it was time to put their collective foot down. Felicien would pay dearly this time.

They sentenced him to be met after school by Pierre each day and put to work at whatever chores had to be done around Treaire. It was Felicien who gave the church and the butcher shop a new coat of paint under the watchful eyes of the priest and butcher. And it was Felicien who swept up after each town celebration, washed the store windows each month at the shops where he had stolen packs of cigarettes, and it was Felicien who cleaned out the barns outside of town, and on and on and on for a year. He was so busy with the demands of completing the chore list Pierre handed him each day that he had no time for trouble. His father was delighted, Pierre was delighted, and most of the towns-people were delighted—even jokingly asking Charles if he could make Felicien's slavery a permanent town benefit.

Felicien smiled to himself as he thought back on it all. Actually, he loved his parents dearly; still visited them often and had them over to his house for lively dinners, good conversation and the enjoyment of several bottles of wine. After his year-of-punishment, he joined his father in his auto mechanic, electri-cal appliance repair, and locksmith business. He had a natural instinct for the mechanical trades—talents which now supported him, his third wife Marguerite and their two children.

God, life is wonderful, he smiled to himself. *God, you are wonderful. You have always given me fun things to do and to top it all off, you had the American Indians come up with tobacco. I love you, God, and your American Indians.*

Felicien even enjoyed the war. Without it, the excitement of being a Resistance rebel would be impossible, frowned upon by everyone. But because of the stupid Germans, he could go about, freely blowing things up, cutting telegraph lines, derailing trains and wind up a hero. *What a life,* he thought, *what a truly great life! I'm going to hate to see this war end.*

The faint sound of an approaching aircraft engine broke his reverie. A hun-dred yards away, Remi tensed, straining to determine if he had heard a plane or just the wind moving through the nearby trees. *No, it's a plane!*

"Light the pots," he yelled. Within seconds, the pots flared to life as the sound of the incoming bomber intensified. "Everyone into the woods," Remi shouted. As they crouched, hidden alongside the open meadow, the sound grew fainter. Remi stood up, held his breath, and listened intently. *Yes,* he thought, *the sound is fading.* "Damn it! They are on the wrong side of the mountain," he cursed.

The pots would only burn for about 10 minutes before they exhausted their fuel. Remi prayed the pilot would quickly recognize his mistake and find their valley. The pilot knew the drop point would be lit. *Surely they won't drop the crate until they see the lights,* his thought a yearning plea.

If they made the drop on the other side of the mountain, it would be virtually impossible to retrieve it—even if they could find it. "Please, God, let him see that he is in the wrong area...please, God, please," Remi whispered. The drone of the plane was now gone completely. Just the whisper of the breeze in the pines broke the silence. They all breathed shallowly, nervous to hear the sound of the bomber's engines. Nothing.

The mountain between them rose to over 12,000 feet. Unless the pilot flew the entire length of its adjacent valley, he would have to climb much too high to be able to accurately place the drop, even if he did see the dimly lit circle.

One of the pots in the center of the circle burned out. It would be just minutes before the rest began exhausting their fuel. Remi sprang from his hiding place and dashed for the vehicles. Additional fuel was in the truck. As he raced past the still-burning pot in the center of the circle he heard the plane emerge over the top of the mountain. The pilot was at over 13,000 feet. He saw the circle of burning pots cleared the mountain peak and put the bomber into a nose dive toward the target. Remi made it to the opposite side of the circle just as the plane leveled out. It was still much too high. The pilot would have to make a second run. One of the pots on the outer circle sputtered and died.

The plane banked, and flew a mile up the valley, then went into a steep turn, dropping dramatically in altitude. It was now wide of the target, heading across the narrow width of the valley rather than flying down its length. *God, he's too low. He's going to hit the far mountainside,* Amaury winced as he watched the plane rushing toward him. Remi's thought was the same, *Pull up, you fool, pull up!* As the black silhouette of the mountain rushed toward them the pilot jammed the throttle full forward and pulled back hard on the stick. Engines screamed in a surge of power, their superchargers maximizing fuel and oxygen to the hungry pistons.

The plane roared toward the *friends,* struggling to increase its climb rate as it swiftly closed the distance to the jutting mountainside. The bomber's black silhouette groaned under full power, its engines tugging desperately at the bulk of the craft. "Jesus, he's not going to make it." Remi shouted, frozen in horror as the heavy bomber thundered overhead.

The pilot threw the plane into a desperate banking turn. The downside wing severed the delicate tops of several pine trees, showering the forest in a downpour of crashing limbs. The engines wailed, as if fighting for their very lives—fire shot from their glowing exhausts. The downside wing topped another of the taller pines. The plane visibly lurched as the impact pulverized the tree top, opening a large gash in the wing as timber and scrapes of torn aluminum peppered the fuselage. The plane dropped from sight, nosing into a small ravine behind the trees. Though out of sight, they could hear the engines roaring in defiance of death. They braced for the impact.

Far down the ravine, the plane slowly growled above the tree tops, skirting parallel to the mountainside not more than a hundred feet above its rock face. The *friends* heard its engines screaming in their continued defiance of death. They saw the bomber's black image rise. They all cheered as they watched the magnificent skills of the aviator and his powerful machine rise into the safety of the frigid night sky. He was banking back toward the valley for another pass at the drop site.

Remi ran on to the truck, grabbed the fuel can and started back toward the center of the ring just as the second center pot went dead. Felicien ran to meet him. Because the pots were hot, they could explode as fresh fuel was poured into them. Felicien would have to light the fuel as Remi poured to avoid the possibility of it exploding—a tricky maneuver, at best.

The instant Remi began the pour, he shouted, "Okay, now," and Felicien dropped a lit match into the pot. It burst into flame. Six pots in the outside ring were still burning and now one of the center pots once again sent out its signal. At the other end of the valley, the pilot got his bearings on the target. He took the plane out several miles, banked, steadied his approach and pointed the nose straight down the center of the valley floor. "It's your airplane", he called to the bombardier, "Do your stuff.

The bombardier took control of the plane. They were almost at stall speed, but still traveling over 160 mph when he dropped the crate. The chute opened immediately, slowing the heavy container to a drop rate of just over 40 feet per second. It was dead on. It slammed into the burning center pot, sending its flaming liquid splashing as the crate crushed the pot. The majority of the fuel hit Remi's back. Felicien also caught several burning drops, but dashed toward Remi the instant he saw the burning fuel engulf him. He tackled him full body and they rolled together on the frozen grass.

With eyes glued to their two flaming comrades, no one saw the pilot rock the plane back and forth several times in salute and goodbye as he climbed into the night and vanished. By the time the others got to their smoldering companions, the two of them were sitting up—Felicien behind with his arms still wrapped around Remi and Remi sitting in his lap. Amaury took one look at the two of them and burst out laughing. Celine also saw the humor in Remi and Felicien sitting there, smudged and smoldering, and soon they all were holding their sides in laughter. Another night for the group of *friends*—united as the Tristan Resistance and dedicated to the defense of liberty—came to a close.

CHAPTER 18

The crate, made of reinforced plywood, had taken the drop well. It's weight and bulk, however, proved challenging for the team trying to raise it into Amaury's, high-bed truck. Alexis' powerful muscular strength was truly missed. Remi's naturally cautious nature demanded they covered their tracks to the greatest extent possible. His insistence on covering their tracks added another hour to the tasks which needed to be accomplished prior to leaving the site. In spite of the drop site's remoteness, he wanted it to look as undisturbed as possible.

They arrived back in Treaire later than planned. The sun's first beams had eliminated the cover of night and even though they kept to farm roads, Remi was anxious about being observed returning to town. The farm road they traveled entered town behind the Bistro, which was the first property after the road became paved. They slipped both the Citroën and the truck into the Bistro's large carriage barn, manhandled the crate out of the truck, pried it open and immediately began hiding its contents. They placed the crate and its parachute back in Amaury's truck and he left immediately for his estate, where he would burn the crate and parachute far back on the property out of sight of curious eyes.

As he drove the highway north toward the estate, he passed a German military truck stranded alongside the road about a mile from the estate's entrance. In compliance with the Germans normal thoroughness, two young soldiers were guarding the marooned vehicle. They had lit a fire in a five-gallon can and were huddled beside it, holding their gloved hands over the flames and hopping from one foot to the other in an attempt to rid their bodies of the freezing cold. *Poor buggers, they've probably been in that truck all night*, Amaury thought.

The fact the truck was beside the highway didn't surprise him. It was the main route between the huge German supply depot at Chambéry and the railhead in Falauge, where equipment was loaded onto rail cars for shipment through the Saint Laurnee Passage on its way to the Italian Front. Almost daily convoys moved south to Falauge. What was surprising was the age of the two guardsmen. Amaury did a double take as he passed. *Good lord, those two can't be a day past 16,* he thought with amazement.

The stalled truck, of course, was of prime interest. Any German equipment the Tristan could get their hands on was highly prized. He decided to check out the situation.

He hurried on to the estate, eased into the truck shed behind the château, instructed his head caretaker to burn the crate and chute on the back side of the property, then went to his room, intent on getting back to the stalled vehicle as quickly as possible. He changed into a Milice Colonel's uniform, which had been stolen from the Treaire Milice armory prior to the Germans shutting down operations there.

Amaury pulled up behind the stranded truck in his four-door Peugeot, a dog of a car when compared to the array of fine Italian, German, and British exotics he now kept out of sight. The Peugeot got him where he wanted to go and did not arouse interest from the occupying Nazis. Hearing the car pull up, the two young guards fearfully peered around the front of the truck. In panic, they clumsily unslung their weapons; the taller of the boys dropped his rifle in the effort. Amaury could tell they were debating whether or not to approach the Peugeot. Their wide-eyed heads kept bobbing out to look at him, then popping back out of sight.

Amaury thought, *I'd better show myself or those fool kids might blow my head off.* He slowly stepped from the vehicle, raising his hands and shouted, "Don't be frightened, young soldiers. I'm a Milice Colonel. We're on your side, remember?"

Both heads appeared. Fretful confusion filled their young faces. "He's wearing a Milice uniform," one whispered loudly to the other.

"What branch is Milice?"

"Not German, Dummkopf. It's the French Nazis. I read about them in a magazine," the boy informed his lanky companion.

The boys slowly stepped around the front of the truck. Both managed hesitating Heil Hitler salutes. Again, the taller of the two dropped his rifle in the awkward maneuver.

Amaury returned the salute, but the instant he started toward them the one still in possession of his weapon raised its muzzle in his general direction, "Who are you, mein Herr Colonel? You must identify yourself, Sir, Colonel, Sir." The taller lad made a lunge for his rifle, inadvertently kicked it in the process and sent it sliding to the edge of the highway. Amaury had to work hard to maintain a straight face.

"I am Amaury Cheever, the District Director of Milice police units in southern France," he lied. "Please, boys, do not be frightened. We Milice work hand in hand with your Gestapo. I stopped to see if I could be of assistance."

The shorter boy lowered his rifle and whispered to his taller friend to go retrieve his. They both approached, still cautiously pointing their weapons in Amaury's direction, but at least they were now pointed at his feet rather than his head.

In reasonable German, albeit considerably modified by his French accent, Amaury said, "I see your truck is broken down and was wondering if you might want me to go into town and fetch a mechanic?"

"No, but thank you, Herr Colonel. We are not allowed to let Frenchmen repair German military vehicles. There will be a team of mechanics here tomorrow morning to make the repairs."

"Not until tomorrow morning," Amaury repeated with a bit of condescension in his voice. "Tisk-tisk, what a shame. You boys will freeze out here tonight. The temperature is expected to drop even lower than last night."

"Yes, Sir. The mechanics are busy repairing some damaged equipment in Chambéry, so we have been assigned to stay with the truck until they arrive."

"And then?" Amaury questioned.

"They will repair the truck just before the next convoy comes through to Falauge. We will be picked up by the convoy, Sir."

"Do you mind shouldering the rifles, lads? It would not go well for you to accidently shoot a Milice Colonel," Amaury smiled.

"Oh, jawohl mein Herr Colonel, Sir. Sorry, Sir," both youngsters fumbling awkwardly as they reslung their weapons.

Amaury could no longer hold his smile. Their ineptness was tenderly entertaining. His smile came across as kindness, as it was intended.

They were good-looking boys, real Aryans. Thick blond hair, sparkling blue eyes, fair complexions—fine examples of Hitler's "special" people.

Amaury said, "So, young soldiers, why you? Why did your commander pick you from all the rest to freeze your butts off sitting in this truck surviving on cold army rations for two nights in a row?"

"You said the reason when you called us *young* soldiers," the taller boy offered. "We are the newest recruits, so we get all the rotten jobs," he grinned.

Amaury's affable personality soon had the boys chatting comfortably. He invited them to sit in his warm car and chat a while. The taller lad was hesitant, but Amaury assured them that being with a Milice Colonel would ensure they would not get into trouble if a German officer showed up. "And," he kidded, "do either of you think a German officer is going to show up on this cloudy, cold day out in the middle of nowhere to see how two young boys are doing guarding a broken-down truck?" He hardly had the sentence out of his mouth as the two started moving toward the warmth of his idling Peugeot. They sat together for nearly an hour, interacting in friendly conversation.

The boys were scared and lonely. Just talking to an adult who showed them a bit of compassion was extremely comforting to them. They accepted cigarettes Amaury offered, although the taller in the back seat coughed violently with the first drag as he forced himself to learn the manly are of inhaling. They relaxed eventually, introducing themselves as Helmut Geer and Roland Packer, both from Ulm.

They told him the disabled truck's convoy had been on its way to Rome for a large buildup. The Germans were convinced the Allies were about to make a major push to take the city.

"We are thankful to God we do not have to go on to Italy with the convoy," Helmut volunteered. "Roland and I have only been in the army for two months, so they are going to put us off at Falauge, where we will take the place of older men who will be sent to Italy."

"So, my young friends," Amaury warmly smiled, "how is it that you wound up here in the French Alps? Did you join up to fight for the Fatherland?"

Roland awkwardly exhaled a long stream of smoke, "Oh, no, Sir. One day two Reich-Wehrmacht officers came into our study class and selected half the boys in the school to be drafted. They had us all count off one-two, one-two. Then they told all of the boys who said "two" that we were now in the army. We were sent home and told to report for duty the next morning…at the city hall building."

"You must obey," inserted Helmut. "There have been stories of boys who ran away or hid. Their parents and brothers and sisters got sent off to labor camps with the Jews. So, we're now here, stranded in the cold in southern France, chilled to the bone, guarding a broken-down truck."

Amaury softened his voice, looked into Roland's eyes and said, "Are you scared?" Roland gave a concerned glance at his friend in the back seat.

"No, Sir. We…we're…" a tear eased down his cheek as he returned his eyes to Amaury. His face tightened and more tears found their way to the surface. Amaury looked over the seat at young Helmut, trying his best not to follow the lead of his crying companion. Amaury's compassionate look was too much. Helmut, too, welled up and tears slipped down his cheeks.

Amaury reached over and patted Roland on the shoulder, "It's okay…I do not blame you. These are scary times. We are all afraid, even I and even your brave soldiers who have seen combat. It is all right to feel afraid and lonely. Even grown men cry in war. War is very difficult. You are brave young men."

The boys took heart from Amaury's encouragement. "I'll tell you what," he continued, "I have business I must attend to in Treaire, so I will have to leave you until this evening. I have a large home just up the road and I was thinking, perhaps when I pass here late this afternoon I will pick you both up and treat you to a fine dinner and some good wine as we sit next to the fireplace this evening."

The car remained silent. The boys hesitatingly shot glances back and forth, trying to assess each other's position on this astounding invitation. Roland broke the silence. "I don't think we should," he said, glancing toward Helmut for reassurance. "I think we can get shot for leaving our guard post." He turned back toward Amaury, "I mean, we can get shot, can't we?"

"Oh, I don't think so…surely not," assured Amaury. "Besides, no one is going to be coming out here tonight to check on you. We'll be gone just several hours after dark. Then I'll bring you back to sleep in the cab of that miserable truck so you'll be here when the mechanics show up in the morning—even if they get here right at dawn."

Helmut spoke up, "Thank you, Sir, but I think Roland is right. You are very kind, but we have been assigned to this post and I am sure we would be in a lot of trouble if they found we had left our assignment."

"Okay...I respect your decision, gentlemen, but I will stop on my way back to the château this evening and the offer will stand if you should change your mind." He gave them his remaining half-empty pack of cigarettes, watched as they trundled back toward the truck, then headed into town to talk to Remi.

Amaury was convinced the stalled vehicle was a communications truck of some sort. Its short, fully boxed-in rear compartment had two rear doors secured with a padlock and from a distance it appeared there was a sealed protrusion on its top—possibly an opening for the attachment of an antenna.

Remi was exuberant. They talked for over an hour, then both went to quarters over the Bistro carriage barn the *friends* had outfitted with cots to catch a few hours of sleep. Just after dark, they assembled with the rest of the *friends* at the cave. They laid out their plans, and at 8:00 pm, Amaury and Celine left for the château.

The night cooperated perfectly. It was freezing cold, with the temperature dropping precipitously. By the time Amaury pulled up next to the truck, its windows were opaque with think frost. It took Helmut some time to slide the side window open after Amaury knocked on it. The first thing that met his eyes was the gorgeous face of Celine, smiling at him from under her pill box fur hat. He struggled to get his stiff legs moving as he pushed himself up in the seat and forced a frozen smile back at her.

Amaury poked his face into view behind Celine, "Hello, Helmut," he smiled. "This is my sister Celine, who lives with me. Have you reconsidered? Will you come up to the house and sit by the fire, have some brandy and a good dinner with Celine and me? Celine is excited to meet the two of you. I am sure it will be all right. No one will be coming by this cold night, and I can have you back by midnight with a full belly and thawed out feet and hands."

Helmut looked over at Roland, "I don't know. What do you think?"

"I think we'll get shot if we are caught abandoning this damn truck."

Amaury overheard the comment. "Roland, I am a Milice officer. I seriously doubt that a German officer is going to wander past on this cold night, but in the doubtful event that should happen, I will speak up for you. I will tell him I invited you. You will not get into trouble."

"Damn it, Roland, he's right. He's a Milice Colonel. He's one of us. Besides," lowering his voice to a whisper, "you should see his sister. She's fabulous! In addition to all that, I'm freezing my ass off. Let's go."

Roland's look of concern weakened and he smiled at Helmut, "She's really pretty, huh?

"Yes, damn it, she's a total knockout."

"Okay, I'm in. Let's go."

It took several minutes for the boys to straighten up and extract themselves from the cab of the truck. "Bring your weapons. That's all right," said Amaury. The gesture further built confidence in the boys. They would be sitting in the back seat of the car with their rifles. What could possibly go wrong?

The young Germans were spellbound as the Peugeot pulled up in front of the massive entrance doors at the château. Aside from government structures, they had never seen a building as huge—the opulence of Amaury's mansion was spellbinding. A butler and a footman, both in white tie and tails, rushed from the house to open the car door for Celine, then immediately pulled open the rear doors for the boys. The youngsters watched in awe as the footman then ran around to take the car.

The warmth that engulfed them as they entered the enormous entrance hall made the trip immediately worthwhile. Dinner and wine would only be a divine addition, further confirming the correctness of their decision to join the gracious Colonel Cheever and his beautiful "sister".

"May I take your guns, gentlemen?" the butler inquired. The boys glanced toward Amaury, who nodded his approval. The rifles were deposited and the butler returned as the boys shed their heavy coats, vest sweaters, under sweaters, scarfs, overalls, hats, earmuffs and gloves. The child-soldiers went starry-eyed as they were ushered into the study. Amaury led the way to a fire roaring in an enormous hearth and out of nowhere a servant appeared with brandy snifters.

Celine engaged the youth in charming conversation, telling humorous stories and offering comforting encouragements to their stories of woe. She was the focus of attention as "brother" Amaury stood by, smiling in approval.

⎯⎯⎯ ⚬⚬⚬ ⎯⎯⎯

Back at the truck, Remi stood watch, constantly searching the road in both directions for signs of headlights. He and Felicien had walkie-talkies, for instant communication should Remi spot trouble—gifts from the plywood crate.

Felicien had quickly picked the padlock and could not believe his eyes as the beam from his flashlight revealed the truck's contents. It was filled with the latest German communications equipment, capable of sending, receiving and recording radio messages. The tuner could pick up a wide range of frequencies—a capability that would dramatically enhance the Tristan's abilities to communicate with the Allies. He quickly surveyed the installation. Its various components were neatly housed in a metal cabinet with just six bolts holding the apparatus to the vehicle's floor. Attached to the wall opposite the radio was a cabinet also bolted to the floor and on the wall was a rack with the multi-piece antenna. *This is so much more fun than stealing cigarettes,* Felicien smiled to himself.

He radioed Remi, "This is incredible. It's the latest technology. Come here. I'm going to need your help getting this thing out of here."

Remi started toward the truck, giving the road one more glance. Total undisturbed darkness in both directions.

"Remi, I'm telling you this is God dropping a gift from heaven in our laps. With this receiver we can pick up radio messages for hundreds of miles. Get to town to get one of Amaury's delivery trucks. I can have everything ready to move in about 20 minutes."

"Okay, I'll radio you if I see any traffic coming toward you from Treaire. Keep the rear doors of the truck open and keep watching for any lights coming toward you from that direction. Be back in 10 minutes."

Remi raced off, pushing the old Citroën to its limits. His objective was a box truck they kept in the Bistro's carriage barn. When he returned, everything was unbolted and ready to move. They opened the rear doors of both vehicles and Remi backed the Bistro truck up against the German vehicle, allowing just enough room for him to squeeze himself in to assist Felicien. They muscled the heavy equipment into their truck and laid the antenna cabinet in the center.

Felicien picked the lock on the antenna cabinet and thrilled when he found four portable VHF line-of-sight propagation radio units neatly packed inside. Remi pulled the Bistro truck forward just enough so Felicien could close and re-padlock the doors on the now empty German communications truck. The entire operation had taken just under an hour and put the Tristan in possession of one of the most sophisticated sets of communications equipment in southern France.

Helmut and Roland enjoyed a truly elegant evening, charmed by the beautiful Celine and made warm and welcome by the gracious Amaury. The dinner, prepared by Amaury's excellent chef and served by his meticulous butler, was exquisite…comparable to any served in the fine restaurants of Paris. The wine was outstanding. The six bottles they consumed came from the well-stocked Cheever cellars, made from choice grapes picked at one of the several Cheever vineyards and then fermented and aged to perfection at the Cheever winery.

By the time the clock struck midnight, the boys were toasty warm inside and out, having spent the most sophisticated social evening of their young lives. Helmut and Roland had dined at a level only enjoyed by the highest ranking officials of the Nazi regime. It was an evening they would remember for the rest of their lives and reminisce about many times over holiday get-togethers with their children and grandchildren.

Amaury drove them back to the truck and bid them adieu, leaving them several extra blankets, which he told them to hide in the woods before the mechanics showed up in the morning. Roland and Helmut drifted off to sleep, feeling loved and cared for for the first time since they had been torn from their parents.

The mechanics arrived shortly after 9:30 that morning. They were a couple of gruff old career soldiers in their late fifties—too old to fight and too young to retire, so were serving out their time while complaining about every moment of it. Their only comment on the youth of Helmut and Roland was to smirk and throw their heads back in one of those *what's-the-world-coming-to* gestures. Still shaking his head in disgust, the heavy-set one went to the truck and yanked open its hood.

"Ja, vhat the hell. Look here, Emil. It's nothing more than a loose distributor vire. Vhat a bunch of scheiß köpfe ve've got fighting for us. The convoy could have fixed this themselves if they vould have just looked under the hood—but, no! That's too much vork for soldiers these days," he grumbled, his head still stuck under the hood. "Okay, Emil, hit the starter," he yelled to his comrade, who was now sitting in the driver's seat. The starter groaned against the cold engine for several revolutions before the engine fired to life.

"There you go, children," he said, pulling himself off the fender and closing the hood. "There is a convoy on the vay. They should be here in an hour or so. At least now you can have a little heat vhile you vait for them." He continued to shake his head in amazement at all of the stupidity filling the modern world as he picked up his tool box and headed toward their vehicle.

The boys climbed back in the idling truck, turned up the heater and waited. The convoy showed up an hour later, just as the old soldier said it would. The officer in charge read Helmut's and Roland's orders. "Sorry, boys, you're not going to get a chance to fight. We're dropping you off at Falauge." He radioed the office in Falauge, informing them that their two recruits had been found, the stalled radio truck had been repaired and all would show up with the arrival of his convoy.

⸺◦⸺

Both Roland and Helmut were part of the team that loaded the empty communications truck onto a flat car for shipment to Italy the next day. It was offloaded in Rome, where it remained parked for several days, waiting to be dispatched to its unit. It eventually wound up in Anzio, an outpost about 30 miles south of Rome, sent there in anticipation of the rumored Allied invasion of Anzio beach.

The German officer who opened the truck's rear doors was furious about the missing equipment, but had no way of tracing when or where it went missing.

Quite frankly, he assumed that through some freak accident it had never been installed in the first place. In his frustration, he had the useless truck sent to the city dump.

After the war, it was appropriated by a destitute Italian garbage man. He had seen the truck sitting abandoned at the edge of the dump for months and decided there was no harm in taking it. He pumped up the tires, got the engine running and drove it home one afternoon. He outfitted it with cooking equipment, left his low-paying job collecting trash, and became a welcome daily addition at Anzio beaches, selling hotdogs and hamburgers (great sandwiches introduced to Italians by GIs), along with pizza, beer and wine to the sun worshippers. He made a good living, eventually adding a truck for his son and one for his daughter. The kids all had good business heads and today his grandchildren own one of the renowned catering businesses serving the discriminating tastes of Anzio's and Rome's elite citizens.

CHAPTER 19

Colonel Andreas Justus Nussbaum III, whose name Celine had used to put the fear of the Lord into Sergeant Steinholt and his group of thugs when they attacked her, was the German officer in charge of the garrison at Falauge. He was a strangely fascinating man. In the fall of 1939, when Germany started the war, he was 41 years of age. He had already endured 19 years in the German military—sufficient time to have developed a well-honed cynicism of the bureaucratic bumbling of the military and the absurdity of Germany's fanatical Nazi politics.

Externally, he was a spit-and-polished German officer—dignified in appearance who carried himself with a majestic deportment that exuded an aura of confident authority. Truly a compliment to the snazzy uniform of a Nazi officer.

Internally, he thought the war was the most preposterous thing Germany had ever done. He was certain that Hitler and his top-level henchmen were all criminally insane, and was convinced their fantasy that Germans descended from a super race of perfect Aryan beings was the most idiotic nonsense he had ever heard.

In spite of his contemptuous attitude toward the military, it was a plausible career for him to follow. All a person of intelligence had to do was show up, have the basic ability to perceive what was happening and deftly stay out of the way. Besides, both his father and grandfather had been military men who served the Fatherland a combined 107 years as loyal and proud officers. The broad path of influence and contacts they had forged in the military establishment offered a path to a secure military career with little effort needed on Andreas' part.

From early childhood Andreas was coached to follow in their footsteps and, being a child bent on finding avenues of least resistance and most reward, he complied willingly. At the age of eight, young Andreas happily waved goodbye to his pompous parents to pursue his education from grade school through college as a star student at the Theresian Military Academy, his grandfather's and father's alma mater.

He graduated three days after Germany signed the Versailles Treaty, officially marking its humiliating defeat in World War I—an event which Andreas found comforting since war can be so distracting to life's pleasurable pursuits, especially for a military officer.

The down side of this scenario was with no war going on there was little opportunity for advancement beyond Andreas' graduating rank of First Lieutenant. This resulted in a bit of a financial strain for Andreas. The family's once huge fortune had been dwindling away for years, and Andreas had a definite taste for the good life—none of which he could afford on his Lieutenant's pay. His parents still lived in their large manor house on the outskirts of Baden-Baden, continuing a lifestyle that denied the reality of their financial condition. They were prudent about their self-centeredness, determined to spend every last bit of the once great fortune on themselves.

With years of education addressing nothing but military studies, Andreas had little choice but to carry on in the soldierly profession of his forebears. He went to work for the quasi-governmental Reichswehr Amt für Informations-Versammlung (Government Office of Information Gathering) as a clerk. He hated the mundane work.

His father advised him to patiently bide his time, predicting that Germany would once again rise militarily and when that happened, Andreas would grow quickly in rank due to the family's military connections. In 1937, his opportunity came. The Nazis tapped Andreas for promotion to Captain and advancement into the intelligence branch of the Gestapo. He was first stationed in Berlin, working in the Reichssicherheitshauptamt (Reich Main Security Office).

While Andreas considered himself an honorable man, he was not above sycophantic kowtowing to attain self-promotion, nor was he averse to moral compromise in order to line his pockets. He had always been so inclined. At

Theresian, he himself was not a cheater, but he unabashedly sold cheat sheets to other students.

As a child, he consistently took advantage of his younger brother, cheating him out of most of his possessions, convincing himself that his brother's own stupidity was the problem rather than his personal greed.

When it became obvious Hitler and his group of demented followers were going to push Germany into war, Andreas immediately took steps to assure he would not be exposed to combat. He promoted himself from Captain to Colonel by manipulating various documents he had access to in the security office. He then did major research on where to assign himself, taking into consideration personal comfort, a post of sufficient importance to protect him from being transferred into combat, and, if possible, a station in a scenic geographical area. Command of the garrison at Falauge, France, fit the bill perfectly. He never really felt guilt about any of this. *How could anyone feel guilt about cheating the repulsive Nazis?*

So, here he was, stationed in the majestic beauty of the French Alps, commanding a group of rail-car loaders and living a rather pleasant life in spite of the war. He had status and authority, wrote his own rules and sported a rather natty uniform to boot. *Not bad*, he thought, *not bad at all.*

When he first arrived in Falauge, one look at the town convinced him not to live there. The place was tiny, offered no amenities, and living there would result in his every move being scrutinized by his troops and officers. He inspected Treaire and was immediately impressed. It was a throwback into antiquity—meticulously maintained and sparkling clean. Its citizens took pride in its medieval rural charm. The town blended so perfectly with the environment, it actually enhanced the area's resplendent natural beauty. It offered a Bistro renowned for its menu and wine list, and a quaint little hotel reminiscent of a Swiss chalet right next door. What more could a sophisticated German officer possibly ask?

He took a room in the hotel, found the food and wine at the Bistro surpassed its reputation, and manipulated the necessary paperwork to assure both his room and meals for him and his officers would be paid monthly by the Reich Ministry of Finance in Berlin.

He demanded his officers live in Falauge, and since French citizens were not doing much travel with the war going on, he often had the quaint hotel all to himself. The innkeeper was delighted to have reliable income, and soon found he could pad the hotel bill without repercussion.

Andreas moved in and settled down for a pleasant enjoyment of the war. *Yes*, he smiled to himself, *I can certainly put up with these inconveniences as a sacrifice to the Führer.*

Colonel Nussbaum and his officers became Bistro regulars, arriving precisely at 6:30 each evening to take possession of a table Amaury kept permanently reserved for them. The first hour or so involved jovial conversation over several beers. Dinner was accompanied by multiple bottles of wine, and the evening was gastronomically settled with schnapps Andreas had shipped in from Germany. Most evenings, the officers would stay late, often lingering until well after midnight, singing rousing gay drinking songs like "Bier Her" and "Beim Kronewirt". Every singing night's final melody was "Du, Du Liegst Mir Im Herzen"—Andreas' favorite and one that he would accompany on the Bistro's old upright piano.

He would then bid his officers auf Wiedersehen, sending them drunkenly driving back to Falauge while he stepped next door and up to his tidy, quiet room for the night. He flirted with the inn's pretty young night clerk, but having been raised a gentleman of traditional military bearing, he never once made an inappropriate advance.

<hr />

Remi found Colonel Nussbaum both irritating and intriguing. The mere fact that he was a German officer made him intimidating to Treaire's citizens. The Bistro's other patrons endured Andreas' and his officers' lively songs and laughter each evening only because they felt they had to. To complain might result in a very unpleasant reaction from the Germans—and no one was willing to risk finding out what form such a reaction would take.

Remi and Celine often observed the Colonel in the Bistro, where they, too, spent many evenings. He allowed his men their fun, but demanded they remain gentlemen and display respect for both the Bistro staff and other patrons. He participated in the buoyant activities, yet always held himself slightly aloof. If his officers began to enjoy themselves a bit more than he thought appropriate, it took no more than a stern look from him to quickly settle them down. There was no question that Colonel Nussbaum was in control. At all times, he was clearly aware of everything taking place in his environment.

He spoke flawless French and made it a point to interact with all of the regular Bistro customers and quickly learned their names. He always addressed them respectfully, by surname and the appropriate Madame, Monsieur, Mademoiselle, or Docteur. Without fail, he stopped by each person's table for a few moments of conversation—nothing deep; just a hello and light social exchange.

In these interactions, he maintained a well-practiced manner. While his conversation was kept at a light and pleasant level, most customers had the feeling the Colonel was studiously analyzing everything that was said. He gave the feeling that even a "hello" was carefully scrutinized to see if it might hold something of potential value for him.

Because of his authority, no one rejected his socializing, yet everyone breathed a quiet sigh of relief once Colonel Nussbaum finished his evening cordialities and moved on to the next table.

Andreas Nussbaum received an extremely interesting call on his private communications line. Top-level messages were communicated over a special secure line to commanders of German headquarters locations. Andreas loved receiving calls on the 'private line'…it gave him a tremendous feeling of importance. Whenever it rang, he puffed up with self-satisfaction and answered the phone with authority, "Colonel Andreas Nussbaum here. How may I be of service to the Reich?"

On this call, the letdown was immediate. It was his brother Wessel calling.

In Andreas' opinion, his younger brother was slow of mind, small of stature and timid in nature—all held tenuously together by a whimpering disposition. Wessel had managed to squeeze through Theresian Academy and graduate as a Second Lieutenant, the lowest rank a Theresian graduate could receive. When the war broke out, he was promoted to First Lieutenant and assigned to the strategically insignificant seaport town of Ancona—a dumpy little backwater town on Italy's central east coast. There, he was in charge of four privates who made up the Third Reich's Military Police unit, a symbolic representation of German presence in the town.

"Wessel, you fool, this is a secure communications line reserved for top military business. How in hell did you get this number?"

"You won't give a damn how I got the number when you hear what I've got to tell you. I've got news that will astound you," he bragged. "It will make us both wealthy." Andreas perked up.

"Yesterday, I was summoned to the Cathedral of Saint Ciriaco by the Bishop of Ancona. He told me that back in the mid-1930s, a German mining engineer employed by the Jagersfontein Diamond Mine in South Africa, walked off with some nine pounds of raw diamonds. The story goes that the enterprising engineer took the stones to Surat, India, where he spent the better part of a year having them cut and polished by an Indian diamond cutter and his young nephew.

"The diamond cutter was amazed at what the engineer had brought him. Almost every stone was of the highest blue-white brilliance and virtually defect free. Apparently, they had all been mined from a uniquely pure vein the week prior to the supervisor stealing them. Not only were they exquisite, they were huge. Andreas, are you there?"

"Yes, damn it. Go on!"

"You were so quiet, I didn't think…"

"For the love of God, Wessel, just tell me the damn story," Andreas almost shouted in the phone.

"Okay, okay, don't get your ass in an uproar. Let's see, where was I?"

Andreas rolled his eyes in exasperation. "You were telling me the diamonds were huge, you idiot—now go on."

"Oh, yeah. The Bishop claims the average weight of the finished stones is an amazing 5.99 carats, with the largest gem being almost 9 carats. When the cutting was complete, there were 1,535 stones, and the lot still weighed an astonishing 4.1 pounds.

"Well, according to the story, the greedy diamond cutter killed the German engineer and his nephew in 1934, taking the diamonds for himself. Then, he set out for Europe to sell them in Antwerp.

"I hope you're sitting down for this... He estimated the value of the gems at 70 to 80 million U.S. dollars." Andreas was now so intrigued and pressing the phone so hard against his ear he was starting to get a headache.

"Well, luck was not with the diamond cutter. While on the sea voyage from India to Italy, he contracted typhoid. He was deathly ill and because of his dire condition upon arrival in Ancona the compassionate priests at the Cathedral of Saint Ciriaco took him in. In spite of their best efforts to nurse him back to health, the diamond cutter died. The priests found the box of diamonds under his bed when they were cleaning up the room.

"You're going to love this. Instead of splitting up the diamonds and quitting the stupid priesthood, the idiots summoned their head man and asked him what to do," Wessel couldn't help himself from laughing. "It turns out he was as stupid as they were! He notified the Vatican, telling them he's going to bring the box to Rome to become property of the church." Wessel was now incapacitated with laughing at the absurdity of the priests not taking the gems for themselves.

Try as he might, Andreas couldn't help but smile in agreement. "Okay, okay, go on," he urged. *Only my brother and I could get a kick out of this.*

Still chuckling, Wessel continued. "Well, the head man from Ancona never made it to Rome. I never quite understood what happened to him, but for years everyone just assumed he wised up and took off with the gems. Now, and here's the amazing part, the box and all the diamonds were recently found in the maze of catacombs under the Ancona Cathedral.

"Apparently, all of these religious idiots have several screws loose! The reason Bishop Bentinelli called me over to the cathedral yesterday was he has decided to send the entire box of gems to Hitler as a gesture of goodwill from the Italian people in support of the Third Reich's plan to rid the world of homosexuals and Jews."

Again, Wessel began laughing so hard he couldn't speak. By now, Andreas was sitting up straight and listening intently.

"Wessel, damn it. Get ahold of yourself," Andreas commanded. "Get on with the story."

"Sorry, I just get such a kick out of blatant stupidity. Anyway, to guarantee the gift's safe arrival, Hitler has tapped General Helmfried Schulmann, some high muckety-muck in the Gestapo, to personally accompany the package to Berlin. Schulmann is to pick up the box eight days from now, and Hitler has arranged for a private train to transport him and the diamonds directly to his office in the Reich Chancellery in Berlin.

They've set up Schulman's train with four cars attached so the train does not appear to be special, but Schulmann will be the only passenger and he'll be in the car right behind the engine. The Reich is trying to keep a very low profile on all of this. The train will pass through Falauge at noon, three days after it leaves Ancona."

Andreas quivered with excitement, "Where are the diamonds now?"

"They are at the cathedral with that idiot Bishop. The point of all of this is, can we figure a way to skim off a few of the diamonds for ourselves when the train comes through Falauge? You know, maybe take three or four for you and three or four for me…just a few so Hitler will never know."

The moment Andreas had heard the diamonds' estimated value of 70 million in U. S. dollars, his mind had been focused on acquiring the gems. "I will work on that, my little brother. Do not mention a word of this to anyone—not even that Italian whore you hang around with. Or have you dropped that pig for another?" Wessel let the double negative comment pass, being all too familiar with his brother's obnoxious personality. "Also," continued Andreas, "do not call me on this private line again. I will contact you as soon as I have developed a plan."

Wessel's voice grew stern, "There's one more thing, Andri. If you try and cheat me, I will kill you. I swear, I will find you and kill you!"

Andreas smiled to himself. *Yes, of course you will, you little twerp. Just like you have always sworn to come and kill me as I cheated you out so many things, so many times.* He did not consider the threat worthy of a response.

"Just keep things to yourself, Wessel. I will be in touch. Goodbye."

Seventy million U.S. dollars, he mused. *Seventy million.* He couldn't shake the thought. *And, of course, Wessel is thinking of taking just a few. What a wimp! Just like him to be unwilling to work hard enough to figure out how to steal the whole lot.* He clasped his hands behind his head, leaned back in his chair and crossed his glistening boots on the edge of the desk. *My God, seventy million. I'm rich!*

CHAPTER 20

9 September, 1943
The Nuremburg Laws
Ordered in Southern France

Felicien had the superlative new German radio receiver operating within a day of stealing it. After transferring it into the Bistro delivery truck, they drove it immediately to the large vehicle maintenance garage on the Cheever estate. With the help of Amaury's chief mechanic, they moved the entire box bed of the delivery truck onto the rear of a four-wheel-drive military truck they had stolen several years ago from the Falauge depot, bolted the radio equipment in place along with some small desks chairs and two cots. They now not only had an extremely sophisticated radio system, but a highly mobile one giving them the capability to efficiently change locations when broadcasting. In addition to varying their broadcast locations each time they sent a message they also broke up messages into in short bursts as they broadcast thus further denying the Germans the ability to triangulate their location.

Their radio signal would only be detectable by the Germans if the Tristan sent messages. If they simply listened to German radio transmissions, their equipment was not traceable. They began their listening immediately.

A late-afternoon message brought the Tristan a whole new challenge.

The critical message came from headquarters in Paris to the attention of both General Hofstetter, Commandant at Chambéry and Colonel Nussbaum at Falauge.

ATTENTION NOTICE FROM THE OFFICE OF:
Field Operations Marshal Ulrich Jager
French Headquarters, FHD, Paris
French Area Military Command,
Paris, France

TO COMMAND AT CHAMBÉRY AND FALAUGE:
ATTENTION: General Hofstetter, Commandant Chambéry
Colonel Nussbaum, Commandant Falauge

SUBJECT: FRENCH THEATER ENFORCMENT OF THE NUREMBURG LAWS

Communique 121-322-105
09 September, 1943 - 14:28gmt

It has come to the attention of the command of the Occupation Forces in France that the implementation of Reich policies, as outlined in the Nuremburg Laws concerning the Jewish problem in France, has not been sufficiently enforced. This oversight is particularly glaring in southern France, although tightening of enforcement is also necessary in northern Zone 1. Now that the Free Zone has been eliminated from southern France, it is crucial the identification, certification and recorded documentation of all Jews in France be implemented at once.

Immediately form a Search & Identify Unit from the ranks of the Chambéry Garrison and a similar unit from the ranks of the Falauge Garrison.

Chambéry unit is to cover a radius of 18 kilometers of the Chambéry depot, and the Falauge unit is to cover a radius of 18 kilometers of the Falauge railhead. The units are assigned to search out, identify and record all persons of Jewish ethnic heritage within their area of coverage. All identified individuals of all ages are to immediately be ordered to wear the official yellow Star of David identification patch.

Completion date shall be on or before 10 October, 1943.

Notify this command when these processes have been fully implemented.

Acknowledge time and date of receipt of this message.
... END...

Because of the excitment of operating the new equipment for the first time, the *friends* had all crowded into the truck to hear their radio transmitter. Several insignificant messages had preceded this one, and the group had been laughing and congratulating each other on the clarity of the reception. As this message rattled its letters onto the page and were crudely translated by Amaury, the group sobered.

Standing next to Felicien as Amaury read the message aloud a second time, Remi grew tense. He took the page from Amaury, glaring at it. No one spoke. Remi ushered them outside the truck and said, "We have been without a clear mission. Ever since Celine returned, I have searched my mind for a clear purpose for the Tristan. We know from mourning the deaths of our friends and neighbors we are not playing a child's game. The seriousness of the consequences of our actions demands that what we do truly makes a difference. Other than just trying to make life miserable for the Nazis, we have had no definable objective... nothing of moral value sufficient to risk our lives for. The Nazis have just solved that problem. We will not let this happen," his emotion was emphasized by the now crumpled message he raised high in his fist.

"We will not stand by and allow the German pigs to assault our neighbors simply because they are Jews. We need time to think about what we should do. We will meet in the cave tomorrow afternoon at five. Think about what this means to our citizens, to our fight for liberty. I will have ideas. I want to hear yours. We will fight this. It is wrong. It is immoral. This is worth our efforts, our lives."

Amaury poured the wine as they gathered around the primeval conference table in the subterranean quiet of their cave.

Remi stood. His seriousness had not abated, "In spite of the horror stories we've heard coming out of Germany, Poland and Holland—the forced labor, the death camps—until now, they have let our Jews live in peace. That, apparently, is about to change. You've had time to think about the message. What action should we take in response?"

"I have many friends and acquaintances among the local Jews," Amaury spoke up. "Most of them are farmers. I purchase meat and vegetables from them. They're good, hardworking people—quiet, honest."

"I don't even know who the Jews are around here. I've never given it a second thought." Felicien said. "How do you tell a Jew from anyone else?"

"We've never had cause to pay attention to Jews in Treaire," Celine added. "Since there is not a Synagogue I'm not sure I know who the Jewish families are, either. Mr. Crémieux has a tiny brass Star of David over the counter at his tailor shop, but I don't recall seeing any other symbolic relics anywhere."

"I wish Alexis were here," Amaury lamented. "He knew everybody for 20 miles of Treaire, what they did for a living, who their folks and grandparents were..."

"And, most likely, the names and ages of any pets they had," Celine smiled.

Remi said, "Well, if the Germans can figure out who the Jews are, then we can, too. We'll set up a constant monitoring of Nazi communications. We've got to stay on top of everything they're doing. Celine, go visit Mr. Crémieux tomorrow. Tell him what is going on. Maybe he can help us."

"So, once we figure out who the Jews are, what's the plan?" asked Felicien.

"I don't know. First things first. Let's find out how many people we are talking about, then we'll come up with how to address the situation," Remi answered, pondering the question.

They sat together for an hour, discussing various ideas and methods they could use to interfere with the Nazis carrying out their assault on the local Jews. Nothing seemed workable. They were powerless against the might of the German army. If the Nazis decided they were going to round-up and eliminate the Jews in southern France, there really was very little the Tristan could do to stop them.

They left the meeting in frustration. Amaury, Celine and Remi went to the Bistro and sullenly watched Colonel Nussbaum casually flitting around to the tables of various customers, as he always did. Remi whispered to Celine as they watched the obnoxious German officer, "How in hell can these bastards be so casual, so jovial on the outside, and carry out such evil?"

Celine shook her head, "What do you suppose they will do once they have identified all of the Jews?"

Without taking his eyes off of Nussbaum, who was laughing at a joke he had just made some customers sit through, Remi replied coldly, "They'll round them up and kill them. Just like they are killing thousands in Germany, Poland and Holland." His response revealed his deep frustration with the situation. The Colonel strolled past their table, giving them a smile and a nod of greeting as he made his way back to his officers, who sat lightheartedly enjoying each other's company. They ordered another round of drinks.

CHAPTER 21

A week later, Remi received a very unexpected phone call. It came from the one person who dined nightly at the Bistro, whom Colonel Nussbaum never engaged in conversation. In fact, *no one* engaged in conversation with Doctor Gasper Chabot, although he was one of Treaire's most intriguing citizens.

The first week Andreas Nussbaum began dining at the Bistro, he made his way around the restaurant glibly introducing himself to the various customers including the reclusive Doctor Chabot. Andreas had been around to several tables and on his way back to join his officers, he stopped at Gasper Chabot's table. "Good evening, sir," he grinned in perfect French.

Chabot slowly raised his head from the technical article he was engrossed in. Looking up over his reading glasses, he stared at the beaming Nussbaum and replied, "What exactly is it, Herr Colonel, that you find so *good* about this particular evening?"

Nussbaum was taken aback. He was not used to Frenchmen being so brazen. It was an affront to his Germanic politeness, his authority, his uniform.

"I beg your pardon, sir," Nussbaum indignantly replied. "I was simply attempting to be friendly and make you comfortable in my presence."

Chabot removed his glasses, keeping his eyes locked on the Colonel's. "It is *you*, sir, who should be uncomfortable in *my* presence. You are an unwelcome intruder in my country. You have forced your will on my people and you are making a mess of Europe by engaging in a senseless war that Germany cannot possibly win. In the meantime, you are intimidating our citizens and, if all of that is not enough, you are interrupting my meal and my reading."

Though shocked, Andreas immediately respected this man. Chabot was in his mid-fifties, physically out of shape, obviously antisocial and absolutely fearless. No one else had dared utter such a rebuff, although Andreas suspected many had similar feelings. He could not help but admire Chabot's spunk.

"I beg your pardon, sir. I see your point; please rest assured I will not bother you again."

"You have now begged my pardon a second time," Chabot replied. "A third begging will not be necessary, as I am now officially granting you my pardon. I suspect that concludes our conversation and our meeting, Herr Colonel." Chabot returned to his reading, thus ending the first and last conversation the two men would ever have in the Bistro.

Gasper Chabot had been living on the outskirts of Treaire for some 26 years, yet no one knew much about him. To say the least, Chabot was a strange fellow—eccentric, peculiar, and reclusive being fitting descriptions. He had fully met all of those classifications from the very day he arrived, characteristics that offered wonderful fodder for all sorts of fascinating speculation by the locals.

Rumor had it he was brilliant, holding doctoral degrees in physics, chemistry and electrical engineering from several highly regarded technical universities. As the story went, the year before he arrived in Treaire, there had been a very messy affair involving some advanced research Chabot was doing in one of the technical laboratories at the University of Strasbourg. Whatever the quarrel was about, it had caused quite a stir in the scientific community at the time, in both Europe and America. The confrontation was eventually settled with the university awarding Gasper Chabot a huge court-ordered financial settlement. Although he walked off with the settlement money, both he and the professor in charge of the laboratory where Chabot was performing his work were promptly terminated as a result of the mêlée. The university put the word out in the scientific community that neither of them could be trusted.

Chabot left the university in a huff. He moved to Treaire primarily because of its remoteness from the spying eyes of competitive research scientists. He brought with him a sizable financial fortune consisting of the court settlement and a hefty inheritance he had received that same year from his grandfather. He purchased a small farm just north of town, and hired contractors from Chambéry to do some remodeling and construct a huge addition on to the property's existing barn.

He had remained reclusive and aloof from Treaire since moving in. The grounds of his property were colossally overgrown, and if any repairs were needed, he always hired people from Chambéry. Not once had a citizen of Treaire set foot on his property. Even groceries, which Chabot ordered by phone, were delivered to an electrically cooled metal box next to the mailbox at the road.

What little of Doctor Chabot's daily routine was known served only to deepen Treaire's curiosity about him. Every day, regardless of the weather conditions, he drove his 1937 olive-drab Hotchkiss sedan the four miles into Treaire, arriving at the Duc de Richelieu Bistro at exactly 6:22 pm for his evening meal.

His table was permanently reserved with one place setting and one chair. By his request, his chair faced away from the entrance to shield him from the distracting comings and goings of other customers. If another Bistro patron passing his table acknowledged him, he looked up from his newspaper, gave an unsmiling nod, and immediately returned to his reading.

Every six weeks, a case of the acclaimed Pétrus Bordeaux was delivered to the Bistro directly from Château-Pétrus. The shockingly expensive wine arrived by truck and was addressed to the Bistro with instructions stamped on the case, *PREPAID – For personal consumption by Dr. Gasper Chabot*. Amaury had the wine placed in a special bin in the Bistro's cellar. Each evening, Chabot consumed one glass of the fabled red wine—drinking half prior to his dinner, then finishing the glass with his last bite. He developed a device that inserted a needle through the cork of his opened bottle and sucked all of the air out after recorking it, keeping the wine fresh for the following evening. Amaury was so impressed with the device that he asked Chabot if he would make one of the devices for him. Chabot answered plainly, "No, I am not interested in manufacturing commercial wine preserving devices, and I do not want the one I have produced used on any bottles except mine."

A copy of "Le Figaro", Paris' oldest newspaper, was also delivered by post to the Bistro each day. Although the newspaper was one day old when it arrived, Doctor Chabot read its headline article and editorial page each evening after he consumed whatever technical paper he was reading.

The Bistro staff knew Chabot's routine by heart. His wine was uncorked at 6:15 pm, allowing it to breathe. It was poured at 6:20 and set next to his folded newspaper to await his arrival two minutes later. He was always served the daily main course, regardless of what it was, and it was served at 6:30, giving him time to drink half of his glass of wine prior to its arrival. The main course was followed by a chopped green salad or the vegetable of the season with one tablespoon of Bionaturae extra virgin olive oil and two tablespoons of Jerez de la Frontera sherry vinegar—both of which he had specially shipped to the Bistro for his personal use. In the winter, when fresh vegetables were not available, the main course was preceded by the soup of the day. Chabot rose from the table at 7:15, tucked his newspaper under his arm and exited.

It happened every day like clockwork. Chabot hadn't missed an evening in over 25 years.

Amaury always sent the bill to Chabot's residence for the month's dining, which was immediately paid. Gasper Chabot was a unique tradition in Treaire, and if he ever changed his ways, it would somehow detract from the picturesque inimitability of the town.

The majority of the townspeople agreed that the large building Chabot constructed attached to his barn was some sort of laboratory. Even with that as the consensus, there was still absolutely no knowledge of what mysterious experiments went on within the walls of the windowless edifice.

Speculation was rampant that he was covertly employed by Britain's MI6 secret service, working on everything from harnessing the power of the sun to building programmable Frankenstein monsters (the monster theories were certainly the most fascinating to Treaire's children on dark, stormy nights).

When Remi answered the phone, the caller said, "This is Doctor Chabot speaking. I would like you to come to my house for a conversation of importance. Would that be possible this afternoon?"

In shock, Remi pulled the receiver from his ear and stared at it, as if looking to the phone for verification of what he just heard. He was one of the 99.7% of the citizens of Treaire who had never spoken to Doctor Chabot. Quite frankly, he didn't know of anyone, other than Amaury and one or two of the serving staff at the Bistro, who ever had.

With a furrowed brow, Remi said, "Hello, hello...who is this?"

In precise repetition and tone of the original message, the voice answered, "This is Doctor Chabot speaking. I would like you to come to my house for a conversation of importance. Would that be possible this afternoon?"

"Doctor Chabot? Doctor Gasper Chabot from Treaire?"

"To the very best of my knowledge, young man, there is only one Doctor Chabot in Treaire, and if you care to check the records, only one Doctor Gasper Chabot in all of France. I am the one everyone in Treaire thinks is making a working replica of Frankenstein in my laboratory.

"You are Remi Rousseau, the handsome young man who is often seated with the beautiful Celine Duval at the second table just to the left of the fireplace in the Duc de Richelieu Bistro most evenings. You are a personal friend of Amaury de la Cheever and Felicien Naffis. You live at 35 Rue Beudant with the attractive Miss Duval, who you married on 2 April, 1940, and you work at Treaire's water pumping works, which you are in the process of purchasing from Monsieur Pippen. Now, would it be possible for you to come to my house and meet with me this afternoon?"

Remi stammered. He was actually speaking with the *Frankenstein* doctor and being invited to come over to the house for a chat. Recovering a modicum of good manners, he answered, "Yes...yes, of course, Doctor Chabot. What time would be convenient for you?"

"Whatever time you care to come before 4:48 pm. I begin preparation for dinner at 5:48 and it will take one hour for our discussion."

"Yes, okay, fine. Should I knock on the door or come around to your...um, your...big building in back...the building next to the barn?"

"I'll know when you arrive. Goodbye." There was a click, followed by... *buzzzzzz*

Remi stood for a moment, waiting for the shock to subside. The phone receiver was covered with grease from the water pump he had been working on. He slowly placed the receiver in its cradle, still shaking his head and trying to affirm to himself that he had just had a phone call from the weird and mysterious

Doctor Gasper Chabot. He wiped down the phone and asked Monsieur Pippen if he might have the afternoon off.

"Just remember we have to get that pump back online by noon tomorrow," Pippen said, implying that his request had been approved. Remi quickly cleaned up and left for the unkempt farm of Treaire's notorious recluse.

As he pulled the car up to within a foot of the front gate, it amazingly swung open. He slowly pulled through, parked and approached the front door. As he stepped onto the porch, Gasper Chabot's voice crackled through a speaker, "Drive around to the barn and pull the car inside. I'll meet you there." Chabot was standing next to a gapping open door and motioned for Remi to pull inside. As soon as the car was in the barn, the heavy doors slid shut in response to his host touching a button on the wall. Emerging from the car, Remi extended his hand to the approaching Doctor Chabot. Chabot passed with the comment, "Not necessary. Let's go to my office," and continued moving in toward a door leading into the adjoining building which Remi assumed housed the mysterious laboratory.

The lab was huge. Sophisticated equipment lined the walls, leaving a narrow aisle down the center of the high-ceilinged building. They entered a small, disheveled office crowded with a cluttered desk and two chairs. Chabot took the one next to the wall, motioning Remi to the other.

"I do not mince words, Monsieur Rousseau, and will come directly to the point. Since you are the head of the Tristan Resistance group, I would like to know if you can help me." Chabot's opening statement was shocking. *How does he know about the Tristan?* Remi panicked. *And, what's more, how in hell does he know I am the head of it?*

Chabot smiled, "You are wondering how I know that you are head of the Tristan. I know a lot of things the people of Treaire don't think I know. But none of that is important at the moment.

"What *is* important is that yesterday I was called on by the local German pigs. They came to the house, asked a lot of obnoxious questions and instructed me to begin wearing their yellow Star of David 'Jew' patch. I am sure you know that forcing Jews to wear the patch is the first step in their eventual annihilation. The Germans will wait just long enough to humiliate us and build up propaganda against us in the gentile community. That way, when they ship us off to death camps or take us all out in a field and machine gun men, women and children, the rest of the townspeople can look the other way and appease themselves that we were really a bunch of rats who needed extermination."

Remi sat dumbfounded. Yes, he had heard about the atrocities being implemented against the Jews by the Third Reich, but his knowledge came from reading articles and hearsay. He had never heard it put so bluntly—and certainly not from a person who was one of its potential victims. Remi could not hide the bewildered look on his face, "I didn't know you were Jewish, Doctor Chabot."

"Of course, you didn't. People don't *look* like their religious beliefs. I haven't practiced the faith for many years, believing that religion is a bit of a fantasy, regardless of which of the fairytales one chooses to embrace."

"I don't know what to say, Doctor Chabot. I really..."

"I am not asking you to say anything, Monsieur Rousseau; I am asking you and your Resistance organization for help. What can you do to protect the Jews in this area from these insane devils who so arrogantly parade about among us?"

"We don't even know how many Jews live in Treaire."

"Twenty-one families in Treaire, six families in Falauge, and five additional families in the immediate countryside," snapped back Chabot. "Counting men, women, children and me, the total individual count comes to 128 and one half. Nureet Suchet is pregnant, thus the half."

Chabot leaned back in his chair, "So, my young friend and freedom fighter, what are you and your little group going to do protect these people from needless slaughter by those Nazi fools?"

Remi looked at Gasper Chabot in the embarrassing realization that he didn't have an answer. There was a long pause. Chabot just sat there calmly, looking at him.

Finally, Chabot spoke, "You don't know what to do, do you?" The comment stung, as it was meant to.

Remi let out a long sigh, "No, sir. We do not know what to do. We picked up the radio-telegraph message several days ago and..."

"How did you receive the radio-telegraph?" Chabot interrupted, with a slight smile spreading across his face.

Remi inwardly groaned. *What the hell, this guy seems to know everything about me and the Tristan anyway.* "We stole a very advanced radio transmitter-receiver out of a German communications truck that stalled on the main highway and was left behind…"

Chabot broke into a full smile. Again, his impatient mind interrupted his guest, "I was *hoping* you'd steal that. I thought to myself as I passed that truck on the way to dinner that night, if the Tristan does not steal that radio-receiver, they are not the skilled Resistance group I have always thought they were."

Remi shook his head in amazement at the amount of detailed knowledge that so casually flowed out of this man. "How did you know there was a radio-receiver in that truck?"

Gasper laughed, "Of *course* there was radio-receiver equipment in that truck. That truck was a Henschel 33D1 Kfz.72. The Kf designation stands for Kommunikation Fahrzeug or communications truck, and I'm confident that what you now own is either the Lorenz AG Er-F or the Telefunken E 52b Koln HF receiver. But if you really hit the jackpot, it will be HF-RRT-652 equipment produced by Siemens. That would be the ultimate. Very advanced stuff capable of auto-encryption as a message is being sent. Even has radar capabilities if you know how to operate it properly."

Remi was smiling. *This man is amazing.* He sincerely liked the quirky Gasper Chabot. There was no doubt he was strange—shrugging off a handshake, his directness of conversation, and his total knowledge of Remi, the *friends* and their Resistance activities was unexplainable. At the same time, there was a delightful warmth to his personality.

"Now, getting back to the fact that you do not know how to stop the Nazis from carrying out the order to exterminate me and the rest of the Jews in the area…I have an idea." Remi's interest immediately intensified. "Have you watched Colonel Nussbaum in the Bistro?" Chabot asked. "I mean, have you really *studied* him?"

"I think so, yes."

Lowering his voice, Chabot leaned forward, looking Remi squarely in the eye, "In my opinion, Andreas Nussbaum is bright and cunning. I see a man who is a Colonel in the Nazi army only for one reason." He paused, letting the comment sink in.

"The only reason Andreas Nussbaum is serving the Nazis is because, at the moment, he feels it is in his best interests to *be* a Colonel in the Nazi army. He is not at war because he believes in the fight or because he has any loyalty to Hitler or that crazy bunch running Germany right now. Colonel Andreas Nussbaum is a man loyal only to himself. Regardless of the circumstances Andreas Nussbaum finds himself in, he will always find a way to maneuver them to his best interests."

Chabot paused, again letting his message sink in. He watched Remi. It was almost as if he were watching to see if Remi's brain was keeping up. He took in a deep breath, leaned back in his chair and said, "You can strike a deal with a person like that, a person that self-centered. You just have to find out what he wants, then figure out how you can deliver it. He will do whatever is necessary to meet his own desires. He will work side by side with whoever will help him meet his needs. If killing Jews is in his best interests, he will kill Jews. If not killing Jews is in his best interests, he will not kill Jews. It is as simple as that," Chabot beamed.

Gasper Chabot had Colonel Nussbaum's personality nailed in every detail. "But, how do we figure out what he wants?"

"Ask him!"

"*Ask* him? Just walk up and ask him what it would take to get him to defy his commander's order to round up all the local Jews?"

Chabot chuckled, truly enjoying himself. "No, don't walk up and ask him… kidnap him first. *Then* ask him."

Remi sat back in his chair staring at his new acquaintance in amazement. *I love this guy.*

CHAPTER 22

What an enjoyable evening, Andreas Nussbaum thought to himself as he inserted the key into the door of his room. He was still chuckling at a joke one of his officers told in parting when a black sack was thrown over his head, pulled down hard, and tightly bound around his waist. "Do not cry out," a muffled voice command. "What you feel pressed against your neck is the silencer on my pistol." Andreas immediately called up his training in panic control, reviewing the steps he had been taught in the class. He focused on his breathing, listened to and slowed his heartbeat by going into to his calming mantra. He put himself totally in the moment.

He sensed there were other people in the room. There was a rustling to his right, then another movement in front of him. A whisper, "They're leaving." The sounds of his laughing officers in the street below slamming car doors, then a growing quiet outside as the car ground into gear and moved off into the darkness.

He took another calming breath, his good sense telling him to be cooperative. Things within the room were silent. The arm of the man behind him remained around his chest, the pressure of his pistol still behind his ear. The quiet continued for several minutes. Not a sound. Not a movement from the man gripping him.

His room door offered its familiar squeak as it opened. The arm swung him around, urged him forward. There had been no other guests in the hotel for several days. Whatever noise they were making, as he blindly stumbled down the stairs in the guiding grip of his captor, would go unnoticed. *The night clerk will either be incapacitated or, more likely, sympathetic to these people,* he thought. *No help there.*

It was widely known that the war was not going well for Germany and they were quickly becoming short of capable officers. Recently, there had been a growing number of incidences throughout France of local citizens commandeering

German officers—taking them to remote locations and shooting them in hopes of depriving the Nazis of critically needed officers. He forced that scenario from his mind. Dwelling on it would destroy his focus on remaining calm. *What in hell are they up to?* he searched. *Stay calm. Focus. Get some perspective on the situation, then negotiate.* He was confident he could talk his way out if given a chance. His main concern was that they would shoot him without giving him any opportunity to negotiate...maybe without even lifting the sack encasing him.

They halted in the lobby as his captors assured themselves all was safe to proceed. Then the arm around his shoulders turned him to the left and urged him forward.

We're in the back hallway, he noted. He had walked this hallway just to find out where it went. It led to a rear door that opened out into the alleyway. Again, they stopped. Again,

quiet...listening. The door latch clicked opened and a loud whisper came from the alley, "All clear." A shove. A few more stumbling steps, tripping on the door's threshold, he was caught by his handler, then pushed into the back seat of a car, wedged tightly between two large men. He strained, trying to determine if the car had a familiar sound...perhaps a car he had heard in town before. He came up with nothing.

They drove for over 20 minutes, making twists and turns until it became impossible to mentally follow their route, even though Andreas Nussbaum had a keen sense of direction and had made it a point to become familiar with the geography of the immediate area. He found the circuitous route encouraging. It was obviously being taken to confuse him.

This probably means they plan on releasing me. While that though was comforting it totally perplexed him as to his captors' motives. He focused back on his training, *Don't try to figure it out. Just stay calm. Keep your wits.*

The car jerked to a stop and he was manhandled out of the seat. They walked a good distance, his captor's arm around his shoulder guiding him. They stopped several times and spun him around to further disorient him. He felt as if they had also doubled back several times, adding to his confusion.

The rustle of leaves against his boots ceased as his heels clicked on a hard irregular surface almost immediately followed by the smell of damp antiquity.

Perhaps a musty cellar, he thought, *but we have descended no stairs.* The arm guiding him turned him right, then a few more steps and turned left. *We've walked too far for this to be a cellar.*

He was jostled left once again, then abruptly halted. A chair was shoved against the backs of his legs and he was pushed down on to it. The black sack was pulled up to his neck and his arms were belted to the arms of the chair. The sack was removed. He blinked several times, finally realizing he was in pitch blackness. Two hands steadied his head and cotton swabs were placed in his ears to muffle voice qualities as much as possible. *These people are well trained,* he thought, *professionals. They pay attention to detail.*

There was a rustle of movement behind him and to his sides. Then silence.

The total lack of light brought a heaviness to the darkness. The silence was total and suffocating as it settled into a nerve-racking wait.

He knew this was purposeful—another in his abductors' series of intimidation techniques. He focused hard on his counter-torture training…slowing his heart rate, steadied his breathing and mentally concentrated on his calming mantra. The maddening blackness and silence dragged on. *You are good at your intimidation,* he thought, *but I know what you are doing and I'll outlast you.* Five minutes passed, then 10. The only interruption was his breathing and the internal mental chant of his mantra.

Suddenly, burning white lights flashed on. He quickly turned his head away from the painful glare, tightly closing his eyes. He squinted, slowly looking around as his eyes adjusted.

The floor was crude wooden planks nailed together like the top to a large crate. To his front, both sides and rear hung floor-to-ceiling black curtains, creating a 10-foot-square room. His chair was positioned squarely in its center. The lights shone in his face and on both his left and right sides. Their brightness was intense. He could feel and smell their heat. Other than the low buzz of the lights' searing filaments, there remained no sound. He strained, attempting to pick up a clue, anything that might give him an idea of his location. Nothing.

All at once, in flawless German, a deep voice from behind the black curtain broke the silence, "Welcome, Colonel Nussbaum, we apologize for any discomfort you may be feeling, but you, of course, understand our precautions."

Andreas did not respond. There was another pause of several minutes. The voice once again broke the silence, maintaining a friendly tone, "Do you know why you are here, Colonel Nussbaum?"

Andreas hesitated, focusing on the voice. He was sure there was some familiarity, but he could not place either the accent or its inflections.

He searched his mind, trying to recall if he had heard the voice before. *The enunciation is excellent*, he thought. *This must be a native German. There is a slight accent—perhaps northern Germany. Maybe even Swedish.* He mentally paged through the voice inflections of his officers and just as quickly, eliminated all of them. *This voice is authoritative*—a quality he considered generally lacking in his officer staff.

He forced a confident tone in his reply, "Not having been sent a formal invitation to this little gathering, I have no idea as to its purpose. I am sure, however, you are not going to keep me guessing much longer."

A pause of perhaps a minute or so, then, still in a friendly tone, the voice replied, "You have been invited to join us tonight because we are disturbed about something and perhaps you can be of assistance to us."

Nussbaum sat for a moment without responding, trying to determine the technique they were using on him. He purposely let time pass. The voice patiently waited. Again, he heard nothing but his own breathing. He finally spoke, forcing a self-assured and somewhat sarcastic tone, "And what is it that you find disturbing, where you feel I may be of assistance?"

"We are disturbed that certain citizens have recently been contacted concerning their religious affiliations, their heritage, and their ethnicity by individuals under your command."

Oh, now I understand. Our absurd racial policy, Andreas disgustedly thought to himself. "And why do you find these contacts to be disturbing?" he asked, his voice steady, still infuriatingly calm.

"Because, Herr Colonel, we do not understand what possible interest your garrison could have in various people's religious leanings or their family heritage. Unless, of course, you feel their religious beliefs to be a threat to the mission of the German army and your assigned duties at Falauge. Perhaps you might take a moment and enlighten us."

Andreas hesitated. *This was an interesting approach,* he thought. *They seem to be opening the door for discussion. Perhaps this meeting can be useful.* He answered, now inserting a tone of inquisitive friendliness of his own, "Do you mind if I speak very directly and bluntly?"

"By all means. That will be most appreciated."

Andreas gave a sigh, as if to say, where shall I begin? "First, I personally do not give a damn about anyone's personal beliefs, who their parents were, what religion they follow, whether they like me or not, or any other such meaningless distractions from my focus on my assignment."

"And just what is your interpretation of your assignment, Herr Colonel?"

"It consists of two distinct functions. First, to see that our military equipment and troops are efficiently loaded onto train cars for their continued trip south into Italy; and second, to the greatest extent possible, we are to protect the trestle and tunnel that make up the Saint Laurnee Passage from destruction by Allied forces."

"So, Herr Colonel, without meaning to put words in your mouth, you see the interrogation of local civilians concerning their religious beliefs and lineage as being, shall we say, a distraction?"

"Of course! It is insanity," Andreas did not attempt to hide his personal disgust with the Nazi idea of ethnic restructuring. "It serves no practical purpose. Assaulting innocent citizens inflames the local population. They're already agitated toward the presence of the German army stomping around in their country; intimidating their Jews only exacerbates their disgust with our presence. It accomplishes nothing positive, just makes my job all that much more difficult. The whole policy is baseless and absurd."

He paused. There was no response from the voice, so he continued, "Now that we have my attitude toward harassing your Jewish friends out of the way, let me move on to a point I believe may piqué *your* interest," Andreas inserted his own pause for effect.

"There is a sealed dossier in my vault at the Falauge headquarters that my aide is instructed to send to Gestapo headquarters in Berlin should I ever fail to return to my office. I placed it there with those instructions in anticipation of the possibility of a meeting such as this." He paused, waiting to see if there might be a response. Nothing.

"The file informs Berlin that I have been investigating a Resistance group operating in this area, which I am almost positive goes by the name of Tristan— an interesting name for such a group. I have been doing some personal research on this organization. The name is the same as the given name of a World War One hero who lived in Treaire, a young man by the name of Tristan Delsenare. According to my investigation, Monsieur Delsenare posthumously received the French National Order of the Legion of Honor for his heroics in personally destroying a German machine gun nest and saving the lives of 17 of his wounded comrades." Again, Nussbaum paused to see if there might be some response. Only silence met his attentive ears, so he continued. "The thing that makes the group's name of particular interest is that Tristan Delsenare was the maternal grandfather of a young—and please forgive me if I sound presumptuous—beautiful Treaire woman—one Celine Duval- Rousseau, I believe.

"This Tristan Resistance group is of considerable interest to the Wehrmacht High Command in France, because several years ago their activities proved quite disruptive to German military interests in this area. Toward the end of that period, several Tristan operatives were killed in a series of raids that went awry. Since then, the group has been inactive." A smile grew on Nussbaum's face, "But I have reason to believe that is about to change.

"A while back, our Sergeant Steinholt and three of his patrol privates went missing. Their failure to show up for inspection did not go unnoticed. I believe they met some tragic misfortune at the hands of some local citizens. I also suspect these citizens are members of the Tristan since they are the only ones in the area bold enough to kill four German soldiers and have the audacity to think they can get away with it.

"Should the Tristan once again become active, their shenanigans will present yet another set of circumstances that will make my job more difficult. I would rather that not happen.

"I reported Steinholt and his men as suspected of desertion, thus, once again, not bringing the wrath of the high command down on the Tristan. It goes without saying, I do not want the irritation of having to deal with a troop of Wehrmacht officers and probing Gestapo idiots rushing down here and sticking their noses into every detail of daily life, including mine." Andreas broadened his smile.

"Now, perhaps I owe you some explanation of additional information in my sealed dossier and how I came to develop it.

"I am fascinated by libraries and historical museums, both of which exist right here in your charming little town," he grinned. "Actually, very conveniently located in your little library is a small room devoted to historical features of Treaire. Although both the library and historical room are small, they are perfectly sized to fit the ambiance of Treaire.

"Well, when I first arrived to take over Falauge, I reviewed the rather shabby files the local Milice had gathered on a mysterious Resistance group operating in the area. No doubt you are aware the Tristan did have a spy at one time, a fellow by the name of Maximilien Dulac. My analysis is that he was a reluctant spy, offering the Milice only the most rudimentary of information— probably to protect members of his family. He did, however, use an interesting term while under interrogation. He used the term 'the friends'. Although he was not specific and the stupidity of the Milice unit did not pursue the term, I found it fascinating that he said *the* friends…almost as if it were a particular organization or a unit.

"I was perplexed until one day in the historical room at your delightful little library, I noticed a small photo of some high school students, all arm-in-arm happily smiling for the camera. Under the photo, scrawled in blue ink, was the term 'the friends'. Needless to say, I was intrigued. With a bit more friendly conversation with the cute white-haired lady who volunteers her time each Wednesday afternoon when the library is open from 1 to 4 pm, I was told the *friends* were a delightful group of five wonderful boys and a beautiful girl—all born in Treaire within two weeks of each other. By the way, your librarian is quite proud of all of you. She speaks of you with the loving pride of a grandparent. She did mentioned that Felicien went through a period of rambunctiousness in his youth, but other than the fact he has been married—if my memory serves me correctly, I think she said, 'More times than I care to count', she radiantly added, 'He is a good mechanic and a sweet young man.'

"She smiled lovingly, telling me these 'friends' have been closely related in a true and admirable unity since their early childhood. She was, however, emotional about the fact that one of the group, one Daniel Laurent, had passed away in what she described as an unfortunate accident.

"The dossier contains much more information. Things like names and profiles of individual members, but no need to bore you with all the details," Colonel Nussbaum was grinning now as he paused, letting his listeners digest his comments. "Would you like for me to continue?"

Sitting behind the curtain, Remi was shocked. *My God. The library,* he thought. He had never given the tiny Treaire library and museum room a thought. The ski masks being worn by the group hid his expression, as they did the concerned expressions on all of their faces. Andreas Nussbaum sat there, looking smugly self-satisfied, a look he often wore when he felt he had a hand up.

Staring at him through the curtain, Remi felt his stomach tighten. He wanted to kill this despicable man—remove his pistol from its holster and unload it into this revolting human being.

Nussbaum, again, broke the quiet, "I take it from the silence I may have touched a nerve. Might that be correct, Monsieur Rousseau?" Only silence followed. "Ah. The silence tells me your little band of followers are present, Monsieur Remi Rousseau. I must say, I had no idea one of you was so flawlessly proficient in German. I must add that information to my dossier.

"Well, I believe I have sufficiently established my point. So, let's be frank. I believe you can see I hold a few more cards than you may have suspected and that puts us all in a very interesting negotiating position, doesn't it?" a smug grin filled Nussbaum's face.

Remi looked over at Gasper Chabot and nodded for him to continue.

Maintaining a steady calm in his tone, Gasper said, "So, Herr Colonel, what is your point? Where exactly to you see mutual grounds for discussion?"

"My point is, I have known about all of you for some time now and, as you can see, I have done nothing. I have gone on about my assignment in Falauge, loading equipment on train cars and all of you have gone on about your daily lives, undisturbed by me. Everything has been happy and uneventful.

"So, you see, you have proof that I can be a reasonable man, a calm man, unlike all of those nasty stories you hear about irrational German officers who unashamedly go about shooting people for no reason. I am sure you will agree that it is in your best interests for me to continue my silence about all of you, rather than bring the wrath of the entire Wehrmacht command down around your necks." The *friends* and Chabot sat quietly, Remi perplexed as to the next move.

Nussbaum broke the silence, "Well, here we are. It is in your best interests for me to continue to sit on my dossier about you, which I am fully content to do so long as you behave yourselves. But that still leaves the question concerning your Jewish friends. I take it from your opening statement you want me to promise not to bother them.

"I may be able to be of service to you along those lines, too. But for that, I need something in return. There, my German-speaking friend, is where I see mutual grounds for discussion."

Chabot responded, "We continue to listen, Herr Colonel."

"My having incriminating information on your organization assures my safety while in your hands. This, of course, brings me considerable comfort. The fact that I have done nothing with this information for some time now, I am sure, brings comfort to you. Therefore, we meet on a level playing field.

"As to my not enforcing the absurd racial and ethnic policies of my government, you doubtless understand that my direct refusal to carry out the order would result in very negative consequences to myself, which I certainly am not going to encourage. That said, I am in a position to substantially slow the process of implementing those orders. I can do that without bringing suspicion upon myself."

The Colonel heard whispering behind the curtain, then the voice spoke, "What do you mean you can slow the process? Please be specific."

Colonel Nussbaum smiled, "I have spent my entire career circumventing the red tape and the myriad ludicrous irrationalities of military bureaucracy. Bringing those highly developed skills into play, I assure you I can slow the process so much that you and your Jewish friends will never know the order exists.

Your Jews will be able to go about their daily business, free from any harassment—including not having to wear the identification patches."

Chabot responded, "How can you do this and keep your superiors satisfied?"

"Gentlemen, and Madame Rousseau, who I presume is also present behind the curtain, no one of any intelligence still believes Germany can win this war. Of course, we keep our troops in the dark, but anyone above the rank of First Lieutenant with a modicum of intelligence knows it is but a matter of time before we are forced to surrender. The High Command is distracted these days, trying to figure out how to cover their asses when Germany loses. They will become even further distracted as the inevitable day draws closer. You may not like our officers, but they are not stupid men. They will not be focused on implementing the government's so-called Jewish Policy any further than absolutely necessary to keep the muttonheads in Berlin off their backs.

"This order came down the chain-of-command because some idiot in Berlin has pushed the issue. Chambéry has washed their hands of it by forwarding the order to their field officers. They will not be pressing for results so long as comforting reports are filed, implying that efforts are being made to carry out the order. I am highly talented at submitting comforting reports."

While it was encouraging to hear a German officer say, with conviction, that Germany was certain to lose the war, the statement was still startling.

Nussbaum continued, "So, you see, the commanders throughout France are more focused on figuring out how to put themselves in the best position possible when we become prisoners-of-war or, better yet, how to escape becoming prisoners-of-war altogether. And that is where you can be of assistance to me."

The thought of helping this man avoid the wrath of the Allies sickened Remi. Everything about Colonel Nussbaum disgusted him. Now he was sitting there, tied to a chair, still making the rules. It was obnoxious! Remi dug deep, trying to reason with his immediate desire to inflict severe pain on Andreas Nussbaum. He fought to calm himself, to force himself to see the benefit of using Nussbaum to protect the safety of the Tristan and the local Jews. Celine sensed his restlessness. She placed a hand on his shoulder. He relaxed slightly.

Gasper continued, "So, you want us to help you escape?"

"I not only want you to assist me in escaping, I first want you to help me steal something."

⌘

The *friends* and their new associate, Gasper Chabot, sat in awe as Andreas Nussbaum described the diamond shipment that would be coming through Falauge in the next 10 days. In his description, he lowered the value to $20 million, rather than the $70 million Wessel had mentioned. He said he would not only turn over all of the incriminating information he had on the Tristan, but would be willing to give them $5 million worth of the diamonds once he was assured of his escape.

Remi had to admit, although he loathed the man, he admired his nerve. Andreas Nussbaum had presented a proposition that could result in all parties coming out whole and parting company without a battle. They took the Colonel back to town in an even more circuitous route than they had driven to the cave. It was over an hour's drive when they dropped him a mile south of the hotel. His wrist restraints were untied and he was told to wait 10 minutes before removing his blindfold once out of the car. He did so, feeling he was probably being watched and there was no sense in aggravating what had otherwise been a positive evening.

He smiled as he walked along the road. *Yes,* he thought, *it has been a very positive evening. I have an extremely astute group of skilled people seriously thinking about helping me. They have the means of assisting my escape. I will give up a pittance in value for their efforts and be safely on my way. Yes, it has been a very profitable evening, indeed.* It was all he could do to refrain from humming to himself as he strolled back to the comfort of his room. He decided *not* to hum a happy little tune, to assure his glee would not be observed.

CHAPTER 23

Gasper Chabot was now the newest official member of the Tristan—and its oldest at more than twice the age of the 25-year-old group of *friends*. He was the first member outside of the *friends* who had ever been allowed in the cave, although, for the time being, they insisted on blindfolding him both coming and going.

Gasper brought a considerable package of useful items to the group. To him, solving knotty scientific problems was a hobby and after moving to Treaire, he continued his research more for his personal enjoyment than contributing to the world of scientific advancement. He experimented with whatever happened to strike his interest at the moment. His pack-rat habit of keeping everything had both his laboratory and much of the barn filled with the most interesting items.

There were literally hundreds of things: a battery-operated button you could use to turn on a light from a distance; candles that would burn for four hours, then automatically extinguish yet could be relit for another four hours; plastic that didn't melt when exposed to fire; wood that would not burn...an endless variety of gadgets and fascinations. He would demonstrate the functions of the items that most fascinated him, then smile with satisfaction as the *friends* reacted in amazement.

After several days of letting them sift through the vast inventory, he gathered them together one evening in his living room. He was grinning as he checked the window blackout curtains to be sure they were all tightly sealed.

"I have a little surprise for all of you," he smiled. "I haven't looked at these for years. Our conversation with Colonel Nussbaum brought them back to mind. They are the results of what I was developing at Strasbourg when the head of my laboratory tried to steal my research. I was so bitter about that fiasco that I put these away and never looked at them again. But now, perhaps, they will finally serve some purpose."

He shuffled over to a magnificent antique hutch, took a tiny key from his pocket and pulled open its doors. He removed a wooden box that was about 12 inches square, set it on the coffee table and with another key, unlocked its lid. Inside was a black velvet bag, drawn tightly closed.

"Celine, would you please lift the bag from the box for us?"

She was surprised at the bag's weight—almost five pounds.

"Now, please untie the bag and pour its contents into this wooden bowl."

As the bag's contents filled the bowl, the group gasped. Out poured hundreds of magnificent diamonds—gorgeous, glistening, flawless diamonds.

Chabot delighted in the wide-eyed astonishment on the faces of his young friends. "I made these years ago when I was still at the University of Strasbourg."

Felicien picked up one of the larger stones, "You can make diamonds?"

"Well, that is what I was trying to do," Chabot shrugged. "This is as close as I ever got."

"But these are the most beautiful diamonds I have ever seen," Felicien said, holding a stone up to the light and watching it flash its rainbow colors from hundreds of sparkling surfaces.

"No," Gasper sighed heavily, "they are *not* diamonds. I failed at making diamonds. These are Zirconium dioxide. I named them zirconia. The shorter name was more convenient for the court case I brought against my laboratory boss who stole my research."

The *friends* were engrossed in the brilliant display of gems filling the bowl. They all continued picking up various stones, holding them up to the light, rolling them in their fingers, delighting in the spectrum of colors gleaming back at them.

Chabot rambled on, although no one was paying particular attention, "Zirconium dioxide does occur in nature in a monoclinic crystalline structure, but it is extremely rare. In its natural state it is known as the mineral baddeleyite, but that's not really important to this discussion." Chabot, now totally in his scientific mindset, was oblivious to the fact he was having this *discussion* with only himself.

With the *friends* continuing to fawn over the display, making comments to each other, Chabot droned on, "The high-temperature cubic crystalline form, which all of you are looking at, is sometimes, but rarely, found in nature as the mineral tazheranite. I was only able to synthesize this form, which I call cubic zirconia in reference to its internal cubic crystalline structure. All of that is, of course, interesting, but the statement of purpose for the experiment was to artificially create a diamond. In in that regard, the experiment was an utter failure. I was just never able to make a diamond," he sighed.

"A failure?" Amaury exclaimed, giving Chabot an amazed look. "These are magnificent!"

Gasper looked up at Amaury with an apologetic expression, "Yes, but they simply do not match up to the attributes of diamond." Again, his mind spun off into his wonderland of science as he re-immersed himself in lecture. "Cubic zirconia, you see, has a specific gravity between 5.6 and 6.0—at least 1.6 times that of diamond. And although it is relatively hard at about 8 on the Mohs scale, which, of course, is slightly harder than most semi-precious natural gems, it doesn't even come close to diamond, which comes in at a 10 Mohs reading. I mean, even Corundum has a 9 Mohs hardness. Yet these have a wonderful refractive index reading of 2.15 to 2.18. Diamond, as you know is 2.42." Remi and Celine smiled at each other, amused by the way Gasper continued his discussion with himself.

As Gasper looked up at his guests, it was obvious no one seemed to be particularly interested in Mohs hardness comparisons and refractive index readings. He sighed, looking a bit dejected as he watched the group pouring over the magnificent gems and continuing to ooh and aah at the display.

Speaking to no one in particular, he said, "I have a whole barrel of these back in the laboratory. I kept them, never knowing what to do with them…until Colonel Nussbaum came along."

They all looked at Chabot at once as he sat there, looking dejectedly at his bowl of failures. "What do you mean?" Celine queried.

Chabot's expression changed to an innocent questioning, "Well, why don't we trade these valueless pieces of synthesized cubic zirconia for the Colonel's shipment of real God-made diamonds? I mean, if we're going to risk our necks stealing the real diamonds from that train car, why let the Colonel walk off with the riches?"

Remi laughed delightedly. It was the best he had felt since he sat helplessly watching the despicable Colonel Nussbaum take control of his own kidnapping.

CHAPTER 24

26 September, 1943
Cathedral of Saint Ciriaco
Ancona, Italy

Obergruppenführer (General) Helmfried Schulmann's uniform was unique—as was he. To the casual observer, the uniform would pass as Gestapo standard issue, but Schulmann had customized it to his own tastes. It wasn't that he had any particular gift of fashion design. His motivation came strictly from an unquenchable need to prove to his fellow officers that he possessed the personal authority within the military pecking order to make such changes in direct defiance of the mandated uniform standards. The alterations were not extensive, yet ample enough to impress others of his above-reproach status...a statement that Helmfried Schulmann was a man to be reckoned with.

He had done other things to prove his power and authority since attaining the rank of Obergruppenführer, like the time he drew his pistol and shot a prisoner-of-war in the head as he trudged along in a line of defeated men. It wasn't that the selected victim was doing anything wrong. It was simply to demonstrate to the group of German and Italian officers Schulmann was walking with that he could pull off the killing and remain immune from any repercussions. The officers gasped in horror as Schulmann calmly re-holstered his pistol and strolled on.

Without question, his tactics were effective. One did not have to witness many such demonstrations to get the point that Helmfried Schulmann was uninhibited by convention, and it was probably a good idea to remain on positive terms with him. In spite of his pomposity, he had a redeeming quality. He was not a financially greedy man. While he would calmly snuff out a human life to prove his power, it was power, and only power, that interested him. Monetary wealth held no attraction. He would gladly pay a king's ransom to gain Adolf

Hitler's accommodation, and he would shoot his own parents to become one of Hitler's favored inner-circle advisors. Money simply held no interest. This quirk qualified him perfectly as the officer of choice to accompany Bishop Bentinelli's magnificent gift of diamonds to the Führer.

Schulmann actually had met Hitler on several occasions. He fondly recalled those meetings and carried a framed photograph of himself in a group with 17 officers gathered around Germany's fanatical leader. Despite the presence of the 17 other officers at that event, all of whom were serving as nothing more than background for photos of the Führer, Schulmann went away with the very imprudent feeling that a personal relationship had developed between him and Hitler.

On a following occasion, he stepped forward at a Gestapo cocktail party into the path of Hitler, who was making his way across the room. Schulmann thrust out his hand, saying how pleased he was to see the great Führer once again. Startled, Hitler reflexively shook Schulmann's hand. Then, as he quickly continued across the room, he muttered to his aides, "Who in hell was that idiot?"

But the meeting Schulmann held most fondly in mind was where he, along with five other Colonels, was promoted to the rank of Obergruppenführer. In Schulmann's mind, Hitler had attended the ceremony because *he*, Helmfried Schulmann, had attained the prestigious rank. Schulmann further fantasized that Hitler personally attended the promotion ceremony due to his interest in guiding Schulmann's career. The fact that Hitler took time for tea with the group after the formal photo session and conversed face to face with Schulmann convinced him the Führer definitely had his eye on him.

Actually, Hitler *did* remember Schulmann from that meeting. He had never met a more conceited, power-hungry individual in his life—a man so thirsty for power that he had virtually no interest in things of monetary value. It was the Führer's recollection of this narrowness of character that came to mind in selecting Schulmann as the man he would trust to deliver the millions of dollars' worth of diamonds from the Cathedral of Saint Ciriaco to him personally in Berlin.

Schulmann swooned with self-importance when he was contacted by a member of Hitler's staff about the assignment. It was no longer simple speculation.

He was convince the assignment was undeniable proof the Führer would be offering him a place within the inner circle. *Perhaps when I get to Berlin,* he mused, *I should play a little hard to get.* He smiled at the thought, concluding, *That little game always makes one of more value.* He could hardly control his excitement as he was chauffeured to the cathedral to pick up the valuable gift.

He exited the staff car and climbed the stairs toward the massive doors, pulling stiffly on his tunic to straighten the dapper uniform. It had been freshly cleaned and pressed in anticipation of meeting with Bishop Bentinelli, and he had held himself stiffly rigid during the drive to avoid creating any unnecessary wrinkles in the jacket.

He was looking forward to meeting this man who was willing to part with 70 million dollars' worth of diamonds in support of the Nazi cause. He had heard rumors that Pope Pius XII had expressed supportive attitudes toward the policies of the Third Reich, and he was hoping to gain some clarification of the church's position on Nazi programs from this obviously enthusiastic Bishop.

The anticipation of his arrival became obvious as he approached the top of the stairs and the huge ornate doors leading into the basilica were swung open by two priests who bowed respectfully. Another priest standing directly in front of him, hands clasped across his stomach, bowed his head in silent greeting, then turned down the long center aisle leading toward the magnificently adorned sanctuary. Schulmann was not only expected, he was an honored guest warranting the most respected welcome. He relished every second of it.

Personally, he had little interest in churchly activities, but he admired the splendor of the sanctuary as his boots echoed their crisp click on its glassy terrazzo floor. The size and elegance of the building's baroque architecture exuded power. It immediately convinced an observer he was in the presence of the awesome might of the church—and it demanded one humble himself to that power. It spoke nothing of God to Schulmann. He attributed the grandeur of what he saw solely to celebration of the power of man.

In monk-like silence, the priest led him through an elaborately carved door adjacent to the altar, and down a dark, paneled hall. He opened a thick wooden door, nodding for Schulmann to enter. As he did so, Bishop Bentinelli smiled. He did not attempt to hoist his huge bulk from his chair, but held out his hand, palm down, displaying his amethyst ring. Dressed in his full regalia of ecclesiastical finery, it was obvious he, too, had a flair for imposing first impressions.

Schulmann found the gleaming gold filling framing one of the Bishop's front teeth distracting. *On second thought, it's a unique and unforgettable aspect of the man's face...perhaps even purposely placed there for that very reason.* He was not about to humble himself and kiss the fat Bishop's ring. Instead, he grasped the Bishop's hand in a curt downward shake. Bentinelli nodded, maintaining his pasty smile. Schulmann's rejection of the ring-kissing ritual gave the Bishop confirmation his guest intended to carry on their interactions as a colleague of equal power. *It will be fun bantering with this stilted little man,* Bentinelli thought.

"It is my distinct honor and pleasure to meet you, Herr General."

"As it is mine to meet you, Bishop Bentinelli," Schulmann countered with a subtle click of his heals.

"Please, Herr General, sit down," the Bishop said, ringing a small bell on the table beside his chair. Tea was immediately served. "I also have some schnapps, if you prefer—Danziger Goldwasser schnapps, which I understand is highly praised in Germany."

"No, tea will be fine," Schulmann answered, thinking, *This man has a peasant's knowledge of schnapps.* "I have been dispatched to accompany your generous gift to my friend Adolf Hitler," Schulmann said, accentuating 'friend'.

The emphasis was not missed by the Bishop, "Yes, of course," he smiled, "But first allow me to compliment you on your personal friendship with the Führer—truly one of the unique personalities of our time. I am most impressed with him, having listened to recordings of many of his inspiring speeches. He is a uniquely gifted man. It must give you great pleasure to consider him in your array of personal friendships."

Schulmann beamed. *What a wonderful knack for overstatement, and it was such superlative embellishment. Besides,* thought Schulmann, *he has no way of really knowing whether Hitler is a personal friend of mine or not.* "Yes, Adolf and I go back a long way," Schulmann lied, "all the way back to when he was just emerging as the esteemed leader he has now become. He has but few friends now whom he can trust with an assignment such as this. He personally asked that I accompany your superb gift and deliver it directly into his hands. He instructed me to extend his most gracious appreciation to you individually and to the Catholic Church."

Bentinelli shifted his massive bulk in his chair, a bit nervously, thought Schulmann.

"Although I am sure the Vatican would look favorably on this gift, Herr General, it would be most appreciated if the Führer not acknowledge to the Pope that I have donated it to the cause of the Third Reich." The Bishop attempted to appear confident, but his look clearly indicated the Vatican was unaware of the gift. It confirmed it was *his* doing and implied that any form of appreciation should come directly to him.

"I understand fully, Bishop Bentinelli," Schulmann smiled back.

Refilling their tea cups, Bentinelli said, "I would not have taken this precaution had I known it would be *you*, a personal and trusted friend of Chancellor Hitler, who would be accompanying the shipment to the Führer. But, of course, at the time I notified him of the gift, I had no knowledge his personal friend would be its guardian.

"As a precaution, I listed in detail the number of stones in order to assure him they would *all* safely arrive. Write it off to the superstitions of an old man," he chuckled. His smile contained a cunning, self-satisfying smirk as he handed a folded paper to Schulmann. "This is a copy of the description of the gems I sent to the Führer. I thought you would want a copy you can hand him with your delivery, thus confirming your honesty and reaffirming your deep friendship."

Helmfried took the paper and unfolded it:

Breakdown of the Gift of Diamonds to
Adolf Hitler, Führer of the Third Reich, Berlin, Germany
from Bishop Bentinelli - Cathedral of Saint Ciriaco - Ancona, Italy:

476 stones @ 4 carats each = 380.8 grams
423 stones @ 6 carats each = 507.6 grams
325 stones @ 7 carats each = 455.0 grams
<u>311 stones</u> @ 8 carats each = <u>497.6 grams</u>
Totals 1,535   1,841.0 grams

You bastard. You fat, smug bastard, Schulmann thought, glaring at the detailed inventory of the diamonds. He had no intention of stealing from his beloved Führer. This ostentatious man, who delighted in passing himself off as a man of God, was implying Schulmann could not be trusted. In Schulmann's mind, the note conveyed to Hitler that the Bishop believed a catch-trap had to be set to assure that Schulmann would not help himself to a portion of the Führer's gift. The look of contentment on the face of the Bishop convinced him the note had been designed to imply exactly that. He seethed with hatred at the toothy, smiling Bentinelli, who seemed to have anticipated exactly the irritation he would arouse—and was immensely enjoying it.

"Excellent precaution, Bishop," Schulmann forced a smile as he looked up from the paper, "however, totally unnecessary. It also has set up an immediate inconvenience."

Still grinning, the Bishop raised his brow, "Please enlighten me, Herr General. How do you feel my note has necessitated an inconvenience?"

"The note makes it necessary for me to count the stones and have a diamond expert verify the carat weight of each one prior to removing the gift from the premises. Surely, you understand."

"By all means, my friend. Hopefully, I am not being presumptuous in using that term. I anticipated you would want to count the gems and have arranged for a certified gemologist to be present. He is waiting in the anteroom now with certified proof of his qualifications—unless, of course, you would care to return another day with your own expert."

Schulmann glared at his condescending host. *Under any other circumstances I would slit your bulbous throat, you pig. You will live to regret this day, my fat Bishop,* he thought.

"You may dismiss your man, Bishop. I took the liberty of having my own gemologist follow me here. He is waiting in the car behind my limousine. If you would be so kind as to have one of your staff fetch him, we can proceed," the muscles in Schulmann's cheeks were beginning to ache from his forced expressions of pleasantness.

The three men spent most of the afternoon inspecting and carefully inventorying the gems. Schulmann's gemologist was awed with their quality. The stones were separated into trays according to carat weight, then counted several times to assure the accuracy of the count. Each group was then placed in separate velvet bags, tied at the top with the bag's cord, and the top was dipped in red sealing wax. The four bags were placed in an ornately carved wooden box of ancient construction, then locked with a small brass padlock, whose key was attached to Schulmann's key chain. They concluded their business just before 5:00 pm, with Schulmann declining the Bishop's offer to stay for dinner. *I couldn't make it through another 15 minutes without killing you, you multi-chinned ass,* he mused as he smiled his goodbye.

Schulmann's limousine drove directly to the train station, where his private train waited on a siding. He dismissed the guard and entered; walked directly to the cabinet, poured himself a glass of American whiskey, downed it, and poured another as he flopped down in a lounge chair. The jolt of the train as it pulled from its siding comforted him. It would take him hours to calm down from his irritation with the Bishop. He *would* eventually calm, but he would *never* forget.

CHAPTER 25

Schulmann looked up from his reading when his train slowed as it passed the sign for Falauge. Irritation flashed as he felt the car jostled onto a refueling siding. *What in hell is going on? We are not to stop for fuel until we arrive in Chambéry,* he grumbled in thought. He was on his feet at the exit door as the car came to a halt and immediately Colonel Nussbaum's smiling face and a snappy Heil Hitler salute peered at him through the glass.

"What is the meaning of this, Colonel?" Schulmann demanded. "I was not to stop for refueling until I got to Chambéry."

Nussbaum dropped his salute, but kept his broad smile. "I am terribly sorry for this inconvenience, Herr General, but a local group of terrorists dynamited a section of track just to the north last night. I have repair crews on the scene as we speak, and have been informed the damaged section should be passable early tomorrow morning. My humble apologies to you, Sir."

Andreas Nussbaum's explanation was not without truth. With his full co-operation, the Tristan had blown up a small section of rail between Falauge and Treaire in order to force Schulmann's car to remain in Falauge overnight.

Schulmann glared at Nussbaum. "If you did your job, Colonel, these gutless bastard French rebels would have been eradicated years ago. Take me into your office immediately. I want to contact Berlin and speak to Führer's Headquarters," Schulmann huffed.

"I'm afraid I have more disappointing news, Herr General," Nussbaum's smile faded, giving way to a mortified look. "As part of their attack, the terrorists also have cut the phone lines and damaged our radio antenna. The damage is not severe, but will take time to repair. We should have communication re-established about the same time as the track will be fixed."

Schulmann's face reddened into a supercilious stare, glaring at this junior officer whose incompetence clearly stood in the way of his carrying out the most important assignment of his career. "You are a disgrace to the uniform and your rank, Colonel. I have heard reports on this group of terrorists who have been operating unchecked in this area for years. You are disgusting. When I arrive at Chambéry, I intend to file a full report with General Hofstetter concerning your inability to control your area of command. I will also deliver a copy of that report directly to the Führer when I see him in Berlin. I suggest you pack your combat gear, Colonel, and pray you are sent to the Front rather than shot for flagrant incompetence."

Nussbaum lowered his head in shame, "I respectfully accept your criticism, General. The terrorist group in question is new to the area. This was their first attack since my arrival at this command. I assure you; they will be tracked down and annihilated with dispatch. This incident will be their last.

"It could not have come at a worse time, however, just as you are passing through. Your esteemed accomplishments and admirable reputation precede you, and I am most embarrassed to have you inconvenienced. I would be highly honored to have you as a special guest accompanying me and my officers this evening. There is an outstanding restaurant not more than three miles from here in Treaire—and for your comfort, I have taken the liberty of booking you a room at the hotel next to the Bistro where I reside. I implore you accept this offer, as it will reward me with a brief time to get to know you and deepen my respect for you."

Nussbaum's words found their soothing mark as they played on every narcissistic aberration Schulmann's warped mind constantly fed on.

Schulmann began to reconcile himself to the miserable circumstances. *Damn, I'm stuck here with this jerk. What the hell, perhaps I can amuse myself with this bumpkin while I'm stranded in this miserable hole. Might as well have some fun with this idiot before I have him castrated.* He let out a resigned sigh, "Well, Colonel, it looks like we will be in each other's company for a while. I will accompany you to dinner, since it appears I have no other alternative, but will return to sleep here in the car. I am assuming you can scrape up a reasonably dependable security guard for my car during our dinner in Treaire?"

"Absolutely, Herr General. My personal guards will be in charge the entire time," Nussbaum smiled. "Shall we go to my office for a brandy?"

Nussbaum cheerfully followed Schulmann toward the office with a satisfying thought, *You have just slid your self-adoring neck into the noose, you pompous ass.*

CHAPTER 26

Colonel Nussbaum had the train engineer sent to the post's dorm for the night and assigned two inexperienced garrison soldiers to guard duty at Schulmann's rail car. Later, when the party left Falauge for the Bistro, Nussbaum sent word to the soldiers they would soon be relieved by the General's personal guards.

An hour later, Remi, Amaury and Felicien emerged from a five-foot-diameter drain pipe that offered them a concealed entrance into the Falauge rail yard. As children, they had often played in this pipe, so were intimately familiar with its location. Back then, they had been able to walk through standing erect; now they were forced to bend almost in half as they awkwardly maneuvered its length. They brushed the cobwebs from the German uniforms Nussbaum had provided them, crawled up the embankment alongside the rail yard, and began scanning the sidings for the General's car. Schulmann's were the only passenger cars in the yard. Felicien spotted them on the far side of the yard across the multitude of parallel tracks where rail cars were parked, awaiting their loadings.

They made their way across the yard, trying to look as casual as possible each time the sweeping search light hit them. Remi approached one of the soldiers Nussbaum had stationed at the car and in his best German, informed the man they were there to relieve him. Detecting his accent, the young man gave Remi a questioning look, started to say something, gave an oh-what-the-hell shrug, and walked to the other end of the car to inform his commerade that General Schulmann's relief guards had arrived. The two stood together for a moment, lighting cigarettes and mumbling to each other, looking back at the Tristan trio.

Amaury leaned over to Remi, "What the hell are they waiting for? Do you think they suspect us?"

"I don't know. I tried to cover my accent as best I could. Actually, I got the impression the guy I spoke to really didn't much give a damn. I'll start walking toward them. I'll guard the door at that end; you take the one at this end." He turned toward Felicien, "Don't enter the car until those two are gone."

Remi started toward the soldiers. He breathed a quiet sigh of relief as they turned and trekked across the yard toward the barracks. Felicien went to work picking the car's lock. To aid them, Nussbaum had placed the General's car off on a remote siding, somewhat protected from the glare of the search lights moving rhythmically over the area.

Felicien entered, closing the door quietly behind him, and Amaury took up his position just outside. Felicien searched the narrow room. The roaming search lights intermittently provided some light, but for the most part, Felicien groped in the darkness, using his flashlight in quick flashes. He flashed the right wall, then the one in front of him.

Where would I put a valuable cargo if I were assigned to deliver it to an asshole? Felicien mused to himself. *Actually, I wouldn't take it to the asshole,* he thought, chuckling at his own humor. He moved down the length of the room. In the center of the car the room narrowed to a short hallway, a door on the right—the bathroom. Ahead, another room. *Aha, the bedroom. Yes, the bedroom. That is where I would hide the asshole's package.* He entered, opened the sliding closet doors, went through the built-in drawers, then stood, perplexed at having found nothing.

The bed's mattress rested on a boxed-in wood frame, its front face made up of five inset panels. He tapped each panel, stopping when the center one rattled. He tapped them all once again. The center one was the only loose panel. Although loose, it remained fixed in place as he searched for a method of removing it without damaging it. He placed the blade of his knife between the panel and its frame, carefully sliding it along the frame—*click.* He smiled as the panel slid open, exposing a small safe. *There you are, my little darling.*

Felicien positioned himself on the floor, shining his flashlight tight on the safe's combination dial. His position was awkward. He had cracked combination safes before, but lying on his side complicated the process. He tensed at the two taps Remi made on the car's door, the signal for all is clear. He took a deep, calming breath, pulled the stethoscope from his jacket pocket, and went to work. He comforted himself that he had all night to work on the safe, knowing the General would not be returning.

CHAPTER 27

Unlike other nights, Colonel Nussbaum did not flit around the Bistro visiting local citizens that evening. His attention was focused on his cherished guest. His keen eye indicated the majority of regular patrons were dining. The reclusive Doctor Chabot sat with his back to everyone—buried in his newspaper, about to finish his wine and abruptly leave; the medical doctor and his wife were at their usual table, sitting unspeaking—each staring off into space; the middle-aged pharmacist and another in his seemingly endless entourage of pretty young women at the table next to the fireplace; the widowed banker and his teenaged son and daughter at their normal table. The couple noticeably missing was Remi Rousseau and his charming wife, Celine, but, of course, the Colonel was not expecting their presence this evening, and General Schulmann would have no idea of their absence.

Schulmann had loosened up considerably since his irritation with Colonel Nussbaum earlier in the day. He actually was beginning to enjoy the Colonel—not enough to forget about filing a negative report against him, but sufficiently to relax a bit and enjoy the evening. He even gave a fleeting thought to taking the Colonel up on his offer to stay over in the hotel, but then thought it more appropriate for him to bed down over his valuable gift for the Führer. Right now, however, a well-endowed waitress with the wonderfully low-cut blouse was bending low in front of him as she poured his fourth glass of a superb full-bodied Cabernet, and he was enjoying the depth of the silken cream valley that seemed to plunge into oblivion between her breasts.

The drug in the wine she was serving Schulmann was of a special design. Chabot had prepared it especially for the General. It would remain dormant until activated by Schulmann's digestive processes when solid food hit his stomach. Only then would it bring on the feelings of nausea. But for now, Schulmann could enjoy himself, savoring the wine and the cute French girl's wonderful bustline. The mellow mood brought on by the wine was comforting. He was glad he had an opportunity to enjoy these few moments of relaxation. *I should allow myself more of these moments,* he thought. *Life is short and I must learn to enjoy it more. Yet I'm sure there will be little time for such frivolity once I'm on the Führer's advisory staff.* He couldn't help but smile at the thought.

He was not only enjoying his time with Nussbaum, but also with his officers. They were a well-mannered group of bright young men—truly able to put a positive face on the Aryan image Germany wanted projected to the citizens of the countries it now ruled. This was true of all of the officers except one. He had not liked Adam Brant the moment he met him. Initially, it was his "Old Testament" Jewish-sounding first name that grated on Schulmann, but Captain Brant's overbearing personality quickly earned him additional and more justified disdain from the General.

Brant was immature, uncultured, boisterous and loud. His mouth rattled on endlessly—emitting trite, commonplace utterings, yet he delighted in his own commentary and followed almost everything he said with a distracting little chuckle. Additionally, he continually made insulting sexual comments toward their attractive waitress, who, in spite of the General's attraction to her breasts, reminded him of his younger sister.

Schulmann prided himself on his gentlemanly manners, which projected a stiff Victorian reserve in the company of women. Captain Brant's crudeness highly offended him, and from the reactions of his fellow officers, they, too, abided Brant only through forced tolerance. Colonel Nussbaum had repeatedly reprimanded Brant on his abhorrent behavior, but each time, Brant's thick-headed wit caused him to quickly fall back into his repugnant behavior patterns. He was an embarrassment to Colonel Nussbaum...truly an embarrassment to his group of otherwise rather sophisticated officers. But, tonight, Andreas Nussbaum remained silent concerning Brant's behavior, knowing he would soon be rid of him.

Dinner was served and, right on schedule, General Schulmann began to feel nauseous urgings welling up inside of him. He excused himself quickly, making his way to the men's room, where he immediately vomited what little venison he had eaten. His stomach spasms continued and while he was bent over the stool,

Celine eased up behind him and in one rapid move slid the long hypodermic syringe into his ear and up into the outer casing of his brain, injecting the vial's contents. She then slipped the needle out, leaving only a spot of blood in the wall of the General's inner ear. The entire procedure had taken but a fraction of a second.

Schulmann bolted up, turning to look at her, and sucked in a breath in anticipation of yelling for help. Before his cry could materialize, the intense pain of his heart abruptly ceasing to function sent his hands to his chest, ripping his jacked open and popping its custom sterling silver buttons in all directions.

Celine stepped back as Schulmann hit the floor with a thud. She stood over him, placing her finger on his neck to test for a pulse. Satisfied her injection had done its job, she turned the General's head and wiped the injected ear with a damp tissue assuring the removal of any trace of blood. Her Special Forces trainer had told her the chemical shut down the heart so quickly that the puncture wound would not have time to bleed. He was right—no blood. She exited the men's room, quickly moved down the hall and disappeared into the closet that concealed the passageway to the cave.

About 10 minutes later, Colonel Nussbaum ordered Captain Brant to go check on the General. It was all he could do to keep a straight face as Brant's wide-eyed, boyish face came screaming back into the Bistro in panic, yelling, "General Schulmann has had a heart attack!"

As he rose from the table, Nussbaum thought to himself, *I'm so glad I sent you, Brant. Your heart-attack announcement was so thrillingly convincing—so beautifully and childishly dramatic.* Again, he had to force his best theatrics to subdue a smile as he followed his officers toward the men's room

CHAPTER 28

Felicien was dripping with the sweat of tension. He stood up, stripping off his jacket and wiping rivulets from his forehead. He always sweated when doing tedious work, and the safe was not being cooperative. Remi's *all-clear* taps had come every 10 minutes, as planned. He had just heard the fourth set.

Damn the Germans and their meticulous engineering, Felicien frowned at the compact little safe. He was sure it was a 4-1-2-1-half combination—four turns left, one right, two left, one right, then half left to the stop position. He had only gotten one tumbler to drop since he started. He desperately wanted a cigarette as he resumed his uncomfortable position on the floor.

Thunk! That time, it came in loud and clear. The second tumbler. He stopped the dial immediately. The point on the dial was 57. He would have to pass that number to the left, preferably in one motion. Slowly, steadily twisting, then *Thunk!* Two more to go. He let go of the dial, took a calming breath, *Okay, krautheads! I've got your brass balls dropping now.* He carefully took hold of the dial and started back left. Remi's all-clear knock came at the instant Felicien thought he heard the next tumbler fall. *Damn it! Was that Remi or the tumbler?* If it wasn't the tumbler and he moved ahead, he would have to start all over again.

He decided to proceed. Turning the dial right ever so slowly to the halfway mark—*Thunk! Yes, that's it!* He turned the latch handle and the metal door swung open. He rolled onto his back, trying to dissipate the aching tension in his shoulders. He turned back, looking into the open safe, where his flashlight revealed an ornate wooden box within the cavity. Its top was locked with a little brass padlock. He moved the flashlight's beam around, searching for alarm wires running across the open cavity of the safe. It would be just like the Germans to cover their asses six ways to Sunday. Detecting no wires, he slowly reached in toward the box, praying the safe's floor was not equipped with a weight alarm. He was in luck.

In less than three seconds, he picked the pad lock on the box and opened it, revealing four wax-sealed black velvet bags. He carefully removed the four bags, replacing them with the single black velvet bag containing Chabot's zirconia crystals. He then latched and locked the box, slid it back in the safe, spun the dial, and slid the wood panel shut. He went to the door to retrieve Remi. The two moved through the darkened car as Felicien quickly checked to assure himself he had left everything in order. They stepped out onto the rear platform. Felicien pulled out an envelope containing a blank sheet of paper from his pocket and handed it to Amaury, who wrote down the safe's combination as Felicien dictated it. Then, with further instruction from Felicien, he added a note in German: 'Safe location behind central panel below bed, open with knife slid along left side of panel.' The note completed, Amaury gave it to Remi to pass on to Nussbaum, then the trio started back across the multiple tracks toward their exit point.

Making their way across the open spaces of the huge rail yard, they bent low, running between sweeps of the search lights scanning the yard and using standing freight cars for cover. Crouched behind one of the parked rail cars on the last siding before they reached the embankment leading down to the drain pipe, Remi froze. He grabbed Amaury's arm and motioned for Felicien not to move. Everything was quiet, but a faint smell of cigarette smoke drifted across the track. A soft cough came from the opposite side of the car, then quiet. They crouched against the large steel wheels, attempting to hide themselves from whoever was on the opposite side of the track.

Remi motioned for Felicien to sit tight with the diamonds and signaled Amaury to move around the car to see if he could pinpoint the smoker. Amaury peered around the edge of the car—no one in sight. He slowly moved toward the edge of the tracks where the embankment steeply fell off, dropping toward the safety of their exit pipe. Mumbled voices. He froze. Peering down the steep grade, he spotted two shadowy images sitting half way down the embankment. He could see the tips of their cigarettes glow as they inhaled drags. *Damn it, now what do we do?*

He started back to inform Remi and dislodged a large ballast rock, sending it tumbling down the embankment. The shadows jumped up, looking toward the sound just missing Amaury scurrying around to the other side of the car.

"What's going on?" Remi questioned in a faint whisper.

"Two soldiers." Amaury whispered. "Maybe guards. I couldn't see if they are armed. They may have seen me…don't know."

They heard the two shadows scramble up the embankment. Looking under the car, they could see the soldier's legs. One went one direction, the other headed opposite.

Remi motioned for Felicien to crawl under the car at his end. Felicien did so quickly, wedging himself against the inside of the car's wheels at one end while Remi and Amaury melted down as best they could under the wheels at the opposite end.

The soldiers rounded the ends of the car. "You see anything?"

"No," his comrade whispered back. "Probably just some night animal out searching for a meal."

"Let's hope so. I don't want to get caught out here smoking after lights out." The two moved off, sneaking back across the wide yard, hoping to make it back to the barracks undetected.

Remi let out a long sigh, whispering loud enough for Felicien to hear, "Let's get the hell out of here—quietly, very quietly."

They moved quickly down the embankment into the drain pipe and disappeared into the night with 70 million dollars' worth of Hitler's diamonds.

———❧———

As the local Treaire doctor pronounced General Schulmann dead of heart failure, Captain Brant kept bouncing up and down, looking over the shoulders of his fellow officers ringed around the body. His face flush with worry and concern, he kept blubbering, "Oh, my God…a friend of the Führer. The General was a friend of the Führer and now he's dead. Oh, my God, my God. What shall we do?" One of his fellow officers scowled toward him, "For the love of God, Brant, shut up and have some dignity, you muddlehead."

Colonel Nussbaum approached the doctor. He conjured a most sorrowful expression, "Your diagnosis of a heart attack is sufficient for my report. We'll respect the dignity of the General by not having an autopsy. Please see the

General's body is taken to the mortuary and properly prepared for burial. I will stop by and make the necessary arrangements to ship it back to Germany."

He then pulled Captain Brant aside, "You have impressed me with your honesty and love of the Führer, Captain. Our Führer knew and respected General Schulmann and..."

"Oh, I know. I know that, Colonel Nussbaum," Brant interrupted, bobbing his head up and down in agreement.

Nussbaum rolled his eyes. "As I was saying, General Schulmann was personally accompanying a gift from the Bishop of Ancona to be delivered to Adolph Hitler. He was a trusted friend of the Führer's and..."

Brant broke in again, "Yes, sir. There is certainly no doubt about that...no doubt at all."

Nussbaum furrowed his brow, "No doubt about what?"

"About General Schulmann being a trusted friend of the Führer's," Brant blurted out, giving his irritating little chuckle and nodding his head repeatedly up and down in agreement with his statement.

Nussbaum forced himself not to draw his pistol and shoot this dimwit right between the eyes. He paused and took a deep breath, forced a smile at Brant, calmed his voice from the torrent of screams he wanted to shout, and said, "Captain, would you please refrain from comment and allow me to finish?"

"Oh, yes, Sir. Of course, Sir...absolutely, please continue. Yes, please."

Nussbaum sighed and forged on, "The Führer expects the gift to be personally delivered directly into his hands. You are trustworthy, Captain. I am appointing you to personally place the gift into the hands of our revered Führer, Adolf Hitler."

Brant stiffened and gasped, bringing both hands to his mouth in adolescent astonishment.

Nussbaum smiled, nodding his confirmation that, yes, Brant had heard correctly. He continued, "Because of this responsibility and my confidence that you will carry it out with the utmost dignity, I will immediately file the necessary forms recommending you for promotion to Major."

Brant's eyes went wide with wonder, his mouth hung open in shock. He staggered backward, literally falling into the chair behind him. He sat, stunned.

Disbelief and excitement filled his face as Nussbaum forced himself to continue smiling down at him. With eyes becoming affectionately watery, Brant choked out, "I…I do not know what to say, Herr Colonel."

"As a matter of fact, Brant, say nothing. Please, I beg of you, say nothing more—nothing to anyone. Did you hear me, Captain Brant? Can I count on you to say nothing about this honor I am bestowing on you to anyone?"

Seriousness replaced juvenile disbelief. His eyes shifted quickly from side to side, making sure no one was within earshot. "Yes, Sir," he whispered. "Not a word to anyone!"

"It is not that I want secrets kept from your fellow officers, Brant, but there is no need to cause them jealousy knowing that you have been selected for this honorable duty." Andreas gazed in amazement as he watched the dumbest officer he had ever dealt with hang breathless on his every word. All at once, Brant shot to his feet, startling Nussbaum. He stiffly thrust out his arm and loudly exclaimed through an emotionally cracking voice, "Heil Hitler!" Across the room the other officers waiting to accompany Brant back to Falauge looked over with amused expressions, shaking their heads in wonder that they shared rank with this imbecile.

Colonel Nussbaum had Brant drive him back to Falauge that evening, telling the other officers that the gravity of the General's untimely death necessitated his returning to Falauge to immediately file reports. Out of earshot of Brant, he also told them he was sending Captain Brant on to Chambéry with the paperwork. Upon arriving at Falauge, Nussbaum had Brant accompany him to his office. He sent orderlies to gather up Brant's personal belongings and had the train engineer awakened to prepare for immediate departure.

He then accompanied Brant to Schulmann's private car, telling him it was critical that not a moment be lost. He gave Brand the notes describing the safe's location and combination which Remi had slipped to him at the Bistro, showed him there was a supply of food in the car and instructed him that when the train stopped to refuel, he was not to disembark until they arrived at the Berlin central station. The engineer was told to proceed on through Chambéry since the train had been fueled sufficiently to take it on to the Dijon refueling siding.

As Andreas turned to exit the car, he felt Brant's hand on his shoulder. There were tears in Brant's eyes. He looked lovingly at Andreas, "You are the very best Colonel in the army, Colonel Nussbaum. If there is ever anything I can do for you, just let me know. I am at your service, Mein Herr."

"Just do your duty," Nussbaum smiled, "and don't worry about us. Somehow, we will carry on without you."

Brant snapped to attention, his face giving way to his emotions. He thrust out a stiff-armed salute, "Heil Hitler."

As the car pulled away, Andreas Nussbaum beamed. He waved in response to Brant's enthusiastic waves of goodbye and thought, *What a truly outstanding day. I have gotten rid of Captain Brant and become a multi-millionaire—all within a period of six hours. Actually, it would have been a very pleasant day just getting rid of Brant. Becoming a millionaire is almost anti-climactic.*

Back in his office, Nussbaum filled out an Absent Without Leave report on Captain Brant. In the Recommended Action section, he wrote:

> *Captain Brant has been acting strangely for the past several months (perhaps the strain of military life) and has been under my personal observation. He has begun to make negative remarks concerning the Third Reich and disparaging comments concerning the Führer, Adolf Hitler. Psychological evaluation would be recommended if and when Captain Brant is captured.*

He smiled as he placed the report in Brant's file. *Things are going swimmingly,* he mused, *just swimmingly!* He then leisurely drove back to Treaire. He had difficulty falling asleep that night, his mind consumed with joyous thoughts of his newly acquired astounding wealth.

While Nussbaum tossed and turned in jubilation, Captain Adam Brant slept contentedly, gently rocked in the comfort of the private train car as it rolled north through the night. Little did he suspect that in less than one week, he would be shot by a firing squad by order of his beloved Führer.

CHAPTER 29

Back at the Tristan's subterranean conference room, surrounded by the *friends* and Chabot, Felicien set the four wax-sealed bags on the table. He had taken care to avoid any damage to the sealing wax. As he placed the last bag on the table, he said, "Remi, I'm concerned. If General Schulmann opened the safe and showed Nussbaum these bags and we break the seals, he will know immediately we have tampered with them."

Chabot spoke up, "Then we will show him these bags." Felicien gave him a quizzical look.

Chabot sat silently, content with himself.

"Okay, Gasper, you have our attention," Remi respectfully nodded, "What scheme do you have in mind?"

"We let the Colonel open each of these bags here in the cave. After he has had a chance to examine all of the stones, we will let him take one of them with him to verify its authenticity. We will keep the rest of the stones with us. The night we put him on a plane out of France we hand him a bag filled with my beautiful zirconia crystals and send him on his way.

"So, Felicien, if the General did show him these bags, when we bring him here to the cave he will be seeing the same bags, still sealed and untouched. He will be the one to break the seals. See, my friends, simple!"

Chabot seems to figure out answers even before questions come up, Remi thought. "Okay. Good plan. We will bring Colonel Nussbaum here tomorrow night."

❦

The next evening, Colonel Nussbaum was particularly cheerful—back in full form filling the Bistro with discomfort and tension as he resumed his round of cheerful evening greetings. He discretely slid a small folded note under the rim of Remi's plate as he passed on his way back to his officers. *I am ready to receive what you owe me.*

As Remi passed the note under the table to Celine, he thought to himself, *We are ready to give you every bit of what we owe you, you bastard.*

Two hours later, as Andreas entered his room, he rolled his eyes and sighed with resignation as the heavy black bag was once again thrown over his head.

"Can we please dispense with the theatrics since we are all working together now?" he protested through the stuffy material. His comment elicited no response, just the familiar firm grip on his arm as he was turned and pushed through the door into the hall. He shrugged in acceptance and wearily stumbled along with his kidnappers.

To his continued chagrin, every step of his previous abduction was repeated just as it had unfolded the first time: down the hall and out through the back door, the long disorienting drive, tramping around in the woods, and finally seated in the black-draped room. This time, however, his hands were not bound to the chair.

He blinked painfully as the sack was removed, exposing him to the glare of the bright lights. To his surprise, sitting across a small table in front of him was a man shrouded from head to toe in black—tight black leather gloves, a black ski mask and dark sunglasses. Andreas shook his head, "Now, really, Remi, don't you think all the theatrics are a bit much?" He continued in a friendly, good-humored voice, "Come on...I am one of you now. We are working together. We are comrades."

Remi sat, silently staring across the table at Nussbaum.

"Okay," Andreas' tone changed to hopeless acquiescence, "play it your way."

From behind the black curtain the German voice spoke, "We have brought you here, Herr Colonel, to deliver our initial part of the bargain."

Remi leaned over and lifted a paper sack from the floor. He placed the four black velvet bags with their tops sealed in red wax onto the table. Andreas beamed in anticipation. The voice said, "These sealed bags are what we found in the General's safe. We will open them tonight, Colonel, for your inspection. We want to be sure you are fully satisfied with what we are delivering to you."

Remi placed a large wooden bowl in the center of the table—the same bowl Chabot had poured his zirconia crystals into the night he revealed them to the *friends.* He cut open the first bag and poured out its gleaming contents. Andreas could hardly control himself as the sparkling gems layered the bowl. The second bag was opened and added to the array, followed by the remaining two. The shimmering gems almost filled the bowl in a mound of amazing wealth. They surpassed Nussbaum's expectations. Not only were there hundreds of them, they were brilliant, huge…genuinely astounding. Andreas reached for one of the larger stones and held it up to the light, stunned at it radiance. He was awestruck in his exhilaration. Lightheaded in his glee, he had to consciously remember to breathe. There was no doubt that what he was viewing was value of immense proportions.

The voice spoke again, "We want to know if you are satisfied with our part of the agreement at this point, Herr Colonel?"

Nussbaum had to shake himself out of his ebullition. He looked past the man in black, answering the unseen voice, "Ah…yes, by all means, *yes.* These are magnificent. Everything I was led to believe they would be."

"Fine, pick one to take with you."

"What?" *Pick one?* Andreas' face flashed surprised anger. "They are *all* mine," he blurted, then quickly caught himself forcing a calmer tone. "Except, of course, the 50 or so I promised to give you for your efforts at the time you arrange for my escape."

"We agree, Herr Colonel. The diamonds are *all* yours, except, as you stated, the '50 or so' you will give us for arranging your escape. We recall you offered us a value of five million in diamonds when we arrange your escape, but we'll not quibble over details at this time. For simplicity, let's say our share will be an even 200 stones at the time we place you on a plane out of France."

"Wait. Where do you come up with 200?" the irritation was noticeable in Nussbaum's voice. "There is no way to know what 200 of these precious gems are worth. They could be worth much more than the five million we agreed on. This is not fair to me," Andreas was almost panicky in his objection.

The voice, still mellow, "You are absolutely correct, Herr Colonel. As you say, there is no way to know what 200 of these stones are worth. They may be worth more than five million—they may be worth less. We are willing to accept 200 of the diamonds as fulfillment of your payment to us. That makes things simple and understandable."

The voice went silent. Andreas desperately worked to calm himself. *I'll still have hundreds left. Still a fortune of incalculable value. I probably could argue until I'm blue in the face and not change these arrogant frog-eaters' minds.*

He breathed deeply, forcing aside his frustration at not getting his way. "Yes, all right, an even 200. I will select them now."

"No," the voice stated, still polite but firm. "They will be randomly selected from the bowl, counted out as you watch and placed in a separate container."

Andreas squirmed miserably in his seat, "Damn you. Damn your greed. All right, damn it. But I take the rest with me tonight."

The voice was calm and steady as it replied, "No, that will not be possible, Herr Colonel."

"I demand so. That was the deal. I demand you adhere to..." Nussbaum's voice rose in panicky anger and he began to rise from his seat. The man in black drew a pistol and the agitated Colonel immediately calmed himself.

"The deal, Herr Colonel, was that we steal the diamonds while you divert the General. It also specified we kill the General, deliver the diamonds to you, then help you to escape from France—for which you will pay us five million dollars' worth of diamonds. Additionally, the deal was that at the time of your escape you will deliver all incriminating information concerning the Tristan that you have on file, and that you will give us your word no additional copies of that information exists. We are meeting our obligation to you, Herr Colonel, and will continue to do so, but we will proceed only on our terms."

The finality of the voice's comment was obvious. More wealth than Andreas Nussbaum ever dreamed of lay immediately before him. He could see and touch it. The thought of parting from it, even temporarily, was unbearable. He strained, trying to come up with a means of taking control of the situation. He was thrust back to those horrible times in childhood when he was not granted his way. His mind shouted no to the very thought of leaving the gems behind, *No. You will cheat me. These are mine. It was my plan. My idea. You would not even have known of the shipment had I not told you.* Everything in him wanted to cry out and he fought to force it down. His face flushed. His left eye gave a slight twitch. He fought for restraint. He knew he had to get himself under control.

The voice remained silent, letting the agitated Colonel settle down. Then, in its calm reassuring tone, it said, "We have not cheated you so far, Herr Colonel. We will continue to follow through on our commitment to arrange your escape from France. We are your only way out of the country. We are sure you are painfully aware of that, but you must understand, if you want to escape with a bag full of gems, you will have to cooperate. We will only continue under our own terms."

Nussbaum had forced his adult consciousness back into control. He began to settle down. The voice continued, "You may take one of the gems with you tonight. Select any of the stones you see on the table. Have it analyzed professionally to assure yourself of its quality. Tonight we will place the remaining stones in two bags, our 200 in one and all the rest for you in the other. We will weigh your bag on a scale. The night of your escape, we will weigh your bag once again so you will be assured the weight matches. Prior to you leaving that night you will also hand us the complete dossier concerning all information on the Tristan and any information you have gathered on our Jewish citizens. Once we have exchanged your gems for this information, we will place you on a plane that will fly you out of France to a neutral country. There, you can make arrangements for the remainder of your escape to wherever it is you decide to go. That is the only way we will proceed."

Andreas had to admit, they were playing it smart. He reminded himself he was dealing with professionals.

"All right," he grudged. "But rest assured that if you do not deliver on the escape plan or if you try to cheat me on my share of the diamonds, I promise your destruction."

There was the hint of scornful teasing in the voice's response, "We understand and respect each other explicitly, Herr Colonel. In order to proceed, we will both have to develop a bit of trust, won't we? Please select the gem of your choice."

Andreas sorted through the stones several times, like a child trying to pick the very best piece of candy. He finally settled on one of the largest, an emerald cut, as his favorite. The man in black took a handful of stones from the bowl, placed them on the table and quickly counted off 200, pouring them into a small black bag. He knotted it, then set a small scale on the table. He placed the remainder of the jewels into a different larger black felt bag, pulled its top string tight and tied it. He placed the larger bag on the scale. The weight was 3 pounds, 10 ounces.

"Please inspect the weight and repeat it aloud, Herr Colonel," the voice commanded.

Nussbaum squinted at the scale, trying to indelibly imprint the figure on his mind, "Three pounds, 10 ounces," he said, "No, wait!" He leaned closer. "Yes, okay, yes. Three pounds, 10 point three ounces," he repeated, still closely squinting at the scale.

"Would it be acceptable to you, Herr Colonel, to settle on an even three pounds and 10 ounces?"

"Yes, damn it, yes…three pounds and 10 ounces. I am agreeable to that. Three pounds and 10 ounces. Okay, yes.

"Thank you for your patience with me. I have always been a very cautious man."

"We understand. To further your comfort, you will also take the scale with you tonight. This will assure that you will be weighing the stones on the same scale at the moment of your escape, and that it has not been tampered with.

"That, Herr Colonel, concludes our business tonight. We will be arranging your escape and during one of your evening social visits to the Bistro, we will notify you the exact time and date and how we will get you to the takeoff sight. Do you have any further questions?"

"At the moment you hand me the three pound, 10 ounce bag, I want time to open it and see that the only thing it contains are gems. Do I have your word on that?"

"That is acceptable, Herr Colonel."

The scale was placed in a small wooden box and given to Andreas. He placed his selected diamond in his pocket, then endured the stuffy sack being placed over his torso and he was once again returned to a spot near his hotel.

Two days later, Andreas had a jeweler in Chambéry inspect the stone he had selected from the dazzling array.

"This is one of the most remarkable diamonds I have ever seen, Monsieur," the jeweler uttered in astonishment as he continued peering into its depths through his loupe. "It is virtually flawless...and the brilliance...it is colorless! I am speechless. Where did you get this, may I ask?"

"You may not ask," retorted Nussbaum. "I did not come in here in the interest of striking up a friendly conversation. Can you estimate the value of this stone or not?"

"Yes, of course, Monsieur, my apologies. It is just that I have never seen a stone of such..." He interrupted his thought as he opened a large leather-bound book and began studying its charts. As he flipped through the pages, he kept making 'hmmm' sounds, furrowing his brow, then the 'hmmm' once again as he flipped back and forth among the reference charts.

"Good God, man! What is taking so long?" Andreas growled.

Not looking up from his charts, the jeweler responded, "I am sorry, Monsieur. The quality of this stone is so remarkable—I must be sure I give you a fair appraisal." Finally, he looked up at Nussbaum, who had dressed in civilian clothes, feeling he would get a more honest appraisal without the intimidation of his uniform. "I have never experienced a gem of this quality, Monsieur. Therefore, I can only approximate a value based on my charts. I put the value at $47,700."

Andreas beamed, "So, you would pay me $47,700 for this stone?"

The jeweler's expression shifted to astonishment, "Oh, no, Monsieur. I place the value of this stone at $47,700 per carat. There is no way I could possibly afford to purchase this stone from you. This stone is worth at least $425,000 U.S. dollars."

CHAPTER 30

The *friends* immediately initiated communication with British intelligence in hopes of arranging the Colonel's flight out of France. Through a series of coded messages sent from various locations using their powerful transmitter, they were able to convince the British that Nussbaum was of value to them. They told of his intimate knowledge of the German defenses protecting the Saint Laurnee Passage, his detailed information concerning the Nazis' plans to destroy the Passage upon their retreat from Italy, and his understanding of the growing dissention in the ranks of Germany's officer corps. While the British did not make a practice of assisting German officers to escape, their desire to interrogate Andreas Nussbaum soon outweighed any reluctance they initially had.

The plan was to pick up the Colonel at a secret location in the Alps, refuel the plane at Saragossa, Spain, then continue on to Gibraltar, where British intelligence would interrogate Nussbaum. It was the safest and most direct route. The only sticking point was the needed refueling stop in Saragossa, requiring the use of Spanish air space.

Spain, under the steel grip of Dictator Francisco Franco, claimed neutrality in the conflicts going on in Europe. While Franco's sympathies generally favored Nazi Germany, he was not above working both sides of the political spectrum if it served his purpose. The British were finally able to gain his assistance by promising Franco 50 of Nussbaum's diamonds. Franco decided a multi-million dollar fee was a reasonable price for allowing the Colonel to pass through his country. With that complication solved, the Brits contacted the Tristan requesting the coordinates and date for Nussbaum's pick up.

Andreas was once again kidnapped and forced to endure the hassle of the stuffy bag and circuitous route of getting him to the cave, tied into his chair in the brightly lit curtained little room and speaking with the calm German voice.

He was furious when told he would have to part with another 50 of his glimmering gems just to appease Franco. He bottled up his anger and sat silently fuming, convinced it was in his best interests to remain calm and in control in the presence of these people he needed so desperately. *Think, Andreas, think. Don't lose it*, he focused. *You're almost there. It still leaves over 1,280 of the gems...that has to be worth 50 million or more. Okay, it's okay. Just resign yourself that it will probably take another million or so to purchase passage from Gibraltar to Argentina. It's okay. Remain calm. You are eminently wealthy.* He acquiesced, realizing these horrifically painful compromises were necessary to get him out of this insane war and comfortably secluded with his massive fortune.

The intensity of his fury paled in comparison to the pangs of terror that gripped him upon being told the British were insistent on interrogating him as their fee for providing him safe passage out of France.

"The British want to interrogate me! About what?" his voice high pitched with tension.

Chabot answered in his calm German diction, "They want information concerning the Saint Laurnee Passage, the defenses in place to protect it and whatever plans exist for its destruction once the German army no longer needs it as they retreat out of Italy. Additionally, they are highly interested in your observations of the growing dissension in the ranks of German senior officers as they become ever more convinced Germany will lose the war."

For the first time, Remi saw true fear in Nussbaum's eyes. "What assurances do I have the British will release me with my diamonds if I cooperate? For that matter, what assurances do I have they will release me at all?"

"None," came back Chabot's calm reply from behind the curtain. "But, Herr Colonel, what assurances are there in life? So far, you are doing pretty well, all things considered. You are discussing the final preparations to extricate yourself from a war you feel your side will lose. You are leaving with a huge number of gemstones. You are being smuggled out of the country by French citizens and the British military—both of whom are avowed enemies of you and your country. We have arranged everything as promised. We are simply informing you your passage through Spain and release by the British have certain price tags attached. We have kept our word to this point, and we feel the British will do the same. There are no guarantees...just good faith."

Nussbaum sat fidgeting for some time. They could see him trying to assess his predicament, trying to make a calm, logical decision. Finally, he shrugged, giving a fatalistic sigh, "Yes, I suppose you are right, but I don't trust the British. They're all a bunch of limey pirates, you know. What exactly do the Brits expect to get from questioning me?"

"Full, accurate disclosure of the geographic coordinates of all German defensive weapons guarding the trestle and tunnel at the Passage, the type of weaponry, its manning, information as to the protective structures housing these weapons, troop sizes at Falauge, details on all sabotage procedures you are expected to use to destroy the Passage once you evacuate the site, and any officers you may know of who might be convinced to become spies for the Allies."

Nussbaum nervously shifted again, "Are they prepared to take my word on these matters?"

The voice sighed, "Herr Colonel, you have a lot of money at stake here. Let's be frank and think logically. If I were in your position, I would give the British as much indisputable information as possible Knowing you Germans' infatuation with record keeping and diagrams, I am sure you have maps, charts, written orders and other documentation that will certainly lend believability to your responses to the British concerning Falauge and the Passage. Also, any written communication you may have of officers who may have confided their frustrations with the Reich or their fears of becoming prisoners of war would be most convincing. I would suggest you take such credible data with you as proof of your cooperation and believability."

There was a long pause as Nussbaum mull over what he just heard. With obvious concern in his voice, Nussbaum said, "I am still uneasy that once I give the Brits what they want they will arrest me as a prisoner of war, steal my fortune, and try me for war crimes."

"That is a risk you have to decide whether or not you are prepared to take," the voice calmly responded. "These are the terms that have been dictated to us by the British for arranging your exodus. Your alternative is to stay here and figure a way to escape with your fortune. We have no other way of arranging your exit. We leave it to you, Herr Colonel. Should we proceed with arranging your flight?"

Andreas Nussbaum was facing the greatest risk he had ever confronted. He squirmed in the chair, tugging at his arm restraints. Several times, he bent his head down to wipe perspiration on his sleeve. His sighs were so deep and agonizing, the listeners felt short of breath. Finally, he looked at the curtain, "Okay. You are right. You have kept your word and I will have to trust the damn British to keep theirs. Arrange the flight. I will gather up the information the Brits want."

"Fine," the voice said.

Nussbaum then added, "I have a request."

The voice replied, "Yes?"

"Is there any way you can inform me of the departure date and anything else we have to discuss without going through this whole kidnapping routine each time?" There were subdued chuckles from behind the black curtain. "At times, life can be fraught with little annoyances, Herr Colonel. Especially when one is on one's way to one's just rewards." The room blinked into darkness, the black sack thrust over Nussbaum's head, and the now familiar and irritating procedure of returning him to his drop point a mile from the hotel again repeated.

<hr />

Eight days later, the drone of a British Lysander moaned in the night air moments before it touched down on a deserted mountain road dimly lit by the Tristan's burning fuel pots. Andreas Nussbaum, looking much less intimidating in a civilian business suit and laden down with supportive documentation for his meeting with British intelligence, had his blindfold removed. He stood in the light of a full moon, surrounded by four ski-masked individuals dressed in black. It was not difficult to identify the trim figure of Celine. He was sure one of the three taller figures was Remi, and he was reasonably sure Amaury Cheever and Felicien Naffis made up the other two. He remained perplexed as to which of them was so meticulously fluent in German.

They weighed the Colonel's bag of zirconia crystals, allowing him to inspect the contents by shining a flashlight into the glittering bag. He checked the scale several times to assure himself it read exactly three pounds, 10 ounces. They handed him a small bag in which he was to place 50 of his gems and hand them to a Spanish officer at the refueling stop in Saragossa.

Nussbaum gave them the incriminating dossier and a second file he said he had come across concerning the Tristan's activities from some years back. He assured them there were no copies of the information he had gathered, but said he had no way of knowing if copies of the information in the older file existed.

Standing beside the idling plane, Andreas paused for a moment. During his life he had never really developed friendships because he had never felt respect for other people. In a strange way, he felt an attachment to these people hidden behind their ski masks. He respected their professionalism, their courage, love of freedom and their determination.

He felt an unexpected sorrow leaving them. He reached his hand out to the one he felt was Remi. Remi shook his hand. Andreas looked into the lenses of the dark glasses covering Remi's eyes and said, "I very much respect you. You and your friends are brave and dedicated, a trait lacking in me. You have shown me a side of humanity I have failed to see before—that there is more to life than just today. It has taught me..."

Sadness filled his eyes. He started to finish the sentence, hesitated, then turned and climbed up into the seat behind his British pilot. Celine pushed the door closed and glanced up at him. He was looking down at her. He gave her a soft smile and a little wave as the engine roared to full throttle, whisking him into the night sky to vanish forever in its blackness.

———

When Colonel Nussbaum did not return to Falauge, his aide went to his safe and found the sealed dossier Andreas had instructed him to mail to Gestapo headquarters in Berlin if he ever failed to return. As he promised, Andreas had removed all of the incriminating information concerning the Tristan. In its place, he had inserted 22 blank sheets of paper accompanied by a handwritten note that said, *Vital information concerning five French Resistance cells in Southern France. All information written in invisible ink for security purposes.* The Gestapo spent months and a small fortune trying to bring the "invisible" ink to a readable state.

Andreas made it safely to Gibraltar. He divulged new and critical information to the British concerning the Saint Laurnee Passage, its defenses, and additional intelligence concerning the German officer corps deteriorating morale in France. The British honored their commitment, allowing him to depart Gibraltar on a private plane he hired to fly him to the Azores. The flight cost him 20 of the zirconia crystals as payment to the civilian pilot. There, he spent another 30 of the worthless crystals purchasing passage on an Iberian freighter that took him to the Falkland Islands, and he was forced to part with another 25 of the fake diamonds in payment for an Argentinian ship's passage from the Falklands to Buenos Aires.

He was extremely disappointed to discover his bag of gems was worthless several days after landing in South America. Still, the single gem he had taken for evaluation fetched $278,000. It wasn't the $425,000 the jeweler in Chambéry had estimated, but was the very best price he could negotiate in Buenos Aires. He learned that the Captain of the Argentinian freighter that brought him to Buenos Aires had discovered Andreas paid him in worthless shiny rocks and was in searching for him. He immediately decided to move on to Porto Alegre, Brazil, determining the move would be beneficial to his long-term health.

The Argentinian ship Captain never caught up with Andreas—nor did any of the others he paid off with his zirconia crystals. A fraction of his $278,000 purchased a large home on a hillside overlooking Porto Alegre offering a marvelous city-lights view. With another portion of the money, he purchased a dry-cleaning business. He worked hard at his new business making an honest living and eventually grew his enterprise to five dry-cleaning shops and a bookstore in the growing seaside city—the bookstore more of a hobby investment, but still quite successful.

He married a charming Jewish girl who had migrated from Germany to Brazil to escape the Nazis when they rose to power in the 1930s. He converted to Judaism, raised two boys and a girl in the Jewish faith, had a loving relationship with his wife and children, and wound up volunteering as a Gabbai in the local synagogue.

Over the years, he often thought respectfully about the Tristan freedom fighters. Yes, they had cheated him of his diamonds, but had provided him with so much more. He came to view his brief relationship with them as a blessing, an event that changed his view of humanity. He felt he was a better person for having known them.

CHAPTER 31

27 October, 1943
Colonel Wilhelm Auchenbach takes
Command of Falauge Garrison

Andreas Nussbaum's self-centered personality and superficial friendliness toward Bistro patrons had certainly been an irritant, but would have been gladly embraced in exchange for the shroud of evil his replacement brought to Treaire.

Golden-haired Colonel Wilhelm Auchenbach descended on the garrison at Falauge like a death knell. Within hours of his arrival, four garrison soldiers were incarcerated for 10 days in one-meal-a-day, pitch black, toiletless, solitary confinement for failure to appear in what their new commander considered proper regulation uniform. Another was cuffed to the inspection yard review stand, unable to attain a sitting position for 36 hours for making a whispered comment to the man to his left during inspection.

The next day, Auchenbach called a meeting of the garrison officers. He had them line up at attention in his office antecom as he walked up and down the line, building his fury.

"Everything here is going to change—*everything*! This is the most despicable, degenerate, lackadaisical and insulting excuse for a German military installation I have ever seen. You are the problem! *You*," he screamed, peppering the face of his senior officer with enraged spittle. He stepped back from the rigid line, shaking his head in condescending disgust. His eyes flashed, his face red with rage. He slammed his riding crop down on the desk, cracking its protective glass top.

He wheeled around to the Captain on his right, bringing the crop down with violent force on the man's neck, splitting the skin. The officer staggered in shock as blood began oozing onto his collar.

"Stand straight, you slovenly pig!" Auchenbach shrieked, hitting the man in the arm with such force the crop tore through the sleeve. It, too, quickly turned red from the severe cut the strike had produced.

"Get that stupid wimp-ass to his feet," he yelled, strutting the line, his voice pitched high with anger. "When a military unit deteriorates, it is the direct fault of the officer staff. You are the officer staff. It is the direct fault of *you*. It is *your* failure. *You are disgusting!* You are an insult to Germany, to the Third Reich and to the Führer! You have so totally failed the ideals of the German military, so totally disgraced its proud tradition, so completely abandoned its pride and honor, I shall report all of you for treasonous acts against the Führer!"

The seemingly endless harangue was punctuated with long silences where Auchenbach paced, allowing his rage to rekindle its volatility. The officers fought the urge to flinch each time the Colonel strutted past them, never knowing if they might be next to be physically brutalized.

The tirade continued for over 40 minutes, as the insanely enraged Colonel repeated over and over the most vile and abusive insults he could muster. Then, without warning, he abruptly turned and stormed into his office, violently slamming the door behind him. The horrified men remained at attention as they listened to their new boss shriek every curse word he knew, interrupted only by the crash of breaking objects as he vented his rage behind the closed door. The diatribe finally ceased when Auchenbach felt the first tinge of pain rising in his stomach. He quickly quieted himself and gulped down several swallows of Kaopectate.

Finally, the Captain, whose bleeding neck and arm wounds had saturated his shirt, slumped forward and lost consciousness, his face hitting the floor with a thud. Two of the men lifted him to his feet and stumbled toward the hallway with their injured comrade. "Get him to the infirmary," commanded the senior officer. The group departed in horror at the prospect of what lay ahead.

———

Wilhelm Auchenbach…35 years old, handsome, toned, blond-haired, blue-eyed, towering in height—the epitome of Hitler's fantasies of a Nordic ethnologically superior being, the embodiment of Aryan perfection. His crystal-blue eyes missed nothing; his steel-trap mind permanently registered it all.

Few other men stood tall enough to look directly into his chilling eyes, and this dominance in height suited him perfectly. When he spoke, the air resonated with the sound of unnerving narcissistic detachment. There was never a smile, an accommodating gesture, a hint of humane compassion to modify the arctic aura that emanated from Wilhelm Auchenbach.

He had always been physically and mentally superior to his peers. Large for his age and quick of mind, he lorded it over the children he encountered in his youth. His mother's feelings of superiority were born into him, and she spent hours affirming those attitudes in his developing mind. She fawned over his every accomplishment, turning the most rudimentary feat into manifest pillars of achievement in his eyes.

His father, too, raised in the luxury of German aristocracy, was convinced of his own noble superiority, treating all others as beings placed on this earth to satisfy his whims. The Auchenbachs flaunted their wealth, their contempt, and their chilling pageantry on everyone. They bought into Hitler's philosophy of a superior race of Aryan beings with relish—in their minds, they stood as its living proof.

Although Wilhelm Auchenbach fancied himself one of Hitler's beloved superior Aryans he suffered from one major flaw: Severe Queasy Stomach Reaction—at least, that's what physicians finally labeled it. It first reared its ugly head when he was just a child. Every time little Wilhelm became too excited, he vomited. His immature temper tantrums almost immediately shot wrenching pains surging through his stomach and upper intestine so severe, he would double over and become totally incapacitated. After months of visiting numerous doctors, the only thing that could successfully help him avoid the pain and vomiting was a quick gulp of Kaopectate. Over the years, he had learned early detection of the oncoming symptoms and kept multiple bottles of the thick liquid within arm's reach at all times. His re-occurring nightmare, however, was to suffer a stomach attack and not be able to get a quick swig of the disgustingly thick pink fluid that flowed from the Kaopectate bottles like life-saving blood transfusions.

Auchenbach could not tolerate the officers he inherited from Colonel Nussbaum. He immediately replaced them with his own staff, convinced the riffraff he found in charge of Falauge were hopeless.

He made good on his threat to file treason charges against all of the original officers, accusing them of dereliction of duties and malicious acts of sabotage against the Third Reich. In their courts-marshal, only one of the officers was acquitted—after he testified against the others and confirmed the trumped-up charges to save his own skin. Nussbaum's senior officer was hanged, and the rest of the convicted men spent the remainder of the war in Berlin's brutal Plötzensee prison. It was a needless loss of experienced manpower when the Reich was in such dire need of officers.

Auchenbach replaced Nussbaum's six officers with a staff of 10 commissioned and five non-commissioned officers. Under Auchenbach, the Falauge garrison had the highest ratio of officers to private soldiers of any unit in the German army. He also transferred 30 of the soldiers he inherited at Falauge to the Italian Front, replacing them with men of his personal choosing. Life for the common soldier at Falauge became a living hell.

Auchenbach continued the practice of taking his evening meals at the Bistro, but without his officers. He had Amaury stock Côte de Brouilly Beaujolais, a wine he particularly favored and often consumed with his meal. Although patrons of the Bistro were spared having to endure Andreas Nussbaum's disquieting evening chats, the new garrison commander's mere presence filled the air with a chill, muting conversations to low whispers and causing patrons to fix their eyes intently on their meals, avoiding eye contact with the menace of this man.

Again following in the footsteps of Nussbaum, he decided to reside in Treaire at the hotel. Auchenbach, however, forced the innkeeper to break doorways through to adjoining rooms, taking over four of the eight rooms at the inn.

He promised there would be compensation for the cost of the renovations and loss of revenue from the confiscated rooms. Bills were endlessly submitted to Nazi headquarters in Chambéry, but neither payment nor acknowledgment was ever received.

One night, as Auchenbach dined at the Bistro, he was approached by the irate innkeeper demanding his money. Colonel Auchenbach rose from his table, towering over the Frenchman. He bent low, whispering in the man's ear, "Your insistence in bothering me and my superiors in Chambéry concerning this trivial matter is tiresome. If you continue, you will one day return to your home and find your wife cut into several pieces." The Colonel pulled back from the little man, gave him an icy stare, and said, "Do we now have an understanding, Monsieur?"

The Colonel's living accommodations suited him perfectly. He did not have to put up with the hassle of constantly rubbing elbows with junior officers, the excellent cuisine and magnificent bottles of Beaujolais were within a few steps of the inn's front door, and he was attracted to the cute young night clerk at the inn. He would give her several more weeks to relent to his advances, after which he would threaten the safety of her family if she did not accommodate his needs.

He assigned pairs of soldiers from the garrison to walk the streets of Falauge and Treaire 24 hours a day. These two-man units were in addition to the motorized patrols plying the pavement. The 10:00 pm curfew was strictly enforced for all non-Jewish citizens, and Jews, now required to wear the yellow Star of David identification patches, were not allowed on the streets after 5:00 pm or before seven in the morning.

Jews bold enough to venture into the streets during their allowed hours were consistently stopped by the patrols, harassed and humiliated. The windows on Treaire's tailor shop, the apothecary, and the laundry were crudely painted with the word "Jude", alerting all to the fact the establishments were Jewish owned. People were not restricted from patronizing Jewish establishments, but every citizen realized that to be seen frequenting one of the marked shops would bring immediate retribution from the street patrols who would red-stamp their papers with the words Jew Lover and begin harassing them relentlessly.

Wilhelm Auchenbach brought the full weight of the extreme cruelty of the Third Reich to southern France with a vengeance.

The citizens of Falauge and Treaire watched the actions of Colonel Auchenbach with increasing alarm. The years of calm they had experienced under the lackadaisical attitude of Andreas Nussbaum had lulled them into a false sense of safety from the more brazen impact of Nazi occupation being endured in other parts of France. They were shocked at the brutality and total disregard for human suffering exuded by Auchenbach and his new team.

Remi contacted Gasper Chabot, who, for some unknown reason, Auchenbach had overlooked in his search to identify and register the area's Jews. The *friends* and Chabot met in the cave shortly after Auchenbach's arrival. Remi prepared them for war.

"Until now, we have rarely been subjected to the evil cruelty of the Nazis. Colonel Auchenbach exemplifies the worst of what we have been spared. There is no way for us to avoid or neglect this satanic beast. No one will be able to stay out of his way, no one—Jews and non-Jews. I have never experienced evil up close before. If we are to survive, we must go to battle, and we must go to battle now.

"We will focus on disrupting everything we can under Colonel Auchenbach's command. We will kill him if we can find a way to get away with it. We will become as troublesome to Auchenbach and his forces as possible, but first we will go underground—disappear from sight.

"Amaury, because of your high profile at the Bistro, you will continue on with your normal daily activities. Be in the bar and restaurant each evening. See if you can open a line of communication with Auchenbach as he takes his evening meals. We have to know as much about his movements and plans as possible. See if you can gain his trust.

"Felicien, you, too, continue your daily routine. Your repair and handyman work gets you in close contact with the people. They see things, hear rumors every day. Pump them for as much information as you can. Relay everything to Celine and me, no matter how absurd the rumor may sound.

"Celine, Chabot, and I will drop out of sight."

Chabot's high-functioning autistic personality made it difficult for him to give up his entrenched routine, but Remi convinced him it was for his own good and the good of the Tristan. They moved his living quarters and laboratory into an abandoned gristmill on the back side of Amaury's estate. The mill itself sat several miles back from the main highway, deep in a wooded valley. Virtually all of the Cheever estate property could be accessed from various back roads out of sight of anyone watching the main highway fronting the estate. The mill had not operated for many years, but, as with all Cheever properties, the structure had been immaculately maintained—its water wheel and wooden gearing still fully operable.

Under Gasper's supervision, his laboratory equipment was moved into the mill, enabling him to continue development of items the Tristan would need in their fight against Auchenbach. The door and window openings of the mill were sealed, allowing it to be fully lit inside at night while maintaining its dark and abandoned appearance from the outside.

At Chabot's property, all of the buildings, including his house, were completely gutted of equipment and furnishings, leaving the property vacant and abandoned. It was only a matter of time before Auchenbach's storm troopers would discover their oversight of Gasper Chabot's Jewish descent. When they showed up at his house, it would appear the odd professor had fled the area.

Celine and Remi moved to an old cottage on the estate that had once housed one of the Cheever sheepherders. This building, too, was in good condition, allowing the couple to set up housekeeping by simply moving their furniture in. The cottage sat even farther back than the mill, making its access an inconvenience but assuring its secrecy. Remi quit his job at the waterworks, informing its owner, Maurice Pippen, he was leaving the area to tend to an ailing uncle in Paris. Overnight, he, Celine and Chabot vanished from the streets of Treaire.

The disappearance of Celine and Remi did not go unnoticed by the citizens of Treaire. Many of them had growing suspicions the couple was the driving force behind the local Resistance group, resulting in concern in their disappearance. With Remi and Celine gone, people somehow felt more vulnerable. In response most town's people further lowered their profiles shunning the streets to the greatest extent possible. Treaire went dead.

CHAPTER 32

Amaury's freshly pressed white apron draped over his black trousers from waist to mid-calf, his black bowtie straight and tidy against his freshly starched collar designed to set a mood of accommodation and respect as he approached Colonel Auchenbach's table. A crisp pressed towel draped over his arm, he extended a bottle of Gasper Chabot's prized Pétrus Bordeaux wine, "Monsieur Auchenbach, may I offer one of France's most esteemed wines as a compliment of Le Duc de Richelieu Bistro?"

The Colonel's cold eyes shot up from the document he was reading. He studied Amaury, not looking at the bottle being presented for his inspection.

His voice devoid of any emotion, "Why?"

Taken aback, Amaury stammered, "Pardon, Monsieur. I do not understand."

Auchenbach, staring piercingly at Amaury, pushed back from the table, continuing his lock on Amaury's eyes. His manner was callous, his look calculating. He furrowed his brow, narrowing his eyes slightly, "Why are you offering me a bottle of Pétrus Bordeaux? I specially ordered Côte de Brouilly Beaujolais. You now stock it. I am pleased with it. So, why are you offering me a complimentary bottle of Pétrus Bordeaux? You're not trying to cover your panicked ass because you let my order run out, are you?"

The moment hung frozen. A hush washed across the Bistro. Amaury's natural confidence vanished. He had never before felt so totally defenseless as the scowl of Wilhelm Auchenbach burned through him. A spasm of fear he had not expected, had never before experienced, suddenly gnawed at his stomach. He felt in peril, as if he might not survive this initially benign encounter.

It wasn't only what Auchenbach said. It was his menace, his icy tone, his totally penetrating stare. Amaury was looking into the eyes of evil, as assuredly as if he were staring into the glare of Satan himself.

A cold sweat enveloped him. His voice broke embarrassingly, as the voice of a terrified child breaks, "I...I meant no offense, Herr Colonel. There was no intent...I had no motive but to make your evening in my Bistro as...as pleasant as possible."

"I don't believe you," Auchenbach monotoned, continuing his arctic stare.

"I...I don't know how to respond," Amaury stammered, further sinking into an aberrant fear of what the next moment might bring. He dug deep. He gathered what strength he could muster, forcing his fear toward anger. As he did, the anger began to subdue his terror. A bit of strength returned. He straightened up, breaking eye contact, now looking at the bottle and thrusting its label toward the beast sitting in front of him.

"I offer you this bottle, Herr Colonel, knowing that you are the powerful new commander of the garrison at Falauge. You have chosen to take your evening meals in my Bistro, and I am honored you have chosen to do so. I realize the power you wield, and I am open to admit that I would like to be on friendly terms with you."

A smirk transmuted Auchenbach's face. He slid his chair farther from the table, glancing down at the bottle's label. Amaury took the Colonel's change in position as a break in the frigid setting, saying, "Are you familiar with Pétrus Bordeaux, Herr Colonel?"

"Yes, it is one of Reichsmarschall Hermann Göring's favorites. I have tasted it once while in his company."

"I hope it suited your taste, Monsieur," Amaury responded, feeling the Colonel's more conversational tone may have allowed him to pass some unidentifiable threshold of disgust that Amaury provoked in him.

"Address me as Colonel, or Herr Colonel. Save your obnoxious French prefixes for Frenchmen," Auchenbach sneered, refreezing the environment.

Amaury seethed with humiliation and anger. He had never confronted such a detached, dispassionate and terrifying individual. All five-hundred facial muscles were called upon as he forced a smile at this hateful being, "Yes, of course, Herr Colonel. My mistake. I should have known better. Please forgive my blundering ways. I would still like to welcome your patronage of my Bistro with this bottle, if the Colonel would be inclined."

"Pour it," Auchenbach commanded, sliding his chair forward and turning back to his reading. As he read, he drank the glass Amaury poured, then recorked the bottle and departed. Amaury watched him leave, tucking the bottle under his arm as he stepped out onto the street.

My God, I have never encountered another human being so terrifying. His body gave an uncontrollable shudder as he relived the encounter with this human aberration. *There has got to be a way to break this man*, he thought. *And it is critical we break him soon or he will consume us.*

<hr />

It was early evening, the last of the day's sunlight wrapping the charming streets of Treaire in its golden glow. Auchenbach stood for a moment on the Bistro's entrance step, taking in a breath of the crisp evening air. He dropped the bottle of Pétrus Bordeaux off at the hotel, instructing the young woman tending the desk to take it to his room. She had been the victim of his leering scrutiny before and immediately avoided eye contact as she saw him enter the lobby. She simply nodded and almost in a whisper replied, "Yes, Herr Colonel." He stood, staring at her. When she didn't hear him leaving, she looked up and he commanded, "*Now*, damn it! Take the bottle to my room, *now*." He watched her immediately grab the wine and scurry up the stairs. He then turned and exited back onto the street.

He strutted along the ancient cobblestone streets, some only wide enough to pass foot traffic. *Definitely a town created without a thought to the future of technology*, he mused. He turned onto a narrow lane tightly flanked on both sides by brightly colored two-story buildings as it dropped down a hill and intersected with Treaire's main street. As he stepped into the intersection, he spotted one of his street patrols approaching. They had not notice him, so he stepped back between the buildings to observe them. The two young men were relaxed, smoking and chatting as they casually strolled their route. Although it was several hours before non-Jewish curfew, the streets were vacant.

The soldiers stopped at a small plaza, beautiful in the late day's fading glow, its little fountain sparkling in complement to the charming surroundings. They had a hearty laugh about something as one of them unslung his machine gun and set it on a bench. He put one foot on the bench seat and leaned over, resting his arms on his knee. His companion slouched down on the bench, flipping his cigarette butt toward the fountain.

Auchenbach approached from behind as they laughed at another of the remarks made in their youthful banter. Moving toward the two, he barked, "You are examples of everything the Führer hates about Germany's slovenly youth." The soldiers swung around, startled; their surprise plunged to stark terror as they saw the Colonel approaching. They stiffened to attention. A cigarette still hanging from the lips of one boy was backhanded from his mouth. He staggered against his comrade, struggling to regain his footing.

"Pick up those weapons, you slobs," Auchenbach sneered.

He calmed his demeanor, clasping his hands behind his back and stood towering over the frightened youth.

"Attitude, gentlemen, attitude," he lectured. "Attitude and discipline are what make a country great. They are the cornerstones of great societies and powerful armies. It is attitude and discipline which I have found totally lacking in you slovenly pigs who served under Colonel Nussbaum—perhaps not directly your fault, as I have come to believe Colonel Nussbaum himself was a slovenly pig. Nonetheless, I intend to correct those shortcomings, and the two of you are going to assist me in doing so." He looked down on his frightened victims. It excited him. He felt his power

"Do you hear me, children?"

A whimpered response, "Yes, Herr Colonel."

"What?" Auchenbach yelled.

"Yes, Sir, Colonel Auchenbach," came back the unified shout.

A sinister smile spread on the Colonel's lips, "Have you boys ever heard of flogging?"

"No, Sir, Herr Colonel," came another unified response.

"It is a disciplinary procedure the British invented to assure their sailors understood the importance of being alert and productive at all times and remained respectful of the authority of their ship's Captain. It was a procedure performed in front of the entire crew aboard ship. In this way, the entire crew learned from the corrective instruction of just one or two of their mates." He paused, "Wouldn't you agree that is a very efficient method of instruction?"

"Yes, Sir, Herr Colonel."

"Well, allow me to explain why the floggings proved so memorably instructive to those who watched. The shirt of the errant sailor was removed, his hands tied to one of the ship's masts, and a whip made of multiple strands of leather with little studs embedded in their ends was whipped across his back with force.

"Through sad experience, the limeys learned that over 40 such lashes often resulted in the sailor's eventual death. This was not an efficient use of crew, so the Royal Navy passed a law stating the maximum number of allowable lashes would be 25."

The boys, now visibly shaking, struggled to maintain their rigid posture. Their panic was exactly what Wilhelm Auchenbach was after. They would project the terror of their impending punishment to the entire garrison filling all the men with the fear that lack of compliance with regimen would meet with severe disciplinary measures.

Auchenbach narrowed his gaze at the soldiers. "Lashing has never really caught on in the German military, although it is not forbidden. We are going to use it on the two of you for having been slovenly in carrying out your assignment on this patrol."

The panic of the severe punishment facing them allowed an unwanted tear to slip down the face of one of the boys.

Auchenbach reached over and gently wiped the tear away with the back of his index figure, "Ah, I see by your expressions that I have your attention. Being a reasonable man, I will only allow 12 lashes each rather than the 25 the barbaric British inflict on their men. You will now continue on your patrol until you are relieved. Upon returning to Falauge, report immediately to Lieutenant Schultz and instruct him that you are to be confined to cells until you are sent for to stand your lashings before the garrison…Dismissed."

Public flogging, he thought as he turned back toward the hotel. *Brilliant! Why didn't I think of that before? I must remember to tell Lieutenant Schultz they are to sit for a few days to let the thought of their punishment soak in—and the rumors of it to thoroughly filter through the rest of the garrison.*

He stopped and turned for another look at the little plaza. *Truly charming*, he thought. *I really must come back here for a visit after the war.* He turned and strolled up the hill. *Tonight will be the night I insist that little desk clerk accompany me to my room. Perhaps I'll share a bit of my Pétrus Bordeaux to help her relax.* He smiled to himself at the thought.

CHAPTER 33

With their move underground complete, the *friends* began monitoring German radio messages daily. The increasing chatter from Nazi command posts in Italy indicated German strength along the Italian Front was becoming tenuous as the Allies continuously pounded their positions. German commanders were screaming for additional troops, equipment and supplies. In response, the largest convoy to date was scheduled to move south from Chambéry to Falauge within a week.

Since the British and Americans were insistent on saving the Saint Laurnee Passage for their own use, the destruction of that critical point was not an option open to the Tristan to disrupt the convoy reaching Italy. Their small numbers ruled out a direct attack as the convoy moved south along the Chambéry-Treaire highway.

The constant barrage of radio communication made it clear this convoy was critical to German defenses in Italy…perhaps *so* critical its failure to arrive could spell a turning point in favor of the Allies there. Celine and Remi met with Amaury, Felicien and Chabot to develop a feasible plan of attack. They left the meeting frustrated. Short of blowing the trestle over the Saint Laurnee Gorge, there seemed no reasonable way for the five of them to stop the massive movement of troops and supplies.

Two days later, Chabot said he might have a solution and requested they all gather at the mill that evening. As they entered, Celine noticed he had that confident little smirk he always wore when he thought he had a clever trick up his sleeve. Despite his look of self-contentment, he appeared exhausted.

She went to him, "Gasper, you look exhausted. Is everything all right?"

"Oh, yes, it's just that I've been up for the past several days. I often do this if I get an idea. Once we are through here, I'll sleep for several days to catch up. Have a seat and I will explain myself.

"I felt badly the other night, thinking there was little we could do to stop the Germans from shipping all those men and supplies to Italy—so I have created a number of interesting toys I think will halt their convoy in its tracks."

Little did the *friends* anticipate the magnificent array of items Chabot called his *toys* as he walked around the large table on which they were displayed?

Holding up the first gizmo, he delighted, "Although this looks like a common bicycle tire pump, this little bottle of fluid attached to its side injects an interesting chemical into tires that causes their interior structure to break down in about 12 hours. Just two pumps are enough to inject sufficient fluid to destroy the tire." He paused, waiting for applause that did not come. Somewhat deject, he moved on to the next item.

He picked up a small bottle containing clear liquid. "This one does a lot of damage to motor vehicles. About an ounce of this poured into a gasoline or diesel fuel tank causes the fuel to thicken into a sticky mass. It, too, takes 10 to 12 hours to work, but that is a benefit. If the vehicle is running as the chemical begins to solidify, the thickening fuel is sucked through the gas lines and into the fuel pump and the carburetor, thus filling the entire fuel system with thick goo. The result," he smiled, "is the vehicle stops running and not only does the gas tank have to be replaced, but the entire fuel system along with it. Can you imagine how long it will take the Germans to replace several hundred fuel systems?"

He had their attention. Remi was beaming, "My God, Chabot has the answers we are looking for."

Remi's comment added a bounce to Chabot's step as he moved on to the next item. "Now, this one you might want to be a little careful with." His eyes twinkled behind his glasses as he held up what appeared to be a small tin can. "Pull the pin at the top of this can, throw it like a grenade and three seconds after the pin is pulled, it releases a fog that causes almost instant nausea to anyone who breathes it. The fog covers about a 50-square-foot area. It's invisible and heavy so it lays close on the ground and doesn't quickly dissipate. But when troops move through it, they stir it up and become sick within seconds. It's good for throwing in a barracks, then slamming the door...or if a bunch of enemies are chasing you, throw it at them and I assure you, it will stop them. It saturates the clothing, too, so even if a soldier leaves the area where the fog is laying, he remains sick and those who come into close contact with him get sick, too."

Felicien interrupted, "These are fabulous! What a great way to wage war. Even more fun than Celine's poisons. You could take over a whole country with this stuff and never fire a shot. To hell with the Germans," he laughed. "Let's attack the United States—better country, nicer people."

The *friends* were thrilled as their weird and wonderful associate joyously moved around the table.

"Oh, here is one of my favorites!" Chabot beamed, I call it boot pepper. Just a squirt into a boot or shoe will result in a painful burning sensation after the boot is worn for a couple of hours. Sweat activates it and spreads it around. It permeates the material making it impossible to wash out, so the boot has to be replaced. The burning sensation dissipates as soon as the boot is removed, but the boots become useless."

He picked up a squirt bottle. "This contains an interesting chemical. When sprayed on any metal surface, it causes extensive rust to form within minutes. Really not good for the firing mechanisms of most weapons," he chuckled. "Spray it inside gun barrels and breaches so the Germans will not immediately notice it.

"Well, my Tristan friends, do you think we can slow up the convoy with these?"

Remi asked, "How many of each of these things do you have?"

Chabot looked over at him sheepishly, "Well, there are four of you, so I only made eight of everything, except the chemicals—the tire melt, boot pepper and the like. There's enough of that to dissolve every tire in Europe and set all the boots in the world on fire."

Remi, Felicien and Amaury were pouring over the items on the table. Celine could almost hear the excitement turning in their heads. Chabot's creations were incredible. They provided an ability to disrupt the convoy and, if they planned their assault carefully, inflict massive damage without bloodshed. *Perfect*, she thought, *this is exactly the stuff we should be doing.* She walked up to Chabot and gave him a hug and kiss, "You are amazing...a God-send to us." To Chabot, Celine's admiration was more rewarding that a five-minute standing ovation from the whole group.

Celine and Remi were still stimulated and amused at Gasper's creativity, as they got back to the cottage and climbed into bed. Tomorrow they would resurrect the Tristan and plan the most destructive sabotage operation against a German military convoy ever carried out by a citizen-organized Resistance cell.

CHAPTER 34

Through their interaction with Andreas Nussbaum, the Tristan had secured enough German infantry uniforms for Celine, Remi, Felicien and Amaury. The problem was, in order to use Gasper's destructive inventions, they would have to infiltrate into the heart of the German supply depot at Chambéry while the convoy was being prepared to move out. Four mid-twenties French-speaking terrorists would never pull that off, regardless of the authenticity of their uniforms. They needed an authority figure—one who spoke fluent German. All eyes turned toward Chabot.

"No, no, you can't be serious," he protested. "No, really, I'm 57 years old."

"All the better," encouraged Remi. "We want to pass you off at least as a full Colonel—better yet, a General...and young men don't hold high rank."

"But, I'm Jewish!"

"So?"

"Not only that, I'm a coward. What if they recognize that I'm a cowardly Jew?"

They all started laughing. "I thought you said there was no such thing as looking like a religious belief," Celine teased the distraught professor. Chabot drooped down in his chair, his head hanging, chin almost touching the table. They had him and he could see no way out. It was one thing to be the invisible voice behind the black curtain in the cave with all these armed young "Turks" standing by your side to protect you. Facing German soldiers—possibly even German officers in the middle of the Chambéry supply depot and pulling off an act of being one of them...well, that was another story altogether. He sat slump-shouldered with his hands folded in his lap brooding his predicament.

"You can do it," Felicien piped up. "Colonel Nussbaum said you speak German better than most Germans. And, besides, we'll all be there to protect you. Celine can beat up anybody—two, three men at a time. I've seen her do it; she'll beat hell out of anybody who gives you any lip. If anybody gives you problems you come tell me, he laughed. "I'll run and get her and she'll beat the crap out of them."

Chabot looked up meekly, "It *would* be kind of fun to see some of my toys put into play, and be right there when it was taking place." The *friends* sat calmly waiting for him to finish convincing himself. "I suppose it really *is* the only way for us to get into the depot.

"You know, I really can't run very fast. We'll have to plan things so there's no running or jumping, of course."

"Well?" Remi queried.

"Yes, if that can be done, I mean getting in and getting back out with no running or jumping, then I think I can do it," he finally concluded. He looked over at Remi, his expression becoming serious, "I think we had better get a least a General's rank uniform. Yes, *at least* a General," he nodded in self-satisfaction.

It was the natty customized uniform of the recently deceased Gestapo Lieutenant-General Helmfried Schulmann that was fitted out for Gasper. After General Schulmann was embalmed, Colonel Nussbaum ordered the casket sealed for its return trip to Germany for burial. As soon as Remi heard the casket would not be opened, he got together with Treaire's funeral director, removed the uniform, and had Schulmann shipped home in his skivvies. Schulmann's sister had passed away, so the family consisted only of an older brother who, quite frankly, didn't really care for his pompous sibling, and ordered the casket buried in the family plot immediately upon its arrival. He did not attend the burial and did not even purchase a headstone, so the once self-aggrandizing, eminently powerful General Helmfried Schulmann now lay molding in his grave—nameless, forgotten, and regally festooned in green-and-blue-striped boxer shorts.

Treaire's Jewish tailor let out the General's jacket and pants a lot for Chabot. He did a masterful job, making Schulmann's trim-fitted uniform fit the egg-shaped professor as if it had been custom made. They also replaced Schulmann's sterling silver buttons with Gestapo standard-issue black, and subdued other customizations Schulmann had made. No sense in calling unnecessary attention to Chabot's charade.

Gasper looked resplendent in the uniform. His gray temples showed just below the black band of his SS visor, lending emphases to the hat's silver piping, skull and Third Reich insignia and giving the perfect impression of experienced authority. He stood before a full-length mirror for hours in the uniform, practicing various stern scowls he felt would be necessary to fulfill his role as a strong, demanding Gestapo officer.

***

According to the continued radio communiqués, the convoy being assembled at Chambéry supply depot was huge—over 100 trucks, 18 tanks, 7 heavy artillery pieces, 13 tracked vehicles, and tons of ammunition, along with a thousand troops. With the approval of the supplies being sent to Italy, the German Italian command began planning a major offensive against the Allies.

At the moment, the Allies in Italy were suffering a setback as a particularly troublesome flu strain swept through their troops. The majority of the German army was not coming down with it. Allied doctors chalked it up to the fact the Germans had been in the area for a longer period of time and perhaps had become more resistant to whatever strain was laying their troops low.

German field officers were using the break in Allied pressure to build up their defensive positions and prepare for the offensive while the enemy was in this temporarily weakened position.

A radio message indicated the convoy was scheduled to move out in two days. The two-day delay was due to the inclusion of a massive railcar cannon Berlin was insisting accompany the convoy. The gun was so large it was built on its own set of railcar wheels. Although not the largest cannon in the German arsenal, this monster was capable of hurling a three-ton explosive shell a distance of five miles. German commanders in Italy kept insisting the gun was useless in the defense of Italy, imploring the high command not to delay the convoy, but Berlin would not compromise, insisting the immense weapon be part of the shipment. German engineers knew it would fit through the Saint Laurnee tunnel, but were waiting to complete their calculations to assure themselves the trestle leading into the tunnel was capable of supporting the weapon's weight.

Felicien was manning the radio receiver the afternoon approval for the rail cannon's shipment came through. The convoy would begin pulling out of Chambéry at 9 am the next morning. All was ready and the Tristan swung into action.

They arrived at the Chambéry staging depot in a stolen Kübelwagen field car at 10 pm that evening in the midst of bustling activity throughout the depot. The entire supply yard was abuzz, fully lit under the yard lights, soldiers and officers feverishly scurrying among the various pieces of equipment to ready everything for the trip south. Amaury was driving as they pulled up to the depot entrance gate. Chabot, radiant in his Gestapo General's uniform, sat stiffly to his right. The remaining *friends* in the rear seat hunched over in their Private's uniforms, trying to look as inconspicuous as possible.

Two guards holding machine guns stood in front of the vehicle and a third emerged from the guard house and approached Amaury. The young guard's face, bored with his duty, sneered, "The sign says to have your papers ready for inspection." Amaury reached into his jacket pocket, fumbling for the forged paperwork.

Chabot leaned across Amaury, exposing his uniform and rank. He read the name tag on the guard's uniform, "I can appreciate your boredom with this duty assignment, Private Brunner, but your job is necessary to assure the protection of this convoy. You are the only safeguard against sabotage by Allied agents or French terrorists. Your attention to your responsibilities is necessary to the success of this mission and to the success of Germany, *so look sharp!*"

The guard sprang to attention, "Yes, Sir, Herr General." He took the papers from Amaury. "Pardon, Herr General, these papers do not authorize entrance to the yard. I must request you go to headquarters and secure..."

Chabot burst from car, interrupting the guard in mid-sentence, "Do you recognize this uniform, young man?" he demanded.

"Yes, Sir," the private shot back, "a General's uniform."

Chabot rolled his eyes, conveying obvious disgust. "What branch of service, *Private?*"

"Gestapo, Herr General," the Private mumbled, growing nervous about where this line of questioning might be leading.

"Good, good, Private Brunner, very good, indeed. And do you know that the primary duty of the Gestapo is to check up on all of the other branches of the military to assure they are doing what they are supposed to be doing?"

The young guard was confused. "No, Sir. I did not know that, Sir."

Chabot shouted at the baffled soldier, "Well, it *is!*" He then lowered his voice, "And the only way we can accomplish that assignment is if we are able to arrive unannounced and do our inspections spontaneously. Now, *open that gate*, soldier, or I will go to headquarters and demand you be reprimanded for standing in the way of a Gestapo General and his inspection staff," Chabot growled with more authority in his voice than any of the *friends* had ever heard.

Private Brunner gave a stiff, "Heil Hitler," turned toward his cohorts, and authorized passage for Gestapo General "Schulmann" and his staff. The two followed Brunner's lead, snapping off crisp Heil Hitlers as the gate slid back, allowing the *friends* and their powerful Gestapo commander access to the largest buildup of German equipment ever assembled in Chambéry.

The flurry of activity charged the air with excited electricity. Troops raced about, readying equipment. Officers shouted commands while soldiers scurried hither and yon in compliance. The *friends* melted into the confusion, hastily going about their business under the shouts of Chabot's yelling commands that added to the general confusion. Over the next three hours they squirted solvent into tires, fuel thickener into fuel tanks, and Chabot's magnificent rust-producing concoction into every piece of artillery they could find.

After two hours they were ready to move on to the supply buildings. Things had quieted considerably, most of the activity in the assembly yard reaching completion. Remi whispered, "Let's get a move on. Things are slowing down. We're going to become a lot more visible."

Felicien quickly picked the locks, opening the supply room doors. The yard lights blazing in through the windows dimly lit racks of new boots, stacks of socks, and bales of underwear—all of which got a liberal dose of Boot Pepper. Celine wasn't sure if Boot Pepper would work in underwear but thought, *What the hell. We have buckets of the stuff and it probably won't hurt to test it on other applications.* She couldn't help but smile, envisioning hundreds of good-looking young German soldiers desperately ripping off their pants and dancing around naked from the waist down, trying to cool their burning body parts.

Finally satisfied they had done their damage, the Tristan exited the same gate through which they had entered. A different set of guards snapped to attention as Chabot exited the car and spoke a few words to the man in charge; the gate slid open.

They drove farm roads back to Treaire to assure no undesirable run-ins with German patrols. As they bounced along the dirt roads they got to laughing so hard about Chabot's charade and their destructive foray that Amaury had to demand they settle a bit so he could maintain control of the vehicle. They parked the Kübelwagen in the basement of the mill, covered it with a tarp and carefully stowed their uniforms. Once again, the Tristan faded into the camouflage of being just common French citizens.

—∞∞∞—

Around 10 am the following morning, while the *friends* and Gasper were still sleeping off the exhaustion of their evening's activities, five miles north of Treaire, problems began developing with the massive convoy rolling toward Falauge. Without warning, the front left tire on the lead staff car experienced a blowout. The driver's quick response brought the car to a safe stop alongside the road. As the senior officer stepped from the impaired vehicle, its right rear tire hissed, slowly giving up its air. The troop truck following the staff car pulled off the road behind it as two of its tires went flat, and a powerful Tiger tank inexplicably stalled in the middle of the road a quarter of a mile back. At almost the same moment, another tank experienced engine failure, immediately followed by three more.

Try as they might, and in spite of frustrated officers shouting at them, the tank drivers could not get their vehicles restarted. Trucks, half-tracks, Kübelwagens, and motorcycles all up and down the line began experiencing engine trouble while their tires hissed air, settling their loads gently on their wheels' steel rims.

All of a sudden, as if in preplanned unison, hundreds of soldiers riding in the troop trucks began screaming. They jumped from the trucks, shedding their newly issued boots as fast as they could pull them off. To their relief, as soon as they removed the boots, the burning sensation subsided. Many also started pulling off their socks, pants, and undershorts, jumping around in the road and holding their crotches. Officers, too, were leaping from their seats of dignified authority, joining the Privates in the highway striptease. Boots, socks, pants, and underwear flew everywhere as hundreds of men continued their roadside dance, naked from the waist down. The few vehicles still running sat on flat tires; every tank had stalled, filling the highway connecting Chambéry and Falauge to the point of impassibility.

Amaury had ordered one of his trucks to leave for Chambéry at sunrise that morning to pick up supplies for the Bistro. The truck returned some two hours late that afternoon due to a forced detour on to some very marginal farm roads. The driver had found the main Chambéry-to-Treaire highway closed by German guards, who, despite questioning, would not divulge the reason for the road's closure.

CHAPTER 35

Thirty-seven troop trucks, 40 half-tracks, 16 field cars, 20 heavy cannon, eight Panther tanks, 10 Tiger tanks, and 52 tons of ammunition came to a halt in the middle of the Chambéry-Treaire highway that day. Additionally, 802 pairs of boots, 736 pairs of undershorts, and 622 pairs of socks became mysteriously unwearable. Closer examination of the heavy artillery pieces found that 14 of them encrusted with such an extensive buildup of rust in their barrels they were unusable. Two hundred and twenty-two tires were destroyed and 111 gas tanks and fuel systems were filled with an unknown sticky substance. Clearing the equipment from the highway took over two weeks. Once hauled back to the Chambéry depot, the majority of it was permanently scrapped. While the rail-mounted cannon did make it to Italy, the German crew setting it up was overrun by American forces who captured and destroyed the massive gun.

The destruction of the convoy marked a disaster for Nazi forces in Italy—perhaps one of the key events that substantially accelerated the Allies' liberation of Rome. With the occupation of that city, and their bout with the flu behind them, the British, Canadians and Americans relentlessly pounded the Nazis as they retreated north toward the Italian Alps. Their one hope being a rapid escape through the Saint Laurnee Passage into France.

Two days after the convoy disaster, an emergency meeting took place at Nazi headquarters in Chambéry. It was attended by senior officers, including the highly respected General Josef Dietrich from Paris and Italy's celebrated Field Marshal, Albert Kesselring. Colonel Auchenbach was also ordered to attend that meeting. The conclusion was that either the Allies had inserted a Special Forces unit into the area, or, worse, a very sophisticated group of French Resistance—perhaps even the hated Tristan—was alive and reactivated.

Due to the highly complex chemicals that had been used to disable the convoy, the theory that a local Resistance group could have pulled off the attack was seriously in doubt. It was concluded the Allies had somehow gotten one of their sabotage teams into the area. The plaguing question was: just how they had been able to get in, get their chemicals into the convoy vehicles, and get back out again totally undetected?

The guard teams who had manned the entrance gate at Chambéry depot were grilled for hours, yet no one could (or would) remember any suspect group that approached the entrance. Soldiers and officers involved in the preparation of the vehicles for convoy were also questioned, with no recollection of witnessing any unusual activity.

Having read previous reports on the damage done by the Tristan several years before, Field Marshal Kesselring fumed, "This is the same crap we confronted in this area years ago, when Reichsmarschall Göring replaced Franz Fettler as Commandant of the French Southern District with *you*, General Hofstetter—the *exact* same crap. Hit Chambéry depot and disappear without a trace. I stake my reputation this so-called Tristan bunch are behind this. What the hell is going on, Hofstetter? You were sent here by Göring to rid the area of this menace."

An icy chill shot through Horst Hofstetter. He had dreaded the possibility of this moment ever since Göring selected him to replace General Fettler. Now the bomb of accusation had just landed squarely in his lap.

He looked into Kesselring's angry eyes, "General Fettler was relieved because he failed to find the so-called Tristan Resistance fighters. Upon arriving at Chambéry, I thoroughly investigated this band of rebels. I found them within four weeks of taking command. Through the Treaire Malice unit we infiltrated their organization, killed at least three of their operatives and have heard nothing of them for the past 20 months. I seriously doubt, General Kesselring, that group has mustered the strength to reunite.

"We are ever vigilant of Resistance activities in the Southern District," he glared at Kesselring, "We have had no indication of such activity in the immediate area surrounding Chambéry and Falauge since the desertion of Colonel

Nussbaum. The few incidents that took place during his command at Falauge were the work of amateurs.

"I also remind you, General, the reports coming back from our chemists indicate extremely advanced chemical compounds were used in disabling the convoy. Not only were they complex in their chemical makeup, but all possessed an element that gave them ability to delay their activation states for hours. The only delayed-action chemicals we know of are used in the rubber industry in the vulcanization of tires. The chemical structure of what our chemists believe is this delay agent is nothing like that used in the manufacture of tires. No one has ever seen such chemical designs.

"The Tristan I destroyed 20 months ago did not come close to this level of sophistication. No, General, this is the work of a nationally backed sabotage effort. Mark my words, the Americans are behind this. They're the only country possessing chemical factories capable of producing compounds of this complexity."

Kesselring leaned toward Hofstetter, "Then, how in the name of Christ did the Americans get in, do their destruction, and get the hell out without so much as a trace of evidence? I'm telling you, Hofstetter, there is a snake in your woodpile...a very dangerous snake. And if you do not find and kill it soon, it will strike you down."

Hofstetter came nose to nose, with the powerful Kesselring, "If *you* were not being pushed around like a bunch of schoolgirls by the Allies in Italy, Herr Kesselring, we would not have had to go to the expense of assembling one of the most costly convoys in the history of the war." The room crackled with tension. Other than the Führer himself, no one took the liberty to speak to Albert Kesselring in such a confrontational tone.

Kesselring sighed wearily, settling back in his chair, "I resent your accusations and your tone, Hofstetter, but tensions are running high just now. We are terribly outnumbered and the Allies have an endless supply of men and materials flowing into Italy daily. You are probably right. No group of citizen Resistance fighters would have the ability to wreak the destruction that was done to the convoy. Regardless of the source, the damage has been devastating to our efforts in Italy."

The meeting broke up with no definite conclusions. It was decided guard units would be beefed up in both Chambéry and Falauge. Several different assembly points would also be used to put together future convoys. To say the least, the attendees left perplexed and frustrated.

CHAPTER 36

As Colonel Auchenbach's train rolled back toward Falauge, he couldn't shake the intensity of Kesselring's accusations that the old nemesis, Tristan, might be alive and well. Leaving the meeting with no plan of action gnawed at him. *There has to be a logical explanation. This type of mass destruction just doesn't evolve out of thin air. And once done, the perpetrators do not vanish into thin air.* It flew in the face of logic that somehow an Allied sabotage team—especially the boisterous, clumsy Americans—had miraculously slipped in, then vanished without a trace. *It had to be a local group,* he thought. As the train pulled into the Falauge yard, he determined he was going to get to the bottom of the dilemma. *Those responsible will pay in bleeding agony.*

He went directly to his office and opened the outdated report on the Tristan that had been reviewed at the meeting. It was the only report he had found in the files— frustratingly lacking in detail. In preparation for the meeting, he had searched every file in the Falauge headquarters in hopes of finding something, anything, on local Resistance activity. He had found nothing except the inadequate information he held in his hand.

The file had been produced by the Malice office in Grenoble, offering sketchy information on a small Resistance group that was thought to operate under the code name "Tristan". It speculated the group was centered either in Treaire, Albertville, or Grenoble—then, almost as an afterthought, it added Voiron as another possible location. There was no information as to the group's size, its membership...not even a description of any activities the group had successfully been involved in. There was one entry of note:

4 July, 1942 – Treaire Milice report of assassinating Damian Descoteaux, male, age 22 or 23, for suspicion of being linked to a Resistance movement operating in the area. Assassination carried out at night and body left in demonstrative manner intended to send a message to the local citizens that Resistance activities will not be tolerated. Information received at Grenoble Milice office – 5 July, 1942 – 14:27 hours by courier from Treaire Malice office.

The file ended with a September entry:

16 September, 1942 – Colonel Jacques Madure, commanding officer, and two high-ranking members of the Treaire Milice office have been reported missing. General Hofstetter, Commandant of the French Southern District, ordered the Milice office in Treaire closed, transferring its responsibilities to the Grenoble Milice operations center in Grenoble.

There have been no Resistance activities in the Grenoble / Chambéry / Falauge operational area since the assassination of Damian Descoteaux. It is assumed he was the ringleader of a small Resistance cell that has now become inactive.

Auchenbach threw the report on his desk, scattering its few pages. *This information is crap. Typical French Milice slovenly crap. Nothing but conjecture.* He sat, staring at the wall, feeling his anger starting to rumble in his stomach. He took two gulps of Kaopectate, waited for the thick minty liquid to settle the rage beginning in his bowels, then left.

On the drive to Treaire he determined he would, once again, dig through every file in Falauge. *There's got to be something more than the file we've got,* he thought. *Christ, the Treaire Milice assassinated a bastard they thought was with the Resistance. Nussbaum was in command of Falauge at the time. He must have known something.* He parked in front of the inn and sat in the vehicle, its engine running as his lightning-quick mind worked incessantly. The longer he dwelled on the destroyed convoy, the angrier he grew. Light pain shot through his delicate stomach. He forced himself to calm, gulped another swig of Kaopectate and went to his room for the evening without eating.

Files were stacked everywhere. All file cabinets in the Falauge administration had been emptied. Aides frantically searched every nook and cranny of the garrison headquarters, then were sent into the culled-file storage areas in the basement to spend hours scanning hundreds of pages of data. Auchenbach demanded every sheet in every existing file be reviewed—whether the file had anything to do with rebel activities or not. There had to be something somewhere that would offer a starting point at digging into the past of this terrorist organization. Nothing came to light. Auchenbach was livid!

He made a trip to Chambéry with two aides to search through the archives there. He did not often work side by side with underlings, but this was different. In the dim lights of the Chambéry archives, they found it. Not exactly what Auchenbach wanted because of the file's sketchiness, but sufficient to give his search for the Tristan a starting point. The Milice file, dated 27 May, 1942, that his aide handed him stated:

> *We have successfully penetrated the Tristan Resistance group of Treaire with Maximilien Dulac's acceptance into the group on 2 April, 1942. Dulac is not suspected by members of the Tristan since he has been a long-time acquaintance of this group of Treaire citizens.*
>
> *Dulac is a reluctant spy. He is working under the threat to the safety of his sister. To date, his information has been of marginal use. He has identified Remi Rousseau as the leader of the group and Celine Duval-Rousseau (Remi Rousseau's wife) as his assistant. Other members of the group have not been identified at this date.*
>
> *We have expanded the threat to the rest of Dulac's family, and recently have physically beaten his younger brother (26 May, 1942) as proof of our willingness to carry out our threats.*
>
> *Improved results expected in light of beating of Dulac's brother.*
>
> *Signed, Colonel Jacques Madure*
> *Treaire Milice Unit T16d*
> *27/05/42 - 15:26gmt*

CHAPTER 37

It fell to Maurice Pippen, the owner of the waterworks that employed Remi, to serve as the starting point of the Colonel's search for the Tristan. The 58-year-old Pippen had to be shaken back into consciousness when Wilhelm Auchenbach entered the small, sweaty room in the basement of the Falauge town hall, which now was used for interrogation of suspect citizens. Auchenbach scowled at the bloody pulp tied to the chair, then turned toward the interrogator, "Has he opened up?"

"I do not think he knows, Herr Colonel. He is convinced Remi Rousseau has left the area. Insists he now resides somewhere in Paris, tending to a dying relative."

"Do you believe him?"

"Why else would he undergo such pain? In the beginning, he said he was upset with Rousseau for backing out of an agreement to purchase his waterworks. I see no reason for him to protect the man."

"Have you permanently injured him?"

The interrogator shrugged, "Who knows? He is old. He will need medical treatment, mein Herr, but I believe he will recover. Perhaps his eyesight has been somewhat damaged."

Auchenbach bent low, pulling up Pippen's puffy eyelids, and stared into the blankness of the man's bloodshot eyes. "Get him treatment. Tell the doctor to give him whatever is necessary for his recovery, then send him back to Treaire. Be sure he is sent back while his bruises and swelling are still showing. He will be a good example to the rest of those snail-eaters that I mean to find this Remi Rousseau, and that no one will stand in my way."

A snappy, "Jawohl, mein Herr," met Auchenbach's back as he exited. As Auchenbach moved into the hallway, a crippling pain surged through his gut. He steadied himself against the wall, knowing it would pass. Then another immense cramp shot through, almost causing him to double over. *Damn this stomach.* He yanked the Kaopectate from his pocket, continuing to curse the affliction. He stood, sweating, leaning against the wall, waiting for the seizure to pass. Finally able to carry on, he slowly moved down the dim corridor, weakly sliding against the slick wall. *Damn you, Remi Rousseau. You are my pain. I will destroy you and your whore wife. You bastards will pay for this,* he snarled to himself.

———

Local reports filtering back to the Tristan were disturbing. Evidence of Colonel Auchenbach's rage was everywhere. Maurice Pippen had been sent back from Falauge in a wheelchair and it was doubtful he would ever recover from his torture-inflicted vertigo. Jewish curfew was tightened allowing them on the streets only four hours a day. Non-Jewish citizens experienced intensely abusive shakedowns from street patrols—several were beaten to their knees in the streets in full public view. Women and teenaged girls were particularly harassed by the patrols, who vulgarly threatened them with sexual abuse. Everyone was questioned about Remi Rousseau and Celine Duval.

"It is only a matter of time before we are found out. The bastard is relentless. No one is immune to his tactics." Remi's nerves were raw with the news that swirled with increasing intensity.

"So he can prove you are the head of the Tristan. So what?" Amaury countered. "You went underground over six weeks ago and apparently your story to Maurice Pippen about moving to Paris held up even under torture. No one knows where you and Celine are. The patrol he sent to find Chabot got irritated that Chabot escaped, and they burned every building on his property to the ground. The idiots burned up any stray evidence we may have left behind at his place. And they don't have a clue about Felicien and me. It's hard to believe, but I think Auchenbach believes the only thing I own is the Bistro. Usually, the Germans are up on everyone of means, but I've become convinced he is totally in the dark as to the château and the estate."

Remi looked up at Amaury, taking some encouragement from him. "Do everything you can to keep it that way. We sure as hell don't need that bunch from Falauge poking around the estate. I'm still worried. It's just a matter of time before those bastards find us. Hell, we're all holed-up just a few miles from town on one of the biggest estates in France."

Amaury shrugged off Remi's concerns, "Nobody remembers the Cheever estate, Remi. None of the buildings are visible from the highway or the railroad tracks that pass through the back of the property. My parents were bent on having everybody for miles around forget we had money. As soon as Grandpa got senile, they stopped hosting the annual Marquee de Cheever birthday celebration at the Bistro. The last one was in 1920—over 24 years ago. That was the last year dear old Gramps could remember who he was...and he was the one who kept that party going."

Amaury smiled, recalling the final birthday celebration and his Grandpa whom he liked. "It was at that last birthday celebration that Grandpa stumbled off the Bistro patio and slammed into big old Madame Bouffeau, pushing her into the horse trough that used to sit there on the street.

"Remember her? Madame Bouffeau? Always sticking her nose into everyone's business. Even my stiff-necked father used to laugh about her thrashing around in the horse trough, cussing old Gramps. Truth is, Grandpa was probably too drunk to realize what had happened."

Dropping his humor, "Gramps got bad that year. Got to the point he couldn't even remember his own name—poor old soul. Finally gave Mother the excuse to shunt him off into the south wing. She never liked the old man, and she sure as hell didn't care for the annual Marquee's birthday celebration—having to mingling with all those smelly townsfolk. From that time on, Mother and Dad holed up right here and accelerated their goal of drinking themselves to death.

"They wanted people to forget we had money. Loved the riches but, for some perplexing reason, were ashamed of our wealth. They did everything they could to hide it—actually did everything they could to become invisible. That's why they had the huge front gate out at the highway replaced with a common farm gate...to hide the fact this was an estate.

"Maybe that's why the Germans seem totally unaware of me and this place. Most of the old folks who remember the wonderful extravagance of Grandpa are dead. The only local people who know about all of this are my workers and their families, and they've all lived out here so long most townspeople don't even know them.

"Hell, Remi, I was talking with our winery superintendent last year and he told me he hadn't left the property in the past five years.

"Take heart, my friend. We're invisible out here thanks to the paranoia of dear old Mom and Dad. To the outside world, this place doesn't exist."

"I pray you're right, Amaury," Remi's cautious nature not allowing him to completely relax, despite Amaury's reassurances.

"Invisible or not, we've got to stop Auchenbach," Celine interrupted. "Maurice Pippen will never totally recover from the beating he took for us. Auchenbach is on the verge of killing people. Probably publicly killing them just to prove how much danger everyone is in if we're not found."

Celine was crushed by the brutality inflected on Maurice Pippen. She adored him and his wife. Kind people, honest and caring. She and Remi had been to their home numerous times. They were a wonderful, loving couple. Now Maurice had been beaten senseless—all because of the Tristan; because of her and Remi. She couldn't shake the deep emotions she felt about that.

"But how?" Felicien's look of hopelessness visible through his cigarette smoke. "How in hell are we going to stop Auchenbach? He controls everything. His patrols are everywhere."

"Not only that," Amaury cautioned, "the man is evil. I've never confronted living evilness before, but I have looked into his eyes and I'm telling you evil truly resides within the man."

"Then we'll kill the bastard." Celine shot back. "I can do it just like I killed General Schulmann," her tone sharp in its frustration.

"Cel, I feel as badly about Mr. Pippen as you," Remi said, "but killing Auchenbach, no matter how we do it, will bring the entire Chambéry command down on us. The Nazis already suspect a Resistance cell is operative in this area. The loss of another of their officers from Falauge on top of Nussbaum going missing and Schulmann dying of a heart attack here in Treaire is going to raise a lot of questions about what's going on here. They're certainly not going to believe another one of their officers just keeled over of a heart attack. Auchenbach is too young and healthy for that."

"Then let's attack the garrison at Falauge and kill Auchenbach as part of the package." Celine forged ahead. "We don't have to take on the entire garrison at once…just pick away at them. Sniper-shoot them one at a time. Scare the hell out of them—and make sure Auchenbach catches one of the bullets."

That's going to bring them down on us faster than just killing Auchenbach," Felicien said.

Celine was not conciliatory. She was sick of being reasonable. The years of anger and frustration bottled up inside of her boiled over at the treatment of Maurice Pippen. "They're beating our citizens," she persisted. "They've set in motion plans to export our Jewish population. Christ, they're not going to send them to labor camps. They're going to ship them off to *death* camps…every one of them—men, women and children—strip them naked, line them up and march them into gas chambers.

"I told you when I returned from training that if we could avoid killing the enemy, we should, because our own citizens might become terrified of us. But now the Germans are beating and threatening to kill those citizens. The Nazi devils have changed the situation. Sympathy will be with us. Any actions we take against the Germans now will be supported by the townspeople. Some of the braver ones may even stand and fight with us. It's time to fight the bastards—fight them to the death, if necessary," Celine's passion flashed in her eyes.

No one spoke. The group sat, absorbing her frustration and rage. There was no eye contact between them as they wrestled with the relentlessness and violence of her recommendation. She was advocating all-out war. War against the entire garrison—killing their soldiers, disrupting their every activity…and doing so in such a way as to inflict as much terror into their environment as possible. There was no doubt the Germans would not stand for such an assault. Yes, they could kill Auchenbach and probably a good number of the garrison's soldiers and officers, but they would bring the wrath of hell down upon everyone.

Remi knew in his heart the time had come to launch the offensive Celine described, but he also knew they could not survive such an attack. Searching for even a flash of hope, an idea that might spare them such an assault, he looked at Felicien. "Have radio messages given any new reports on the British and

American advances in Italy? Is there any hope of them breaking through into France any time soon?"

"The Germans seriously needed that equipment we sabotaged. They are being pushed back daily now—almost to the Alps. Messages from field commanders keep saying they do not think they can hold the line; return messages from Paris and Chambéry tell them to fight to the death."

"Fight to the death," Remi repeated, startled. "Are you saying their commanders are telling them to fight until every last man is killed?"

"Paris command claims those orders are coming directly from Berlin, directly from Adolf Hitler. They are to fire on their own troops if they retreat."

"Dear God," Remi grimaced. "Children soldiers, shoot those who retreat, fight to the death, kill the Jews. What in hell is the world coming to?"

Celine had calmed a bit. She looked over at Remi, saw the deep concern in his eyes and felt his turmoil of not knowing what to do. As she reached out and placed her hand on his arm, he looked at her.

"Remi, the Allies will beat the Germans back in Italy. The question is how long it will take."

Turning her attention to the whole group, "My outburst was my own frustrations coming out. I apologize for that. I know attacking the garrison is assured destruction, but perhaps we can still take some action. What can we do to get all of the Jews to leave the area—all of them, quickly, quietly? It would shock Auchenbach. Maybe stagger him a bit. But if we could pull it off, we assure they won't be sent to the death camps, and we put Auchenbach in a position where he is made to look inept in carrying out his orders to gather up all the Jews."

"All the Jews?" Felicien questioned. "How many are there?"

"One hundred and twenty-nine," Chabot answered. "Nureet Suchet had her baby. But prepare yourselves. They can be a stubborn bunch."

CHAPTER 38

While Gasper continued producing his wonderful array of destructive innovations, the *friends* divided into teams. Remi and Celine making up one; Felicien and Amaury the second. With Gasper's help, they determined the location of all Jews in the area. Twelve families were in Treaire, eight families in Falauge, five rural families west of Falauge and six farming in the area immediately surrounding Treaire. Over the next several days they visited every Jewish family informing them of the impending dangers and imploring them to leave the area immediately.

Gasper's assessment of the stubbornness they would encounter was not understated. The *friends* showed them copies of radio messages ordering the garrison to round them up and ready them for transportation to work camps. The teams pointed out the so called work camps were most likely death camps relating stories of the horror taking place in other parts of France, Holland, Germany and Poland. The Jews politely listened, thanked them for their concern, and stayed put.

The following week the Tristan teams went back again virtually begging the people they visited to run for safety—repeating their warnings of forced labor camps leading to impending extermination. Having lived through three years of German occupation with no repercussions the local Jews just could not bring themselves to accept the realities of what they were being told.

Surely, the Germans do not mean to kill every Jew in Europe, they protested. *No one in their right mind could even conceive of such a thing. We pose no threat to the Germans. They have had a garrison at Falauge since 1940, over three years now, and aside from implementing their curfew and these silly yellow badges they have not bothered us.*

Besides, if we leave, where will we go? How will we survive? The food and clothing we can carry is only enough to keep us for a week. Where will we live? We have little children—and the elderly, what about the elderly? Surely, they will not demand we leave for a labor camp. The children are too young to work in labor camps.

Frustrated, the Tristan sat in the mill late in the evening. Felicien complained, "We got nowhere. They are so used to Nussbaum's lackadaisical attitude they cannot be convinced it will be any different under Auchenbach."

Amaury added, "One of them said that if the Germans were going to do anything against the Jews they would have done it long before now. They just don't believe anything drastic is going to happen."

"It's the women who are resisting," Celine stated. "I am convinced of it. I see it in their eyes and I see the men's resigned willingness to accept their wife's hesitations. The women cannot see how their families will survive with no place to live, no source of food and shelter.

"The women are petrified about tearing up their families, dragging them off without any means of providing for them. No food or shelter. No secure destination—it's terrifying to them."

"What makes you so sure of that?" Amaury probed.

"Because it is exactly how I would feel. Especially if I had small children or Remi and I were caring for old people. So far they have not been threatened by the Nazis and the thought of tearing up their homes with no real plan of where they are going is untenable."

"If you're right, Celine," Amaury thoughtfully spoke, "If providing them a destination, a roof over their heads and the ability to feed and keep their families together is the hesitation we may be able to fix that.

"There are only 129 of them. There are livestock barns at several locations on the estate. They would need cleaning out and some patching up to accommodate people, but they could easily hold that number. The barns are not visible from the highway or the tracks. If we could get them to move in, I'm confident we can keep them hidden."

That night, the Tristan laid a plan to house all 129 Jews at the Cheever estate. Amaury's trucks began stockpiling supplies. He started sending two trucks a day, rather than just one, to his black-market restaurant suppliers. He had supplied the Germans with bribe money to keep the Bistro well stocked. Now, the fruits of that bribe money would be used to feed their hated Jews.

The trucks were a common sight on the highway and went about their business uninterrupted by the Germans. Two barns located in an isolated area on the far backside of the estate were cleaned out and fitted with crude bunks and wood-fired stoves. The supply trucks drove discreetly onto the estate via back roads. Once again, the Tristan made the rounds to the Jewish families to spread the good news. They were shocked. The resistance continued.

It was the clumsiness of garrison soldiers from Falauge that finally changed their attitude. The garrison cook dispatched a team of four soldiers and an officer to confiscate two cows from the countryside. Occasional garrison theft of local livestock had occurred since the Germans had arrived. Previously, the thefts had been carried out without incidence—livestock stolen out of sight of their owners, resulting in nothing more than the vain protests of the farmers whose livestock had been appropriated.

This day was different.

Rolling down a country lane, the officer spotted two cows contentedly grazing on the farm of Isaac Zeldmeyer, the fifth generation of Jews to operate the small cheese making farm. In spite of the fact these cows happened to be grazing close to the milking barn the impatient officer decided to proceed with the theft. When Isaac ran from the barn and yelled as his cows were being led toward the German truck, a startled soldier shot him. The shot alarmed Isaac's wife and daughters, who rushed from the house in horror. They, too, were dropped dead in a volley of machine-gun fire coming from two nervous soldiers before the officer could get control of them. The Germans panicked, racing off and leaving the Zeldmeyer family's bodies where they fell.

A neighbor witnessed the horror from a nearby wood lot, and details of the cold-blooded murders spread in a matter of hours. Amaury was contacted at the Bistro that evening that the Jewish community was ready to evacuate into hiding. The exodus took place over a period of 36 hours, quietly and furtively.

The rapid disappearance of all of the Jews in the area was the first solid proof Colonel Auchenbach had that the local Resistance was once again active. He had not been surprised when he learned that several families, including the reclusive Doctor Chabot, had left the area, but learning that every Jew had vanished virtually overnight, left no doubt that such a mass migration implemented with such speed was the result of a highly organized effort.

Just the previous week he had reported to Chambéry command that he had set the date round up and transport the Jews to their assigned labor camps. Now having to report that he had lost track of all of them propelled a powerful surge of convulsive pain ripping through his gut and sent send him racing for his stomach-soothing pink drink.

That evening, dining in the Bistro, Auchenbach called Amaury to his table. "An interesting development has taken place in the area, Monsieur Cheever, and I was wondering if you could shed some light on it?"

"But, of course, mein Herr," Amaury smiled, bending low in compliant respect. "How may I be of assistance?"

"It seems every Jew in the area—men, women and children—all of them have vanished. One day they were among us, the next they were gone. Have you heard anything, Monsieur Cheever, concerning this abrupt disappearance of our local Jews?"

Amaury pulled up straight in shocked disbelief, "I have not, mein Herr. Every Jew...*all* of them?"

"Yes, just as I said, *all* of them," irritation was evident in Auchenbach's voice at having to repeat himself to this stupid French restaurant owner.

Amaury bent close to the Colonel's ear and whispered, "Good riddance, I say, Herr Colonel. While I wish it would not have taken our country being conquered to rid us of the scourge of the Jews, I applaud Germany in this respect. I have always been disgusted by the Jewish pigs, and now, thanks to you, they have run off into the rat holes where they belong. Thanks to you, Herr Colonel, and thanks to your leader, Adolf Hitler," Amaury's eyes filled with satisfaction as he regained his upright position.

Colonel Auchenbach pushed back in his chair, staring critically at the restaurateur. He was convinced a man's truth could always be quickly detected in his eyes. He saw only the twinkle of sincerity emanating from his host's contented face.

"Perhaps the Colonel would accept another bottle of Pétrus Bordeaux in celebration of this cleansing event?"

Auchenbach's acid scrutiny continued. *Is this French bastard lying?* he questioned. He studied Amaury, but detected nothing but radiant satisfaction that the Jews were finally gone from Treaire. *Perhaps this Frenchman can be useful to me,* he thought, nodding. "Yes, Monsieur Cheever, a bottle of Pétrus Bordeaux is appropriate. Perhaps you would join me to share a glass?" Amaury went to the cellar for the wine, nervously repeating to himself, *I must be careful —very, very careful.*

As they conversed, Amaury's suspicion that Colonel Auchenbach was completely unaware of his wealth and property holdings was confirmed. The Colonel had no knowledge of the vast Cheever properties in the area, was shockingly unaware of the estate just two miles to the north. He had Amaury pegged as simply a small-town tavern owner. While delighted, Amaury was amazed that the Colonel hadn't done his homework concerning the citizenry he was responsible for. He spent his entire glass of Pétrus reinforcing the notion in the Colonel's mind that he was nothing more than a modest commoner of parochial intelligence. He spent his second glass reaffirming his loathing of the Jews, and his glowing support of the fascist philosophies of the Third Reich.

When he offered Auchenbach another bottle of Pétrus to take with him, the Colonel allowed him a third glass. For the next hour they chatted with Amaury enthusiastically agreeing with everything the Colonel had to say about anything. They parted, both continuing a cautious attitude toward each other, but with the hope they had instituted what possibly could become a mutually useful relationship.

CHAPTER 39

Positioned uncomfortably in the chair in front of the radio transmitter, her feet propped up on its desk, Celine was startled from her sleep-deprived doze by the warning beeps emanating from the radio's speakers. She had eased the radio truck in behind one of the cheese barns just outside the tiny six-house village of La Bérarde at 4 am, miles from Treaire. There she anxiously waited for the expected communiqué from the British.

She lunged for the receiver's switch, hitting it just as the third beep finished its last irritating resonance. Ten seconds of coded data spilled onto the printer then abruptly ended, followed by the symbol (>), indicating additional information would follow. Twelve minutes later, a second short burst, ending with the same *additional-info-to-follow* mark. *Damn it's going to be light soon,* she fretted.

Constantly monitoring the radio waves the Germans were aware a message was coming into the area but the short interrupted signals denied them the ability to pinpoint the receiver's location. Ever since Auchenbach's arrival, the Nazis had been patrolling a large area around Treaire with an observation plane, searching for the Tristan's radio transmitter. The plane would be sent aloft as soon as an unidentified radio signal was detected. Celine had parked the truck so it was not visible from the road and would be impossible to spot from the plane in the dark, but her location was exposed to aerial surveillance if she were forced to remain after daybreak.

Her first transmission, alerting the British she was ready to receive their transmissions was sent over an hour ago. Their long delayed response had used up much of the stealth of the night's darkness. Hopefully, the next transmission would complete the message's data stream. All she could do was sit and wait. Eying the first gray of dawn edging the eastern horizon, she anxiously glanced at her watch…5:33.

She chastised herself for not selecting a spot that would have better concealed the truck from the air, but talked herself out of seeking a more concealed spot fearing that if she missed any incoming transmissions while moving the truck, the entire effort would have been a waste.

The first rays of orange sun lit the tops of the taller pines. At 6:02, another data burst flowed through followed by the infuriating continue-to-sit-there-and-wait (>) symbol.

If the plane spied her, it was all over. The light weight Fieseler Fi 156 Storch observation plane had been fitted with a 50-caliber machine gun. The heavy gun compromised the maneuverability of the tiny Storch but she and the truck didn't stand a chance of surviving its fire power if she was spotted.

She cranked down the cab windows in hopes of hearing the plane if it was in the area. The brisk air felt good. The receiver lit up again at 6:10; another burst of code ending with the *more-to-follow* mark.

She stiffened. Her peripheral vision caught a movement outside. The blur quickly ducked out of sight behind the corner of the barn. She drew her pistol, jumped from the truck, and eased herself to the spot where the shadow had vanished. Carefully peered around the corner. No one. Her heart pounded. She scanned the area. Nothing—not a sound.

Pistol extended, she moved toward the barn door, cracked it open, slipped quickly inside pulling the door shut behind her. She bent low, then held motionless, listening intently as her eyes took time to adjust to the windowless barn.

Suddenly, a rustle to her right. She whirled toward the sound. A shadowy figure rushed at her. The prong of a pitchfork pierced her skin at the hip. She staggered, landing hard on her back. She groaned as the prong was ripped out of her side. The dark figure raised the implement for another thrust. She fired two rapid shots, the figure jerked back at the force of the bullets' impacts. There was no movement from the shadowy figure lying on the floor. She strained to her feet, holding the painful flesh wound in her side.

Her gun pointed at the body on the floor, she moved carefully forward and gasped in shock at what the dim light revealed. The beeping signal faintly emanated from the radio receiver. She hesitated a second, then raced to the truck. She flipped on the receiver in time to pick up the last several seconds of the transmission. The message segment finally included the symbol (...), indicating message's end.

She slumped down in the chair, pulled up her shirt and slid her slacks down to expose the wound. It was shallow, turning black and blue, but the bleeding was slowing. *Lord only knows what infectious filth might have been on that damn pitchfork.* She squeezed the area in agony, encouraging increased blood flow in hopes of cleaning the wound as best she could. She pulled herself to her feet to face the horror of what she had seen in the barn.

Leaving the barn door open, she made her way to the figure. Laying there in a pool of blood was an emaciated old man…a *very* old man. Her heart broke. She dropped to his side, took his head in her arms. "I am sorry," she whispered, tears flowing from the tragedy of a mistake that could not be reversed.

His ancient eyes slowly opened and he whispered, "Why did you come to steal my cheese?" His eyes closed again, "I would have given you the cheese if you are hungry." He sighed, looked into her eyes, and died.

The irreversible tragedies of her war torn world fell upon her with unbearable weight. She had become no better than the oppressors. She instinctively killed an old man—perhaps taken the life of his wife's only companion. Perhaps eliminated the joy of a child's grandfather. Everything in Celine gave way. Tears burst forth from agony filling her heart. She melted in excruciating sadness. Hopelessness filled her mind. There was nothing to be done—no way to correct the disaster. Her only choice was to leave the scene.

She lowered his head, gently stroked back his silver hair, painfully rose and drove back to Treaire. She cried most of the way, unable to suppress her misery. She would deal with this tragedy alone, telling no one. If she could keep her wound from Remi, she wouldn't even tell him. It was a tragedy born of the insanity of war. An incident that, if exposed, would be discouraging to her teammates, distracting to what they must focus on. The trauma of what had happened, its tragic innocence would live with her forever.

———✸———

Celine went directly to the cave. It was mid-morning when she arrived and she knew no one would be there. She needed time alone to deal with the wound. The puncture was not deep. It had penetrated through exiting on the opposite side. She searched the medical supplies kept at the cave, took several anti-bacterial liquids from the cabinet, gritted her teeth and swabbed out the wound, pushing the swab in as far as she could stand the pain. She poured alcohol into the wound and screamed aloud, knowing no one would hear.

The intensity of the burning pain was excruciating. She felt dizzy and purposely allowed herself to slump to the floor to avoid falling. It was almost noon when she opened her eyes, finding herself stiff and chilled. To her relief, the searing pain had abated to a dull throb, and there was no further bleeding. The puncture appeared almost cauterized.

Intense pain reignited with certain movements, but the constant agony was gone. *I can deal with this*, she thought. *No one has to know. Just have to work at keeping it from Remi.* She redressed the wound, tightly wrapping gauze around her waist, and was satisfied from her image in the mirror the dressing was not noticeable under her loose sweater. She went to the cottage, changed clothes, then went to find Remi to relieve his worry.

⸎

That night, the decoded message lay on the conference table in the cave as the *friends* and Chabot gathered around:

> TO: TCP-3.965
> FROM: HMN-O-37
> 1 October, 1943
> FROM: *The field office of Major General Mark Wayne Clark, U.S. Army*
> SUBJECT: *Victory-Naples, Italy*
>
> *Allied forces breaking through German defenses-capture Naples Italy (>)*
>
> *German captives in the thousands. German troop and equipment withdrawing to the north. Watch for possible German rail evacuation through the Saint Laurnee Passage expected soon (>)*

Allied push toward Rome underway (>)

- - - tect saint Laurnee passage at all costs from German sabotage and destruction (…)

"Well, there are our orders. Protect the Saint Laurnee Passage," Remi's exasperation clear in his comment. "I wish I'd never heard of the damned Saint Laurnee Passage. How in hell are the five of us supposed to keep the Nazis from destroying the thing if they want to?"

Remi pushed back from the table, went to the chalkboard and drew a crude image of the Passage, showing the tunnel and trestle. "If I were them, I'd place explosives inside the tunnel and at both ends. Blow it to bits. Try to seal it permanently."

"I would also place explosives in the center of the trestle," Chabot added, "in hopes of bringing the whole thing down. A damaged trestle can be fixed, but a collapsed trestle is not repairable…at least, not quickly. If they are able to accomplish either the Passage becomes impassable."

Remi agreed, "The challenge is, how do we prevent any of that from taking place? How do we prevent them from doing even the slightest damage that will slow the Allies kicking their asses all the way back to Berlin?"

Celine sat silently, fighting to look natural and breathing lightly to avoid the pain each time she inhaled. She was normally full of ideas and hoped her lack of participation would go unnoticed. Her appearance did not seem to be raising any concerned questions, but it took her constant focus to maintain the façade.

Chabot broke the pondering silence, "Could we find a way to eliminate the garrison? Perhaps kidnap them, just as we kidnapped Colonel Nussbaum?"

"The whole damn garrison?" Felicien marveled. "Good lord, Gasper, they have 80-some troops and a dozen officers over there."

His increasingly confident look indicated Chabot's growing fascination with the idea. He sat there with his 'I'm thinking, don't bother me' look the *friends* had become so familiar with. They could almost hear the wheels turning in his brilliant mind. With a contemplative expression glued on his face, he raised a finger as if trying to hook it on to the ring of his thoughts.

"Wait a minute," he said, "waaaait just a minute." He slowly continued. "Perhaps we do not have to capture the whole garrison; just the officers." All of a sudden, Chabot literally bounced with excitement, "The Germans are a very hierarchical society. Their military is structured that way, too. It is well known by the Allies that if you can kill the commanding officers, the troops almost always fall into confusion...they literally become dysfunctional. If we could remove the officers, the garrison soldiers would become virtually directionless."

Amaury interjected, "They have 10 commissioned officers, dear Doctor, plus five non-commissioned and Auchenbach to boot. We still are five versus 15 very capable Nazi officers." Amaury was now humored at the audacity of the whole idea. "Perhaps we could invite them all over to the chalet for tea one afternoon and poison them."

In irritation at Amaury's frivolousness, Chabot grumbled, "We don't have to deal with the non-commissioned officers. Once the senior officers are eliminated, the Sergeants and Corporals become just about as directionally clueless as the enlisted troops. I'm telling you, if we can take out Auchenbach and his senior officers, we can force our will on the garrison troops. I haven't thought through all of the details yet, but I assure you, if we can remove the commissioned officers from Falauge, the garrison is ours."

Chabot's look was so self-assured, the *friends* began to let his determined confidence argue with their doubts.

"If Gasper is right," Remi said, "that means we only have to deal with Auchenbach and his 10 senior officers. That may be doable."

Chabot spoke up again, "Having to retreat from Italy, the Nazis have only one way to come through the Passage. They must come by train. That is the only transportation capable of evacuating large numbers of men and equipment efficiently. They will not attempt to destroy the Passage until the last train passes through. That gives us time before they sabotage things. We have time to think of how to do this.

"Now, I am going to go to bed so I can think of the way we're going to do this." With that, Gasper abruptly rose and exited the room.

Celine forced past her throbbing pain, "If we could eliminate the officers, there are all kinds of ways to terrorize a bunch of directionless troops, snipe off several each night, blow up one of the barracks. Maybe run them off into the woods."

As with all of Chabot's wild ideas the more the group struggled with it the more it intrigued them.

Amaury added, "We'd have to grab all of the officers at once. Picking them off one at a time will alert them to trouble. They'll call Chambéry for reinforcements."

"How do we grab the whole damn group at one time?" Felicien mused. "Auchenbach never lets his officers come to town the way Colonel Nussbaum did. Hell, none of us have ever seen most of his officer staff. They're kept like a bunch of school kids in the compound at Falauge."

Remi searching for a method, glanced over at Amaury, "Maybe we can get him to reconsider that. Is there anything we could do to get him to bring the officer group to Treaire one evening? You know, a rewarding night out." Celine excused herself telling Remi she was tired and would meet him at the cottage. The rest opened another bottle of wine, Felicien confident the answers to capturing the garrison at Falauge would be found within.

CHAPTER 40

For the next several evenings, Amaury approached Colonel Auchenbach with invitations to have his officer staff come for dinner at the Bistro. He even offered to provide the meal free of charge, in recognition of his support and friendship with the German occupiers. While his relationship with the arrogant Colonel had at least made it to the level of being able to approach the man, it had not warmed to the point of Auchenbach taking the bait of the invitation. The force of his final refusal, the third time Amaury had proposed the invitation, closed the matter completely.

"Your continued invitations to entertain my officer staff is annoying, Monsieur Cheever. I do not dine with subordinate officers, I do not socialize with subordinates, I do not enjoy their slow mental response, nor do I easily tolerate their base humor. Quite frankly, Monsieur, the vast majority of subordinate officers disgust me—and that includes most of those I personally selected to assist me at Falauge. They exist to carry out my orders; not to be entertained by me. I hope I make myself sufficiently clear that this will be the last I hear of this absurd invitation. If there is anything confusing about what I have just told you, then I will begin to lower my opinion of your intelligence, which I do not hold in very high regard anyway."

⚬⚬⚬

With the option of bringing the officers together at the Bistro out of the question, the Tristan once again wrestled with to how to round up the Falauge command in one fell swoop. Then, one evening, Chabot excitedly demonstrated the results of his latest tinkering, bringing new hope to the plan.

He had them drive the communications truck to the mill. On the table he had arranged a seemingly disjointed array of electronics. A confusion of wires connected multiple electrical boxes from which protruded glowing vacuum tubes, various dials, tiny flashing red and yellow lights, and several-hundred paper tubes standing in rows like soldiers, each neatly wrapped from top to bottom in thin copper wire. The entire table was covered with the electrically buzzing contraption. Chabot stood smugly glowing as the *friends* stood bewildered and wondering at his newly introduced creation.

"Okay, Gasper," Remi said, "we have had time to inspect this and, as usual, none of us knows what we are looking at. So, why don't you begin your explanation and, if possible, please try to keep it in plain French."

Gasper held the silence just a few seconds longer, allowing sufficient time for his audience to settle and quiet themselves so as not to miss a single confusing word.

"This, my lady and gentlemen, is how we will capture the Falauge officer staff, including Colonel Auchenbach." he beamed. "I have created a radio-wave trap. Actually, I have substantially improved on the well-known and rather common crystal radio-wave trap we are all familiar with."

Felicien laughed, "Yeah, my wife and I were just discussing radio-wave traps with our kids last night. But, of course, we were talking about the standard run-of-the-mill traps, you know, the common ones we are all familiar with."

Chabot ignored the comment and Amaury's chuckle. "The common radio-wave trap is designed to exclude unwanted signals or interference from a receiver. They've been around for years. Basically, it is a tuned circuit placed in the antenna path to a radio. It traps and then dissipates the signal, or at least the majority of it, thus allowing you to reduce interference between stations. It is a device that can remove, filter out or exclude noise and interference from a wave—usually, a radio wave. It may also be called a rejector circuit for radio systems." The group patiently waited for Chabot to get to the point of just exactly how this array of electronic gadgetry was going to round up Auchenbach and his officers.

"I have simply advanced the basic concept several steps further. Not only does this array of electronics modulate radio waves being sent from one receiver to another, this one feeds them off into a completely different channel and frequency." As usual, the friends remained quiet in their puzzlement not providing Chabot the bounding excitement he was waiting for.

"Give it to us in terms we can understand," Remi prodded.

Chabot sighed, thinking, *You have to spoon-feed these children everything.* He resigned himself to try to get down to their level. "Okay. If the Colonel at Falauge sends a radio transmission to Chambéry, this device grabs it, changes the frequency and side-tracks it off into a different channel. Think of it as a train being switched from the main track onto a siding. Once the wave is side-tracked, it is recorded on this wire recorder. When we turn on the recorder, we can play back the message and then we have a choice to send it on in its original form or make changes before we send it on. We can also grab messages transmitted from Chambéry to Falauge. For that matter, we can trap and change any radio message coming into or going out of this area," he beamed.

Felicien said, "So what?"

"So what? *So what?* Chabot gasped. "This device will grab the message and make any changes we want to it before we send it on. This puts us in a position to send whatever orders we want to Colonel Auchenbach and send whatever response we want to Chambéry! Both will think they are communicating with each other and will have no idea we are the ones in control."

Celine lit up, "So, we could create a message of our own and transmit it to Auchenbach as if it had come directly from the German headquarters in Chambéry?"

"*Yes,*" beamed Chabot. "And we can send a message to Chambéry as if it originated from the Nazi high command in Paris or, for that matter, as if it came from Hitler himself. This device puts us in complete control of all German communication coming into and going out of this area. We can send orders to them, countermand previous orders—tell them whatever we want to tell them. They are *ours,*" Chabot was practically bursting with triumph.

Celine further questioned, "So, no matter the content of a message being sent back and forth between Chambéry and Falauge, we can change it to say whatever we want it to say?"

"Absolutely. That is what I just said."

All at once, the excitement Chabot was craving broke out among the group. Felicien lit up a cigarette and broke open a fresh bottle of wine. "Let's send them a message from Hitler, telling them all to immediately return to Germany."

"There is one catch," Chabot warned. "All of this has to be put into the truck with our radio-receiver. Once it is hooked up, we cannot send radio messages to the Allies without the Germans immediately receiving them." Remi gave Celine a concerned look.

"And there is one more thing," he added. "Even though the Germans will no longer be able to pinpoint our radio's location, we will have to man the machine 24 hours a day." A second concerned look passed between all the *friends*.

"And, Gasper sheepishly added, "Since all messages between Chambéry and Falauge will be captured, we will have to listen to every one of them and either change it or pass it on immediately. Otherwise, the Germans will catch on to the fact that something is interrupting their communications."

"What do you mean by immediately?" Felicien asked.

"Within 5 to 10 minutes of the originating transmission. Right away."

Celine shrugged, "Well, that will be no problem since we will be sitting right there in the truck all the time."

Chabot gave her an uneasy look, "Yes, but the incoming message will be in German and the response must be in perfect German…and its content must fit our plans."

The enveloping disappointment was immediate. This magnificent device was useless to them. Chabot was the only Tristan member sufficiently fluent in German to man the equipment, and it was impossible for him to continuously be at the radio.

Amaury spoke up, "We can have Jonas and Wilhelmina Schultz help us, but, Remi, you are going to have to let them know all about the Tristan if we do."

Remi gave Amaury a perplexed look, "Who in hell are Jonas and Wilhelmina Schultz?"

"They're two of my Jewish friends in hiding over at the barn." Amaury answered. "I have purchased eggs and produce from them for years. They are first-generation Germans. German is all they ever speak to each other. They fled Germany in the early 1930s, as soon as Jonas felt the Hitler bunch had the possibility of gaining control. Jonas is very bright…a mechanical engineer, I think."

Celine asked, "How long have you known Jonas and Wilhelmina, Amaury?"

"For years. Delightful people, and I trust them completely."

"Will they do it?" Remi asked.

Amaury leaned back, "I have been to the barns frequently since the Jews have gone into hiding there, just to check on things. See how they are doing. They are frightened, the whole bunch, Remi, very frightened. They see now that we are their only hope of survival. They are ready to fight and if this will help us beat the bastard Nazis, you can bet they'll do it. They'll do whatever it takes to help."

Remi sat for a moment, then turned to the others. "Except for Gasper, we have not allowed outsiders into the Tristan since Daniel's death. Daniel died because I let outsiders into our ranks. Max and Damian died because of that, too. We have suffered betrayal at the hands of the outsiders. It was my fault. I put all of you in danger. If we allow these people in, we will have to open up to them. They will know who we are and virtually everything about us."

Gasper encouraged, "I think if we have two other Germans to man the radio, I can fill in and still have time to work on things like this."

"Remi," Celine said gently, "the death of our comrades was not your fault. You have to get over that. We are in a dangerous business. Just like Alexis, they were casualties of a hideous war we did not start. They died fighting for liberty, our liberty. They died for the Jews we are hiding. They would all tell us to do whatever will help us win against the Germans. We need help, Remi, and if Jonas and Wilhelmina Schultz can help us now, we should bring them in."

Felicien raised his glass, "Here's a second to that on my part."

"Okay," Remi's anxious look remained. "We will bring them in for this purpose, but it must be for this purpose only. They are not to be made aware of any of our activities, other than what we want to accomplish using the radio trap."

Chabot interrupted, "I am afraid it will not be that easy. Whoever works the radio will have to know everything. They will come to know us because one of us will have to be with them in the truck at all times, and they will come to know what we are doing when we dictate our response to the messages we capture from Chambéry and Falauge. If this is to work, the people manning the radio must know the plan completely."

Remi groaned in frustration. Of course, Gasper was right. The Schultzes would quickly come to know everything and everyone. His stomach tightened at the thought of, once again, exposing the Tristan to strangers.

Celine saw the agony tearing at him and asked the group if she and Remi could converse together. This was not the first time they had privately conferred. She was his confidant, his love, mate, and his champion. Her council was critical in helping lift the stress he constantly felt. They excused themselves and stepped out onto the mill's second-story landing.

They no sooner closed the door behind them when Remi burst out, "Cel, I know what you say about those deaths is right, but I can't help it. They weigh on me as if I killed all of them myself."

"You cannot allow yourself that privilege. Whatever it takes, you have to be stronger than that. This is not just your personal fight, Remi. Yes, you were the one who brought us all to arms against the Germans, but we have all committed to this battle. We are all as dedicated as you are. It is *our* war. We are fighting for *our* destiny, *our* dignity and *our* freedom."

Her words were firm and on target. They offered reprieve. "You are our leader. You know what has to be done, and these people are our only hope in accomplishing our objective. They are probably our only hope of saving us and themselves."

There was no denying Celine's comments. Either they sought help from others now or the fight was lost. They returned and a slightly more confident Remi addressed the group. "Amaury, you have dealt with the Schultz couple for years. Apparently, you are sure they can be trusted. We will open up to the Schultzes, but only to them. We've got over a hundred people in hiding. There is no way we can expose ourselves to all of them. I cannot allow that. You must get them to come along without revealing any of the details until you get them alone. They must be sworn to secrecy, and we must be certain they will not divulge anything they are doing with us to their friends in hiding. Are you convinced we can count on them for that?"

"Look, Remi, all I can say is their lives are on the line, just like ours. If we die, they die...their children die, their friends and relatives die. They have the same incentives we do. What else I can tell you? It's a risk, yes, but one I feel we have to take."

"Okay. Tomorrow, Amaury, go to the barn and ask the Schultzes to help us. Do not discuss any details in front of the others. Take them off, remote from the others, and briefly outline that we will need them to assist us 24 hours a day. They will have to live away from the barn. It is too risky for them to go back when they are not working the radio. Their friends will ask questions and probe for what they are doing. Sooner or later, they will slip and let the word out. I will not take the chance of letting them continue living at the hideaway."

"Okay. They can live at the cottage where you and Celine live now," Amaury decided. "The two of you can come to the château."

Felicien chimed in, "Amaury, are you sure? Won't it cramp you not having all 70 rooms to yourself?"

"This is war, Felicien," Amaury retorted, "Certain sacrifices simply have to be made."

Felicien smiled, "Wow, what a guy."

Remi did not lighten up with the banter going on between Felicien and Amaury. Amaury said, "It is going to concern everyone when the Schultzes get their belongings and leave the barn without explaining in detail what this is all about."

Remi took a deep breath, trying to calm himself, "Look, damn it, my concern for our safety isn't naïve or unjustified. Regardless of whose fault it was, people we liked—people we loved—died because I let my guard down once before. Figure out what they're supposed to explain to all the others, but we're not opening up to the whole damn bunch of them."

"Okay. I hear you. I can do that," Amaury's confident reply took some of the edge off the atmosphere.

The first step in the plan to destroy the garrison at Falauge was underway.

CHAPTER 41

Jonas and Wilhelmina Schultz, a quiet and unassuming couple in their early fifties, were eager to help. Amaury's explanation to the others in hiding, that the couple was needed in the fight against the Nazis, was met with total acceptance from the others in hiding. No questions were asked. One of the young men approached Amaury as the Schultzes were packing up, "I want you to know we are capable and eager to help in any way possible. Whenever you need us, no matter what the assignment, we will come. We will come willingly. Do not hesitate to ask anything of us—any of us."

"That call may very well come," Amaury patted the man on the shoulder. "In the meantime, lay low and take care of your people."

The Schultzes were bright, proud to have been chosen for the task. Remi's confidence in their ability to do the job and their trustworthiness grew as he and Celine discussed the details of their assignment manning the radio. Chabot spoke to them in German, assuring Celine and Remi their enunciation was perfect.

Jonas said, "Wilhelmina and I—all of us—we are ready to stand with you, Remi. We know nothing of fighting, but we can learn. You will find us brave. Willing to die, if necessary. We thank God you have come to our aid, and are proud we may now come to yours."

Jonas then opened a whole new avenue of opportunity. "I want you to know, Celine and Remi, there are other German-speakers at the barn: the Zollermans, Albert and Margret and their twin sons, Adrian and Anton. The boys are now 23, strapping lads, lean and handsome…"

Wilhelmina poked Jonas, "Just tell them, Jonas. They're not interested in knowing the boys are lean and handsome."

"Oh, yes. Sorry. The Zollermans speak perfect German. The boys despise the Nazis. They blame them for disrupting their young lives and were incensed at having to leave the farm to go into hiding because of being identified with a religion they had never practiced," he chuckled. "They call the Nazis 'bastard Boche'. They would be good fighters, if you want them."

⟞⟝

That evening Felicien, Gasper, Jonas and Wilhelmina all squeezed into the communications truck that was now also packed with Gasper's message-grabbing equipment. Chabot delighted in demonstrating how to operate his creation, then stayed on with Felicien and Jonas for an hour after they teamed up to take the first shift. The initial plan was to simply pass on each communiqué in its entirety. They would spend time learning to flawlessly operate the equipment before attempting to manipulate any messages.

⟞⟝

In spite of the powerful control Chabot's wonderful radio contraption had placed in the hands of the Tristan the plan to capture the entire officer corps of the garrison, was still fraught with multiple hazards. Colonel Auchenbach's hand-picked officers would be exceptional, disciplined, observant—not likely to be easily fooled by a flawed plan.

In one of his rare semi-friendly conversations, Auchenbach divulged to Amaury that he had also brought 20 enlisted men with him when he took command of the garrison. These men, too, were expected to be highly skilled and assumed to be combat experienced. Celine and Remi could only pray Gasper Chabot's theory would hold true that once the officers were gone, the enlisted men would become directionless. If any of Auchenbach's specially chosen enlistees ran counter to that theory and took command, the tiny Tristan did not stand a chance of subduing the garrison. Celine and Remi had to assume a worst-case scenario, realizing that men like Wilhelm Auchenbach left nothing to chance. Their survival, and the lives of all those now under their protection, would depend on meticulous preparation. Every detail had to be anticipated, every potential problem analyzed and planned for.

Remi continued his apprehension about exposing so much to so many people, but saw no alternative. He pushed aside his concerns, allowing Albert and Margret Zollerman and their sons, Adrian and Anton, into the inner circle. He and Celine spend hours hashing over details; how to make the capture, where to imprison the officers, how to deal with Auchenbach's hardened enlistees, how to manage the garrison in the absence of their officers.

As soon as the officers were neutralized, it was critical to immediately take control of the garrison communications room at Falauge in order to free up their radio truck for communication with the Allies. The operation was multifaceted, complex and delicate—certainly the most complicated and aggressive action the Tristan had ever contemplated.

As they wrestled with the numerous dangers, every now and then they would exchange looks that implied, *Are we crazy to proceed? Is this whole idea simply crazy?* Each time such doubts arose, one of them would push ahead, encouraging the other. If successful, the mission would assure the safety of the Saint Laurnee Passage, eliminate the Falauge garrison and stop the Nazis from sending any additional troops and supplies to their forces in Italy. If it failed, the Tristan would be annihilated and, most likely, Falauge and Treaire would become explosive battlefields, devoid of people…the entire area nothing more than a smoldering memory.

CHAPTER 42

Having five more people fluent in German added immeasurably to the capabilities of the Tristan. Along with Gasper's impersonation of a Gestapo General, they could now add Jonas Schultz, Albert Zollerman, and his two sons as German military impersonators. They also had Wilhelmina Schultz and Margret Zollerman. Both women were bright and capable of interpreting and creating messages between Falauge and Chambéry.

Several challenging problems remained. There were not enough German uniforms for all of their new German-speaking recruits. They had Gasper's Gestapo General's uniform and six enlisted men's uniforms, but that left Schultz and the Zollermans still to be clothed. The plan required the addition of a Colonel's uniform to fit Albert, two Captain's uniforms for Anton and Adrian, and a Sergeant's uniform for Jonas.

There was also a question of vehicles. Although they had successfully gotten away with Gestapo General Chabot riding in a lowly VW Kübelwagen to get into Chambéry and destroy the convoy, his showing up in anything less than a Mercedes or a Horch limousine for this caper would not pass scrutiny. Chabot would be arriving in Falauge in broad daylight and had to project the image of his rank and authority.

He would be traveling with an entourage of staff. As the plan was now designed, it called for General Chabot to be accompanied by Privates Remi, Celine (disguised as a male), and Felicien, Sergeant Jonas Schultz, Captains Adrian and Anton Zollerman, and their father, Albert, dressed as a Colonel. This team would arrive in Falauge immediately following the capture of Auchenbach and his officers. They would take command of the 80-troop garrison, hopefully convincing them that General Chabot and his team had been assigned as the replacement command officers at Falauge.

During the raid on the convoy at Chambéry they had seen several prestigious staff cars stored in the yard. With luck, they might still be there. One successful raid might fill both their need for vehicles and the necessary uniforms. They would again hit the Chambéry depot relying on Chabot to once again pull off his previously impressive charade.

With the Schultzes and Zollermans now trained to operate the radio and fully aware of the details of the plans, the *friends* and Chabot donned their uniforms, packed into the Kübelwagen and headed toward Chambéry. They stuck to back roads to avoid any German check points that might be halting traffic on the main highway. The winding country road approached the massive Chambéry depot from the rear.

When the Germans first came to Chambéry, they leveled several acres next to the depot's rail sidings for their storage yard. They bulldozed tons of dirt, creating a 15-foot-high embankment along the back of the property. The mound now thick in grass and weeds conveniently hid the road on which the Tristan approached.

Amaury killed the engine, letting the little Kübelwagen silently roll to a stop at the base of the embankment. Remi and Celine crawled to its top to assess the scene. As before, the yard was ablaze with floodlights and teeming with personnel. Peering through the tall grass, they could see most of the complex, including the entrance gate. The rumors they had heard about beefed-up security were highly understated. Remi studied the front gate through his binoculars.

"There's no way we'll make it through the front gate Cel. They have totally changed the entrance. Now there is a second gate about 50 yards beyond the first. The headquarters building sits between them." He continued watching as a supply truck made its way through the gauntlet of guards and gates. Finally, he said, "They let that supply truck through the first gate, then made the driver go into the headquarters office. Probably to clear his papers before they let him through the second. Both gates have four guards and there are two gun towers adjacent to the front gate. It looks like the gate's made of steel rather than the wood that was in place when we bluffed our way in. We'll never pull this off, Cel. Not a chance."

He handed the binoculars to Celine. She watched a second vehicle move through the complicated entrance process, and agreed with Remi's assessment.

They hand signaled to Amaury and the others to stay put, then crept along the crest of the embankment toward the center of the yard. The entire yard was surrounded by a wire cyclone fence topped with multiple strands of barbed wire. Toward the far end of the embankment was a length of approximately 20 yards where the fencing was shrouded in darkness from the shadows of two supply buildings located just inside the yard. The buildings and the shadows they cast offered some cover. This appeared to be the only point at which an entrance could be made with a reasonable chance of success.

They were about to move down the back side of the embankment to rejoin the group when Celine caught the gleam of a flashlight coming around the south corner of the fence. She grabbed Remi's arm and they dropped to the ground.

Two guards and a German Shepherd were making rounds, walking just outside the fence and surveying it as they progressed along its length. They watched the trio move along, stopping every now and then to let the dog sniff whatever attracted him. The guards moved casually, obviously bored with their task—indicative they had repeated the assignment multiple times.

Celine and Remi breathed shallowly as the guards passed in front of their position on the embankment. Though they were well hidden at least 50 feet from the fence, the dog looked their way, sniffed and barked. He tugged violently on his leash, continuing to bark in their direction. His handler pulled him back, but the animal continued his agitation, tugging on the leash. His partner queried, "Shall we go have a look, Jörg?"

The handler looked in the direction of the dog's interest, "It's probably just some night animal. I'm not hiking up that damn hill to satisfy this mutt's curiosity." He yanked hard on the leash, pulling the Shepherd back with force. The dog got the message and settled down as the three trudged on their way. Celine and Remi remained frozen. It took another several minutes for the guards to round the far corner of the fence. Remi rolled on his back, breathing a long, hushed sigh of relief. Celine looked over at him and whispered, "We will have to stay and observe how often those guards make their rounds. There is no way we can break in tonight. It's a totally different situation than when we attacked the convoy."

She winked at him, "Sometimes our own successes wind up complicating our lives. Take the others back to Treaire, then come back for me. By the time you return, I will have had time to observe the guard schedule and we can decide how we're going to pull this off."

Remi hesitated, "Cel, they're not going to put that dog off the next time."

"I'll move down to the corner of the fence. That will put me downwind. Once I see them round the far corner, I'll move back into the woods long before they get close enough for the dog to pick up my scent. Now, get going."

Once again, Remi had to remind himself that Celine was probably more capable than he of defending herself if it became necessary. He gave her a quick kiss and scooted down the embankment, vanishing into the night.

———— ❦ ————

The following night, Celine stood before Jonas Schultz, the three Zollermans, the *friends*, and Chabot, "The Chambéry depot is a very different place than the yard we broke into when we attacked the convoy. Much tighter security. The entire entrance procedure is too secure for us to enter there."

She had drawn a rough sketch of the rectangular yard on the chalkboard, showing the fence and the embankment with the country road running behind it. She drew a couple of short hash marks at a point on the fence, "This area, a span of about 20 yards along the back fence, is cast in shadow from these buildings. I remember these buildings from when we broke in before. They contain various supplies. We broke into both of them."

Pointing to the south building, she continued, "This one contained mostly repair parts…things we are not interested in, but the north building housed clothing. It's where we sprayed all the boots and underwear with the Boot Pepper." The thought of the naked dancing soldiers *still* made her smile.

"I remember seeing uniforms hanging on some racks in the back of the building. I know there were hangers with low-rank uniforms. I think I remember several uniforms of higher rank, but I can't be sure since we weren't concerned with uniforms during the last raid. At any rate, if officer's uniforms are stored here, it will be no problem to slip in and quickly change into them while we're in the building.

"It's the vehicles that concern me, but I'll come back to that in a moment." She moved to the table, sat, and continued, "They've established patrol units that walk the perimeter of the fence—two men and a dog assigned to this duty. It takes the patrols about 45 minutes to complete one round of the perimeter. They are looking for breaks in the fence and, of course, the dog will pick up any scent of a human intruder. The men seem bored. They're sloppy about their duties. They don't pay attention to the dog's warnings—just yank it back into place and move on. It appears they are required to check in at the headquarters building each time they pass. I'm sure whoever they report to checks the time. Knowing the Germans, they probably keep a detailed log on the check-in times. I'm confident that if a guard unit doesn't check in within a certain time slot, they'll send another unit out in search.

"If we take out the guards immediately as they come around the south corner of the fence, we'll have about 30 minutes before they would be expected to check in at headquarters. We have to get in and back out during this 30-minute window."

She moved back to the board, "The guards circle the yard counterclockwise. Both shifts did this." She pointed to the south rear corner of her chalk drawn rectangle, "If we take them out here, just as they turn up the rear side of the yard, it will give us the full 30 minutes before they are expected back at the headquarters checkpoint. We can have one team take out the guards and dog and another team get over the fence in the shadows of the supply buildings.

"Now, the vehicles," she continued. "Remi and I have been doing a lot of thinking about them. We have to have Chabot and his support staff chauffeured in appropriate vehicles if we are going to be successful in convincing the garrison of his legitimacy."

She turned the floor over to Remi, "We must keep in mind that we are going to call the entire garrison to assembly when we take command of Falauge. We are going to be standing in front of 80 armed soldiers. Nussbaum told us when the garrison is called to assembly they are required to show up with their weapons. They're going to be edgy. We'll be a group of new faces—officers and staff they've never seen before. We're going to be giving them orders that we have to have them follow without question, so we've got to look convincing.

"We also have to assume the group of Privates that Colonel Auchenbach brought with him when he took command of Falauge are seasoned soldiers. No doubt, they are highly dedicated to Auchenbach. Being good soldiers, they will be disciplined, but should they detect the slightest flaw in our performance, they will challenge us.

"Okay, Cel, brief everyone on the Chambéry break-in."

Celine returned to the blackboard, "I will be positioned here, on the embankment at the south corner of the fence, with a sniper rifle. I will take out the guards and the dog and signal you when they are down. You will be here," she pointed to the supply buildings on the drawing. "You will be in the shadows. We're going over the fence. We don't want to cut through it and leave evidence of our break-in. We'll hinge two ladders together at one end. Lean them against the fence and as the first person goes up he'll swing the hinged section over to go down the other side. You will dust out your tracks leaving no evidence of entering the yard. Once you're all in you'll pitch the ladder back over the fence and I will retrieve it before I leave.

"All of you will enter at this point. Chabot will be dressed in his Gestapo uniform; Remi, Felicien, and Amaury in our Private's uniforms. Felicien, you will go first and move directly to this building. Check the door and pick the lock if necessary. All of you enter the building except Felicien, who will stand guard. Once inside, Albert will suit up as a Colonel, Anton and Adrian as Captains, and Jonas as a Sergeant. Remi is familiar with what the uniforms look like and will help you get the right ones. You will have to do this using only the light coming in through the windows. Make sure they fit properly and carefully replace any you try on and reject. Those who change into uniforms will place their civilian clothes in a canvas bag that Jonas will heave over the fence where the ladder is. The whole process—over the fence, entering the building and suiting up—can take no more than 10 minutes. Remember, you have only 30 minutes from the time of my signal to get suited up, get vehicles and get out.

"I will remain here on the top of the embankment, surveying the fence, and will take out anyone that comes along. I am your backup."

She nodded to Remi to take over. The joint presentation assured the group they were in complete agreement about every detail. Remi went to the board, pointing to an area near the supply buildings, "About 50 yards from the supply buildings there are two Mercedes, four Opel staff cars and seven Kübelwagens parked adjacent to the north fence. They are parked behind several tanks and supply trucks, hiding their view from the center of the yard.

"The cars look like they have not been used for a while. We are hoping this is the case so they will not be immediately missed. These will be our targets. We will steal one of the Mercedes, one of the Opels and a Kübelwagen. These are appropriate vehicles for us to show up in at the garrison, and will support Chabot's image as a Gestapo General to the garrison troops.

"Once we are in the vehicles, Amaury, in his Private's uniform, will drive General Chabot and Colonel Albert in the Mercedes. Felicien, as a Private, will drive Captain Anton and Captain Adrian in the Opel. I, also as a Private will drive Sergeant Jonas in the Kübelwagen. That gives us at least one person in each vehicle fluent in German."

Felicien let out a long whistle, "You have got to be kidding me." He tilted back in his chair, lighting a cigarette, having forgotten about the one smoldering in his ashtray on the table. "And just how do you suggest we exit the supply yard?" he mused. "By driving out the front gate?"

"Exactly," came back Celine's immediate and somewhat impatient reply.

"Hey, I'm always up for a good heist," Felicien laughed, "but this is ridiculous. The krauts will nev…"

"*Stop* it!" Remi shouted. The strength and intensity of his voice brought instant seriousness to Felicien's flippant tone. "We are dead serious, Felicien. If all of us do not accept the seriousness of this mission, we will certainly wind up with bullets in our heads." He glared around at the others. "Felicien's joking comment has no place here. Everything we are describing is serious—deadly serious."

Appropriately sobered, Felicien immediately understood that Remi and Celine were deeply concerned that his frivolous attitude could undermine the confidence of the newcomers or, worse, encourage a casual attitude in them.

Remi continued, his tone maintaining its seriousness, "We have got to approach this with complete determination and confidence. You've got to believe that we not only *can* but we *will* pull it off without a hitch."

Celine added, "Sitting here, talking about this in safety and comfort is easy. When you're inside the fence at the Chambéry depot, you must be totally vigilant, totally on top of your game, in control and able to think fast if anything goes wrong. You will not feel the full tension until the night of the raid, and you must keep yourself calm and in control. The slightest mistake can make the difference between success and death. What's more, if we fail, we are sealing the deaths of every one of our friends and relatives in hiding." The room was quiet. Remi, still glaring at Felicien, slowly returned to his seat as Celine continued.

"Remi and I realize we are asking a lot. He and I went back to Chambéry last night and watched the activities at the depot most of the night. Although guards are posted at the front gates all night, there is a certain relaxed attitude that settles in after midnight. Gate traffic slows considerably around 11:00. After midnight, the guards passed some vehicles both in and out without making the drivers check through the headquarters office.

"Perhaps at that time of night the headquarters office and the gates are manned by lower rank people who are less dedicated and should be easier to intimidate." She looked over at Felicien, "We are confident we can drive these vehicles right out through the front gate if we look and act the part of demanding, no-nonsense German officers...and if we all maintain total control."

Felicien said, "I am sorry, my friends. I was taken aback at the thought of so dramatically pulling the wool over the Germans' eyes." He smiled, "Actually, it will be great fun and, of course, as always, I am in." The apology, while well met, did nothing to reduce the tension in the room.

Celine spoke again, "There is one more detail. It will take nine of us to pull this off. That means we have to drive two vehicles to Chambéry—our Kübelwagen and the Citroën. Also, I will need help disposing of the guards and dog after I take them out. We will take the bodies with us, drive them back to Treaire and bury them. That way, there is no evidence we killed them. This part of the plan is as critically important as all the rest.

"We know from what Colonel Nussbaum told us there is a general feeling at Chambéry that Germany is losing the war. Since he told us that, we have heard rumors there have been desertions taking place in Chambéry, particularly among the lower ranks. When the guards fail to show up and their bodies are not found, we are hoping they will be assumed to be another case of desertion. This will further cover our tracks.

"So, I need some strong lad who can drive a vehicle to help me carry the bodies up the embankment, hoist them into our vehicles and retrieve the ladder."

Anton spoke up, "Ask Gavriel Zander."

"Fill us in," Remi said.

"Gavriel Zander is around 30, a good-size fellow. He left Germany about eight years ago, almost as soon as the Nazis started first harassing the Jews. He didn't have a penny to his name, walked from Mannheim to here. He was sick with the flu or something when he got here and was nursed back to health by the Ferbers. He's been working with Solomon Ferber ever since—almost is like a surrogate son."

"Can he be trusted?" Remi questioned.

"Gavriel? He's not real bright, but I'd trust Gavriel with my life."

Surprising everyone, without hesitation, Remi said, "We'll take him."

Then, he turned to Chabot, "What about you, Gasper? There's a lot of risk in this. Are you in?"

Gasper's eyes grew sad and contemplative. His normal hesitation before answering was slightly longer than usual, then, in a soft voice, he said, "I am not a brave man. I was not brave as a child, and I have not acquired bravery as an adult. I am shy and uncomfortable around people. I often lie awake at night, wishing I could be different, but I have come to accept that I am me and these things will not change.

"You all have shown me that liberty and freedom come at great expense and sacrifice. You have taught me that these things are worth fighting for and, maybe, even dying for." He paused, looking at Remi and Celine, "An interesting point about liberty…you can't see it, you can't smell it, you can't wear it, you can't buy or sell it. But when you have it, you can taste it, you can feel it, you can revel in it. The Germans have shown me that once it is taken from you—once liberty is gone, it is very painful and difficult to get back."

After another contemplative pause, he said, "I am very afraid to go with you on this raid. To think about it when I am alone at night will make me shake uncontrollably. I am most afraid of failing you, of getting you into trouble. I am also afraid for myself. I do not want to die and I particularly cringe at the thought of being tortured, but I am with you. I am more afraid of losing our liberty. I will go with you and, God help me, I will do my best."

The *friends* fondly stared at Chabot. He had put into words the force that drove them—the emotion that inspired them. He had come to understand there was something more. Something beyond himself, something worth fighting for, worth risking everything for…in spite of his fear.

The meeting broke up quietly. Celine and Remi walked hand in hand, "How do you think it went, Remi?"

"As well as can be expected, I guess," he sighed. "I pray we are not sending everyone to their deaths."

"We are not, Remi. Our plan is good. We know how to completely cover evidence of our break-in at Chambéry. That will give us time. The depot is so huge that if we're lucky, they won't even miss the uniforms and vehicles…at least, not for a while."

"My concern is the Zollermans and Jonas Schultz. They are all so new, totally inexperienced. Taking them into the Chambéry yard, having to rely on them to stay calm…will they hold up?"

"They'll hold up. I'll work with them," Celine responded. "We have two days before we attack the depot. I can show them the basics and I'll talk them through their fears. I'll be able to tell if they show weakness. So far, we are both impressed with these men. They are smart and dedicated."

Remi stopped, took her into his arms and hugged her. "Cel, you are my strength, my constant support. Thank God you are here with me every day. I couldn't do this without you."

"Remi, so often you chose to carry the responsibility for all of us by yourself, as if this is your fight…just yours. As if the only reason the rest of us tag along is because you somehow drag us into it against our will. Your view is not reality.

"Yes, you are our leader and, yes, without you, we probably would not have had the foresight to see the brutality the Nazis have brought on us, but in opening our eyes, in making us aware, we have all become committed to the battle— as committed and dedicated as you. At this point, we fight on of our own free will. It is *our* fight, Remi. We are all responsible, now."

CHAPTER 43

Celine's training of the new recruits began at 5 am the next morning. The group responded well. Anton's and Adrian's raw hatred of the Germans motivated them, but unchanneled, it could be dangerous. During the martial arts training, Celine could see the young men's aggressiveness boiling through, even having to tell them to ease up on each other.

The ages of Albert and Jonas demanded a calmer approach, yet they were deeply committed. Albert was certainly the more timid of the two. She wondered how well he would fare in the face of intimidating German officers. Still he was the best choice to play the part of Chabot's aide. Jonas' demanding personality was perfectly suited to the gruffer Sergeant role.

Gavriel Zander was a bit on the slow side mentally, but sincere and definitely trustworthy. Celine immediately fell in love with the many remembrances he brought of Alexis. His sweet face, always overly concerned he was doing the right thing, pleasing her, performing the way she wanted him to. After the first session, alone with her memories of Alexis so vivid in mind, she cried. Her heart spilled over with sad longing for her giant, loving friend. Feeling Gavriel would display the same hesitation in a fight that had resulted in Alexis' death she was relieved his only tasks would be behind the scenes, away from the action.

The night of the raid they were blessed with miserable weather. A drenching rain had started late that evening and by 1:15 am, as she and Gavriel lay positioned atop the embankment, waiting for the appearance of the patrol guards, the downpour's haze and noise enhanced their concealment. Celine had attached a rain deflector to her Mauser K98k sniper rifle sights as she lay in the wet grass under a black oilcloth. Chabot crafted a silencer for the rifle—not a good idea for sniper rifles—but the K98k had an accuracy of over a thousand yards, and she would be taking down the fence guards at one-tenth that distance, so the reduction in range would not be a problem.

She would first take out the single guard, then the dog handler, followed by the dog. Three quick shots. She was confident about taking out the men, and prayed the dog would remain calm long enough for her to nail him.

Gavriel nudged her, pointing toward the fence line. She spotted the three-some sloshing miserably through the slop with their rain hoods pulled down tightly over their helmets. The man in charge of the dog pulled on its leash, in no mood to tolerate the animal's irritation at being out in the miserable weather.

Change of plans. Celine decided to take out the handler first since he was several paces behind the single guard. Perhaps she could bring him down before the lead man even knew his team mate was hit. *Thunk.* The dog handler fell backward. The dog yelped in surprise. The single guard spun around in response to the dog's cry just as a 7.92 mm bullet pierced his spine, sending him face down in the mud.

The dog reared up. Something was wrong, seriously wrong. The humans had died. He jumped, tugging at the leash. He began to pull free from his master's dead hand. Celine fired. "Shit!" Missed. The animal jumped, did a circle, tugged. She frantically fought to reload, dropped the cartridge, fumbled for it, jammed it into the breach and took aim. The dog broke loose, hesitating for a moment. *Did the master need attention?* The impact of the bullet impacting with the animal tumbled it head over heels several times, sliding to a stop in a muddy ditch. Celine dropped her head onto the rifle butt. Her body trembled. The tension in her shoulders shooting pains into her neck. She nodded to Gavriel to signal the team several hundred yards up the fence. A quick blink of his flashlight. The ladder was quickly positioned and they started over the fence.

The storm's intensity dimmed the depot's lights coming through the windows of the supply building, and the hanging uniforms were further obscured under dust covers. Remi cursed under the added complications. It was taking too long for the team to lift the covers, search for the right rank uniform, then carefully place them back over the clothes. Finally, Jonas whispered, "These are officer uniforms—two Colonel's but only one Captain's."

"Albert and Anton, get them on," Remi instructed. "The rest of you, keep looking. We need one more Captain's and a Sergeant's."

From the doorway, Felicien gave the all-clear signal. Amaury whispered, "Over here." The dust cover he was holding up revealed several Sergeant's uniforms.

"Get into one of those," Remi ordered ¯onas. "Has anyone found another Captain's outfit?" No response.

"We've been through every rack. No more Captain's outfits." Remi held his wristwatch up to the dim light, struggling to see how much time had elapsed since they had entered the building.

"It's okay, Remi. Only 12 minutes, so far," Felicien said, knowing his boss was nervous to get the uniforms and move on to the vehicles, "Take your time. All's clear."

Remi looked over toward Anton, "Grab the other Colonel's uniform and take it with you. Fill that dust cover with three other uniforms so it looks undisturbed. To hell with the Captain's uniform, Adrian, put on the other Colonel's outfit. Jonas, grab two more Sergeant's uniforms and let's get out of here."

The rain had eased. It was still heavy, but less than the barrage that had engulfed them as they made their way to the building.

The group was following Remi as he moved on toward Felicien, who was almost to the cars.

The area where the vehicles were parked was cast in spotty shadows from the tanks and troop trucks parked in front of them. Felicien slipped on to his back on the driver's side floorboard of the Mercedes, shining a penlight up under the dash to look for the ignition wires. Yanking them from their switch, he hotwired them together. The engine moaned under the sickening groan of an almost depleted battery, "Not this one," he said to Remi as he slid out.

Jonas and Amaury had just arrived in the area, "Get the Opel and the Kübelwagen started," he instructed, "Those cars have push-button starters...no need to hotwire."

Felicien slid into the second Mercedes, found the ignition wires and clamped them together. This car, too, moaned, much like the first. *Maybe a bad contact.* He pulled the wires apart and reclamped them. Still just a moan. The engine sluggishly turned over. He separated the wires, pumped the gas pedal several times and reattached the wires. Another slow grown, followed by another, then *ignition*!

"We're all started."

Remi looked around to assure all team members were present. "Get yourselves positioned in your vehicles. Wipe any mud from your clothes. The Mercedes in the lead, then the Opel followed by the Kübelwagen." He turned and went over to Amaury, who was now sitting in the driver's seat of the Mercedes, "Take it slow and easy. Make it look like Chabot owns this stinking hole. No panic. Got it?"

"I'm so cool I could freeze icicles!" Amaury shot Remi his *'I got this all under control'* smile as he shifted the big car into gear. Remi joined Jonas in the Kübelwagen. Adrian leapt from the Opel at a startled German soldier who had suddenly appeared beside his car from between the tanks. The man cried out as Adrian spun him around and slit his throat—a deep raking cut, almost a beheading. Blood shot everywhere, splattering Adrian's uniform and the immediate area. Remi jumped toward the struggle as the nearly decapitated soldier hit the ground.

"What the hell," he exclaimed in a voice a bit louder than he had intended.

"He just appeared between the tanks. He saw us. He was startled and going to cry out."

"Good God, Adrian, look at all this blood. It's all over the car and the ground. It's a sure giveaway that we were here," irritation clear in Remi's voice. Leaving a pool of blood behind was a disaster that would put German forces in the area on alert making the next phase of the plan unworkable.

"Damn it, Adrian," Remi continued, right in Adrian's face, "look at this damn mess. You've splattered blood all over your uniform, the truck, the ground, everything. That's just sloppy. It could compromise the whole operation."

He yanked Adrian into a beam of light that was filtering through the space between the tanks. The entire front of his uniform was soaked in the soldier's blood.

Adrian glared into Remi's eyes, "Go to hell, Remi. Go straight to hell. I *saved* the whole operation and you know it, you bastard." He yanked away from Remi's grip, turning toward his vehicle.

Remi spun him around, "Don't you *ever* cuss me and turn your back on me, Adrian. I am your commanding officer and you will force yourself into military discipline whenever you are working with me. Now get out of that uniform, shove that body into the trunk of the Mercedes, and climb in with it, because that's the only way we'll get out of here alive."

Anger flashed in Adrian's eyes. Grudgingly, he shed the uniform, grabbed the body and threw it into the Mercedes' trunk climbing in beside it. Remi took the blood-soaked uniform over to a gushing down-spout and drenched it. He wrung out the coat, re-drenched it several times, then dumped the soaking uniform on the floor of the Kübelwagen, telling Jonas to push it out of sight under his seat. The rain was dispersing the blood on the ground and hopefully it would continue long enough to totally eradicate it.

Remi tapped on Amaury's window, "You've got a dead German soldier and Adrian in the trunk. You can't let the guards inspect the trunk or we're all dead. Tell Albert and Chabot, then drive up to the gate slowly. Keep it slow and calm. We'll follow."

The skies burst open again as the vehicles made their way toward the brightly lit front gates. Rain pounded on the vehicles with deafening force. *Bring it down, God,* Remi prayed. *Bring it down by the buckets full.* God didn't disappoint him. An enormous bolt of blue-white lightning lit the yard with an accompanying ear-splitting crash. The guard at the first gate threw up the gate arm from inside his guard shack and waved them through. They inched ahead, lining up bumper to bumper between the two gates. The vehicles sat idling, unacknowledged— trapped between the gates. The pounding rain and steamed up windows made it virtually impossible to see what was happening outside.

Remi fought to keep himself calm. It would be totally inappropriate for him, a Private driving a Sergeant, to leave his vehicle and question the guards. Several agonizing minutes passed.

Jonas, peering through his passenger window, had a slightly better view of the guard shacks and headquarters building. "Nothing's happening. No one is coming." He cracked the window a bit more, squinting through the slit as rain splattered in his eyes, "No, wait. Someone just opened the headquarters door." Through the blur of the windshield wipers, Remi saw a figure wrestling himself into a heavy rain slicker just outside the headquarters' office door. The man slipped and slid down the wooden stairs to the muddy driveway.

Remi tensed. When he and Celine observed traffic moving through the gates, the guards had always approached vehicles from the guard shacks, not the headquarters building. Hopefully, this change was weather related rather than some new beefed-up inspection procedure. Remi unsnapped the holster flap on the pistol strapped to his side and rested his hand on the weapon. The soldier, tented in rain gear, sloshed his way over to the passenger side of the Mercedes and shined a flashlight beam on Amaury, "Your papers."

Albert pulled himself forward so the soldier could see his Colonel's rank. In his perfect German, he shouted above the noise of the downpour, "This is a Gestapo inspection unit. We have been inspecting the depot. Standard inspection. We enter and leave all Wehrmacht installations by direct order of the Führer—no papers, direct order of Adolf Hitler. Open the gate. Wave us through."

The soldier tried to snap to attention, almost losing his balance in the slippery goo, "Yes, Sir, Herr Colonel. But since we had a raid here at Chambéry a while back, the depot command demands that no vehicle passes through the gates without papers. We are not allowed to make exceptions."

Without warning, Chabot threw open the rear door and bolted into the rain as he shouted, "Follow me, young man!" Without waiting for a response, he briskly headed through the mud and up the stairs taking refuge under the tiny gable projecting above the headquarters' entrance door. He stood, indignantly brushing water from his uniform and waiting for the guard to catch up. The soldier arrived and snapped to attention as best he could due to his slippery footing. Chabot positioned himself under the small roof, forcing the soldier to stand in the drenching rain.

It was all Remi could do to keep himself from racing up the stairs to see what was going on. Chabot and the guard stood face to face for several minutes. Jonas had pushed his side window open farther, better able to make out what was going on.

"What the hell are they doing?" Remi asked.

"Just talking…or, rather, Doctor Chabot is talking. The guard just seems to be standing very stiffly, nodding his head and listening."

"God, I hope Chabot doesn't agree to go into the office. We don't know who staffs the place at this hour—hell, it could be Hitler's girlfriend for all we know," he lamented. Jonas nervously pulled his rifle toward him and Remi placed his hand on Jonas' arm to calm him. All at once, the guard gave an abrupt Sieg Heil salute—again, almost losing his balance attempting to click his heels as Chabot briskly descended the stairs and re-entered the Mercedes. The soldier made his way down the stairs and proceeded toward the lead guard shack. The gate slid open as the Mercedes eased toward it. The three vehicles slowly rolled out of the depot, picking up speed as they proceeded toward the Chambéry-Treaire highway.

⚬⚭⚬

It was 4:27 am when they eased the stolen vehicles out of the continuing rain and into the huge maintenance barn on the Cheever estate. "Leave the cars here," Amaury ordered. "I'll have the mechanics go over them in the morning."

Remi called over his shoulder to Amaury, "Get Adrian out of the trunk; strip and bury that German soldier."

Chabot was brushing and then carefully drying his uniform with a dark towel as Remi approached him, "What happened back on the headquarters' landing?"

Gasper continued his fastidious cleaning, "With the young soldier, you mean?"

"Yes, *of course* with the young soldier. The two of you stood talking for what seemed like hours."

"Oh, I am so sorry. I didn't realize you were in a hurry to leave," Gasper muttered, still paying more attention to a smudge on the jacket than he was to Remi. "I simply told the young man he had better read page 33 of his NZA-357 manual defining Gestapo authority and authorization to enter and exit all Wehrmacht military installations without papers. Then I demanded he reach into his pocket and hand me his NZA-357 manual." Gasper was now rubbing on another stain on the uniform.

"Well, did he?"

"Did who do what?"

Remi sighed in exasperation, "Did the soldier hand you his NZA-357 manual?"

Chabot looked up in surprise, "Of *course* not. There *is* no such manual. The lad was dumbfounded being caught without his manual in the face of a Gestapo General," Chabot grinned. "I thought the boy was going to have a coronary right there in the rain. So I became enraged. Told him every Private is required to have his NZA-357 manual with him at all times, and that to be caught without it by a Gestapo officer was a court martial offense. I demanded he immediately summon his superior officer."

Remi's jaw dropped, "You *what*?"

"Just when he turned toward the door to the headquarters' office, I said, 'Wait a minute, how old are you?' He abruptly stopped and told me he was 19. I managed the best pained expression I could and said, 'The same age as my son who is fighting on the Russian Front.' I deepened my pained expression, almost going to tears. Let him stand rigid at attention, thinking I was mulling over my son fighting on the Russian Front. Finally, I gave him a big resigned sigh and said, 'Okay, you are young. Perhaps you deserve another chance. I will not report this tonight. I will, however, pull your file and review if you have been a loyal soldier, dedicated to the Fatherland and supportive of the Führer. If I find your record clear and if no word reaches me that you and I have had this conversation, then I will not press charges. To protect yourself so that there is no record of you're having been confronted by a Gestapo General, you are to pass us through and fill out the headquarters log sheets that three supply trucks passed through the gate...not a Gestapo inspection unit. That way, no one will ever have to know I confronted you. Do you understand?' He shot me a stiff Sieg Heil, almost falling on his butt in the process. You know the rest. The gate opened and we left."

Remi just shook his head in awe, patted the amazing Doctor Gasper Chabot on the arm and left the building.

CHAPTER 44

The rainwater from the downspout had rinsed virtually all of the blood out of Adrian's Captain's uniform. Teams at the hideaway were assigned to cleaning and pressing all of the uniforms and were able to get all stains out of the uniforms of both Adrian and the soldier he killed. Uniform brass and silver were polished, boots spit-shined. Chabot's Mercedes was waxed and even the Opel and Kübelwagen washed and polished. If nothing else, the imposters would have a crisp, professional look when they stood before the garrison at Falauge.

In the communications truck, a message cracked through from Chambéry, addressed to both Falauge and Paris:

ATTENTION NOTICE FROM THE OFFICE OF:
Lieutenant-General Horst Hofstetter,
Chambéry Headquarters
Militärverwaltung in Frankreich,
Chambéry Area Authority,
Chambéry, France

TO COMMAND AT FALAUGE AND PARIS:

SUBJECT: TROOP DESERTIONS
Communiqué 56-372-004
09 May, 1944 – 11:21gmt

It has come to the attention of Chambéry command that three enlistees and one schooled guard dog are reported missing. The perimeter walls and fencing surrounding the Chambéry depot has been thoroughly inspected and has proven secure of any external interference. It is concluded depot security

has not been breached. Subjects are suspected of having deserted their posts.
They are to be apprehended and taken by force if necessary. Description of
deserters:

Ditmar Shamburg – 728-776, age: 20 years, rank: Private, weight: 180,
*   height: 5'- 11", eyes: brown, hair: brown-wavy, mole right cheek,*
*   DOB: 20-2-24*

Klaus Britzmuller – 1033-192, age: 18 years, rank: Private-First Class,
*   weight: 192, height: 6'- 0", eyes: blue, hair: light-brown, trained*
*   Attack/Guard Dog handler, DOB: 13-1-26*

Peter Kurtz – 1293-977, age: 17 years, rank: Private, weight: 171, height:
*   5'- 8", eyes: hazel, hair: light-brown, DOB: 17-5-27*

Attack/Guard Dog – Answers to Luddie, trained attack dog (danger-
*   ous), age: 4 years, male, breed: German Shepherd, color: mixed brown/*
*   black, collar number: 2737-6, handler: Klaus Britzmuller, NOTE:*
*   Trained attack dog – shoot on sight.*

---------- END ----------

Wilhelmina and Celine were tending the radio and simply replied a curt
ACKNOWLEDGED to the captured message.

Several minutes later, a follow-up message came through from Paris
Command:

ATTENTION NOTICE FROM THE OFFICE OF:
Field Operations Marshal Ulrich Jager
French Headquarters, FHD, Paris
French Area Military Command,
Paris, France

TO COMMAND AT CHAMBÉRY AND FALAUGE
SUBJECT: TROOP DESERTIONS
Communiqué 171-976-521
09 May, 1944 – 22:33gmt

Re: Communiqué 56-372-004

NOTE: APPREHENDED DESERTERS ARE TO BE SHOT ON SIGHT.

Desertion is punishable by death (Reich Wehrmacht Order – 1272-19). You are instructed to correct previous communiqué (Communiqué 56-372-004) relating the named deserters. Deserters are to be shot on sight. This communiqué supersedes previous instruction.

---------- *END* ----------

Jonas had told Wilhelmina about the killings that took place during the depot raid. Tending the radio reinforced the news of the deaths, put names and ages on the slain, brought her face to face with the death, destruction and cruelty surrounding them. She was no longer distanced from the viciousness that held Europe in its grip.

That night, as he and Celine sat together, Remi verbalized his anger about the confrontation he had had with Adrian in the depot yard.

"Right there in the middle of the operation, Adrian gets defiant. He starts arguing with my authority. Maybe I should have waited to chew him out, but the way he killed that soldier was so sloppy it could have destroyed everything. If it had not been for the rain, there would have been no way for us to clean up the blood splattered all over on the ground. I'm still not sure it all got washed away. Sure as hell, if they take a dog back there, it'll pick up the scent. All he had to do was stab the bastard, not cut his damn head off."

He paused, rubbing the stiffness in his neck, "I am not comfortable with him, Cel. Adrian's a hothead. He'll blow under pressure. We have him playing a Captain's role. When we're standing in front of the garrison at Falauge that puts him above you and me in rank. As far as the garrison is concerned, Adrian's calling the shots. You and I are just a couple of lowly Privates in their eyes," he stretched his neck from side to side, trying to get the muscles to relax.

"He's young and inexperienced, Remi," Celine tried to sound calm and reassuring. "He was nervous. We haven't trained him how to kill cleanly. I'll work with him."

"Oh, no, it's more than just being young and inexperienced. He's an angry hothead. He loved slitting that guy's throat. I saw it in his eyes. He enjoyed every second of it," Remi's voice was sharp reflecting his continued irritability. "He's a child. He's not in control of his emotions. Whatever pops into his stupid head comes charging out and to hell with everyone else. That bastard will blow the whole operation—get the whole damn lot of us killed."

Adrian's impulsiveness was definitely a problem, but Remi's nervousness about the delicacy of the Falauge operation was coming through loud and strong. She tried to ease his concerns, "We have to have him in a command position because of his German. I'll talk with Margret and Albert. If you are right, if Adrian is short-tempered, they'll have had to deal with it in the past. They'll have some suggestions. I think what he needs is a good spanking. He seems spoiled to me—a 23 year old child," she critically smirked.

Celine's voice calmed Remi. It always did. She soothed him. Settled him. Through an exhausted sigh, he acquiesced. "Yes, do talk with them. See if you think I'm right about that idiot hotheaded son of theirs."

He rose and poured himself another glass of wine, "Albert is a good man and will understand. What about Margret? How do you feel about her?"

"She is bright. A tough lady. She has the guts for war. It doesn't faze her like so many of the others. If we ever have to kill the entire German army, I want to be the one feeding bullet belts into her machine gun."

Remi missed the quip. He was too edgy. The Tristan was into killing now—the close-up, eye-to-eye, hand-to-hand kind of killing. It bothered him, perhaps more deeply than either of them had anticipated. He was displaying his normal hyper-concern about others, still holding himself much too responsible for everyone involved in the plan.

❦

Celine's discussions with Albert and Margret confirmed their suspicions. Adrian had always been short-tempered, confrontational, and quick to make a scene when he didn't get his way. A belligerent child. Albert and Margret kept the peace by giving in to him.

As Celine was leaving, Albert called her aside. "Adrian has always been a problem. I had to punish him so often it began to cause tension between Margret and me, so I backed off. I shouldn't have. He is spoiled. Too many times he has gotten a pass when I should have given him a good beating."

Celine looked Albert in the eyes, "What are you avoiding telling me?"

He looked down at the ground, shook his head then looked her in the eye, "Remi is right to be concerned. Adrian may not be reliable under pressure if he is made to feel insulted. He will lash out without thinking."

Celine told Adrian she wanted to have a special martial arts training session with him—just him. He smiled at her, accepting the invitation. He presumed she recognized his superior natural talent for the art, and this was her acknowledgement of his skill. He prided himself on how deftly he had mimicked the complicated Aikido moves. He felt sure she had been watching him out of the corner of her eye, admiring the precision of his moves. Her desire to work privately with him confirmed his suspicions. He was physically attracted to her. Perhaps she, too, felt the attraction, hence the private session. Early the next morning, he strutted into the gym with a confident smile, eager to show his stuff and fantasizing about how she may want to conclude the session.

Celine walked over to him, stretching out her hand, "Good to see you, Adrian. How are your folks?" As he reached to shake her hand, she spun violently, twisting his arm painfully over his head, flipping him on his back. He landed hard on the mat, knocking the wind out of him. He lay there, shocked, gasping for breath. She stood over him, arms folded across her chest, sneering down at him, "You pathetic little child. You pitiful excuse for a man."

Anger exploded in him, adrenaline surged. He jumped to his feet as his mind shouted, *You may be Remi Rousseau's bitch, but I'm going to kick your ass*. The veins in his temples pulsed as he glared at her. "Pissed off because I stood up to that wimp bastard husband of yours, aren't you? Well, he's an asshol..."

His tirade was cut short as her foot caught his left leg behind the knee. She hammered his solar plexus with her palm, paralyzing his breathing as he plummeted backward. Lying on his back, he fought to inhale. His impact shocked lungs refused to expand. Panic surged, his body crying for oxygen that did not come. Celine bent close, "Having trouble catching your breath, little man? Here, let me help you." She brought her fist down on his stomach. His lungs gasped in response.

She rose slowly, shaking her head, a look of pitiful disgust on her face. She stood easily within reach, defiantly goading him to make a move. He sluggishly rolled away from her taking a long time to get on his feet.

Still bent over, his hands on his knees, he stared up at her from under his brow and growled, "You bitch. You arrogant, nasty little bitch. You'll pay fo…"

A move flashed so swiftly, he didn't see it. Adrian hit the mat face down. He pushed himself up on all fours, panting. Celine stood two feet from his bent head, taunting him, "Humiliated, Adrian? Angry, Adrian? You look so laughable there on all fours. Like a whipped little dog."

He sprang to his feet, charged in rage. She stepped to the right, caught his ankle in the curl of her foot, and brought an elbow to the middle of his back, sending him off the mat, skidding face down on the wood floor. Three more times the stubborn anger boiling in him overshadowed his common sense; each time, the result was painfully repeated. Crashing to the floor, thrown against the wall, flopped over a table. Finally, bruised and in pain, he lay panting, physically spent.

Celine snarled down at him, "You're all show. No brain. Think you can take me, little man?" She dropped a knife at his side, "Go ahead, worm. Go for it!"

Her insults, her scorning attitude, her condescending innuendos pumped angry power to his exhausted muscles. His mind exploded, *Nobody treats Adrian Zollerman with such disrespect. You want to get cut, you little bitch? You're going to get cut.* He grabbed the knife, surged to his feet and lunged at her, whipping the blade at her throat. She pulled back, inches from the blade, grabbed his wrist, twisted, kicked him hard in the groin, and spun him against the wall, flat and hard. Immediately, he sprang back at her. She flipped him over her head, grabbing the knife as he crashed to the floor on his side.

Instantly, she was on him, her knee pressing heavily on the side of his neck and the knife's blade bringing a drop of blood at the point where it contacted his throat.

"I should kill you right now, you miserable, irresponsible brat."

He groaned. Pain radiated everywhere in his body. He was dizzy, nauseous, fighting for air.

"You are a *child*. You *act* like a child. Your anger is that of a child. Your temper is that of a child. You are nothing more than overgrown baby. I do not trust a child to be able to protect me and my comrades from harm. *That* is why I should kill you." She felt the urge to proceed. It could easily be explained...an accident. It would be excused. She forced herself to calm.

He lay in utter exhaustion, totally emotionally humbled and physically defeated. He had been brought to the point of death by a woman 70 pounds lighter and several inches shorter than him. Celine's knee remained pressing on his neck, affording him only shallow breaths.

"I am sorry," he managed.

She shouted, "Not good enough! You cannot be sorry when Remi is dead, when your father is dying, when the garrison attacks us. Sorry won't count then. Get over being sorry, little boy. *Grow up!* Become a man—like Remi, like your brother, like your father, like Chabot."

She rose releasing the pressure on his neck. He groaned. Rolled over. Ever so gradually, he got to his knees. She reached down to give him a hand, and he shied away. "It's over," she said. "You can take my hand and I will help you up."

He gained his feet, staring at her. Still breathing hard, "I understand what... you just did to me. I want to...to be part of the Tristan. I will...do as you say."

"Yes, little baby boy," she scoffed back at him. "You know *what* I just did, but do you know why?"

Still panting heavily, he nodded, "I...I think so."

"*Why?*" she spat back.

"I think you and Remi are *(pant)*...worried about my attitude."

"*What* about your attitude?"

"I think you are worried about my temper. Not being able to control my temper."

Celine came up very close and looked Adrian in the eye. He stiffened. "Your temper, your little-boy self-centered temper and defiance will get us killed—all of us on the mission and all of those in hiding. You have been a hothead all of your life. You are spoiled. You think of no one but yourself. We need you, but we need you as a man, not as a self-serving, juvenile brat. You've got to grow up and get control of yourself, and you have to do it within the next few days. Can you get yourself ready mentally?"

"I think so."

She slapped him hard in the face, "*No!* Thinking so is not good enough!" she yelled.

He lurched back, surprised at the sting of the slap—surprised she was still so angry. Emotion began to rise. He had never been so disgraced, so embarrassed. Worst of all, by a woman he was sexually attracted to. He pushed the feelings down.

He bent, placing both hands on his knees and looking at the floor. Breaking eye contact helped him deal with feeling so completely mentally broken. He continued staring down as he spoke, "You will not be sorry. Not now…not later. I will do my assignment well, like an adult. With a calm attitude. I will fight with you, for you…for you and for Remi."

Celine moved toward the door not looking back, "If you don't, I will kill you."

Alone in the empty massive room Adrian sank to the mat. He could hold his tears no longer.

CHAPTER 45

Celine and Remi were in the parlor adjacent to their suite of rooms in the château. Amaury sat with them, none paying attention to the warm gaiety of late afternoon sunlight sparkling through the windows. Remi exhaled from the long drag he had just sucked from his cigarette. "Everything is physically in place—the cars, the uniforms, our German speakers." He sighed, "But we are not ready...not by a long shot."

Amaury looked perplexedly irritated. *More of Remi's overly cautious fears,* he grumbled to himself. "For Christ's sake, Remi, it's time to move. Everyone is motivated and ready to go. Stop with all your hesitation, damn it. It's never going to be the perfect time..."

"No! This operation is so delicate, so complicated it stands the chance of falling apart with the slightest misstep. We are depending on a huge number of people—more people than we have ever had to rely on to back us up. One misstep, one single slip, Amaury, and the whole damn thing blows up in our faces."

Celine watched the tension between the two of them, unusual for Amaury. Remi continued, "I have been observing everyone—the Schultzes, the Zollermans, everyone involved. They are good people. I'm glad to have them, but they are not ready. Not to stand up in front of the garrison shouting orders and keeping a bunch of edgy young Nazis in line. I insist on more training, play acting...call it whatever you like, but until I'm satisfied, we are at no go."

Amaury glumly shook his head, "Damn you, Remi, you always do this." Such irritation coming out of Amaury was rare—more an attitude they would expect from Felicien.

"What's concerning you?" Celine asked gently, searching Amaury's face.

"Hell, I don't know. Having to endure that horse's ass Auchenbach every night is more than I can bear, and to have to continue to do so is unthinkable. I'd like to castrate the son-of-a-bitch," his tone was both angry and hopeless.

"Amaury, I can't remember ever seeing you so upset," Celine probed. "What's this is all about?"

Amaury stared at his half-empty glass of Bordeaux. "Nothing," he grudged, continuing his despondency. She waited seeing Amaury wrestling with his equivocation.

"No," he said, "it's *not* nothing." He sighed deeply, his eyes filling with tears. He took a handkerchief from his pocket, blew his nose and wiped his eyes. The room remained quiet as his pain began to emerge. It puzzled Celine and Remi.

He took a sip of wine, coughed, and steadied his voice, "You know Aimée… Aimée Laroque, the girl who tends the night desk at the inn?" His chin trembled. He sighed painfully, trying to hold everything in, then pushed down hard on emotions that were fighting their way to the surface.

"He's…Auchenbach is forcing her up to his room at night, threatening to have her parents arrested. He's…he's…

"I love her. I know she's too young for me. Only 18…but I love her. I have for a long time, and that Hun bastard is raping her time and time again. That Hun bastard, son-of-a-bitch is *raping her*!" Amaury lowered his head and sobbed. Celine went over and wrapped her arms around him.

"We had no idea, Amaury," she whispered "Why didn't you ever say anything about Aimée?"

"She's too young for me," he repeated. "I've been in love with her ever since she started working at the inn. She was only 15—my God, only 15. I'm so embarrassed," he welled up again.

"Amaury, you're only 25," protested Celine. "You are *not* too old for her. Maybe when she was 15, but she's 18 now. I think she would be thrilled to know you care so deeply for her."

"I see now why you want to get on with taking Auchenbach out of the picture," Remi said. "Look, Amaury, we cannot speed up our plans because of this, but we don't have to let this continue. We will fix this, my friend. Immediately."

The next afternoon, after Amaury knew Aimée had left for work, he and Remi knocked on the door of the Laroque home. Her mother answered, friendly, but with a look of surprise. She knew them both, but only in passing. She was further perplexed when they asked if they might come in and speak with her and Mr. Laroque.

Gabriel Laroque gave them an enquiring look, setting down his book as his wife entered their tiny living room with the unexpected guests. It was a complicated, emotional and trying conversation. Aimée's parents listened—shocked, violated, angry, and heartbroken.

Gabriel finally spoke, "Mr. Cheever, we are honored at your affection for Aimée, and your respect for her and us. You are Treaire's leading citizen and if Aimée..." his eyes teared as his affection gave way to his daughter's agony. "Oh, what can I do? How can I protect my beautiful Aimée?" he cried.

"We have a way, Monsieur Laroque. We want to remove Aimée from the situation," Remi's voice was strong and respectful. He described how she could go into hiding, and offered the couple the ability to do so as well. The Laroques sat, bewildered at the complexity of events that were falling upon them with such suddenness. They agonized in the torment their daughter was enduring and now the possibility of leaving their home. Their calm world had instantly turned to chaos, their daughter abused—living in pain and agony to protect them from a threat they hadn't known existed.

Gabriel Laroque's anger boiled, his guilt tore at his heart as his mind searched for a way to protect Aimée—his beautiful daughter. How to get at Auchenbach, and dissipate his burning internal fury. He was the man, the father—the one responsible for providing for and protecting, yet there seemed nothing he could do but run off and hide. "I will butcher that bastard," he raged. "I will cut him to ribbons..."

Remi latched onto Gabriel's anger, "We will help you do that. We will give you the opportunity to vent your frustration and avenge Aimée. Join us. We are about to rid Treaire of these Nazi swine."

It was 2 am when Amaury entered the inn through the alley door. He deftly moved down the hall. She was there, thank God, dozing in her chair—hopefully, having been left alone tonight. He looked at her adoringly. His heart pained for her.

She was startled when he gently touched her arm, but did not cry out. He whispered that her parents were waiting in the car and they were taking them all to safety, away from Colonel Auchenbach to a place the Nazis could not find them. She teared up, ashamed her parents now knew but grateful she could escape. They moved quietly down the hall and out to the waiting car.

⁂

For the next seven weeks, Chabot, the Zollermans, Amaury, Felicien, and Jonas Schultz were drilled in martial arts, weapons instruction, playacting standing in front of garrison troops, studied sections of German military manuals concerning uniform dress codes, proper salutes, orders of rank and protocol. The rehearsals seemed endless as Remi insisted on perfection, "It has to look natural", he demanded, "as if you are doing things effortlessly. Any hint of playacting is not acceptable." Those directly involved in the capture of Auchenbach and his officers and those who would take command at Falauge were drilled repeatedly, tested verbally and in written examinations. Scores were kept to focus the training on weak spots. Off hours the troop memorized hundreds of minute details that could mean the difference between success or death at Falauge. Celine and Remi spoke privately with Adrian several times—pleased at his new positive and determined attitude.

Those in hiding not involved in the training prepared the meals, did the laundry, gave moral support, and tended the children and the elderly. Preparations went on late into the night and the Tristan did frequent night inspections, assuring the windows of the barns, the mill and other buildings on the estate were properly sealed to assure they suggested no hint of night activity.

The stolen vehicles were gone over in detail by Amaury's mechanics assuring no unexpected breakdowns. Activities were intense; spirits were high. Everyone was working together, the common cause uniting hearts and minds. They were all involved—all participating in fighting back at their oppressors— taking charge of their lives and standing up for their freedoms.

Everyone, including Chabot, Celine and Remi, now took their evening meal together in the barn dining hall. Joy erupted the night Wilhelmina Schultz stood, proudly holding a radio message aloft, "The Allies have attacked Cassino, Italy!" she shouted. Cheers erupted so loudly Remi jokingly worried any German patrol aircraft within miles might have heard the cry. Not long afterward, another night of celebration broke out as Celine announced the Allies had landed on Anzio beach just south of Rome.

Spirits soared with the news of Allied advances in Italy. Perhaps the end of the Nazis was in sight. Remi expressed to Celine, "Wouldn't it be great if the Allies came busting over the Saint Laurnee trestle and blew the Falauge garrison to hell?"

"Oh, how disappointing," Celine smiled. "All of our hard work wasted."

Their hard work would not be wasted. The counter offensive mounted by Generalfeldmarschall Albert Kesselring at Cassino and Anzio assured the battle for Italy would grind on for months.

⸺ ⸎ ⸺

Celine, Remi, Amaury, Felicien and Chabot gathered around the table in the mill. It was late on the moonless mid-March night. Humid warmth offered the first teasing of the coming spring.

"We are ready," Remi said. "There is nothing to be gained by further training."

While eagerly awaited, the impact of the announcement fell on sober ears. There was no misconception of the danger in what they were about to do. Remi wanted to be sure he was not misinterpreting the silence, "Are we all still committed?" Every head solemnly nodded yes.

"Good. Day after tomorrow we send the message."

Thirty-six hours later, Remi and Celine were in the communications truck when Chabot sent the message to Colonel Auchenbach at Falauge:

--- *ATTENTION --- NOTICE FROM THE OFFICE OF:*
Lieutenant-General Horst Hofstetter,
Chambéry Headquarters,
Militärverwaltung in Frankreich,
Chambéry Area Authority,
Chambéry, France

TO: COLONEL AUCHENBACH AT FALAUGE
SUBJECT: PREPARATIONS FOR ALLIED INVASION
OF FRANCE
Communiqué 56-374-077
07 July, 1944 - 10:47gmt

SPECIAL BRIEFING MEETING:

A briefing will be held in the assembly room at Chambéry Headquarters at 13:00:00, Saturday, 08 July, 1944 concerning defensive instruction, assignments, and operations to be implemented in southern France relative to the possibility of Allied armies' assault into the region.

Colonel Auchenbach, you will have in attendance with you all of your officers, except two left in charge of the garrison at Falauge. Please select your most trusted and capable officers to remain at Falauge garrison headquarters.

You and your officers are instructed to travel by railcar to Chambéry Hauptbahnhof where staff cars will transport you directly to Chambéry Headquarters. Allow 30 minutes to be seated and ready for presentations from Field Marshal Ulrich Jager and General Joseph Ault. Expect the meeting to last 2 hours, then return immediately by railcar to Falauge.

Acknowledge receipt and confirm.
---------- END ----------

Within minutes, they captured the acknowledgement message confirming that Auchenbach and his officers would be in attendance at the appointed time.

The count-down on the battle of Falauge began ticking.

CHAPTER 46

The locomotive lurched, giving Colonel Auchenbach and his officers a jolt as it started from its siding toward the main line to Chambéry. *Why in hell can't train engineers start off without half breaking their passenger's damn necks?* Auchenbach checked his watch—*10:45, perfect.*

He sat toward the front of the car, separating himself by some six rows from his officers, sitting stoically behind him. The car jostled from side to side as it picked up speed, heading toward Treaire. There the track made a leisurely curve and then headed north toward Chambéry.

Auchenbach settled down to review his file of contingency plans dealing with an invasion of Allied forces moving north from Italy, through the French Alps and up into France. There was also a set of maps dealing with a possible Allied invasion onto the beaches of southern France. The documents were several years old and addressed scenarios considered purely hypothetical at the time. When the file was originally prepared, the Allies were being beaten bloody by Rommel in Africa. The thought of Germany having to fight them in France was almost laughable.

My, how the situation has changed, he thought *I would not have believed the Allies had the will or would be able to work together to make this all happen.* Thinking about the Allies working together brought a disgusted pause. The stories of the hatred existing between Britain's self-adoring General Montgomery and America's arrogant General Patton were widely publicized. Both men carried massive egos and were constantly chaffing at each other, delivering cutting remarks about one another to the press. But in spite of all their immaturity, Generals Eisenhower and Marshall had kept them pointed relatively in the same direction, and they were now knocking on the door of southern France. Auchenbach had little doubt they would eventually penetrate German defenses in Italy.

While it saddened him to think of his cherished Fatherland being pushed around by the scummy British and the disgustingly mixed-race Americans, he was excited about this meeting. Future plans might offer him the opportunity of leading the garrison into battle against them. *Should that happen, they will find they have run into a very capable field commander,* he mused. As a Lieutenant, he had briefly led a platoon during the six weeks it took the Germans to bring Poland to its knees. Stimulated by the violence of that one-sided battle, he looked forward to, once again, spill the blood of Germany's enemies.

He set the file on the seat next to him, staring out the window at the passing countryside. *What a shame,* he thought. *Such a beautiful area. Soon, it will be pretty much demolished.* He smiled, thinking of how he would dig in his troops and fight the despicable Limeys and Yankees until every last one of them lay dead. *Yes, they will pay,* he mused. *They will pay dearly for every inch of French soil they attempt to take from Wilhelm Auchenbach.* He relaxed, suddenly feeling drowsy—stretched his legs out onto the seat facing him and leaned his head back against the head rest. *Time for a morning snooze before we get to Chambéry.*

<hr />

Coming out of the long turn toward Chambéry the engineer increased speed in anticipation of the almost 20 miles of straight track ahead. Although Auchenbach was unaware of it, for two miles after the turn, the track ran through the Cheever estate, dividing the property into east and west sections. None of the estate buildings were visible from the tracks; the view was obscured by giant ancient pines growing close to the right-of-way on both sides of the track. The Cheever barns, now brimming with citizens in hiding, lay a short distance beyond the tree line to the east.

All at once, one of the mammoth pines crashed onto the tracks a thousand yards ahead of the speeding train. The shocked engineer reacted instantly, locking the engine's huge wheels and throwing the air brakes on the tender and passenger car. Sparks shot from the grinding of steel against steel as the train's wheels slid down the tracks.

Auchenbach was thrown from his seat. He hit the floor with a thud, shattering his pleasant dream state. His file scattered to the floor beside him. One of the two sentries he had stationed on the car's platform just outside the front door was thrown forward, lost his footing and fell to an instant death as he hit the tracks between the moving car and the engine's tender. The engineer reversed the locomotive's drive wheels, giving another abrupt jolt as the train screeched to a stop just feet from the enormous tree resting across the track.

As a blast of steam shot from the engine's rapidly depressurizing boiler, 30 of the hideaways from the barn emerged from behind the trees on both sides of the track. Ominously clad from head to toe in black, their faces hidden behind black ski masks, they stood silently, weapons trained on the railcar.

Auchenbach struggled to his feet, caught sight of the hoard of terrorists, and dropped to his knees. Seeing the armed band outside, his officers ducked down trying to get out of sight of the windows. Auchenbach crawled down the aisle to the rear door, rose up on his knees and peered through the window just in time to watch another of the great pines crash across the tracks 30 yards behind the train. The two guards he had posted on the rear platform raised their hands high in response to the throng of armed opponents lining both sides of the track. They threw down their weapons in surrender. Auchenbach dropped to the floor. "On the floor!" he shouted to his stunned officers. "On the floor *now*. Do not return fire."

The surviving guard on the front platform cried out, "Don't shoot," flinging his weapon toward one of the figures in black. Auchenbach sprang to his feet, hunkered low, shouting for his officers to clear the aisle as he moved to the front of the car. He cracked the door open, attempting to shoot the surrendering soldier. He missed, but one of men in black, thinking the shot had come from the guard, instantly shot him dead.

Auchenbach again dropped to the floor, commanding his officers, "Stay down! Below the windows. There must be 50 of them. Our sidearms are useless against them." He was sure the car was about to be riddled with bullets—or, worse, would erupt in exploding shrapnel from multiple grenades hurled through the open windows. They lay there on the floor of the car for several minutes. Nothing…no sound, no movement. Only the periodic hiss of steam releasing the pressures of the engine's boiler broke the silence.

A voice finally called out in German, "Stand so we can see you. Throw your weapons out of the windows. Lock your fingers behind your heads and move toward the rear of the car. Wait at the rear door for me to call to you to exit. We know you have eight officers with you, Colonel Auchenbach, so do not attempt to leave someone behind in hiding." There was a pause as the voice waited to see if there was any movement from within the car. Auchenbach and his men held their positions.

The voice continued, "If you fail to comply, the railcar will be fired upon by two 20 millimeter Solothurn anti-tank rifles. You are familiar with the Solothurn rifle's ability to pierce armor, so you know the railcar will not protect you. Now, stand so we can see you, throw out your weapons, and move single-file to the rear of the car."

Every officer aboard was familiar with the Solothurn's destructive power. Its projectile would easily pierce the car's metal sides and explode upon entry, turning the car into a death trap. The question in Auchenbach's mind was, *Do they really have such weapons, and, for the love of God, where on earth would these peasants have gotten them?*

The officers remained on the floor, waiting to see if their Colonel was going to comply with the demands they had been issued. He hesitated. *They have got to be bluffing,* he thought. *No Solothurns have been reported missing from either Chambéry or Falauge.*

The voice called out again, "Colonel Auchenbach, killing you and your officers in the railcar will save us a lot of time and effort. We are not reluctant to do so. Stand…throw out your weapons and move toward the rear of the car—*now!*"

Still, Auchenbach did not move. *How in hell do they know my name, and how do they know I have eight officers with me?* The questions infuriated him. *And who in hell is that son-of-a-bitch yelling at us in perfect German?*

All of a sudden, a huge blast blew one of the larger trees on the far side of the right-of-way off of its trunk. There was no mistake about it—that was a Solothurn.

Auchenbach slowly rose, motioning for his officers to follow his lead. He leaned over a seat and pitched his sidearm out of the open window. His officers did the same, then locked their hands behind their heads and shuffled toward the rear door with Auchenbach the last in line. The troops in black stood some 20 yards to the sides of the car, maintaining the safe distance—just in case the Solothurns were required to open up.

The voice called out, "First man, exit now." The door opened and a Captain stepped onto the rear platform, his fingers clasped behind his head.

"Exit the platform to your left." He did as instructed, awkwardly jumping the four feet from the platform to the ground while maintaining his hands behind his head.

The voice called for the next man. The exit procedure continued one by one, with every other man exiting to the right or left side of the track as directed. As soon as they hit the ground, the officers were grabbed, blindfolded, gagged, and their hands were tied behind their backs. As Auchenbach stepped onto the platform, the buzz of multiple chainsaws broke the silence. He looked up and a team of men in black were attacking the tree that had been felled behind the train.

Those bastards are going to move the train back to Falauge. The thought filled Auchenbach with fury. His anger and humiliation soared, pounding in his head. He longed to kill these black-clad dogs…slowly and painfully. His heart raced as anger and raw emotion engulfed him. All at once, a searing pain shot through his gut. *Oh, God, no.* He doubled over, falling from the platform hard onto the ballast rock. He lay there, bent in half, cramping in response to the pain growing in his gut. He was yanked to his feet, a rag stuffed in his mouth and tied tightly with a gag. He was then blindfolded and his hands were tied behind his back. As another excruciating pain surged through his gut, he panicked. Without a quick swill of Kaopectate, he would vomit.

Auchenbach frantically jumped up and down, trying to yell through the gag, mumbling as loudly as possible, desperately trying to alert his captors to his dilemma. They pushed him forward, angered at his theatrics. He felt the explosion welling up from deep within his gut. The erupting fluid shot up his esophagus, filling his throat and impacting against the rag plugging his mouth. It recoiled down his windpipe, the acid of his retching stomach searing his lungs with agonizing pain. He screamed as loudly as the gag would allow. He doubled over as a second wrenching spasm sent its regurgitation surging up, filling his lungs. He dropped to his knees, then on to his face, where his body convulsed for several minutes as he suffocated in his own stomach fluids.

That afternoon, the remains of Colonel Wilhelm Auchenbach, still gagged and blindfolded, were dumped into a pit dug by one of Amaury's maintenance tractors. His naked body hit the bottom of the pit—his uniform, identification papers, wallet and sidearm now were in the possession of the Jews he so despised. His junior officers and the guards who had surrendered spent the first night of what would become a very long stay locked two men to a horse stall in a stable about 50 yards from the barns where the Jews were housed. They, too, had been stripped of their uniforms, left only in their undershorts. The chill of the night was distressing as they pathetically snuggled up to one another on the dirt floor in search of warmth.

The troops in black shoved the officers into the cell-like stalls and bolted the doors before telling the prisoners they could remove their blindfolds and gags. As their captors left, one of them shouted over his shoulder that someone would bring them supper later that evening. But the victory celebration the officers heard coming from the adjacent barns turned into a gala affair, and whoever the "someone" was must have forgotten the promised supper—an unforgivable oversight. But, then again, had the circumstances been reversed, the Germans may have forgotten to feed the Jews, too.

CHAPTER 47

Auchenbach's train had been halted at 11:17 am. Anxiously waiting in the radio truck with Wilhelmina, Celine, dressed in a Private's uniform with her hair pulled up under her helmet so she resembled a young German recruit, sighed in relief when word of the successful capture of the Falauge officers came through.

She nodded to Wilhelmina, "Okay, they've done it. Send the message." Wilhelmina's nimble fingers keyed in the code and sent the message. It was designed to look like the message had been sent from Paris to both Chambéry and Falauge, but it was sent only to the radio receiver at the Falauge garrison headquarters:

ATTENTION NOTICE FROM THE OFFICE OF:
Field Operations Marshal Ulrich Jager
French Headquarters, FHD, Paris
French Area Military Command,
Paris, France

TO COMMAND HEADQUARTERS AT CHAMBÉRY
AND FALAUGE
SUBJECT: DEFENSE OF PARIS
STATUS: CRITICAL – CRITICAL -- CRITICAL
Communiqué 225-576-773
08 July, 1944 - 11:22gmt

--- DEFENSE OF PARIS --- DEFENSE OF PARIS ---
DEFENSE OF PARIS ---

NOTE:
ALLIED FORCES SUCCESSFULLY LANDED IN FRANCE
AT NORTH SEA PORTS OF
PAS-DE-CALAIS AND BOULOGNE-SUR-MER

The garrison at Falauge is being immediately transferred to duty in the defense of Paris.

Prepare full garrison for transfer within 24 hours — combat dress — weapons and ammunition to accompany troops — transfer by troop train to Gare de Lyon station in Paris without delay.

Stand by for instructions from Falauge Commander Colonel Wilhelm Achenbach following this communiqué.

ACKNOWLEDGE AND CONFIRM RECEIPT IMMEDIATELY
---------- *END* ----------

The radio operator at Falauge had no sooner delivered the shocking message to Captain Gersten and Lieutenant Osterhagen, the officers Auchenbach had left in charge, when he came racing back with the second phony message. This one informing them they were to meet up with Colonel Auchenbach and the rest of the Falauge officers in Paris.

ATTENTION NOTICE FROM THE OFFICE OF:
Lieutenant-General Horst Hofstetter,
Chambéry Headquarters,
Militärverwaltung in Frankreich,
Chambéry Area Authority,
Chambéry, France

FROM: COLONEL WILHELM AUCHENBACH
TO OFFICERS IN CHARGE AT FALAUGE:

ATTENTION:
CAPTAIN KARL GERSTEN AND
LIEUTENANT DAVID OSTERHAGEN

SUBJECT: TRANSFER OF FALAUGE GARRISON TO
PARIS
Communiqué 146-972-388
08 July, 1944 - 11:27gmt

*As directed in communiqué 225-576-773 from Paris command, prepare Falauge
garrison, all troops and officers, for immediate transfer to Paris-Gare de Lyon.
Prepare to exit Falauge for Paris no later than 24:00:00 – 08 July, 1944.*

*Schedule arrival time at Paris-Gare de Lyon no later than 09 July, 1944 -
15:00:00gmt*

*Paris command sending Gestapo Lieutenant-General Helmfried
Schulmann and his staff to assume command of the Falauge railhead.
Schulmann and staff will secure Falauge to await final troop trains retreating north from Italy. Lieutenant-General Schulmann is presently in
route to Falauge. Follow Schulmann's orders and instructions upon his
arrival.*

*Begin garrison transfer preparation immediately; do not wait for arrival of
Lieutenant-General Schulmann and staff. Your troop train will proceed
nonstop from Falauge to Gare de Lyon-Paris station.*

*NOTE: I will meet you upon your arrival at Paris-Gare de Lyon, where
I will resume command of the garrison.*

SIGNED: COLONEL WILHELM AUCHENBACH,
COMMANDER FALAUGE GARRISON
ACKNOWLEDGE AND CONFIRM RECEIPT IMMEDIATELY
---------- END ----------

Gersten and Osterhagen stood dumbfounded, staring at each other. "My God, the Allies have landed in France," Gersten uttered, amazed.

Osterhagen shook his head in fear and disbelief. He looked to Gersten, "What the hell do we do?"

"We follow orders, Lieutenant. The second message says to get the garrison on trains and meet Colonel Auchenbach at Gare de Lyon-Paris station. So, that is what we do."

"This is absurd," Osterhagen, still in shock, protested. "We are to abandon Falauge? That is stupid. We're supposed to rush off to protect Paris with 80 raw troops? It's insanity."

Gersten smiled at his junior officer, "Let me ask you a question. Is this the first stupidly insane order you've ever been told to obey?" They gave each other a look of hopeless submission, then headed off in different directions to prepare their underlings to follow them into stupid insanity.

Runners were sent out to the troops manning the defensive gun emplacements at the Saint Laurnee trestle and tunnel, ordering them to leave their posts and line up at assembly in the Falauge yard within one hour. Garrison platoon leaders were notified to prepare their units for combat readiness, assembly in the yard in one hour and departure within 10 hours.

The atmosphere at Falauge exploded in frenetic activity. Soldiers ran helter-skelter, grabbing weapons and ammunition, getting together various field combat items, and stuffing clothing and supplies into duffel bags for the trip north into a very frightening unknown.

Both Captain Gersten and Lieutenant Osterhagen fought to keep their mixture of irritation, dread and astonishment in check as they stripped their living quarters and filled their travel trunks for transfer to the waiting train cars. As troops finished packing, they were assigned to attach a second coal and water tender to the engine and overload both with fuel. The trip was to be made with all due speed and the excess fuel would allow a straight-through run without requiring a refueling stop. It was in the midst of this turbulent activity that Chabot and his entourage pulled up at the Falauge garrison entrance gate.

The gate stood unattended—no guard, no personnel in sight. Following proper protocol, Remi told Sergeant Jonas to go back to the Mercedes and inform General Gasper Chabot and Colonel Albert Zollerman that he would open the gates. While Jonas was attending to the gate, Remi went to Chabot and told him to be enraged at the fact there was no guard posted at the gate. "Find the officers that Auchenbach left in charge and dress them down." Chabot nodded and smiled, "I am really starting to enjoy reprimanding German soldiers. Doing a couple of officers will be great fun."

Jonas pushed the gate open and General Chabot's convoy rolled into the yard. At the sight of the Mercedes with General insignias fluttering from its fender staffs, several scurrying soldiers halted in their tracks, stiffened to attention and saluted. Chabot had Amaury stop the car, exited his rear seat, moving quickly toward the soldiers, and shouted, "Get the officers in charge immediately!" A quick *Jawohl, Herr General*, and one of the young men dashed off into the din of tumultuous chaos. Chabot shouted to the remaining soldiers, still holding their rigid positions, to carry on. They instantly vanished, relieved to be out of the General's sight. Within a minute, Captain Gersten and Lieutenant Osterhagen dashed out from the corner of a barracks building, moving quickly toward Chabot. By this time, Colonel Zollerman had come to the side of General Chabot, further enhancing Chabot's authority. The two junior officers came to attention in front of Chabot, snapping off *Heil Hitlers* in perfect unison.

Chabot did not return the salute, but immediately began yelling at the distraught officers, "What in hell is going on here? No guard at the gate, no orderly discipline, no organization? You are fools! Your men are out of control! The Italians are better organized than this. This will be reported to the general staff in Paris and *immediately* to Colonel Auchenbach. Now, get your men to assembly immediately!"

"But, Sir," Osterhagen blurted, "we are under orders to immediately…"

Chabot glared at the young officer, "I don't give a *damn* about what orders you think you are under! I just commanded you to get these soldiers to assembly. Now *get them to assembly*…before I impound you for insubordination."

"Jawohl, Herr General," and the officers sped off. Within minutes, the yard's horn sounded its three blasts, calling the troops to assembly. As Albert and Chabot climbed the five stairs and took their places in the center of the review stand, Albert said, "Well, that went well. Now all we have to do is stand here in front of all 80 of them and act angry." Chabot smiled to himself savoring the thought of it.

Celine, Remi, Amaury, Felicien and Jonas lined up in front of the review stand, facing the assembly field. They stood at authoritative ease, their hands loosely resting on the machine guns slung across their chests and praying they would not be forced to begin shooting the gathering throng that was quickly taking their assembly positions in front of them.

Soldiers rushed in to the assembly yard from every direction, in whatever state of dress they found themselves in when the horn sounded. Several showed up in nothing more than undershorts. With the troops assembled, Sergeant Jonas boomed out, "Attention!" The garrison smartly stiffened, all eyes focused on Chabot. Colonel Albert stood just to the right of Chabot; Captains Adrian and Anton stood to his left and one step behind. The foursome projected an impressive and intimidating corps of distinguished officers. At Chabot's direction, Jonas bellowed, "Assembly…at ease," and with a snappy unified sound, the garrison assumed at ease positions.

Chabot stood, critically eyeing the troops. They were curious, *Who is this Gestapo General? Why have he and his staff called us to assembly?* Chabot held his silence. He placed his hand behind his back and strutted several paces to the left, visually reviewing the troops. He turned, abruptly moving back to center stage. Captain Gersten and Lieutenant Osterhagen stood at the front of the assembled troops—in as much confusion about what was happening as their men.

The yard was silent as Chabot continued his theatrics, glancing back and forth at the lines of men. Remi's nerves began their acceleration toward a frayed state. With his back to the review platform he had no idea of what was going on with Chabot. *God, has he clinched? Has he frozen in the face of these troops?* As the silence continued, a general nervousness engulfed the assembly. It was almost as if every soldier began to hold their breath in anticipation of whatever fate awaited them.

At the top of his voice, Chabot shouted, "You are a disgrace!" Again, he fell silent, letting the echo of his blast fade.

"I have never…*never*…come upon a German military facility in such a state of disarray as this. It is *totally inexcusable*. I will not tolerate it, and it will not be tolerated by the Reich." Then, in an unexpected twist that came as a complete surprise to Celine, Remi, Amaury, Felicien and Jonas, Chabot shouted to Jonas, "Sergeant, place the officers in charge of this garrison under arrest and hold them for disciplinary court martial."

The order was so unexpected, so unplanned that the Tristan members stood confounded in their positions. All eyes focused on them, waiting for them to carry out their General's order. Celine stepped forward, directing her machine gun at the two officers, who had stiffened to attention as Chabot issued the order for their arrest. Remi immediately followed, then Amaury and Felicien leaving Sergeant Jonas very confused as to what he was supposed to do as he moved toward the two stunned officers.

Celine gave Jonas a quick little nod, prodding him to take over and carry out Chabot's order. "Step toward me," he commanded, not knowing what to follow that feeble demand with. "Step to the base of the review platform, then about-face and face the garrison," he clumsily commanded. Celine, Remi, Amaury, and Felicien moved to the new position with the officers falling into place on either side of them. The whole procedure lacked finesse, but the rank and file of the garrison were so mesmerized at the proceedings they just stood watching in awe as the events unfolded.

Chabot then ordered Jonas to remove the men's rank insignias—a procedure which, in reality, would never have been performed in the German military in front of regular soldiers. Jonas came to attention, faced the two officers and tore the rank designation patches and hardware from their uniforms. The act was the epitome of humiliation to the officers, and shocking to the troops watching the degradation. Both Celine and Remi were on the edge of panic. Chabot was dramatically overplaying the situation. Celine grew uneasy, seeing the dismay on the faces of the men assembled in front of her. *Damn you, Chabot, end it,* she agonized.

"Now," shouted Chabot, addressing the entire assembly, "you see that the order and the honor of the Third Reich have been restored." He snapped his heels and performed a magnificent *Heil Hitler.* In relief of the sizzling tension filling the air, the entire garrison snapped to attention, exploding with a triumphant return salute and yell echoing Chabot's lead. Remi thought, *My God, he's got them! They have just watched their two commanding officers stripped of rank and they're shouting loyalty to Chabot.* Celine just stood in amazement, working hard not to smile at the ridiculous scene Chabot had just pulled off.

Chabot held his posture for several moments then, shouted, "At ease."

He yelled to one of the garrison Platoon Sergeants standing to the right of his troops, "Have the men been informed of the reason for all of the activity?"

"We have only been told to dress in combat gear and assemble for further instructions, Herr General. That is all, Sir," the Sergeant shouted back.

Chabot glanced down at the defrocked officers, shaking his head in disappointment at them. "Then, it is left to me to tell you what is going on. The Allies have taken a beachhead in northern France. They have landed at Pas-de-Calais and at Boulogne-Sur-Mer. While we are confident Wehrmacht forces will drive them back into the sea, we are taking no chances with the defense of Paris. Various troops from other locations in France are being ordered to Paris to set up defensive positions. This garrison has been ordered to transfer to the Paris defense immediately." There was a stir among the soldiers. Standing at the side of Chabot, Colonel Zollerman shouted, "Stand at ease!" bringing the assembly, once again, to order.

Chabot continued, "At 23:30 hours you will board a troop train here in the yard for transfer to Paris. You are to be dressed in full combat-ready gear, including full allocation of weapons and ammunition, as assigned to infantry troops. Your train has right-of-way and will be supplied with sufficient fuel to carry it at top speed nonstop to Paris. When you arrive at Gaue de Lyon station, your commander, Colonel Auchenbach, will meet the train and lead you to your defensive positions. Stand proud, my sons. The Fatherland calls to you." The last statement brought a noticeable puffing of chests and determined looks to the youthful faces at assembly.

Chabot glanced down at his wristwatch. "It is now 13:57. You have plenty of time to prepare for your departure. I expect to see orderly conduct…not the frantic running about I witnessed when I arrived. Now, in a disciplined manner, continue your preparation for departure." Zollerman shouted, "Dismissed!"

As the soldiers broke from the yard, Chabot and the Zollermans descended the platform. Chabot walked up to the disgraced officers. "Does this post have disciplinary holding cells?" he demanded.

"Jawohl, Sir," responded Lieutenant Osterhagen.

"You will be held there," Chabot continued. "You will not accompany the troops to Paris. I will assign my Captains as their temporary officers for the trip. But before you go," Chabot's face turned to a scowl. He stood, looking at the men with near-compassion and concern. "What were you thinking? The gate stood unguarded. Your troops were running recklessly about. No direction, no discipline. You are distinguished German officers. What if someone besides me, someone from the outside had seen this embarrassment to our proud history of military bearing?"

The shattered looks on the faces of Gersten and Osterhagen displayed heart-felt shame. They had let down not only General Chabot but the Fatherland as a whole. Their heads hung in shame.

Chabot continued, his tone reflecting the disappointment of a dedicated General who had hoped to see more from subordinate officers, "The panicked disorder I saw when I arrived left no doubt you were not in command of your troops, a responsibility Colonel Auchenbach felt you were capable of handling. Losing command of your men at a garrison post is one thing; losing command of your troops in combat will cost them their lives.

"Your court martial will be the lesser of your sentence. Your punishment, Mr. Gersten and Mr. Osterhagen, will be lifelong knowledge that you failed those who counted on you to lead and protect them—those who trusted you." Turning toward Jonas, he said, "Take these fallen officers to the holding cells. If there is more than one cell, place them in separate cells and tie them with their hands behind their backs!" He turned back toward the now emotionally destroyed officers. "May God forgive you."

Chabot and Albert Zollerman went to the Falauge communications room and relieved the soldiers manning the radio, telling them to get packed for their transfer. Captains Anton and Adrian Zollerman wandered the yard, answering questions and shouting orders to maintain the dedication and discipline Chabot had instilled at the assembly. Chabot sent word to the Tristan's communications truck that he was in command of the Falauge radio room and to allow all future communiqués from Falauge to pass through as written.

At 11:15 that night, the Tristan sounded the assembly horn. The 80 soldiers, now dressed in combat gear, helmets drawn low over their eyes and laden with their assigned weapons, came to stiff attention in front of the assembly platform. Still delighting in his authority, Chabot descended the review platform, strutting up and down the rows of rigid soldiers.

Several times, he stopped in front of various men to straighten their uniforms or tell them to button the top button of their shirts. Zollerman, who was accompanying General Gasper Chabot—the little Jewish professor who was so enjoying his dominance over these all-powerful warriors—fought to keep a straight face as Chabot played his role to the maximum. Finally, Chabot finished swashbuckling down a row of the combat-ready men, briskly turned toward the platform, mounted the stairs, and turned to address his assembled soldiers. Zollerman shouted, "Assembly at ease."

Gasper brought himself to his full five-foot, six-inch height, puffing up his chest and clasping his hands behind him. He seemed to glow in the yard lights illuminating the night. He slowly let his eyes take in the entire assembly standing intently ready to listen to his every word.

"You are examples of Germany's finest," he boomed. "Do not be afraid. The Allied forces—the Americans, the British, the Russians—are inferior in every way to Germans. But they are tenacious fighters. Do not underestimate them. Do what you have been trained to do and you will prove victorious."

He turned his eyes toward the garrison Sergeants standing beside their platoons. "Upon dismissal, Sergeants, march your platoons to the train at the rail siding. You will find three troop cars directly behind the engine's tender, followed by two supply cars and, finally, the officer's car. The supply car directly behind the troop cars is already loaded with defensive supplies needed by Paris command. It is locked to assure safe arrival of its contents. Check all of your weapons and ammunition into the second supply car—the one directly in front of the officer's car, then you and your men, take your seats in the three troop cars. I am assigning my Captains to accompany you to Paris. They will be riding in the officer's car. Good luck and Heil Hitler."

Zollerman shouted, "Platoons are dismissed to your Sergeants."

Wilhelmina Schultz checked her watch. She was sitting in the Tristan communications truck hidden in the woods just off the Treaire-Falauge road. It was 11:43. She sent the message Remi had prepared to assure the Falauge troop train would be allowed to pass through Chambéry without being stopped.

ATTENTION NOTICE FROM THE OFFICE OF:
Field Operations Marshal Ulrich Jager
French Headquarters, FHD, Paris
French Area Military Command,
Paris, France

TO COMMAND AT CHAMBÉRY AND FALAUGE
SUBJECT: FALAUGE GARRISON TRANSFER
Communiqué 203-102-398
08 July, 1944 – 23:43gmt

NOTE: PASS THROUGH NOTICE – TRAIN NUMBER 766
Between 24:00 and 00:30 special train number 766 will pass through Chambéry railhead on main track number 02 heading north. This train has Pass-Through-Authorization and will not stop for inspection at Chambéry. Train 766 will be moving at high speed. Open all switches to clear main track.

REPEAT - TRAIN NUMBER 766 WILL PROCEED THROUGH CHAMBÉRY AT FULL SPEED – CLEAR MAIN RIGHT-OF-WAY

ACKNOWLEDGE THIS MESSAGE IMMEDIATELY
---------- END ----------

At 11:48 pm-gmt, Chambéry acknowledged the message, thinking they were clearing the main track for a train ordered north by Field Operations Marshal

Jager at Paris headquarters. Wilhelmina smiled to herself, *Here I am, a common Jewish farm woman, and I just ordered the Chambéry command to pass my train through without stopping it. My, my, the marvel of modern communications.* She sat back in her chair and continued darning several pairs of Jonas' socks.

At the stroke of midnight, the huge steam engine, with the number 766 displayed in large black numerals on a white porcelain plaque attached to its front, chugged to life. A puff of brown smoke surged from its stack and its wheels spun several times in search of traction on the silver rails. The three passenger cars directly behind the engine held the garrison troops and non-commissioned officers. Immediately behind the troop cars was a locked empty supply car, followed by the supply car holding all of the garrison's weapons and ammunition. Captains Anton and Adrian Zollerman rode in the trailing officer's car. The troops were joyous, in high spirits—off to defend Paris for the Führer. Their unified voices singing the national anthem of the Third Reich wafted from the open windows as the train chugged out of the yard and headed north.

As it picked up speed on the straightaway toward Chambéry, the troops settled down. Many began to doze, in anticipation of a long ride through the night. Anton and Adrian left their car, crossed over into the supply car filled with the garrison's weapons and ammunition, and squeezed through its narrow aisle. They opened the car's front door and stepped out onto the platform between the two speeding cars. The car in front of them, the locked empty supply car, rolled along between them and the troop cars. Anton held tight to his brother's belt as Adrian bent over and struggled to release the coupling pin. After several unsuccessful tugs, the pin pulled loose.

As they watched the troop train and its empty supply car fade into the blackness, the twins could no longer control themselves and doubled over in laughter. The thought of the garrison happily riding off to Paris, where the Paris high command would have no idea of why they were there, combined with the knowledge that they would be arriving without *any* of the garrison's weapons, was simply too hilarious.

They were still laughing and making crude jokes about the stupid Germans as they made their way back through the loaded supply car and into the officer's car. They stepped out onto the rear platform and watched the headlight of one of Falauge's steam engines grow brighter as it approached in the distance. Felicien was at the throttle and would soon be pulling them back to Falauge.

PART III

CHAPTER 48

Remi was moving quickly, almost running toward the Falauge communications room. *We've got to get a message to the Allies. Tell them we've taken Falauge. Got to convince them to send us help—just a few well-trained commandos. Somebody, anybody who knows what to do now,* he worried.

It would be about 15 hours before the garrison troop train pulled into Gare de Lyon station in Paris. They might get a few more hours of reprieve while Paris command tried to figure out what was going on. They could keep things confused a while longer since they had total control of all radio messages coming into and going out of the area but, sooner or later, troops from Chambéry would be sent to see what was going on at Falauge. Then all hell would break loose. The Tristan's assurance of safety could now be measured in hours.

Celine was in the communications room. Remi burst in, out of breath, "We've got to get a message to the Allies as soon as…"

"Chabot is already disconnecting the radio trap in the truck and Felicien should be back any minute," she interrupted. "We've got to get Chabot some rest…he looks beat. Are you and Felicien up to a long drive out of the area to send the message to the Allies?"

"We'll have to be. Anything come through from Chambéry concerning the pass-through for the troop train?"

"They simply acknowledged the message, so I assume our troop train is blowing through Chambéry just about now."

"Okay, stay on the radio. As soon as Chabot unplugs the trap, we're back on open communications with no way to grab their messages. Who's coming to interpret for you?"

"Margret," Celine answered.

Remi did not respond as he left the room. Moving across the street, he spied Felicien, chugging into the yard pulling the two cars. Anton and Adrian, still standing on the officer's car platform, cheered and saluted as they passed Remi. *I just hope we have good things to cheer about two days from now,* Remi fretted, quickening his pace toward the slowing engine.

"Felicien, Chabot just about has the trap unplugged. We've got to take the communications truck out of the area and get a message to the Allies. Get to the truck as soon as you get the engine shut down."

Felicien wearily nodded, "Be with you in 20 minutes."

At 4:07 am, 50 miles west of Falauge, Felicien and Remi flashed their appeal for help out into the night air in hopes of getting a positive response from the Allies:

> FROM: TCP-3.965
> TO: HMN-O-37
>   08 July, 1944
> *Falauge railyard and Saint Laurnee Passage captured – Tristan Resistance fighters in control (>)*
>   four minutes later -
> *Only a small force of Tristan available to hold Falauge. Need assistance ASAP (>)*
>   six minutes later -
> *Repeat – desperately need assistance; cannot hold Falauge and Saint Laurnee Passage without support (>)*
>   eight minutes later -
> *Paratroopers can land in Falauge railyard safely during next 24 to 48 hours – send help immediately (>)*
>   three minutes later -
> *ACKNOWLEDGE - NEED ASSISTANCE AS SOON AS POSSIBLE (...)*

Thirteen minutes later, the radio sprang to life:

> FROM: HMN-O-37
> TO: TCP-3.965
> 08 July, 1944
> *Hold position at Falauge switchyard. Protect Saint Laurnee Passage trestle and tunnel (>)*

three minutes later –

Support backup not available at this time. (>)

five minutes later –

Allied forces moving toward Rome. Will send commandos to assist you but cannot specify time/date (>)

seven minutes later –

Hold Falauge yard. Protect Saint Laurnee Passage at all costs. (...)

"Hold Falauge?" Remi yelled. "Hold Falauge? Who do those bastards think they're talking to, the U.S. Marines? Damn it to hell, we can't hold Falauge! Once the krauts figure out they've been fooled..." He sprang to his feet in angry frustration, slamming his head hard on the roof of the truck.

Felicien lit a cigarette. "We've worked miracles before, Remi. We can do it again. You and Celine will figure out something. Maybe we should just vacate Falauge, just fade into the mountains."

Remi remained silent, rubbing the aching spot through his hair, not listening, cussing under his breath.

They drove back in silence. Felicien was not as despondent as Remi, but he knew any further conversation would fall on deaf ears—probably re-kindle Remi's ire. As they made their way back Remi sulked, staring silently out of the side window. Felicien was relieved Remi left him alone to hook the radio trap back up upon their return.

Unaware of the garrison troop train speeding toward Paris, German high command sent a supply train south out of Paris in hopes of beefing up their besieged Italian forces. At 5:02 am, 30 minutes before sunrise, 150 miles north of Chambéry, the troop train rounded a bend at full speed and was met head-on by the southbound supply train.

Neither engineer had time to react. Both engines were delivering full power as they collided, their superheated boilers shattering in a massive blast. As the engines left the track, the heavily loaded cars of the supply train collided with the coal tenders and troop cars, igniting tons of ammunition. An enormous explosion engulfed the wreckage, blasting a huge crater in the right-of-way and sending a searing fireball 180 feet into the air. Napalm canisters burst, ejecting their sticky flaming liquid skyward and the ensuing fire, whipped by its own superheated winds, ignited brush and trees on both sides of the track, reducing everything within a mile to smoldering ash.

A message transmitted from Paris describing the massive collision was captured by the Tristan's radio trap around noon. According to the communiqué, the Germans were in shock, having no idea where the northbound train had come from or why it was on the track at the same time as the supply train. The reports indicated no survivors and devastating damage to the rail line. Chambéry responded, telling Paris of the troop train from Falauge, which they had been ordered to pass through. Chabot's, radio trap captured the message and it never was sent through to Paris.

As additional dispatches trickled in throughout the afternoon, the Tristan was able to piece together a picture of the scene of the crash. Everything that did not disintegrate in the impact had burned to powdery gray dust. The intensity of the explosions had blown a crater in the middle of the track 70 feet deep and 150 feet in diameter. Track lay grotesquely twisted from the intense heat, ties and ballast rock had been blown to powder, and the gaping hole in the path of the right-of-way was fast filling with water from an adjacent stream. German engineers who had raced to the scene estimated that, even if repair materials could be found, it would be months before the rail line could re-open.

A Paris communiqué the following day alerted Italian field commanders and Chambéry high command that because of the total destruction of the rail bed, shipments of supplies from Paris would now be dramatically curtailed. Chambéry was instructed to ration their stocks of ammunition and supplies, and was told to order Falauge to do the same. Paris also made it clear that motor convoys could not take up the slack due to insufficient numbers of vehicles that could be pressed into service. The Tristan passed these dismal messages through to Chambéry unchanged.

Remi could not keep the smile of relief from spreading across his face as he reviewed the messages. Both Paris and Chambéry remained in the dark as to the origin and makeup of the northbound train and so far nothing had warned them to suspect that anything was amiss at Falauge.

The charade remained intact...at least, for the moment.

———◦⦿◦———

The destroyed rail line combined with a continued weakening of Germany's war production severely cut military supplies moving into Italy. Chambéry had depleted most of its stocks of equipment and supplies in the ill-fated convoy destroyed by the Tristan. What usable ammunition and equipment had been recovered from the convoy, along with re-outfitted troops, had been placed on trains and shipped on to Italy weeks ago, leaving the Chambéry depot with few supplies, and a yard packed with inoperable trucks, tanks and artillery pieces. The giant depot, once teeming with personnel and equipment, stood quiet and impotent in the summer sun. The 175 troops at Chambéry bided their time, searching for ways to pass the boredom of manning a supply depot with no supplies and a railyard vacant of the comings and goings of trains.

At Falauge, the *friends* and Chabot took shifts working with whoever was manning the radio room. The focus was to interpret incoming messages and assure outgoing communiqués continued the impression of normal garrison activity. Several times, Chambéry's General Hofstetter radioed seeking confirmation from Colonel Auchenbach that he was prepared to destroy the trestle and tunnel of the Saint Laurnee Passage if given the order. Each time, the Tristan returned assurances that the garrison was busy planting explosives that would close the tunnel and totally destroy the trestle. In reality, teams were out daily, searching for and disabling the demolition charges that Auchenbach's troops had put in place.

Things quieted. Days passed without incident. It seemed as if the war had gone into remission. Remi settled down, Chabot got the rest he needed, and Celine intensified and expanded her training to a much broader group of those in hiding. Men, women, boys and girls over the age of 15 were brought into the training process. Remi, Amaury, and Felicien focused on teaching marksmanship with everything from pistols to machine guns, and Celine worked on defensive hand-to-hand combative moves.

As time passed without incident, Remi's normal worry index began to rise. "Things are too quiet, Cel. It's almost as if the war stopped."

"It's okay, Remi. Everything is fine. You may rest assured war is still going on. Messages coming from German commanders in Italy sound more desperate every day. Last week, we got word British bombers virtually destroyed Hamburg, Germany, and American bombers are pounding the Ruhr Valley almost daily. The Reich is crumbling. That's why we're not feeling pressure right now.

"If you want something to occupy your worry time—what are we going to do once the Allies push the Germans out of Italy? They're probably going to evacuate north on troop trains, all of them chugging right through Falauge. Now, there's a tricky little scenario that should keep you challenged for a while," she mused, forcing a little laugh in an attempt to take some of the edge off of Remi's tension.

He smiled at her. A smile of appreciation for how she always worked to keep his spirits up. "You're right," he relented. "It just bothers me…sitting here, responsible for the whole damn Falauge railhead and the Passage with a bunch of untrained men, women and kids. No news from the Allies. Nothing. I'm not looking for trouble, but its nerve-wracking sitting here with everything so quiet."

Jonas Schultz knocked on the door with more force than usual. Not waiting for an answer, he poked his head into the room, "Sorry, but I thought the two of you would want to see this message immediately."

Remi read aloud, "Message from American Command, Italy… July 15, 1944 – 08:11gmt

"German troops beginning to pull out of Turin, heading north.

"Germans presently loading troop trains with men and equipment.

"Estimate as many as several hundred armed troops per train.

"Expect additional retreating German troop trains to follow – unknown dates, unknown sequence.

"Will notify you as information becomes available.

"German troops also retreating into the Alps.

"Allies will pursue Germans into France as they evacuate north.

"Allied landings on French Mediterranean beaches a possibility.

"Hold out and protect Saint Laurnee Passage at all costs."

Remi poured over the message, "What does 'Germans presently loading troop trains with men and equipment' mean? Nothing about when they'll show up here. Immediately? Tomorrow? Next week?" He glanced over at Celine, as if looking to her for answers. "And what does 'armed troops' mean? Heavy weapons cannon, tanks, armored half-tracks, ready to blow everything to bits upon arrival?

"What in hell is all this supposed to mean? Damn the Allies. No response to our request for help. What in the name of Christ are we supposed to do—kill the whole retreating German army for them?"

"There, you see, my love," Celine teased. "You can start feeling much better. The war is back."

"How are we supposed to know when the Allies will come through for us?" Remi exclaimed in complete exasperation. "They want us to save the Passage, which means those German troop trains are going to roll right into Falauge. Then what? What in hell do the Allies expect us to do—entertain them with a beer and bratwurst party until they arrive?"

Celine couldn't help herself…she started to giggle. Remi was so stressed, and the mental image of their Jews gaily having a songfest, beer and bratwurst party with several-hundred Nazi troops struck her as funny. Remi glared as her giggles turned to laughter. Then, he shook his head, smiled at her and began to laugh, too. Their situation was so unsustainable—had so instantly changed from boredom to frustration and terror that laughter was the only reasonable response. She went to him, took him in her arms and gave him a kiss. "We'll make it through, my love. God is with us and we'll make it through." They stood for a moment, then pulled up two chairs at the large conference table and went to work.

After months of bitter fighting, the war in Italy had finally turned in favor of the Allies. Certain German troops continued to fight retreating north into the

Italian Alps. Other units were ordered north into France to set up offensive positions there. These German troops were to be transported by train, the fastest method of moving hundreds of men. Those trains would pass through Falauge. They would need fuel, and the troops on board would be eager to disembark, leave the stuffy cars and stretch their legs.

No train could be allowed to linger at Falauge for a refueling stop. Refueling could take up to an hour. It would quickly become obvious to observers on the retreating trains that the Falauge complex was missing its garrison. That revelation, with armed German troops mulling around in the yard, was a situation that had to be avoided at all costs. Celine and Remi's planning session would have to come up with a way to move the retreating troop trains through Falauge as quickly as possible…no refueling, no troops getting off the trains.

Hours later, using Chabot's magnificent radio manipulator, they sent the following message as if it had originated from the Paris command center.

ATTENTION NOTICE FROM THE OFFICE OF:
Field Operations Marshal Ulrich Jager
French Headquarters, FHD, Paris
French Area Military Command,
Paris, France

TO COMMAND AT CHAMBÉRY AND FALAUGE
SUBJECT: PROCEDURE TO PROCESS REASSIGNED
TROOP FROM ITALY
Communiqué 445-366-887
15 July, 1944 – 08:52gmt

-----DO NOT DELAY TROOP TRAINS----
----NOTE TO FALAUGE----
Pass all troop trains directly to Chambéry for refueling
Refueling yard at Falauge too small and will cause trains to back-up – DO
NOT REFUEL IN FALAUGE TO AVOID CONGESTION.
----NOTE TO CHAMBÉRY----

Refuel troop trains in Chambéry's multiple refueling yards.
Notify Falauge if fuel runs low and have Falauge deliver fuel to the
Chambéry yard as needed.
Once refueled, immediately pass all troop trains through to Paris. When
trains reach the damaged track area, troops will be transferred to trucks for
transport to assigned defensive positions throughout France.
---------- *END* ----------

The Tristan printed off multiple copies of the fictitious message. Hopefully, the official looking document would be convincing. The plan seemed a bit feeble as Celine and Remi reviewed it.

"Remi, if you were a battle-weary Nazi officer and were handed this order, would you believe it?" Celine questioned, looking at the fake radio reprint. "These men are going to be exhausted. They're going to want off of that train at the first opportunity."

"It's the best we've come up with, Cel. Orders are orders. If the bastards follow Hitler's orders to murder thousands of Jews, following an order to refuel your train 20 miles up the road should be a cake walk. The communiqué looks official. It might piss me off if I were a Nazi officer and expected to refuel at Falauge, but I'd still be looking at what appears to be a legitimate communiqué from Paris headquarters. I'd follow the order."

At 10:00 that evening, the walkie-talkie cracked to life with a scratchy voice transmission from the lookout the Tristan had planted to watch for incoming trains two miles south of the Saint Laurnee tunnel entrance: "Slow-moving train pulling five troop cars proceeding toward the Passage tunnel. Arrival at Falauge yard estimated in about 15 minutes."

Decked out in their German uniforms, all the players raced to their assigned positions. Expecting to refuel, the engineer would bring the engine to a stop directly under the water tower adjacent to the coal chute. The cars would be positioned alongside the long wooden passenger platform overlooking the Falauge assembly yard.

Albert Zollerman, in his Colonel's uniform, and his sons, Anton and Adrian, standing at his side in their Captains outfits, positioned themselves where they estimated the officer's car would come to a halt. If these trains were put together like all other German troop trains, the officers would be riding in the last car—well behind their soldiers. Jonas, in his Sergeant's gear, along with Remi, Felicien and Amaury, dressed as Privates, waited up front at the water tower, ready to hand a copy of the order to proceed on to Chambéry to the engineer. Chabot sat inside the headquarters building in his immaculate General's attire, waiting in reserve if the additional influence of his rank was needed.

Celine lay prone position on the roof of one of the barracks buildings, her sniper rifle steadied on a sandbag and her scope trained on the position where Albert, Anton and Adrian would be talking with the officers. The Zollermans were instructed to stand to the side of the officers as they presented the phony orders, giving Celine a clear line of fire at the German officers if that terrible alternative became necessary. The signal to take out the officers would be Albert removing his hat—a signal they prayed would not come.

Celine fought to calm her raw nerves as the engine lumbered into sight. It seemed to take forever as it crawled toward the refueling station spitting its steam and smoke. She was concerned. In the absence of Chabot, Albert had to carry the lead in facing the German officers. He had been exceedingly nervous as they prepared to take their positions on the passenger platform. Adrian had talked with him. It seemed to calm him a bit, but tension was obvious on Albert's face—and his eyes betrayed sheer terror.

The engine eased up to the water tower, exhausting an ear-splitting hiss of white steam as the drive pistons released their pressure. The engineer stretched, then started down the ladder. Jonas called up to him, "Halt. You will not be refueling here. You are instructed to move on to Chambéry to take on fuel. It's just up the line about 20 miles."

The engineer looked over his shoulder with a surprised expression, "That is not my orders," he yelled back over the still-hissing engine. "I was told to stop here, at Falauge, refuel and allow the troops to stretch, then to proceed on." He grudgingly climbed back up into the cab, retrieved his original orders and started back down the ladder. He handed his papers to Jonas and they read just as he had explained. Jonas handed him the phony message instructing that all troop trains move on to Chambéry for refueling, told him to wait there and he would get clarification. He whispered for Amaury to wait with the engineer, and motioned for Felicien and Remi to accompany him as he started toward the officer's car.

"Nice night," said the engineer. "Just a shame we are having to run from those bastards down in Italy, huh?" Amaury understood 'Nice night'. He caught 'bastards in Italy' but the rest of the sentence slipped past in a garble of quickly spoken German. *Now, what the hell do I do?* he thought. He decided to just smile and nod as the engineer yawned, stretching once again.

"You been stationed here at Falauge for all of the war?" the engineer queried. Amaury picked up 'station – Falauge – all – war'. *My God,* Amaury panicked, *I've never heard this accent in German. I can't understand him.* Again, Amaury smiled and nodded. He unslung his rifle, giving the engineer some pause. He didn't exactly point the gun at the engineer, but rested it on his arm with the barrel pointing at the man's crotch. He kept his eyes trained directly on the now nervous engineer.

The man stood there, uneasily watching at Amaury. Amaury just scowled back at him. Finally, the engineer gave a long sigh, "Well, I'll go back up in the cab and wait." He turned toward the engine, shaking his head and thinking, *No wonder we're losing the war with such stupid soldiers and all of these senseless changes in orders.*

As Jonas, Remi and Felicien made their way down the passenger platform proceeding past the string of cars, several of the troops were already standing on their car's exit platforms, impatient to disembark. Apparently, they, too, thought this would be an extended stop. As they passed each group, Jonas, using his Sergeant gruffness, said, "Keep your pants on, boys. You're going on to Chambéry for refueling."

Groans of displeasure came from the men. "It's only a few miles. Just a 20-minute ride," Jonas shouted back. The battle weary troops were not easily dissuaded from their desires, especially by a Sergeant they didn't know. Some of the older ones were hanging so far off the side of their cars, they were just inches from putting a foot down on Falauge territory.

Down at the officer's car, things were not going much better. A Colonel had disembarked to meet Albert. He introduced himself as Colonel Wentz and immediately objected to the message Albert handed him ordering the train to move on to Chambéry.

"My orders are explicit. We are to disembark at Falauge to refuel. This message is dated today at 8:52 this morning. We left Turin at 18:23 when I was handed my orders. See." He thrust his paperwork in front of Albert. "My orders came after your message." Albert hesitated, his anxiety quickly rising. He and the boys had positioned the Colonel so Celine had the clean shot they wanted, but should he go for his hat? There was no way the officer could be dropped dead on the platform without the whole train exploding in a flurry of armed Nazis shooting everything in sight.

Looking through her rifle scope, Celine detected Albert's hesitation. She adjusted the scope's focus, placing its crosshairs on the forehead of the Colonel. Adrian stepped forward. Celine's heart skipped a beat. *What in hell is that hothead doing? Damn him. He's right in my line of fire.* She glared into the scope, almost trying to move Adrian aside with the strength of her will as she held her breath and waited.

Adrian looked the Colonel directly in the eyes, "Our orders are straight from Field Operations Marshal, General Ulrich Jager at Paris command. With all due respect, Herr Colonel, we do not know who issued your orders, but I am sure there is a lot of confusion right now, trying to get all of the troops transferred from the Italian Front and repositioned here in France. You can see that General Jager wants your men to proceed directly on to Paris. No doubt, he is familiar with your men's valor under pressure and wants them positioned as close to Paris as possible. But if you would like me to go and wake Gestapo General Schulmann, I will be happy to do so."

Adrian calmly maintained his fix on the eyes of the Colonel. His look was firm yet respectful. Colonel Wentz glanced back down at the message Albert had handed him. "Damn it to hell, the whole army is falling apart." he muttered. He turned on his heel toward the car and, looking up the line of cars at his men leaning toward the platform, shouted, "Get your butts back in your seats. We're going on to Chambéry." Then, under his breath, he grumbled, "No damn wonder the Allies are kicking the shit out of us. We can't even figure out where we want our retreating trains to refuel."

As the officer reboarded, Jonas turned back toward the engine, shouting for the engineer to proceed on to Chambéry. The engine gave a powerful chug, and the train jerked forward. Celine rolled over on her back, trying to ease the tightness in her shoulders. *Thank God they are leaving.* She was trembling. *Not a good sign; not acceptable behavior. Where in hell is the calmness they taught me in training?* She tried to force herself to calm down. She continued to tremble.

As the last car disappeared from Falauge, the group of German impersonators reassembled. All of them were shaken, congratulating each other with nervous smiles and compliments on the performance. Adrian looked at his father, "Don't let those German assholes intimidate you. Remember, you are a Colonel...the same rank as them. Argue with them. Don't take their bullshit."

Celine asked, "Is there any way to include Turin in a message that the trains are supposed to refuel at Chambéry rather than stop here?"

"I've already looked into that," Chabot said, "but unless we know the call numbers of the Turin receiver, we have no way to contact them. I looked in the communications room, but apparently the Turin radio they are now suing is just temporary. They must be using mobile communications. Perhaps the permanent unit has been knocked out of commission."

As they broke up, Celine approached Adrian and asked him what he had said to the Colonel that convinced him to reboard and move on. He repeated his conversation. She nodded, impressed, "Nice job. That took guts. I'm proud to serve with you." He felt good about himself as he returned to the barracks.

<hr />

Two more trains followed over the next 14 hours. The first came through in the early morning before dawn, and the weary German officers climbed back on board without protest. The real tension arose when the next train pulled to a stop in broad daylight, offering a commanding view of Falauge devoid of its garrison. The Tristan imposters were in their normal positions, but the rest of the huge yard remained unnaturally silent—devoid of any human activity.

A Captain stepped from the officer's car onto the passenger platform, reiterating the same orders about an hour's stop at Falauge for refueling. He looked over the document Albert handed him, shrugged his shoulders, and was about to turn back to reboard, when a second Captain stepped onto the platform. He walked up to Albert, saluted Albert's superior rank, and said, "We have been watching the yard from the train. Where are your soldiers?"

Celine and Remi had rehearsed this possibility with the group. "All of the men are busy in the surrounding hills, planting explosives that will close the tunnel and destroy the trestle after the last evacuation train comes through. We go in shifts. The night shift is now sleeping while the day shift is working."

The Captain furrowed his brow, a questioning expression on his face.

"With respect, Herr Colonel, isn't it risky having a facility this size almost vacant of defenses?" the Captain retorted as he continued to survey the uninhabited facilities.

Again, Albert was shaken. Once again, Adrian stepped forward, taking a position in front of the Captain and blocking his searching eyes, "We are following the orders of our commander, Captain. We are all shorthanded due to the Allies now breathing down our necks and about ready to push into France due to your inabilities to stop their advance through Italy. We are the ones who will be left here to finish the job you and your men failed to do there. It is disturbing to see you, who are in full retreat in the face of our advancing enemies, questioning the directives of our commander. I would suggest you get back on your retreating train and get your ass out of here before I go and get Gestapo General Schulmann and inform him of your condescending criticism of his orders." As he spoke, Adrian had moved closer to the shamed Captain and was now standing with his face only inches from the officer.

"Okay, okay, Captain," the belittled officer replied. "No offense was intended. But let me assure you, our men fought brilliantly, heroically…many, to the death. Your insinuation that we are retreating because of failure of courage is insulting. I watched men, boys in their teens, soldiers I respected, die in agony. We are in retreat because of overwhelming force being brought against us by the Americans—and because of Berlin, which has failed to adequately support us. Not because of a lack of will."

Adrian could see the Captain fighting to control his emotions, not fighting to hold anger but, rather, raw passion. He saw a sincere caring for his men in the Captain's eyes—felt the emotion in his voice. Adrian immediately softened, seeing that this man, this hated enemy, had feelings of loyalty and affection for his men. He felt the dedication of this defeated officer. It was not a dedication to the Nazis, not to their destruction of the Jews, not to the insanity of Hitler and his henchmen…just to his troops who had risked everything and died fighting simply because they were asked to. For the first time, Adrian had listened to, and heard, the other side of something that angered him. For the first time, he understood that everything was not simply black and white—there may be aspects of another opinion worthy of consideration.

He stepped back from the Captain, relaxing his expression. "I apologize, Herr Captain. My words were selfish and angry. Please forgive my belligerence and my lack of maturity." As he looked into the Captain's eyes, he no longer saw an enemy combatant but, rather, a compassionate human being feeling the deep pains and stress of war. His feelings of hate gave way to empathy for another man who was merely trying his best to handle the terrible job he had been assigned. Adrian continued, "Please understand we, too, are operating under very difficult circumstances."

The Captain slapped Adrian on the shoulder, "It's okay. I understand. God be with you." He nudged his fellow officer, motioning toward the train. The two officers waved to the engineer, reboarded and vanished back into the murky oblivion of war.

CHAPTER 49

16 July, 1944
50 miles northwest of Dijon, France
Location: Point where the supply and
troop trains collided five days earlier

Complying with the Tristan's phony orders, the evacuating troop trains sent on from Falauge were refueled at Chambéry. They then continued north to the point where the track had been destroyed, expecting to meet up with truck convoys for transport to Paris. The first train hissed to a stop 20 feet from the huge crater in the roadbed at 5:27 am.

Colonel Wentz, the senior officer, exited, followed by his aid. To his right, a dirt farm road paralleled the track. Vacant. No convoy. Nothing but quiet, rolling countryside, the eastern horizon painted a soft peach by the rising sun.

"What now, Herr Colonel?"

Wentz couldn't help showing his irritation, "We wait, Lieutenant." His attitude wasn't so much directed at his young Lieutenant, but, rather, at the failure of Paris command to live up to its promise of having a convoy waiting. His mind cursed the growing ineptness he was experiencing at the hands of his superiors. *I've got a train full of exhausted men. Where in hell is the damn convoy?*

"Perhaps we should return to Chambéry, Sir?"

"Other trains are following, Lieutenant. Sure as hell, one of them is on its way behind us. Paris says they'll send a convoy. We wait for the convoy. Get the troops off the train into whatever shade they can find. Those cars are going to turn into ovens once the sun hits them. Position the wounded in the coolest spots and have the medical corpsmen make them as comfortable as possible. Find out how much drinking water we have."

Wentz seethed as he walked toward the engine. *They don't send supplies to Italy. They don't send the convoy for my troops. The whole damn army is falling apart.* He called up to the engineer, who was busy with the final stages of shutting down the boiler, "Where in hell are we?"

"About 40 miles north of Dijon, Sir."

"How far to the next city?"

"Troyes? Not much of a city, Herr Colonel. About 45 miles. Nothing but farmland from here to Troyes. Same all the way back to Dijon."

"Can you radio and ask where the convoy is?"

"Sorry, Sir. We are out of range to either of those stations."

Six hours later, the second train came to a stop behind the first. Its officers conferred with Wentz. Still no convoy. They would continue to wait. Ten hours later, the third train pulled up behind the second—but this train offered hope. Two motorcycles with sidecars had been packed into one of its supply cars. Both were low on gas but operable.

Unloading the motorcycles, they assigned two men to each, ordering them to find the Dijon-Troyes highway. One team would head north; the other south. The goal was to find the nearest town and get word to Paris…find out where in hell the convoys were.

A fourth train showed up eight hours later, carrying some severely wounded men. One of its cars had been crudely outfitted as a hospital car, with two attending doctors who were anxious to get to Paris so their patients could get much-needed medical attention. The four strung-out trains now span almost a quarter of a mile.

Twenty-four hours had passed since Wentz's train came to a halt at the crater and still no convoy. The motorcycle teams had been gone for eight hours. Food was running low and drinking water was fast approaching critical levels as the daily sun scorched the stranded troops. Teams were sent out in search of nearby farms, ordered to secure food and water.

The locals knew the trains were there. Those whose farms were closest watched the stranded Germans through binoculars. Their attitude was to stay as far away from the Nazis as possible, hiding from them if necessary. They were the enemy—thieves, torturers, rapists. *Let the boche-bastards rot,* they thought. When the teams of soldiers fanned out in search of assistance, the locals vanished. Every farm they came upon was abandoned. Houses locked, livestock gone, well pumps chained, farm vehicles disabled. Any attempt to break into houses or barns was met with immediate gunfire from concealed positions. The small search teams quickly retreated from these deadly confrontations, not knowing how many Frenchmen might be taking aim at them.

———— ·⊙⊙⊙· ————

No word or help ever returned from the motorcycle teams. Twenty minutes after the duo heading north started up the highway, its gas gauge was bouncing on empty. They turned on to a farm lane, drove a mile off the highway and knocked on a farmhouse door to ask the distance to the next town. *Perhaps the farmer might even have some petrol he could spare,* they hoped. Coming face to face with two Nazi soldiers as she opened the door, the farmer's wife panicked, screamed, and ran into the house, yelling for her husband.

In a vain attempt to calm the distraught woman, the two young soldiers pursued her. As the first followed her into the kitchen, the woman's husband stepped from behind the wall and plunged a carving knife deep into the soldier's chest. The boy's legs buckled and he fell to his knees, blood gushing from the wound.

His stunned companion, trying desperately to unsheathe his sidearm, was grabbed from behind by the woman's huge teenage son, held in a bear hug, and lifted off his feet. While struggling to free himself, he, too, was stabbed by the same knife that had brought down his teammate.

As the two soldiers lay dying on the kitchen floor of the isolated farmhouse, the family froze in terror. Nazi retribution would be swift and severe. They would be hanged, shot by a firing squad, perhaps tortured. The farmer ran to the front door. No other soldiers were in sight. He called to his son to help him drag the bodies from the house and ordered his wife to clean up the blood.

Within an hour, the bodies were buried behind the barn—a heap of manure mounded over the graves. The two sweating farmers hitched a horse to the motorcycle, pulled it into the center of the farm pond, and stood in relief as it bubbled down below the surface. They dragged a grading rake over the long dirt lane leading from the highway to the house, and the woman rewashed the kitchen floor several times. By evening, there was no evidence the two soldiers had ever existed.

━━━∞∞∞━━━

The team heading south fared no better. Arriving at a small village some 35 miles down the road, they entered the town's tavern seeking fuel and directions. As they spoke with the tavern owner, a patron slipped out the side door. He pushed their motorcycle into a barn behind the tavern, ran across the street to his home, got his shotgun, and, in revenge for the Nazis having hanged his brother two years earlier, shot the two at point-blank range as they emerged from the tavern.

Several village citizens, also victims of previous Nazi abuse, helped him clean up the blood and bury the bodies and the motorcycle. The little town returned to normalcy. Two more young German soldiers vanished from the face of the earth.

CHAPTER 50

Another train came through Falauge at 10 pm that night, carrying mostly severely wounded soldiers. The officers on this train sported bloody, bandaged wounds. There was no complaining from them. When handed the falsified orders to move on to Chambéry, they apathetically nodded their compliance, got back on board, and moved on. The train's occupants indicated these troops had been in heavy combat prior to escaping. Its medical cars—or at least cars that had been fitted out to the best of the retreating army's limited ability to accommodate the severely wounded emitted moans of suffering. Even in the troop cars, where soldiers were forced to sit up during the long journey, men agonized in blood-soaked bandages.

The few sketchy radio messages the Tristan received indicated the Allies were now right on the heels of the retreating Germans. The Americans apparently had most of Turin surrounded. The German troops that weren't being transported north were withdrawing into the rising Alps, where they would continue to fight vigorously as they futilely attempted to stem the Allied advance. Severe fighting raged in Turin within a several-block perimeter around the main train station, where the Germans were dug-in trying to protect their escaping troop trains.

Both Remi and Celine were sleeping restlessly when Margaret Zollerman shook Celine and handed her an incoming message from Allied command:

FROM: *HMN-O-37*
TO: *TCP-3.965*
18 July, 1944 – 02:26gmt

Last German troop train left Turin at 02:14, 18 July, 1944 (>)
nine minutes later –

No more operable trains left at Turin station. (>)
    twelve minutes later -
Final evacuating train damaged by Allied machine gun and cannon fire as it left Turin – extent of damage unknown (>)
    nine minutes later -
We believe this train carries high-ranking officers who will press for destruction of Saint Laurnee Passage once their train passes through (>)
    seven minutes later –
They may demand inspecting placement of demolition charges
    six minutes later -
Be prepared to dissuade them. Protect St. Laurnee Passage at all costs (>)
    three minutes later –
Ground operations now pushing north in pursuit of Germans moving into defensive positions in the Alps (>)
    seven minutes later –
Allied landings on Mediterranean French coast to commence shortly (>)
    four minutes later –
Can Tristan mount an offensive and move south into the Alps?

ACKNOWLEDGE
END (…)

At 5:00 am, the *friends* and Chabot gathered to hear Remi's assessment of their situation. "If that train left Turin at a quarter after two, it's going to be here around noon," he said. "That means they are going to see this place vacant in the middle of the day, but this one is different. The Allies believe this train is carrying high-ranking officers who are intent on seeing that explosive charges are in place to destroy the Saint Laurnee trestle and tunnel."

Felicien interrupted, "We've placed fake explosive packages on the trestle supports and around the tunnel entrances, but if those officers insist on inspecting them, it will take at least an hour just for them to go out, have a look, and return."

Amaury added, "They may not only want to *see* the explosives…they're probably going to want a demonstration. If I were them, I'd want to watch the whole damn Passage blown to hell."

Ever since taking control of Falauge, Celine and Remi had struggled with the frailty of their situation forcing them into the need to fight. They would try to move this train on peacefully as they had successfully done with the others but the chances of success were slim.

⁓⧉⁓

At 6:00 am they assembled everyone in the garrison's mess hall. Men, women, teenaged boys and girls, the now-experienced Zollermans, the Schultzes, Chabot and the *friends*—53 in all. Celine faced the group.

"We do not belief we can get the troop train, which will arrive here at noon today, to move on to Chambéry peacefully. There will be Nazi officers on that train who will expect to disembark and take part in the destruction of the Saint Laurnee Passage trestle and tunnel. We cannot let that happen. We have trained for this possibility. We will definitely try to talk the officers into moving on but this time we will take our positions to defend Falauge and destroy the train if necessary.

"The young children and elderly are to go to the camouflaged hiding place in the woods, along with the four teenaged boys and girls who have been assigned as their protectors. You have all seen the hideaway. You helped stock it with supplies. You know it is a good distance from here and so well hidden you can be standing 15 feet from it and not know it is there. The boys and girls assigned as protectors have been trained how to keep watch, and they know when to take the children into deeper hiding if German troops come searching for them.

"We have given them a sealed envelope they are to open if they have to leave the hideaway. It will lead them to an even more secure sanctuary. We are convinced the present hideaway is so well hidden they will not have to use the information in the envelope, but they have it just in case." She did not reveal that the map in the envelope would lead them to the Tristan's cave, their last hope of safety.

"Take the children and elderly to the hideaway immediately after this meeting, then return here to your assigned positions."

Tension rose among the listeners, who were hearing the initial instructions of a call to battle. Celine saw the growing concern and signs of fear, particularly on the faces of some of the women and youngsters. *The fear is all right,* she thought. *It gets the adrenaline going. Not good if it turns to debilitating panic. Address it. Calm the nerves now.*

She quieted the whispering comments racing between the people, "We will use everything in our power to get the officers back on the train, but if they refuse, our plan is to move the train out of Falauge without giving the troops on board a chance to fire a shot." Curiosity was rising, fear momentarily on hold.

"You have all been trained how to fire your assigned weapons. Every one of you has done well. You would not be sitting here this morning if you had not.

"You all know how to shoot—how to jump up from behind cover, take quick shots then drop down again. You know how to reload your weapons. You know to stay low behind your cover when you reload.

"The way to keep the troops on the train and keep them from being able to fire at us is for us to shower the cars with a continuous barrage of machine-gun and rifle fire. Your target is the whole train car. If you can fire through the window all the much better, but keep peppering all of the troop cars with bullets. You are working in pairs so when one of you drops down to reload the other is to pop up and fire at the cars. We have plenty of ammunition and you will all have adequate supplies of reloads at your cover stations.

"The signal for you to jump up and fire at the troop cars will be when you hear my sniper rifle fire. With that shot, I will take out one of the officers on the passenger platform. Adrian, Anton and Albert will be on the platform and I will back them as they take out the other officers. As soon as you hear the shot from my rifle, the first team member jump up and begin firing at the windows of the troop cars. The troops on board will be forced to drop for cover, but keep firing, keep them down, keep them frozen on the floor of those cars.

"Remi, Jonas and Amaury will take out the engineer. Felicien will climb aboard the engine and get the train moving. He will set the speed at maximum and before the train gains too much speed, he will jump off and return to us. Properly done the troops on the train will be pinned down until the train leaves the yard. By the time it clears the last of the yard it will be moving too fast for any of the troops to jump off. They will be trapped on the train and it will proceed through Chambéry at full speed.

"I repeat...once you begin firing, do not stop shooting at the cars, even after the train starts to move. Keep up the barrage until the train is fully out of the yard, past the north gate.

"As soon as they hear us start firing, Margret and Wilhelmina will send off a message to Chambéry, telling them the officers on the train insisted in refueling here and warning them the train will be coming through on the main track at full speed. We've successfully sent one other train through Chambéry at full speed by sending them a similar message, so there is no reason to think they will not allow this one through. Besides, with this train moving at 60 miles per hour, they have no choice but to get out of the way and let it pass.

"We think it will have sufficient fuel to take it 15 to 20 miles past Chambéry. The area where it will run out of fuel is farmland. Whatever troops survive our attack will be stranded there.

"By winning this victory, we will have successfully sent the last of the troop trains through, putting us in the position of simply having to hold on here at Falauge until the Allies arrive. Of course, we will radio the Allies and describe our situation, urging them to send troops to our aid as soon as possible."

As Celine addressed the group, Remi studied them and agonized at what he saw. Youngsters—boys and girls in their mid to late teens, middle-aged men and women, a pregnant young girl clutching to her equally young husband...people who knew nothing of war and had never anticipated being swept up in one. A group of people they were now going to ask to attack other human beings, possibly kill them and who they were going to ask to die, if necessary.

The message had indicated the train now heading toward them had been damaged by Allied gunfire as it left Turin. The extent of the damage remained an unknown. He knew that if this train was similar to the last two, there would be wounded soldiers aboard—hopefully, so badly wounded they would be incapable of waging a fight. However, there would also be healthy, battle-hardened men used to killing...crack shots, brave in the face of gunfire. Men who long ago lost any hesitation they might have had about killing another human being.

There was no information as to how many troops the train was carrying or the ranks or numbers of the officers on board, but none of this really mattered. Their plan was frail, plagued with weaknesses, but it was the best they could do.

Remi slowly rose to his feet, "You have all been assigned your places of cover in the yard. Every location has a good view of where the troop cars will come to a stop. When you drop behind your cover positions you will not be visible from the train windows. When reloading stay down. Stay calm. Quickly reload, wait for your team mate to drop down to reload then immediately pop up and begin firing.

"Among you, you have 40 machine guns and 50 rifles. You each have dozens of loaded magazines. Those of you firing on the exit doors of the train cars must continue to fire if any troops open those doors and attempt to exit. You must shoot them without hesitation. Keep in mind, you are protecting your loved ones, your children and yourselves.

"It is normal to feel afraid, but do not let your fear overcome you. Do not let it paralyze you. Do not shy from saving yourself and your children by killing German soldiers. Remember, if given the chance, they will kill you without hesitation." He paused. His message was the most direct description of the seriousness of their situation so far. He saw rising commitment and resolve in the eyes of some, rising fear in others.

"While we know the Allies will pursue the Germans, we have come to understand not all of the German troops are being evacuated by train. Some are moving up into the Alps, where they will fight the Allies every inch of the way. We must assume that we will be left here to protect ourselves and the Saint Laurnee Passage...at least, for a while. If we simply run off, the Germans will destroy us, the Passage, everything here in Falauge, and everything for miles around." Remi stopped, searching for anything else he could possibly say... anything that might encourage these people, anything that might anger them sufficiently to overpower their fears and give them courage in the face of the approaching enemy.

"Are there any questions?"

A hand went up several rows back. A small, timid woman nervously stood, "This all sounds very complicated. What if it doesn't work? Who will warn the children and the old people?" Her husband tugged on her sleeve, trying to get her to stop her questioning. It was obvious from the look in her eyes and the tone of her voice that she was fighting to control panic. She slowly sat down and to Remi's relief, Celine immediately rose to answer her questions.

At first, Celine addressed the woman directly, "Your question is fine. It is not out of place. It is natural if you are feeling afraid and nervous. You do not have to be embarrassed about that." She then broadened her comments to the entire group, "There are risks. We know that. But the risk of us doing nothing will surely result in all of us, our elders, and our children being hunted down and murdered by the Germans. The five of us who make up the Tristan are experienced in doing things like this. We have been very successful in the past, and we have carefully planned this operation.

"As for the children, they will be safe in the hideaway. When I took you there and we were only several yards from it, I asked you to locate it…remember? You couldn't find it. We have trained the lookouts so in the unlikely event the Germans get through us and go looking for the children and the elderly they will have plenty of time to escape to a location where they will never be found. Remember…by us keeping those German troops on that train they will never get a chance to search for the children and our elderly. We are the first line of defense."

Celine surveyed the group, "Fight your fears. Fight to control them, but realize they are natural and give you the energy to perform. The way we have laid out this plan puts the odds strongly in our favor. But you, every one of you—must do your part as you have been trained to do. Use your fears to build your strength and resolve, but don't let fear take control of you." She was looking straight into the eyes of the timid woman as she finished, and in those eyes she saw a growing determination.

She dismissed the group, saying, "We all know what to do. When we disperse, take up your assigned positions. Check your weapons. Be sure they are loaded. Be sure you have your extra ammunition clips with you. Breathe deeply to calm yourselves. Be confident and we will succeed."

With that, Celine assumed her sniper position on the roof of the quartermaster building. She checked her weapon, bolted a round into the chamber, sighted-in her scope, sent a test message on her walkie-talkie to Remi, then rolled over onto her back and stared into the beauty of the summer sky.

Marvelous puffy white clouds slowly drifted through the azure blue above. The day was quiet, peaceful. The birds sang their songs of life, as a refreshing breeze brushed her cheek. There was no war at this magnificent instant in time—just God's beautiful world basking in the quiet of the day.

CHAPTER 51

With the words of Celine and Remi ringing in their ears, the small band of citizen fighters nervously took up their practiced positions within view of the passenger platform, dropped behind their protective cover, and waited. Remi, Felicien and Amaury visited each of the teams, giving encouragement and assuring that everyone was out of sight of the platform, their weapons loaded and ready to fire.

Returning to their positions beside Jonas at the water tower, Remi noted, "I've never seen them so afraid. Maybe we were too direct with them. I pray they will not hesitate if it comes to a fight."

"They will fight, Remi. They have even more to lose than you. They have families," Jonas said. "It's our only chance if Chabot and his team are unable to get the officers to move on to Chambéry. You'll see. They will fight."

The train was expected sometime between 11:30 am and 1:00 pm. 11:30 no train. The sun burned hot in the thin air. The people's edginess further complicated by aching muscles longing for a bit of shade. 12:10 still no train. Remi walked the yard to assure himself the team's restlessness hadn't jeopardized their concealment. His own uneasiness tugged at him. He started down the platform toward Chabot and his men, mostly to settle his own nerves. About halfway his walkie-talkie crackled out its ring. The train was in sight. He turned toward the yard, shouting, "Everyone out of sight. The train will be here in a few minutes. Do not shoot until you hear Celine's rifle shot. Be ready." He whispered a small prayer and hustled back to his position.

The throbbing rhythm of the engine unnervingly pounded in their chests before its rumble reached their ears. White smoke bellowing from its stack became visible over the tree tops as the giant black monster made its way across the trestle and took a toehold on the sheer rock face of the Falauge side of the gorge. The engine pulled hard against the rise in grade as it steamed into the yard toward the water tank in search of its drink. It grumbled past Colonel Albert, Captains Anton and Adrian, and Gestapo General Chabot, shrouding them in its cloud of steam as if hissing its defiance of their false authority.

There were two more troop cars than on previous trains. As the cars passed Chabot and his greeting committee, it became apparent the additional length of the train would position them far up the platform from where the officer's car would stop.

Chabot motioned to the group, "Come, we must move down the platform. We must be standing right in front of the officers who get off so they do not have time to focus on the empty yard."

Adrian glanced toward the roof where Celine was positioned, "That's going to eliminate Celine's ability to take out the officers with her sniper rifle."

Chabot, already briskly on his way down the platform, replied, "Then it will be up to you, Anton and Albert, to take them out with your knives. Kill them with pistols if you have to. We've got to be in the face of those officers when they step off this train. Now, move it."

They quickly followed Chabot's lead, arriving at the coupling between the two officer's cars as they rolled to a halt. Adrian looked in the direction where Celine was positioned. Several trees stood between their new position and her view. Her ability to back them up was gone.

Three officers made their way up the aisle of the last car toward the exit door. *Damn*, thought Adrian, *that's a Lieutenant General. That reduces Chabot's ability to order these guys around.* According to formal Nazi protocol, Chabot's Gestapo uniform should give him authority over officers of the same rank in other branches of the military. But whether the so-called "formal protocol" would be acknowledged by these battle-fatigued men was pure speculation. Under the circumstances, it would depend on the senior officer, now disembarking, to subjugate himself to Chabot's protocol position.

Another concern, perhaps more serious, there were three officers stepping off the train, rather than the expected two that had confronted them from each of the previous trains. Both Adrian and Anton knew their father and Chabot would be useless in a physical confrontation. Albert didn't have the will and Chabot was so out of shape that any combative move on his part would prove useless. Adrian looked over at Anton and could tell by his expression that he, too, was concerned. With Celine's inability to back them any potential clash was going to be considerably more complicated than they had planned.

The disembarking officers had been in the thick of things. Their uniforms were beat up and dirty. One of the Colonels had a torn right sleeve stained in blood from where he had taken a flesh wound. Looking through the windows, several of the other officers wore bloody bandages. In both the troop and officer cars, many of the windows were shattered and the steel sides pocked with bullet dents; a large hole gaped in the roof of one of the troop cars. There was no doubt this train had been under heavy attack as it fought its way out of Turin. The exiting trio of officers gave minimal salutes to Chabot as they approached.

The disheveled Lieutenant General removed his hat, glaring disappointedly at its unkempt condition. He was pounding dust from it. Without looking at Chabot he began to speak, "We were fighting Allied forces right up to the main train station in Turin—some of their troops entering and shooting up the inside of the terminal as we pulled out." He shook his head in irritated sorrow, "I was forced to leave our most badly wounded behind—lucky to get on the train ourselves. The bastards probably shot our wounded when they entered the station." He pulled a blood-spotted rag from his pocket and wiped the dust from the hat's leather visor. Now looking at Chabot, "You can see they were shooting hell out of the train as it pulled out. Thank God they were not able to blow the engine... the bloodthirsty bastards.

"We have orders to stop here for refueling, Herr General. I want my men to disembark and want them brought water. And later beer, if you have any. Also alert your physician to come out? Some of the men need medical attention." He once again looked at his hat now wiping the grime from its inner leather band and certainly not anticipating any disagreement with his requests.

Chabot snapped his fingers at Albert, who handed him the fake orders calling for the train to move on to Chambéry. The Lieutenant General jerked his head up at the sound of the finger snapping, an irritated look on his face.

Chabot remained calm, "We realize you and your men are exhausted, but our orders from Paris command demand that all trains continue immediately on to Chambéry for refueling." In a look of defiant disbelief the Lieutenant General squinted his eyes at Chabot. The Colonel with the arm wound reached for the orders Chabot held in his hand. He quickly read the orders and nodded his confirmation of Chabot's description of the document.

The aggravated Lieutenant General grabbed the paper, read it and looked at Chabot. In a voice trying but failing to conceal his rage, he growled, "Well, Herr General, we are weary and we have been cramped up on this hot train for six hours. We have some badly wounded men who need attention. Because of the bumbling of the same idiots in Paris who issued this order we have gotten our asses beaten for the last three months in Italy. So! To hell with what Paris wants. We are going to stop here. My men are exhausted. Even to move them a few more miles on to Chambéry is not going to happen."

Chabot's face filled with compassion, "I couldn't agree more with you, Sir. If it were in my power to accommodate you I would, but we have no fuel. It has all been sent on to Chambéry. Both our coal and water supplies are depleted. You are welcome to come and inspect the coal bins and water tanks for yourself," Chabot bluffed. "Besides, my garrison is busy at the trestle and tunnel readying explosives to close the Passage to the Allies now that your train is safely through. We are in no position to serve your men water or beer, and this garrison has never had the benefit of having its own medical doctor. With no fuel to provide you, it is futile to have your men go through the trouble of disembarking and re-embarking. Chambéry is but 20 minutes to the north. It is a large depot and is in a position to meet all your needs."

The Lieutenant General gave Chabot a look of resigned disgust. The look was not so much directed at Chabot but projected an expression of his frustration at the overall lack of support and consideration he felt he was receiving from German High Command. He looked back down at the orders and crumpled them in anger, slapping his hat back on and muttering his irritation as he abruptly turned and started back toward the car. Just as his accompanying Colonels turned to follow, one of the hidden Jews, trying to relieve the stiffness in his cramped position, unintentionally fired his rifle. The three battle-experienced officers instinctively ducked, turning toward the sound of the shot as they went for their sidearms. Officers and troops inside the train mechanically dropped to the floor in response to the rifle report.

At the sound of the shot, Adrian drew his knife and before the Colonel nearest him realized what was happening, he was dropped to the platform with a deep gash across his throat. Adrian then moved immediately toward the startled Lieutenant General. Anton took a moment longer but reached the second Colonel as he drew his Lugar. He was able to drop the Colonel at the same time Adrian knifed the General, but the Colonel fired his pistol, bringing down Chabot with a bullet searing through his thigh.

Two of the officers on board jumped to their feet, shouting warnings of the attacks. Adrian lobbed a nauseating gas bomb through one of the car's shattered windows. The officers on board intuitively dropped to the floor, thinking the gas canister was a grenade and instantly fell victim to severe nausea as it quickly engulfed the car in its potent fumes.

Having been instructed to begin showering the train cars with gunfire at the sound of Celine's rifle shot, the hiding civilians leaped up at the sound of the misfire and began riddling the troop cars with machine-gun fire. Chaos broke out as the cars were filled with a storm of bullets screaming through the windows. Soldiers at the windows were instantly cut down; those who could, sought refuge in the aisles. Even many of those who made it to the protection of the aisles succumbed to ricocheting bullets and flying glass as the car's shattering windows and interior lights filled the interior with a rain of deadly projectiles.

Remi grabbed the startled engineer standing next to him and shot him, shouting to Felicien, "Get the train moving!" Felicien raced up the engine's ladder and pushed the shocked brakeman out of the cab toward Remi and Amaury on the ground. The man tumbled backward, falling the 10 feet and landing with a bone breaking crunch hard on his back. Amaury shot him as he hit the ground. Felicien instantly released the brakes and pushed the steam throttle forward. The massive wheels shot sparks as they spun on the tracks in response to the powerful input of steam surging into the drive pistons. The train lurched, cars jerked, lurched again.

The citizen machine-gunners were concentrating most of their fire power on the first three troop cars. In the excitement the abandon team-work training. Rather than one popping up and firing while his team-mate reloaded they all were standing and firing in unison. Being relatively free of incoming fire the alerted troops in the fourth car grabbed their weapons and raced toward the exits. The majority of citizen machine-gunners emptied their magazines at the same time, giving the troops in the cars a momentary break in the hail of bullets. The first German soldier able to exit the train jumped onto the platform toward the yard and was brought down immediately. His comrades immediately began leaping to the opposite side of cars, using the train as cover, and raced into a wooded area near the side of the roadbed.

As the train increased its speed, several more soldiers successfully exited the third car and troops were now pouring out of the fourth car, escaping into the cover of the woods. Several were brought down from gunfire by the civilians who had begun to fire on the exit doors, and Celine was able to drop several more, but the sniper rifle was slow to reload, severely limiting her effectiveness.

As the first and second troop cars passed the water tower, Amaury lobbed nauseous gas canisters through the windows. Both he and Remi took cover behind a coal bin, enabling them to take down several more men attempting to exit the rolling train. The train was slowly gaining speed, but troops continued to pour out of the fourth car, jumping to the side opposite the yard and quickly making their way into the woods.

As the third troop car approached, Remi jumped back onto the platform and threw another gas canister into it as it passed. He held his position, waiting for the fourth troop car, but abruptly dropped as a bullet pierced his arm. He struggled to his feet, pulled the safety ring on a gas canister and hurled it into the fourth car.

The increasing speed of the train was finally giving the soldiers pause about jumping. One did, immediately falling victim to a broken leg. The last car now cleared the platform and the shooters in the yard were able to fire on several escaping soldiers before they could reach the safety of the woods. Holding his bleeding arm, Remi jumped from the platform, falling to his knees when he hit the ground. Amaury dashed from behind the coal bin, grabbed him and dragged him back to a protected position. The train was finally moving fast enough so none of the soldiers who had made it to the exit platforms were willing to risk a jump; those still in the cars were violently sick.

With the train now past the platform, the German troops in the woods had a clear shot at the civilians. A salvo of German gunfire burst forth. Incoming fire whizzed past Remi and Amaury. A bullet grazed Amaury's head, causing him to drop from instant searing pain. They were exposed…had to get to better cover. One of the Jewish youth, seeing Amaury's exposure, opened up on the Germans and, using the cover of his fire, dashed to the fallen Amaury, grabbed him by the collar, and pulled him to cover. He opened fire on the Germans again and returned for Remi, took hold of his good arm and led him to Amaury's position. He stood and lobbed a grenade toward the Germans, and ducked down to tend Remi and Amaury. While painful, neither Remi's nor Amaury's wounds were serious… no broken bones. The boy stayed with them continuing to protectively pop up and spray the woods with machine gun fire then drop back down to tend to his heroes.

The Germans, now better protected in the woods, were beginning to find their targets among the civilians. One of the men on the supply building roof cried out as a bullet found its mark. His inexperienced roof-mate rose up in horror, seeing his friend die before his eyes; he, too, was instantly brought down. For the most part, the civilians were fighting back, but Remi watched two more die because they were not fully protecting themselves behind their cover. Amaury, regaining his bearings, stepped from behind the coal bin and lobbed an explosion grenade into the woods. There was a scream as it detonated. The Germans began to spread out, moving farther back out of grenade range.

Celine abandoned her sniper position, hit the ground and ran toward a water-cooled machine gun set up in the yard. She jumped behind its protective sandbag ring, swung the heavy gun toward the woods and began strafing the low brush. She took out five troops in the first burst of fire. Several more dropped to the left as the powerful weapon cut through their protective cover. Fire coming from the woods slowed and eventually ceased as the troops there were forced back by Celine's continual assault on their positions.

⁂

Back in the train, Felicien worked feverishly to fill the boiler with as much coal as he could fit in the fiery opening. He pushed the steam lever forward as far as it would go. *She's probably capable of about 60 miles per hour,* he estimated, figuring they were doing about 30 miles per hour. *Still jump speed, but fast becoming marginal.* He climbed down the engine's ladder standing on the last rung, looking for the softest spot possible. When he spotted one, he went for it, rolled clear of the wheels and managed to land in a patch of tall grass. Quickly, he checked for injuries, got to his feet, moved up close to the passing cars and lobbed an explosive grenade through the window of the first officer's car. The immediate explosion showered him with debris. He pulled the pin on a second grenade and successfully got it into the second officer's car.

It would take another mile or so for the train to hit full speed, topping out at just over 60 miles per hour. It would run full out until its fuel was exhausted.

As the Germans busied themselves with pulling deeper into the woods the battle quieted. Celine raced from the machine gun nest toward the garrison's radio room. She shouted to Margret Zollerman, "Send the message on to Chambéry." The machine immediately began to rattle out its falsified orders:

ATTENTION NOTICE FROM THE OFFICE OF:
Colonel Wilhelm Auchenbach,
Falauge Garrison Headquarters,
Falauge, France

TO LIEUTENANT GENERAL HORST HOFSTETTER,
CHAMBÉRY COMMAND
SUBJECT: FINAL TROOP TRAIN COMING THROUGH
CHAMBÉRY
Communiqué 67-921-246
18 July, 1944 - 12:49gmt
ATTENTION - - - - ATTENTION - - - - ATTENTION

Senior officers insisted on refueling at Falauge and moving as rapidly as possible on to Paris defense. Train cars show damage inflicted by an Allied attack when leaving Turin.

*ONCOMING TRAIN WILL <u>NOT</u> STOP AT CHAMBÉRY
FOR FUEL*

*REPEAT – ONCOMING TRAIN WILL <u>NOT</u> STOP FOR
FUEL AT CHAMBÉRY*

*TRAIN WILL PASS THROUGH CHAMBÉRY YARD AT
FULL SPEED*

*CLEAR MAIN TRACK AND CLEAR SWITCH RAILS
FOR
HIGH-SPEED PASS THROUGH IN TWENTY MINUTES*

ACKNOWLEDGE RECEIPT
--------- *End* -------

The emergency siren wailed at Chambéry. Intercom speakers throughout the huge railyard blasted out the message to clear the main line for an express train high-speed pass-through expected within the next 20 minutes. Privates, Sergeants, Lieutenants and Colonels ran into the massive railyard, shouting to clear the main track. Switch engines were throttled up as idle freight cars were pushed out of the way. In the switch tower, men frantically pushed and pulled heavy steel handles, clanking switch boxes up and down the main track and sliding rails into place to accommodate the oncoming troop train. Within minutes of the all-clear signal indicating the main line had been cleared the speeding, driverless train came into view. It sped toward the vast Chambéry railyard at 63 miles per hour.

A spontaneous atmosphere of patriotic reverence overtook the yard. Emotion swept everyone as they watched the train approach, carrying fellow soldiers returning from the brutal fight in Italy who were determined to immediately move on to the defense of Paris in honor of the Führer and the Fatherland.

Almost simultaneously, every man in the yard came to attention and raised his arm in salute. The yard erupted in the singing of the Nazi National Anthem.

The patriotism in the yard was joined by the voice of the man in control of the loudspeaker system, singing into the microphone and filling the Chambéry yard with stirring song.

As the war torn train thundered past, those standing in reverence in the yard could see a few of the men frantically waving and shouting from its shattered windows. They could not hear what the passengers were yelling, but in the emotion of the moment they were sure they were shouting encouragement and phrases supporting Adolph Hitler and the Nazi cause. The men in the yard hollered back in response to these brave souls speeding on to Paris and the defense of Germany, "Heil Hitler" and "God bless the Fatherland".

The train dashed on past Chambéry and continued another 37 miles north, where it ran out of fuel and coasted another three-quarters of a mile before coming to a gentle stop in the middle of heavily wooded countryside. The few troops alive inside were still ill, although the nausea was now more from the results of their retching in the cars. Those able to stumble out of the stinking coffins were met by blistering heat of the late-July afternoon. They groped their way to the side of the tracks and fell weakly to the ground in hopes the subsiding nausea would continue to dissipate.

The train had rolled to a stop miles from the nearest road. Just two officers were alive, both with minor wounds. They ordered the men to stay put, then separated—one heading north and the other south, hiking the tracks in hopes of finding some means of assistance. Neither of them was ever heard from again.

CHAPTER 52

Celine raced back into the yard, shouting to Amaury, "Get a team together. Search the woods. Kill any of the Germans who won't surrender." She motioned to several of the civilians to gather around her, "We're going into the woods after the troops that got away. Our first approach is to get them to surrender; if they won't, do not hesitate to kill them. Has everyone got ammunition? Let's go."

As they moved toward the woods, Felicien appeared walking up the tracks toward the yard. Celine yelled to him, "Get a team together. Follow us into the woods. Track down the troops that escaped." A shot rang out and the man next to her dropped to his knees. Another burst of fire. Felicien scurried toward them and lobbed a grenade in the direction of the shots. As the explosion sent smoke and a cry of agony into the air, Celine bent low and ran forward motioning to the others to follow. Rifle fire erupted from the woods. One of the civilian youth sprayed the area with machine-gun fire and dashed forward. As the young man advanced, a German soldier jumped up with his hands in the air. The startled youth shot him. Another German yelled, "Surrender, surrender!" Throwing his weapon clear and holding his hands high over his head, he stood in clear view. A shot rang out from behind Celine; the surrendering German grabbed his chest and dropped.

"What the hell are you doing?" she screamed, turning toward the shooter. "He had his hands up and his weapon was gone!"

"My wife was wounded by one of these bastards. Screw all these kraut son-of-a-bitches. I'll kill every one of the bastards I can find."

Celine turned toward the killer, her rifle pointed at him. "Head back to the yard. *Now.*"

"Screw you, bitch."

Celine's bullet caught him in the left shoulder, its force and the shock of its surprise throwing him on his back. "Take him back to the yard. Patch him and his wife up as best you can."

Off in the distance to the right, rifle and machine-gun fire erupted. Amaury's team. A white handkerchief tied to a rifle barrel waved 25 yards ahead. "Stay low," Celine instructed. "We'll move toward that surrender flag. Be prepared. It could be a trick. Shoot to kill if you get any indication they are faking."

An hour later, her team returned to the yard with three prisoners. Amaury's group brought in two more. Celine went over to Amaury, "What's your count?"

"With these two and the dead we found, there were six."

She shook her head, discouragement showing, "That makes 11, counting the dead we found and the ones we killed. Damn it, more got off the train than that. I counted 17 as I watched them from the roof; there may even be a few more. They'll make it to Treaire within the hour. If any of them get word to Chambéry our cover is gone. Your head wound is filled with dirt. Find Remi, get yourself and him patched up and meet me in the conference room as soon as you can get there."

She took off in search of Chabot.

Casualties taken by the Falauge combatants were discouraging. In addition to the two men killed on the roof of one of the garrison's buildings, a middle-aged woman, an 18-year-old girl and two men in their twenties lay dead. Several others had been wounded. Anton and Adrian quickly changed into their civilian clothes and drove to Treaire in search of medical assistance. They returned with the town's two doctors. With the exception of Chabot, the majority of the wounds were not serious. Remi's arm had sustained a wound that would substantially slow him down, but with the bone intact it would heal completely.

Chabot's leg wound was severe...his upper thigh bone had shattered and he had lost a lot of blood. He was splinted and bandaged at Falauge, and hurried back to Treaire for further treatment. Two of the civilians, including the man Celine had shot for insubordination, were treated and would be capable of further combat, if needed. Along with Chabot two other civilians were transported back to Treaire in critical condition.

The cost of the battle had been high. The grieving of the civilians burying their loved ones was agonizing, Chabot's condition rested heavily on the *friends*. An onerous sadness engulfed the tiny band of Falauge defenders.

Teams wearily cleaned up the railyard, burying the German dead and removing as many signs of the battle as they could. The *friends* planned on trying to continue to pass off Falauge to the Germans as if it were operating normally for as long as they possibly could. They sent mundane messages to Chambéry, hoping that the illusion of Colonel Auchenbach and his garrison still being in charge could be maintained until the Allies arrived.

An hour after Celine watched an unconscious Chabot driven off to Treaire, Amaury, Felicien, the Zollermans, and the Schultzes gathered in the conference room, looking to Celine and Remi for where to go next.

Weak from his wound, Remi addressed the group, "We have taken terrible losses—personal losses—but we have survived. We still have sufficient numbers to fight, if it comes to that."

Celine added, "Both Remi and I feel it is just a matter of time before the Germans determine there is something wrong at Falauge. We are hopeful the Allies will arrive before then, but there is no indication of when either of those things will happen. In the meantime, we hope for the best and prepare for the worst.

"Go to your friends and families and comfort them. They need your bravery and encouragement. Remi and I will see where we go from here and will let you know as soon as we turn up with something."

⤜⤛⤛⤜

Remi began sending repeated messages to the British, calling for immediate assistance. Surprisingly, the transmissions went unanswered. Since the Tristan had captured the German radio truck, every message had been acknowledged. All had been answered within a short time. Remi kept sending their plea for backup, waiting only 15 to 20 minutes between transmissions. His discouragement grew with each unanswered transmission.

He was bolstered by the civilians. When they were told the Tristan would continue to hold on in hopes of the arrival of the Allies, no one asked to leave. In spite of the pain of their losses, the citizen soldiers had gained courage from the leadership of Celine and Remi, and had found dignity in that courage. They were no longer victims—no longer willing to submit to the humiliation of prejudice they had felt all of their lives. The *friends* were impressed and honored at the bravery of their citizen soldiers. The Tristan no longer stood alone.

Remi informed everyone that his calls for help from the Allies had gone unanswered. "I don't know why we have not been answered, but the lack of response implies we may be left here for some time to come. I'm deeply moved at your bravery, your willingness to stay. May God be with us."

CHAPTER 53

A nerve-wracking two days passed. No message from the Allies. No indication of a response from the Nazis. Remi and Celine continued to wrestle with how to best defend the railhead.

The Falauge fighters waited nervously. July 19th, hot and oppressive, hung thick with tension as it slowly passed into night. July 20th was fading into dusk when at 8:37 pm, Chabot's radio trap clicked to life.

ATTENTION NOTICE FROM THE OFFICE OF:
Field Operations Marshal Ulrich Jager
French Headquarters, FHD, Paris
French Area Military Command,
Paris, France

TO COMMAND AT CHAMBÉRY
SUBJECT: FALAUGE INSURRECTION
Communiqué 972-824-021
20 July, 1944 – 20:37gmt

FALAUGE RAIL DEPOT SUSPECTED OF BEING UNDER ENEMY CONTROL
It is believed the Falauge Rail Depot and the Falauge garrison have been compromised and are under enemy control. Enemy combatants dressed as officers and soldiers of the Third Reich have attacked and slaughtered German troops and officers passing through the Falauge railhead.

Numbers of enemy troops holding Falauge unknown. Possible infiltration of Falauge by British special forces or American OSS combatants or both.

Enemy holding Falauge is heavily armed – in possession of Panzer attack weapons, heavy cannon, gas bombs, and possibly heavy armored equipment.

Increase security at Chambéry Depot immediately. Go to extreme alert status.

Prepare all Chambéry combat vehicles for convoy to Falauge.

Convoy of 300 troops and heavy armor being assembled in Paris for assault on Falauge.

Prepare 200 troops at Chambéry for combat assault on Falauge. Chambéry troops will join convoy when it passes through Chambéry.

Expect convoy arrival at Chambéry within next 48 hours.
ACKNOWLEDGE
---------- END ----------

The stranded troop trains had been discovered. The last train to come through Falauge, which had caused all of the casualties among the *friends* and their supporters—the train that was now referred to by the Nazis as '*the death train*'—had recently been located by a German patrol. All of the soldiers capable of walking away from that train had dispersed into the countryside, leaving the carnage behind. The cars so reeked of death they were pushed onto a rail siding, soaked with gasoline and set aflame, leaving only their twisted metal hulks as memorial to their battle.

The once seemingly invincible Tristan now numbered just four. Remi was wounded; Felicien, Amaury and Celine were exhausted. There was no word on Chabot's condition. The captured message from Paris foretelling the massive German retaliatory strike being assembled against Falauge was crushing news. But it was the lack of response from the Allies to Remi's repeated pleas for assistance that was so utterly demoralizing.

Celine, Remi, Felicien and Amaury sat gloomily considering their options. There was no doubt the massive force being assembled by the Germans would overpower the small band of Falauge defenders, resulting in the inevitable destruction of the Saint Laurnee Passage. So many lives already sacrificed in its defense, the lives that would be lost in the coming battle...all lost in vain.

Without lifting his eyes from a dejected stare at the table top in front of him, Amaury said, "The question is, should we stand and fight? We're not going to be able to save the Passage. That's what we've all been fighting and dying for." There was no response from the others.

"Why in hell should we continue? The damn Allies don't even care enough to answer our messages," he added, giving Remi a quick glance in hopes of a reaction. "Hell, Remi, why don't we just fade into the forest and forget the whole damn war?" he implored.

Dismal silence hung heavy in the air as Remi took a long preemptive breath in response, "Because that's not who we are. We didn't go into this thing to back out in the final struggle, Amaury. We're not just fighting for the Saint Laurnee Passage. We're fighting for our freedom—our liberty. We're fighting to give those children in hiding a future safe from tyranny—to give our *own* children a world they can grow up in, free and safe.

"You have all teased me over the years about being so idealistic—so wound up in my romantic ideas of liberty. But I tell you, freedom and liberty are everything. There is no life worth living without it. If we give up our fight for liberty for a moment of temporary safety, we deserve neither. To starve for liberty is worse than starving for sustenance. To starve for liberty is to starve the soul.

"Our brothers, Daniel and Alexis, both died for these ideals. All of the others—those we know and thousands we will never know—are fighting and dying for these ideals. At the innermost level of my being I have always believed these things. God placed this commitment deep within me, and I will stand and fight alone in defense of these principles if need be."

Amaury stood and slowly walked over to Remi. He put his hand on his friend's shoulder and softly said, "I am with you, my brother. Whatever you and Celine decide, I will stand beside you."

—◦◦◦—

That evening, the four reassembled and included the Zollermans and the Schultzes. Remi's surprisingly upbeat tone was encouraging. It was the most determined they had seen him in a long time. They were going to fight. They had heavy weapons and knew the territory well. Perhaps there *was* a chance. Yes, with the right attitude, perhaps there was a chance.

Remi addressed the group, "We know from intercepted radio messages the Allies are pushing north every day. They're now past Turin, driving the Germans up into the Alps. We caught fragments of a message this afternoon, something about American troops either planning a landing on the French Mediterranean coast or already having come ashore there. There is no question the Allies are moving toward our position. If we can manage to somehow hold on, if we can just prolong the coming Nazi attack on Falauge, there is a chance the Allies might arrive in time to relieve us. There has got to be a reason we are not getting a response to our messages.

"We now have an idea of the attack we are facing and when. Amaury, I want you and Felicien watching the Chambéry depot when that convoy arrives from Paris. Get a count of the troops, the types and numbers of heavy artillery they bring, and see if you can tell how many infantry are going to join them at Chambéry. If I remember correctly, the only tanks we saw at Chambéry were those we disabled when we destroyed the convoy. I don't think Chambéry has any useable heavy weapons it can contribute."

"Square with us," Adrian said bluntly. "If the Germans attack Falauge, what are our chances?"

Remi thought about how to answer that question for a moment, "That all depends on what the Germans are prepared to throw at us. We know they will not be able to send any more troops from Italy. They could mount a train attack south from Chambéry, but troops inside train cars are sitting ducks. They've already had a taste of what we can do to troops trapped inside train cars, so I'm convinced they are not prepared to risk that. The only alternative is a ground attack—infantry, perhaps supported with heavy armored vehicles.

"Because of the Saint Laurnee Gorge to the south, the only approach to Falauge for ground troops is from the north. Due to the forest to our east and west, any heavy equipment can only attack us by coming up the road—through the front gates.

"They will have to attack from the east and west using infantry. The west side is wide open. Once troops leave the woods they have to cross several rail beds, where they are exposed to fire, before they reach cover of the passenger platform, the water tanks and coal bins. Our greatest vulnerability is the east perimeter. There the woods come right up to the yard and troops have a lot of cover behind barracks and supply buildings once they leave the tree cover.

"From radio messages we know German ground troops are in short supply. The entire Wehrmacht is stretched at this point—not just here in France but all over Europe. I doubt that Paris is going to be able to send the full complement of 300 ground troops they promised. We'll have a good count on that once Amaury and Felicien return from Chambéry.

"We know the personnel at Chambéry are not battle tested. They're mostly a bunch of freight handlers, and there aren't all that many of them. I'm hoping they'll not be able to send battle-experienced soldiers from Paris.

"That's a lot of supposition on my part, Adrian. But if we position our weapons properly, we may be able to hold them off, maybe even kill them in a fight. If we can sting them badly in their first assault—get them to fall back and rethink their strategy, we may be able to hold on until the Allies show up. In spite of our not getting a radio reply from them, I am convinced they are on their way. But I'm not going to lie to you. If the Nazis send seasoned troops and any kind of sophisticated heavy artillery, things do not stand in our favor.

"We'll continue to resist here at the yard as long as possible. If we see we cannot hold Falauge, we will disband into the woods. If that scenario takes place, Celine, Felicien, Amaury and I will lead teams in different directions. We know these woods intimately, and our chance of escape in small groups is excellent. I do not expect the Germans, as stretched as they are with the Allies now invading France, to pursue us very far into a forest they are unfamiliar with. That's the best I can offer. When we explain the plan to everyone, we will offer the opportunity for those who wish to escape now."

Remi studied Adrian, the young man who so recently thought of nothing but himself. "What about you, Adrian? What are you going to do?"

"It is our battle now, too, Remi—all of us. We are going to stay and fight with you. When you explain all of this to the others, you'll see—they will stay and fight."

"Okay," Remi smiled. "Let's get to work."

Civilians not physically able to participate in combat roles were led to holding positions deep in the forest. These would serve as rendezvous points if the battle teams were forced to evacuate Falauge. The elderly and children were moved to the cave. In addition to their original teenage leaders, two adult women were assigned to the group and for the first time since Remi had discovered it, the *friends'* secret hideaway became known to outsiders. The cave was supplied with adequate provisions for a long stay, and its occupants were told to remain in hiding until they were positive the Allies had liberated Treaire.

One of the Solothurn anti-tank guns was positioned to cover the front gate. The other was set inside a steel-walled freight car that was rolled down the main line to a point where it could cover both the road leading to the yard's entrance and the track from the north. Both of the Solothurns were surrounded by as much sandbag cover as possible. The water-cooled machine gun was carried to the roof of the administration building. From behind the building's two-foot parapet walls it could strafe the entire yard and the east woods.

"We've got plenty of weapons and ammunition, Remi," Celine announced. "Everything the garrison left behind—plus, half a supply building full."

"Good, stock everybody up to the hilt. Move anything shooters can use as cover into positions that will give our people direct fire power into the woods where foot soldiers will come through. Give them rifles for distance and machine guns for any troops that get close. What do you think? Can we trust them with grenades?"

Celine's expression was skeptical enough to answer Remi's question. "I can work with some of the stronger boys—Adrian and Anton know how to use them, but the rest…"

"Okay, train grenade throwers and place them between our shooters. Get the others moving cover into position along the east and west perimeters."

The doctor from Treaire tending the wounded at Falauge reported Chabot was mending satisfactorily. He said in spite of Gasper's years of limited exercise, he was in remarkably good health. He would limp and probably be in pain with every change of weather for the rest of his life, but he was going to make it. Remi's wound was also healing. The bullet had exited cleanly through the thin part of his shoulder blade, but the bone, other than now having a hole in it, had not shattered. He was regaining considerable movement and could even hold a rifle aloft for short periods of time. He would be ready to fight when the time came.

Felicien and Amaury returned at 3:25 pm on July 23rd. They found Remi, Celine and most of the civilians busy fortifying the yard. Twenty minutes later, the *friends* met in the conference room.

"Your hunch was right, Remi. From what we could see, the Germans haven't been able to put together as strong a force as their original communiqué indicated," Amaury reported. "Felicien watched the troops disembark the trucks through his binoculars and counted off as best he could. We're not sure we got an exact count, but think Paris only sent between 90 and 100 troops. We have no idea how many Chambéry is going to be able to spare, but from the best we could tell, it looked like about 100 Chambéry guys mulling around in battle fatigues.

"But get this…" Felicien smiled, "the tanks Paris sent were two beat-up old Panzer IIIs and what looked like a heavy machine gun mounted in a Kübelwagen."

"Panzer IIIs?" Remi questioned. "Hell, those tanks have to be 15 years old."

"Maybe so," said Felicien, "but I guarantee you what I saw were Panzer IIIs. And, Remi, the heavy machine gun looked like a World War I MG-08—you know, the one with the slotted cooling barrel…not even the water-cooled model," he laughed. "And it was mounted in a busted-up old Kübelwagen, to boot! All we have to do is come near that Kübelwagen with the Solothurn round and that old 'granny' machine gun is scrap metal."

Amaury continued, "The troops, on the other hand, seem well equipped with up-to-date rifles, machine guns, three and four grenades hanging on their jackets…good outfits, looked new. I think the riflemen are equipped with grenade launchers; probably have some portable anti-tank weapons, too. We know from our own information none of the Chambéry troops have any battle experience, but, of course, the experience of the Paris group is an unknown."

Felicien added, "From the fact they have such outdated crap for heavy weapons and only sent around 100 troops, I bet Paris was stretched to the limit assembling this force. It would surprise me if any of the Paris group has battle experience."

"What about officers?" Celine queried. "Did you see any officers?"

"Two, we think. Maybe three, but we couldn't tell if the third was simply a Chambéry guy or part of the attack group" Amaury answered. "Everybody was mulling around. It was difficult to get a good count at our distance. Couldn't make out their rank, but I'm sure they were at least Lieutenants…maybe Captains."

Felicien said, "I estimate it's going to take them a day to get prepared at Chambéry. That would put them leaving there sometime late tomorrow or the next morning. They don't know the terrain around Falauge, so I don't think they'll attack at night."

"Our biggest problem is the whole damn depot is exposed on the east and west sides," Remi lamented. "Hell, on the east perimeter the damn trees almost come up to the edge of the yard."

Felicien smiled, "So, let's fence it off."

"Yeah, right, Felicien. With *what*?"

"Remi, there's half a freight car full of barbed wire on one of the sidings."

"What? Where?"

"I was snooping around one afternoon and found it. I don't know how much area it will cover, but we can sure secure some of the more vulnerable perimeter with it."

"Why in hell didn't you say something before now?"

"You didn't ask," Felicien shrugged, "and we didn't need it."

"Well we sure as hell need it now. Get some teams and string as much as there is. Start on the east side. At least to the west the bastards have to run across the tracks before they get to cover. We may be able to keep that pretty well strafed with the water-cooled machine gun. Cel, check that gun. Make sure you've got a good view of the east perimeter and enough ammunition to shoot for a week."

Margret Zollerman broke into the room beaming and waving a piece of paper, "Remi, an answer to your messages!" She thrust the message into his hand.

TO: *TCP-3.965*

FROM: *HMN-O-37*

23 July, 1944 – 16:37gmt

NOTE: Message sent from British 8th Army communications center by request of:

General A. Patch, U.S. 7th Army to:

Unknown Receiver-TCP-3.965

Apologize for lack of response to previous communiqués. Our radio receiver was destroyed.

Presently confronting heavy resistance from Germans in the Alps. Slow going through heavy terrain. Nazis are fighting to the last man. We're taking casualties.

I am in the process of assembling a special forces unit for possible parachute drop into Falauge. I have the volunteers, but do not have delivery plane at this time.

Working to clear last German resistance around the Turin railroad station. When Turin station clear, will start sending troops north by train.

To date, the rail line at this end is intact.

Inform us of condition of Saint Laurnee Passage tunnel and trestle immediately.

Will transmit when an arrival (train or air-drop) at Falauge can be estimated.

Hold on – we're coming.

Alexander Patch, General, Seventh Army, United States

Remi was shaking with joy. He handed the message to Celine, tears forming in his eyes and hope welling in his throat.

"Margret, get a message back to General Patch immediately," Celine ordered. Inform him that the Saint Laurnee Passage remains intact—undamaged."

Finally, there was a possibility they could pull it off. Survive. If they could just hold on... General Patch was coming!

CHAPTER 54

25 July, 1944
The Battle of Falauge
Falauge, France

Felicien's suspicion was correct. Nazi Paris command was stretched to its limit trying to assemble an attack force for the assault on Falauge. The 104 inexperienced foot soldiers they rounded up fell considerably short of the optimistic 300 battle-ready troops they had envisioned when sending their initial communiqué. With the Allies having successfully established a beachhead at Normandy on June 6th and now pushing toward Paris, every German battle unit was committed. British and Canadian troops had recently taken Caen, the Americans had finally taken Saint-Lô, and Alexander Patch's 7th Army was about to start its rapid and relentless march north from the French Mediterranean coast.

The troops Paris came up with consisted of men whose only war service had been spent performing administrative duties. Typists, file clerks and switchboard operators were grabbed, told to get into combat gear and meet their newly assigned officers in the assembly yard. The two very outdated Panzer III tanks and the World War I MG-08 anti-tank gun Felicien saw mounted in the Kübelwagen—all cumbersome to reload, slow moving and of limited fire power—had to provide what limited armored support those raw troops could rely on.

Chambéry was not able to contribute any improvements. They offered up 87 men who had served as freight handlers; they were in better physical condition than the Paris clerical crew, but offered no additional combat experience. Chambéry also scrounged up a dated light cannon, but could come up with only six rounds of ammunition.

The only hope in the attack group rested with its officers. The assignment had been handed to Captain Alfred Muntz and Lieutenant Kurt Laufer, both battle experienced and still highly dedicated to the Fatherland. Muntz had been awarded the Order of the Knight's Cross for bravery, then reassigned to Paris Headquarters after a serious wound suffered on the Russian Front disqualified him for further combat. Laufer, awarded the Order of the Iron Cross and the Order of the German Cross for bravery and excellence of command, had been retired to administrative duties following a wound he received in the battle of Sicily. Laufer was widely respected for his successful combat attack strategies.

In spite of the attack force's woefully inadequate infantry and outmoded artillery, the sheer size of the 191-man force was fearsome compared to 31 civilian defenders fretfully waiting at Falauge.

The massive damage the Tristan and their citizen fighters had recently inflicted on the Nazis had the Germans convinced Falauge was occupied by battle-wise combatants. The Germans assumed the Falauge defenders' numbers were not large, but remained wary in their assessment of the battle group's capabilities. Paris knew the Allies were intent on preserving the Saint Laurnee Passage which led them to believe they would willingly risk the deployment of highly skilled combatants to assure the Passage remained intact. It was assumed that whatever the makeup of the Allied force at Falauge, they would be clever, capable, and fierce defenders of the railhead.

Despite the paltry assemblage of troops and equipment Paris had committed to the attack, the High Command's orders were simple and direct: overwhelm whatever forces were holding Falauge, secure the depot, and destroy the Saint Laurnee trestle.

Muntz and Laufer huddled together, studying topographic maps as their convoy rumbled south toward Chambéry. The complicated logistics of the terrain surrounding the Falauge depot, their inexperienced infantry and severely outdated artillery made the attack plan considerably more challenging than Paris' insouciant "overwhelm the bastards and take charge" demand.

The officers quickly realized the only route to get their tanks and the Kübelwagen into the railyard was up the main road and through the front gate—an absurdly exposed and vulnerable route of guaranteed destruction. They would have to take out whatever heavy fire power Falauge had first, then bring up the tanks and MG-08 to mop up. They decided to hold the Panzers and 08 back...

hidden down the road until the infantry was able to take out whatever heavy guns the defenders might possess. It was a bit risky. Probably would get a bunch of troops killed. Still, worth the cost. The tanks and 08 had sufficient fire power that once inside the depot, they could quickly deliver the winning blow. They agreed they would abandon Chambéry's light cannon as soon as the convoy was out of sight of Chambéry command.

They decided to split the infantry into two groups, one team approaching through the forest on the east side of the depot, the other from the west. Their maps indicated the forest ran right up to the depot's east edge, spanning the entire length of the facility and offering excellent cover to within a few yards of the depot's buildings, parked train cars and other objects of cover. Once into the yard, the east attack force could move in quick, short advances, finding cover behind numerous protective objects. It would be their assignment to identify any heavy weapons manned by the defenders and take them out. Muntz would command that group.

The west perimeter with its exposed area between the woods and protective cover was more challenging. In addition to the passenger platform there were also two refueling water tanks and coal bins. Each of these points of cover required a run of some 30 to 40 yards across open ground. The advantage of the western position, however, was a clear view of the yard and the ability to observe most of the yard's buildings from a distance. They decided the west team would provide crossfire—hopefully, holding down the defenders as the east team advanced to take out the heavy weapons. Laufer would command the west team.

He looked up at Muntz, "A bit risky, don't you think? My men firing across the yard in the direction of your advancing troops."

"Ja, not the best. But with the layout, it is the only logical approach. Have them fire high. Be sure they understand their purpose is to hold down the enemy combatants. If you can see any gun emplacements from your position, direct fire on those. Perhaps you can hit their heavy weapons with grenade launchers."

"Laufer, you are the one known to be a great strategist. If you have a better idea, speak up."

Laufer looked again at the map, shrugged finding no better suggestion. He looked up at Muntz with a questioning expression on his face, "Okay, I agree, it's not the best, but a pretty good plan. You think we can pull it off with these clerks and freight loaders?"

"Ja, for the most part. But we're going to return home without most of them."

Laufer frowned, "Ja. I think you're right. The biggest problem is getting these old tanks and that stupid Kübelwagen into a position where they can do some damage. Two years ago I would never have thought we'd be going into a battle with such scheiße."

Muntz let the frustrated comment pass. "If Command is right and we're facing trained combat forces, they're going to have their heavy guns well protected. They'll fight like hell to keep them functional. The Kübelwagen hasn't got a chance. One hit, it's gone. We'll try to roll it in behind the Panzers. Once they start to move the tanks will have to come up the road fast, firing all the way. They're old, slow to reload. We'll move them up side by side, have one fire while the other is reloading. It will expose them more, but it's the only way we can keep them shooting as they make a run for the entrance. We'll have the Kübelwagen's 08 fire between them. First the Panzer III on the right fires, then the one on the left, then the 08 and then sequence again. The Kübelwagen won't be able to hit anything, but it will help keep the defenders pinned down."

Muntz let out a fatalistic sigh. Laufer looked at him, "Like I said, you think we can pull this off?"

"This is war, Kurt. We have our assignment. We will do our best. Say your prayers."

The convoy rolled out of Chambéry at 5:17 pm on July 24th. The troop trucks offloaded the infantry on the road a mile from the Falauge depot's main gate at 6:33 pm. Muntz's team, East Team, moved into the woods to the left; Laufer and West Team went to the right. The teams moved into the thicket just far enough to be hidden from the road, then sat quietly and waited for full darkness. The Panzer IIIs were pulled into accommodating openings in the woods to the right and left of the road, visible but well protected by the huge trees. The Kübelwagen backed in next to the tanks, its smaller size allowing it to move further into the protection of the forest.

At 9:15 pm, both teams move out slowly, quietly. East Team circled wide to the east; West Team well into the forest to the west of the depot. The teams paused often, with Muntz and Laufer moving ahead short distances—searching, listening, assuring themselves they had not been detected then moving their men forward. Within sight of their final attack positions, the two teams hunkered down. Muntz and Laufer each took two scouts and crawled soundlessly up to edge of their wooded cover.

The Tristan had done their job well. No defensive weapons or combatants were visible. The yard appeared vulnerable, dark and deserted.

The German commanders moved back to their teams, then communicated by radio. Their short-wave frequency was not picked up by Chabot's radio trap.

Laufer, whispering in his radio, said, "I saw no defenses. Nothing. No heavy weapons, no troops. The yard is totally dark. Not a sound. How about you?"

Muntz replied, "The same here. There is barbed wire strung along this perimeter near the woods. Other than that, the depot looks totally unprotected."

"We saw no barbed wire on this side," Laufer noted.

"Still," Muntz warned, "remain cautious. There may be tricks in place. Perhaps tripwires. Move your men into position, closer to the edge of the wood. Silently. In small numbers. Spread them out along the length of the yard. Keep a distance of at least 10 feet between them. All of them behind cover. Have each pick his next covered position…the one he will move to once you order them into the yard. Let me know when everyone is in position. Be quiet. I will buzz you when we will begin the attack at dawn."

Over the next four hours, small groups of soldiers silently moved to their attack stations. Both Laufer and Muntz were surprisingly impressed with their troops' stealth.

Laufer's phone buzzed at 4:47 am, just as the sky's first dim-gray lighting announced the approach of a rising sun. Muntz's voice, a whisper, was difficult to understand, "Send scouts to crawl the length your attack area. Search for trip lines, loose soil of recently buried mines, any impediments we were unable to see in the dark. Be sure they crawl quietly. Buzz me when they have reported back."

At 5:17 am, Muntz's phone buzzed. "We find nothing here," Laufer's tone revealed his surprise. "No trip lines, no wire, nothing."

"Good. But be warned, they probably have the greatest fire power focused on your line, then. I am sending teams to cut the barbed wire in several locations. Do not call back. Watch the whole area as we attack. See where they open fire. Get your troops firing as soon as you hear gunfire. Focus your grenade launchers on any heavy weapons you see. Also on the barracks and the supply buildings…try to get them burning. Keep up the crossfire until you hear from me or until you feel right about advancing. Then, advance your men. Small groups. Just short distances at a time, from one protected position to the next."

Muntz sent three teams to cut the barbed wire. He wanted multiple points along the east perimeter where he could quickly advance troops to cover within the yard. The two men in the center team arrived at the wire first. They lay close together—touching. The lead man reached for the wire with his clippers. Sparks shot from the wire cutter as it bit through the wire Felicien had hooked to a high voltage line. Both men shuttered in spasmodic electric death as falling sparks ignited the thick bed of tinder-dry pine needles covering the ground. Flames raced across the brittle pine needle carpet covering the ancient forest floor. Burning ash rose skyward on the thermals of the intensifying heat bursting low branches of rain-starved pine saplings into plumes of flames. The tree's higher branches erupted into a 15-foot super-heated torch; heat waves racing upward swayed the branches of the sapling's larger neighboring trees just seconds before they, too, exploded. Directly under the expanding flames, Muntz's troops scattered right and left, splitting the attack force. The wire-cutter teams abandoned the now-dead barbed wire, scooting back to their original positions.

From her position atop the administration building, Celine opened fire with the water-cooled machine gun on the panicking German troops. Muntz's men were still concealed in the woods, but her blistering barrage of 30-caliber bullets tore through any light cover, bringing down the terrified troops in screaming agony. Watching their fellow combatants being riddled with machine-gun fire, others down the line began to bolt. Muntz screamed for order and ran toward his retreating troops, shouting for them to drop to the ground, take cover, and hold their positions. Celine saw the officer moving among the trees and tried desperately to take him out. She dropped several more troops, but couldn't bring Muntz down.

A rain of rifle fire from the west side of the yard thumped into the sand-bags protecting her position—their distance giving them an angel of fire. Celine whipped the gun around and strafed the west woods. In the terrifying confusion of her incoming fire, many of the inexperienced troops abandon their positions, scurrying across tracks and into the yard areas in search of hiding places. Her strafing fire dropped six men caught out in the open. Others starting to run pulled back confused as to where to go. She raised her line of fire and caught several more in their frozen state of bewilderment. Those who made it to the cover of the passenger platform and the protection of the water tower and coal bins now came under fire from the civilians hidden in the yard, who were popping up, shooting off short bursts, and then immediately dropping back down. As several dropped down, others popped up. Their trained rhythm was working and their previous experience firing on the cars of the death train was beginning to show.

Laufer screamed at his panicking troops, "Hold your positions! Fire on the machine gun on the roof! Hold your positions! Do not run!" Those within range of his voice hunkered down. Curled up. Stopped firing.

Adrian, manning the Solothurn in the yard vainly searched for targets. Nothing. No heavy armor in sight and he could not hit the troop positions to his west. His natural impulsiveness got the best of him. He grabbed his machine gun, abandoned the Solothurn, dashed across the open yard and took cover in the supply building, positioning himself at one of the windows. From there, he could view the entire yard. He knocked out the glass and quickly brought down two exposed German soldiers. Turned to his left and nailed three more behind the water tower which was not exposed to his position.

Seeing his troops continuing to scatter into the yard in search of reprieve from Celine's devastating machine-gun fire, Laufer jumped up and followed them. Making it to the edge of the passenger platform he slid in with several of his men. "Hit the barracks and supply buildings with your grenade launchers," he yelled.

Adrian dashed toward the center of the supply building for a better view of the yard as a grenade crashed through the window immediately to his left, instantly followed by another one just two windows down. The explosion sent flames and red hot metal ripping through the structure. Adrian dropped instantly as the first grenade burst into the building. Its shrapnel caught his legs. The second grenade exploded against the far wall severing a roof beam and bringing the section of roof directly over Adrian down with crushing weight. At his direction Laufer's other two grenade launchers sent projectiles into the barracks building on the left. The explosions blew out windows in fiery spirals of super-heated black smoke.

Muntz had pulled his troops back from the fire, moved them down toward the depot's entrance gate, personally cut a new section out of the now electrically dead wire fence, and ordered his troops into the yard. His men followed him through, rushing for cover behind the burning barracks building. He split his men, directing teams to each end of the building, and ordered them to fire on the exposed backs of the civilians in the yard. Celine could see Muntz's men pouring into the yard, but could not reposition the heavy water-cooled machine gun to fire on the troops at the barracks. She watched helplessly as the German soldiers opened fire surprising the civilians from behind. Those not immediately killed were caught in the crossfire from Laufer's troops at the refueling tower. Within seconds, the majority of the civilians in the yard were annihilated. Several threw up their hands in surrender, but were brought down by the overwrought German troops. Celine was able to take down one of the German soldiers with her sniper rifle, but her shot sent the rest running for cover and out of sight.

Remi had been in the burning barracks building. He cursed Adrian abandoning his position at the Solothurn ran toward the exit door and made it out just as the second grenade come through the building's center window. He shot two surprised German soldiers as he burst from the building then dashed to the Solothurn. Jumping into the sandbagged ring he swung the powerful gun toward the end of the barracks where Muntz was continuing to pour his men into the fray. His first shot blew a sizable section out of the corner of the building—right near where Muntz was directing the troops. Several more shots from Remi's Solothurn and the entire end of the barracks would disintegrate in a rain of burning debris onto Muntz and his tightly gathered troops. Muntz dropped down, halted his troops and radioed the Panzer IIIs in to the battle.

The old tanks lumbered forward, clanked into their assigned side by side positions and the Kübelwagen slid into formation inches behind. One Panzer fired. No particular target. Just cover fire. The second Panzer fired, again haphazardly. The Kübelwagen's mounted MG-08 fired, its gunner trying to space his firing between the Panzer rounds in hopes of keeping any return fire pinned down.

Manning the Solothurn in the rail car, Felicien had a full view of the armored trio moving up the road. He took careful aim, squeezed the trigger and vaporized the Kübelwagen. The Panzers, unaware of Felicien's hit on the Kübelwagen, sent off another coordinated set of wayward blasts in the general direction of the depot entrance gate. Felicien reloaded, took aim and fired. As soon as he did, he wished he had targeted the other tank. His shell took out the Panzer that had just fired. The impact of the explosion alerted the second Panzer crew to the danger. Now loaded, they swung their turret toward Felicien's rail car.

Watching the tank's gun swinging in his direction Felicien frantically grappled with the Solothurn, ejecting it's spent round. He quickly inserted the reload, pulled back the breach, and slammed the powerful shell into the gun. The Panzer's shell pierced the rail car's siding, exploding as it entered; a searing shower of shrapnel engulfed the interior of the car. A live Solothurn shell consumed in the blistering heat exploded. The rail car leapt in a sickening inferno of deafening flame, its wheels leaving the tracks. Flames shot skyward; bending steel groaned as the car fell across the tracks, and flame whipped black smoke bellowed from its twisted frame.

With the rail car Solothurn destroyed, the surviving Panzer ground its way toward the main gate. Remi saw it coming, aimed his Solothurn, fired…and missed. The tank rattled through the entrance gate and pulled to the left, out of sight behind the burning barracks. Remi waited. Positioned the gun where he thought the tank would reappear. Nothing. *The bastards have stopped,* he cursed. He rose up on his knees attempting to see if he could get a fix on the tank.

The rest of Muntz's troops had now circled around the still-expanding forest fire. Celine was doing her best to take out as many as she could, but they raced along just inside the woods, well protected. Only flashes here and there as soldiers dashed between the tightly packed trees. They were making their way to the far end of the yard emerging to the rear of the administration building, again a position she could not fire on due to the location of the water-cooled gun. She was strong enough to move the weapon, but its barrel was now too hot to touch.

She swung the gun around, looking for targets and strafed attackers now streaming across the west perimeter. The smoke from the barracks and burning supply buildings obscured her view of much of the target area. Remi again fired the Solothurn at the barracks where he thought the Panzer was hiding... another huge chunk of building disintegrated. *Maybe I can bring that whole damn end of the building down.* He reloaded and fired hoping for a take-out shot. His fire drew the attention of Laufer, who was now positioned behind some of the cover the civilians had been using in the yard. Laufer grabbed a nearby soldier with a grenade launcher, pointed at the position of Remi's Solothurn and yelled for him to take out the gun. The unskilled Private fumbled with the weapon, dropping the grenade as he tried to mount it on his rifle. Remi sent off another Solothurn round into the barracks and the entire end of the structure collapsed, submerging the Panzer and a dozen troops huddled around it under burning timber. Laufer grabbed the grenade launcher shoving the panicked soldier aside, took aim at the Solothurn and fired.

The grenade hit high on the sandbag enclosure surrounding the Solothurn. It embedded in a bag and exploded. The impact knocked the Solothurn from its mounting and deluged Remi in its molten shrapnel. He rolled onto his side. Numb silence filled his ears. There was no feeling. His mind shut down. His eyes closed. He did not move.

The Panzer, now exposed, wrenched forward, seeking additional cover. Its jerky movement shook off the burning materials from the collapsed barracks building, as its clanking treads rolled over the burning soldiers who seconds ago had sought its protection. The tank crew was unaware the Solothurn was no longer a threat. Muntz's troops, also now exposed by the collapse of the barracks' end section, scurried into the yard, dashing for whatever cover they could find. Celine strafed the incoming soldiers, scattering them and dropping several as her cartridge belt fired its last shell. She yanked another ammunition box into position, opened the bolt on the gun burning her hands on the hot metal and feverishly struggled to feed the cartridge belt into the smoking weapon. The

Panzer now had her position. Its turret slowly swung up in the direction of the administration building, its gun barrel rising toward her position on the roof.

As the tank commander aimed to fire, the vehicle began to shake violently—from the impact of 50-caliber M2 Browning machinegun rounds that peppered its side, followed immediately by the roar of an American P-51 fighter plane pulling up hard, then laying over on its side for another pass. The tank shook again as a second P-51 pelted it. The Panzer commander fired on Celine's position the moment the tank's driver threw the vehicle into reverse in a desperate attempt to escape from the incoming P-51's fire power.

The Panzer shell hit high on the parapet wall of the administration building. With its aim disrupted by the attack of the P-51s, the shell exploded three-quarters of the way down the roofline. Celine saw the tank fire and dropped face down inside her ring of sandbag protection. The exploding shell vaporized the air around it. A supersonic shockwave blasted across the deck of the roof, picking Celine up and then slamming her back down with tremendous force. The noise of the battle grew muffled, faded, went silenced. A light gray fog filled her eyes, slowly darkening as blackness eased away her consciousness.

Celine did not see the P-51s that showered both Muntz's and Laufer's troops in death. She did not see the two German officers die for their Fatherland, or look skyward at the billowing white parachutes dropping U.S. paratroopers sent by Alexander Patch.

She floated in a dream. Most of it was quiet, comforting. Sometimes it turned violent and terrifying. There were voices...at least, they sounded like voices. Mumbling, incoherent, yet seemingly caring. Every now and then there were often children, other children. Yes, other children her age, but their faces were not clear, she could not determine who they were.

All of a sudden the dream went still. *Where did it go?* She wondered. *Wait, there's a voice. I must be quiet. Listen. See what it is saying...*

"Drrrrrr. Docrrrrr. Doctor, doctor..." *Someone is calling. Calling for a doctor. Maybe calling for Chabot. Wait. There are other sounds. Other people. What's happening?*

A low tone. Comforting. An American accent. An American speaking French. She smiled. *I love their accent,* she mused.

"Hello, Mrs. Rousseau. Can you hear me? Can you open your eyes?"

Her eyes flickered, squinting. The light glared. *So bright. Too bright. Painful. My head aches.* Again, eyes squinting, "Where…where am I?" *Oh, I'm so weak. My head pounding… so tired.* Her eyes were closed, yet the light still seemed so bright, assaultive.

The American accent spoke again, "You have been wounded. Wounded in the war," the man's voice was soft and comforting.

Oh, yes, the war. "Where is Remi?"

"We will take you to him later, but now you mus…"

The room darkened. The light was still there, but a gray fuzzy ring began slowly closing around it—slowly…ever so slowly. *Thank God, it is shutting out the blinding light.* The voice became a humming murmur—still comforting, but undistinguishable. The gray ring continued to close and darkened. It was soothing, as if it were there to protect her.

CHAPTER 55

Three weeks had passed. Actually, they vanished…disappeared into that undefinable caldron where unlived time goes. Celine slowly regained consciousness. The impact of the exploding Panzer shell and of being thrown onto the roof of the administration building had broken her left arm, several ribs and left her with a serious concussion. She had been in various states of unconsciousness during the weeks since Alexander Patch's paratroopers had come to the rescue at Falauge. She had no recollection of their arrival or of being transferred first to an American Army MASH hospital near Saint-Brieuc, then on to England.

Her unconsciousness spared the knowledge that she hovered near death on two occasions, as well as the agonizing knowledge of Remi's traumatic wounds. Both she, and Remi, now lay in an American military hospital in England. The doctors were amazed that they—and, in particular, Remi—had survived the transfer, yet it had been the only hope in saving them.

For the first seven days in England Celine waxed and waned between consciousness and unconsciousness. In the times of relative alertness, she had no recollection of who she was or how she had come to be in the hospital. Initially her attending doctor worried she had permanent brain damage, but with each ensuing semi-conscious state her improving actions began to convince him otherwise.

This particular morning, she woke alert—a first in the weeks since her trauma. She opened her eyes, knew she where she was and had that she had been injured in the war…a war in France. The attending nurse immediately called the doctor.

"Mrs. Rousseau," his charming American accent was soothing to Celine's ears, "your nurse says you know you are in England."

"Yes."

"Do you know why you are here? How you got here?"

"I was in the French war. Some war we are fighting in France."

"Who are you fighting in France?"

"The Italians, I think...yes, the Ital...no... no wait. Germany. Yes, the Germans. The Nazis. We are fighting the Nazis. Remi, Felicien, Amaury, Daniel, Alexis and I. The *friends*. We are fighting the Naz..." Panic filled her eyes, "Remi. Where's Remi?"

Startled at her own question, she tried to sit up, rising several inches from her pillow, then fell back dizzy and lightheaded.

"We will take you to see Remi, Mrs. Rousseau. He is here. Here in the hospital on a different floor. You are both healing from wounds you received in the war. I think this afternoon we will see if you can sit up without becoming nauseous. If you can do that, tomorrow we can put you in a wheelchair and take you to see Remi."

"Oh, please, doctor. Let me see him now. *Please*, now!"

"No. You are still very weak. We'll go tomorrow, if you are able."

She placed her hand on his arm, "Is Remi all right? Is he going to be okay?"

A slight hesitation then, "Remi was badly wounded. He is a strong man, Mrs. Rousseau, a very strong man. He is making progress and you can see him tomorrow." He patted her hand then turned, gave the nurse some murmured instructions and left the room.

That afternoon, when the nurse propped her up, Celine fought the instant sickness she felt rising in her stomach from the dizziness that started the room spinning. *I've got to calm this. He won't let me see Remi unless I can sit up. Oh, God, no!* The nurse held her head as she vomited into the porcelain pan.

"It's okay, dear. I didn't think you'd make it today. We'll give it another try in the morning. Maybe if you can hold your breakfast down, he'll let you see Remi tomorrow afternoon."

Celine failed again the next day, but the third afternoon, she made it. Sat up and, although she developed a pounding headache, the dizziness was gone and the nausea did not erupt. She was excited that evening. Felt stronger. Was able to eat a bit of the solid food. *Tomorrow he'll let me go to Remi*, she smiled. Before her wonderful thought had faded, the doctor knocked softly and entered.

"I did it, doctor. Sat up for half an hour. Didn't get sick and no dizziness," she beamed.

"Yes, I heard. I'm thrilled for you," he replied, smiling at her excitment.

"So, tomorrow I can go see Remi?"

"Yes, and that is what I came to talk about with you." He pulled a chair up close, cranked her bed up slightly and sat down. His expression took on a look of seriousness. Each time she had asked if she could go to Remi, he had promised she could…when she was able. Now, his previous hesitations about the visit gave Celine an uneasy feeling. She had purposely not asked for details about Remi's condition, fearing what she might be told. His solemn look forwarned of news she yearned to avoid.

"Remi is badly wounded, Mrs. Rousseau…very badly wounded. Quite frankly, I am surprised he survived the transfer from Saint-Brieuc."

Celine welled up. Her eyes teared. She began losing the emotional battle she had been suppressing since the first day he seemed hesitant about her request to see Remi.

"His body is filled with shrapnel. The MASH team at Saint-Brieuc did a miraculous job saving his life. They removed pieces of metal in and near his vital organs and, amazingly, those critical wounds appear to be healing. While I am encouraged by that, he still has a tremendous amount of damage throughout his body—too much for us to deal with all at once. We will have to pray he heals, then go after the next worst areas and repeat that process many times until he is sufficiently clear of the shrapnel."

Celine sat silently. Tears rolled down her cheeks. "What are his chances?"

He dropped his eyes from hers feeling himself welling in sympathy of her deep sadness, "Not good,", he said.

"Will he make it until I can see him tomorrow?"

"There is no doubt of that, Mrs. Rousseau. He is usually more alert in the morning. We will take you to Remi tomorrow."

Celine hadn't cried for a long time—too long a time. She cried herself to sleep that night, waiting in anguish to see her beloved Remi.

⸙

Two nurses gently lifted Celine into a wheelchair at 5:25 the following morning. They wrapped a warm blanked around her legs. As they wheeled Celine into the corridor, her nurse said, "Your man is strongest in the morning, Mrs. Rousseau. We begin giving him morphine as his strength gives way to the pain, so it's best to see him now." As the elevator door opened onto Remi's floor, his attending nurse met them, "He's awake. Pretty alert this morning. I told him you were coming. He smiled when I told him."

Celine had tried to prepare herself for what she saw as she was wheeled into the room. Most of Remi's body was heavily bandaged. Multiple tubes delivered life sustaining supplements through both arms. Gauze bandages covered his forehead, chest upper shoulders and legs. He lay unmoving, eyes closed. They wheeled Celine to his bedside, but sitting in the chair, she could not see his face...could not look into his eyes.

"I want to stand. I want to look at him."

The nurses exchanged a brief questioning glance, then, without protest, helped Celine to a standing position. She leaned on the side bar looking down on her beautiful man, her soul mate and lifelong friend. She choked back the sadness aching in her throat and fought the tears filling her eyes. She reached out and gently caressed his cheek. He slowly opened his eyes. At first, he stareing at the ceiling, then slowly rolled his eyes toward her.

"Cel," he whispered. A fleeting smile appeared, as his eyes closed once again.

She leaned over the rail, the nurses steadying her, and gently kissed him. She let the tears run down her face. There he was. Her Remi—so handsome, so strong—so helpless and so damaged.

His nurse whispered, "I have never seen him smile before today. It is good you came. Let's try again tomorrow."

<hr />

Celine was wheeled up to Remi's room each morning. The nurses were encouraging, telling Celine that much of healing is the patient's own internal will to heal. Remi seemed to be pushing that will. His alert time with lengthened; with growing frequency he could looked at Celine for several minutes at a time.

He smiled when she spoke…would slightly nodded his head when she said, "I love you."

On her seventh visit, he whispered ever so softly, "Cel, we did it…we won. I love you."

She bent close to him and kissed his lips. He smiled a small smile of joy. Then, she whispered in his ear, "Remi, get well. We're going to have a baby who will need your love." As she pulled back, he breathed deeply, a look of peace fill his face that she had not seen before. He had heard…he understood.

⸎

Celine was released from the hospital on August 29th and at the suggestion of her doctor was offered a room within a block of the hospital by the British government. Her wounds were healing and, aside from a bit of dizziness and an occasional headache, she was rapidly regaining her strength. She was at Remi's bedside every morning as his nurse woke him.

One morning he whispered, "I'm happy about our baby. When will it come?"

"In about six months," she grinned. "When you are well again."

Over the next several weeks Remi stabilized. His pulse grew stronger, his heartbeat more consistent. His doctor talked with Celine about the need for the next operation. Apprehensive, she asked if it might not be better to wait and let Remi gain more strength, but he said he didn't think that would be wise. X-rays indicated several pieces of shrapnel near his heart were attempting to work their way to the surface, and major vessels were in danger of being punctured if the sharp metal pieces were ignored. There was no doubt Remi had improved since the day she first saw him, but he certainly did not look up to the trauma of major surgery.

"What are his chances?" Celine uneasily asked.

"We have no doubt that if one of the heart arteries is punctured, Remi will die within minutes of the event." The physician pointed to a bright white triangular object on the X-ray. "This is the piece of metal we are most concerned about. You see how it is pressing on this artery? It could slip past, but right now it doesn't look good. Once we're in there we are going to remove it and these three other metal pieces."

Staring at the X-ray Celine repeated, "When are you going to operate, and what are his chances of making it through the surgery?"

"We're giving him only a 10-percent chance of making it without surgery... and a 30-percent chance of surviving an operation."

The operation lasted six hours. Emerging into the waiding room at 1:30 am the two surgeons said things went as well as could be expected. Both were encouraged that Remi survived the operation. It would be several days before he would be out of danger. The only thing to do now was hope his body would stabilize and once again begin to heal.

For the next three days Celine did not leave Remi's room. She whispered encouragement to him almost every hour; each time she did, his vital signs improved momentarily. The fourth night, during a time Celine drifted off to an exhausted sleep, Remi died. His body, so riddled with damage, just did not have the strength to withstand its latest assault. He passed in the painless sleep of unconsciousness. He had given everything for the love of his country and his belief in the freedom and dignity of his fellow man. He left behind a world he tried to make a better place and a loving wife who gave birth to his son on February 28, 1945.

FIVE YEARS LATER

June 1950
Avenue de Lumignon
Lyon, France

Celine looked up from the half-written letter on her desk and smiled as she peered through the parlor window. The little boy she watched ordering his playmates around out in the yard touched her in so many ways. It was Remi—just as he had been at the age of five. Confidently in command. Always knowing what was best for the group, what game to play, who best fit each role in his childhood fantasies. Just as his father had ruled the *friends*, so many years ago. *Hopefully*, she thought, *I will live to see him grow beyond the age of 25. I will enjoy knowing would have looked like as he grew older.* She smiled. *Remi left me the best gift he possibly could…his son tucked safely inside of me. My little Remi to hold, to laugh with, to love.*

AN AFTERWORD

Amaury and Aimée survived the war and married a year after the battle of Falauge. Chabot survived, too. Felicien, his wife, and both ex-wives perished. Aimée's parents died at Falauge, too. Anton, Margret and Albert Zollerman made it, although Albert died of a heart attack in the spring of 1945. Jonas and Wilhelmina Schultz survived and adopted Felicien's children. Amaury was so touched by the Schultz's gesture he converted the mill into an orphanage for all of the children whose parents had given their lives at Falauge. Next to the mill, he built a magnificent schoolhouse and hired qualified caretakers, teachers and administrators to staff the facility. He appointed Jonas and Wilhelmina Schultz as Headmaster and Headmistress and built them a home next to the orphanage.

The Tristan and their ragged little army of citizen soldiers had saved the Saint Laurnee Passage. They had delivered the passage to the Allies, intact, as requested. They had fulfilled Remi's dream, given their all for liberty, for freedom, for France.

After the war, the Americans came back to help rebuild war-torn Europe. One of their projects replaced the aging Saint Laurnee trestle, widened the tunnel and built a parallel second track, allowing faster trains to negotiate the route between Italy and France. The improved rail transportation made Treaire and Falauge favorite resort towns for skiers from all over Europe.

Amaury continued to run the Bistro. He re-instituted the Marquee Douzième Chapiteau de Cheever birthday celebration, but he moved the event to July and expanded the party to a two week festival in order to bring tourists to Treaire during the slack ski season. He became mayor of Treaire, successfully insisting that all new buildings must complement the town's medieval architecture—a rule followed to this day in the quaint ski village.

He gave Chabot and Celine the diamonds, which proved to be worth even more than the originally estimated $70 million. Chabot gifted $15 million to the University of Strasbourg—a generosity that fully expunged any continuing tensions that may have lingered at the university toward him. He returned to Strasbourg in 1947 to head up a rather unique laboratory on the University of Strasbourg campus...perhaps unique among all the universities of the world: the Chabot Laboratoire de Recherche Gratuit (Chabot Free Research Laboratory). Although the lab was housed in university buildings and was equipped by the university, it was free to pursue whatever line of research it desired, totally independent of university oversight in deference to Chabot's stanuch independence.

Chabot did walk with a severe limp for the remainder of his life and as the Treaire doctor predicted, any change of weather caused him pain. But in spite of those inconveniences, he seemed immensely happy. Every month without fail, he wrote Celine and Amaury long, rambling letters. Most were filled with unintelligible descriptions of whatever invention enamored him at the moment. A recent one, however, contained a surprise. Chabot mentioned he was seeing a lady, stressing emphatically that she was only a friend and imploring them not to let their lewd and lascivious imaginations race away with them.

Celine did not move back to Treaire. Instead, she chose to raise little Remi in Lyon, a city she had always liked. She was comfortable there, active in civic affairs and became the city's first woman vice-mayor for one term of office. She declined when asked to run for mayor, not wanting to give up that much of her time and privacy.

Amaury and Aimée came to Lyon with some frequency, welcome guests at Celine's large home overlooking the city's picturesque La Saône River. Celine enjoyed their visits. Aimee was delightful...so caring of Amaury. Their children and little Remi adored each other. Amaury's upbeat attitude brought back all that was good in Celine's memories of the *friends*.

Celine was warmed by Amaury's parting comment as he, Aimée and their children departed one Sunday afternoon. She often let it replay pleasantly in her mind, "My God, Celine, the little one is Remi all over again."

Amaury's comment, along with so many everyday things, often sparked Celine's remembrances of those wondrous childhood days filled with the beauty of Treaire and the joyous camaraderie of the *friends*. Her thoughts of Felicien, Alexis, Amaury, and Daniel were as clear as if she had just returned from being with them. And little Remi—his voice, his tousled hair, his free spirit and curious imagination—brought his father into her heart every day.

In her moments of reflection she basked in the warm splendor of the *friends*. She considered her relationship with them a unique blessing, a blessing from God—a special undeserved gift He had somehow decided to grant her.

She had come to peace—peace about the war and peace that Remi had played out his dream. He had provided his son the liberty to grow up free.

CELINE HAD LANDED, ONCE AGAIN.

ABOUT THE AUTHOR

Steven A Segal spent his professional career as CEO of a family-owned, industrial cutting tool business in partnership with his brother. Now retired, Segal says he doesn't miss the stress of the long hours or the pressures of economic volatility. "What I do miss," he says, "is the daily interaction with the hard working dedicated people who helped John and I build our company into the dominant supplier in our industry."

Segal has always found the dramatic events leading up to, and unfolding during, World War II fascinating. *Celine's Landing* is his exploration of the evil tactics of power-crazed governments and those who successfully dedicate their lives fighting tyranny to maintain freedom and liberty for mankind.

Segal and his wife, Lavonne, live in Phoenix. He is author of the historical novel *Ida's Story*, a member of the Arizona Author's Association and serves on the Forest Highlands Foundation board of directors in Flagstaff, Arizona. He enjoys cabinet making, building museum-quality model cars, photography, cooking, writing, and spending time with his eleven grandchildren.

CELINE'S LANDING

UNABRIDGED AUTIO EDITION

The full-unabridged edition of Celine's Landing recorded at the renowned Altissimo Recording Studios of Scottsdale, Arizona; and narrated by professional narrators, Marty Manning and Mary Jo West boasts an industry-first dramatic and emotional audio ending.

The audio delivers a full 14 hours of high quality narration recorded under the guidance of author, Steven A Segal, and recording engineer, Bill Hammers. Available audio downloads bring this action packed drama to life in easy to navigate formats where listeners will eggerly look forward to each listening opportunity,

A wonderful gift for your traveling, or vision impaired, friends to enjoy the all of the thrilling drama of this popular World War II novel.

Celine's Landing Audio Edition is available at Amazon.com, Audio.com, and on all popular book sales websites. Audio formatting can be downloaded from iTunes, Amazon, and Audible.com and is downloadable to your iPhone, iPad, Android, Kindle Fire and Windows Phone.

Immediate download—you'll be listening in seconds.

IDA'S STORY
by Steven A Segal

THE SAGA OF AN
INCREDIBLY STRONG WOMAN

Born into poverty in 1880, Ida enters a world devoid of love. Her spirit and drive is her only salvation from being swallowed up in the quagmire of struggle which surrounds her. Never allowed the privilege of a formal education—unable to read and write, Ida falls victim to con-artists who steal her home and all her positions following the tragic death of her husband. The year is 1915, and Kansas City is little more than a wide open wild city totally lacking in the rudiments of social structure which should have protected her. She is railroaded into an insane asylum and torn from her four young boys who are sent to a brutal orphanage.

Only through the assistance of Tom Pendergast, Kansas City's political crime boss, does Ida obtain release from the entrapment of the asylum. She re-emerges into a world where her children are scattered. Two of her boys have escaped the orphanage and remain estranged from Ida for years being raised in a strange and secret location just blocks from where Ida raises her two youngest sons.

Throughout her life Ida socializes within the highest levels of Kansas City's Pendergast political machine with its gambling, bootlegging, open support of prostitution and political bribery.

In spite of having been born in poverty, uneducated, swept up in the winds of social change, Ida juggles her common past with an uncanny ability to interact with Kansas City's most sophisticated socialites, wining and dining with the famous, infamous and Hollywood's elite stars. Through it all Ida maintains her dignity and epitomizes the strength and magnificence of the human spirit.

Ida's Story is available in paperback and digital formats at Amazon.com and can be ordered for three day delivery wherever fine books are sold.

See a sample of Ida's Story reviews on the next page

READER REVIEWS – IDA'S STORY

Amazon Reviews

Diana Christy   **Rating: 5 out of 5 stars**
This review is from: Ida's Story (Paperback edition)

This is the story of a woman who shows incredible strength in the face of adversity. She begins as a young girl living in a poor immigrant neighborhood but the love of a young man changes the course of her life. You will celebrate the joys in her life and marvel at her courage through the tragedies. All the characters are so well developed that I felt like I knew each one of them. I enjoyed the weaving of the characters' lives with the history of the early 1900's. I highly recommend reading this book.

Carlos   **Rating: 5 out of 5 stars**
This review is from: Ida's Story (Kindle Edition)

An incredible story of love, pain, loss and gain. Decades of American history and how a family struggles to sruvive dramatically entertains.

Margart Kilmartin   **Rating: 4 out of 5 stars**
This review is from: Ida's Story (Kindle Edition)

A real picture of the trials and tribulations of life. A choice between victim or survivor. A journey with threads masterfully interwoven.

Marsha   **Rating: 5 out of 5 stars**

What a great story. Thumbs up to Steven for such a captivating story. I literally could not put this book down. A must read for anyone who loves books about overcoming adversity!! I can't recommend this book enough. You will not be disappointed!!

Julie   **Rating: 4 out of 5 stars**

Received as a GoodReads Giveaway... thank you! What a beautiful story! it is filled with so many emotional situations and struggles. Having many ancestors come to America from abroad, it is truly relatable. Very enjoyable.

www.ingramcontent.com/pod-product-compliance
Lightning Source LLC
Chambersburg PA
CBHW060148260626
47160CB00001B/173